ROOTED IN DANGER

A BLACKTHORNE, INC. NOVEL

ROOTED IN DANGER

TERRY ODELL

FIVE STAR
A part of Gale, Cengage Learning

GALE
CENGAGE Learning®

Detroit • New York • San Francisco • New Haven, Conn • Waterville, Maine • London

GALE
CENGAGE Learning

Set in 11 pt. Plantin.

LIBRARY OF CONGRESS CATALOGING-IN-PUBLICATION DATA

Odell, Terry.
   Rooted in danger : a Blackthorne, Inc. novel / Terry Odell. —
1st ed.
    p. cm.
   ISBN 978-1-4328-2585-0 (hardcover) — ISBN 1-4328-2585-2
(hardcover) 1. Missing persons—Fiction. I. Title.
PS3615.D456R66 2012
813'.6—dc23   2011047021

Published in 2012 in conjunction with Tekno Books and Ed Gorman.

Printed in Mexico
1 2 3 4 5 6 7 16 15 14 13 12

To Amy, who brought home the reality of
"orphan diseases."

ACKNOWLEDGMENTS

As always, writing a book relies on the kindness of others. Thanks go to:

Tony Cartledge and Anna Campbell—thanks for your help with all things Aussie.

Amy Daraghy for all things Oregon, and for finding the "real" lodge where Torie and Fozzie stayed.

Ryan Carter—your piloting knowledge was indispensable. Any errors or liberties are my own.

Mukund Nori for answering my questions about pharmaceutical research. Again, errors and liberties taken with the process are mine.

Tom Fuller for your help with anything combat related.

Sergeant Josh Moulin for some of the realities of cell-phone tracking.

To Wally Lind and everyone at the crimescenewriters Yahoo group for answering any and all questions.

To Mark Carter, brother extraordinaire, for picking the perfect restaurant for Fozzie to "propose" to Torie—even though they never got there.

Steve Pemberton and Karla Lang—phenomenal crit partners with keen eyes. And extra thanks for Steve for all things coming within ten feet of a computer or other technology. Any errors are mine.

Jessica Odell, for her brainstorming help, and her fight-scene choreography.

Acknowledgments

Special thanks to Debra Webb and Cindy Gerard for taking the time to read the manuscript.

And many, many thanks to my editor, Deb Brod, for her keen eye and open mind. The book is stronger for her help.

And of course, Dan, who always understands when I'm "wording" and is willing to read my daily output.

CHAPTER ONE

"Say again, Fozzie. You're breaking up."

Foster Mayhew slapped the radio. He took a calming breath and wiped his palms on his cargo pants. Several hundred feet below him, in the dense foliage of the tropical island jungle, Hotshot, the team medic, had their target. A few minutes and they'd be aboard the helo. Safe.

Focus. Almost clear. His heartbeat ticked away the seconds.

Fozzie kept his voice steady. "Another storm band is closing in. Fast. Get her up here," Fozzie barked into the radio. "Now."

Endless seconds ticked by. "Target is ready for transport," Hotshot said.

"Thank God," Fozzie whispered under his breath. He keyed the radio. "Hotshot, hold the hell on. Manny, start winching."

All too slowly, the litter rose from the jungle below. Blackthorne, Inc. had been hired to get the target out, and that's what they'd done. However, *alive* was understood to be part of the deal, and from the look on Hotshot's face when he brought her on board, it wasn't a given. Yet.

"All accounted for," Manny said. "We're clear."

Grinch, the pilot, did the helicopter equivalent of pedal to the metal and they were off.

"Another successful mission, mates," Fozzie said with forced bravado. "Chalk one more up to Blackthorne, Incorporated."

When he didn't get a response, Fozzie glanced over his shoulder. Hotshot knelt over their target. Kathleen? Katherine?

Didn't matter. Keeping them anonymous made the job easier if things went south. And since people trusted Blackthorne for its discretion, Fozzie preferred to know only what was necessary for the mission. Getting the target out of the jungle was their job, and they'd done it.

"How's the patient?" Grinch asked.

"I wouldn't know. Hotshot's the medic. Me, I'm just the one who saves your arses."

"And we're glad you do, them being mighty fine asses and all," Grinch replied.

"Shut up and fly," Fozzie said. "I'll alert the boss."

An ambulance waited at the airstrip. Four men rushed a gurney to the helo. Within seconds, the ambulance tore away, sirens screaming, lights flashing.

"She gonna be all right?" Fozzie asked. "Did we get her in time?"

"I hope so." Hotshot's grim expression sent a knife through Fozzie's belly. "She's dehydrated, running a high fever. The local specialists are probably familiar with whatever bugs lurk here."

"Hey, mates, we did our part. It's out of our hands." Fozzie brushed his palms together and wiped them on his pants. "How about a beer?"

"You're buying," Grinch said.

Torie Stoker held her breath against the smell of sickness and disinfectant as she pushed open the door to Kathy's room. Bleeps and hisses filled her ears. The fact that this hospital happened to be on Isla Caribe, a tropical island where Torie was on vacation, didn't reduce the creep factor.

She stared at the figure in the bed near the window. Her knees shook. Her stomach roiled. Residual effects of the bad clam, she told herself. Not because it was Kathy lying in the bed, full of tubes and swathed in bandages. A second bed lay empty, and Torie perched on the edge of the plastic-covered mattress, exhaling and inhaling. If not for that pesky clam, she might be lying in the bed, not sitting on it. Composing herself, she rose and crossed to Kathy's bedside. Gently, she touched her friend's arm, avoiding the IV tubing.

Kathy's lids fluttered. They were swollen and red. Her eyes slitted open. "Hey."

"Hey, yourself."

"You okay?"

Torie suppressed a laugh. "I think that's supposed to be my line."

"Looks worse than it is," Kathy said. "They're pumping me full of antibiotics." She smiled. "And some very nice, happy medicine."

Torie cast a quick glance over her shoulder to make sure the door was closed. She pulled the visitor's chair close to the bed and sat. "You were gone four days. I didn't know who to call, or even if I should call anyone. What happened?"

"No biggie. Fell. Landed in a stream. Hit my head. Wrenched my knee, couldn't hike out. Picked up some local infection from the water, I think."

"Sheesh, Kath, that's definitely biggie territory."

"I'll be fine."

Torie took in Kathy's flushed face, her labored breathing. Thoughts of her best friend lying helpless and in pain for days flooded her with guilt. "I should have been there."

"It's all behind us. I was the one who decided to wander off the trails looking for new specimens. I should have been more careful." She reached for the water glass at her bedside.

Torie jumped up. "Let me help." She maneuvered the flexible straw into Kathy's mouth.

After she drained half the glass, Kathy smiled. "Thanks for

11

calling out the search party."

"It wasn't me. I was sick as a dog for almost thirty-six hours and totally out of it for at least another twelve. When I could think again, I figured you'd hooked up with someone, or I'd missed a message. I didn't start worrying until yesterday. When the hospital called this morning, I rushed right over."

The beeps from one machine got faster. Kathy exhaled a shaky breath. "God, Torie, this was supposed to be a vacation." She gasped, as if breathing were difficult. "Everything got screwed up."

"It wasn't your fault there was a bad clam in my paella. I should have stuck with the pasta."

Kathy's eyes were closed, but the machine's beeps hadn't slowed. Torie watched the monitor. Ninety-two. Ninety-six. Would that summon a doctor? Her heart pounded as if trying to match the rhythm of the readout. She squeezed Kathy's hand. "It'll be all right. You need to get well."

"My notes?"

"I still have them, but I haven't looked at them yet. Sorry."

Kathy's face paled. Her breathing grew labored. "Keep them safe."

A slender man in a blue lab coat entered the room. "I'm sorry, but it's time for Miss Townsend's treatment. I'll have to ask you to leave. Afternoon visiting hours begin at two."

"Treatment?" Torie said. "What kind of treatment?"

"We must make sure the dosage of the antibiotic is correct and that her lungs are functioning properly. I must draw blood, and she must do breathing exercises." He raised a contraption that looked like a mug with a thick flexible straw coming out of the bottom, then set it on the bedside table. "But, first, the blood."

Torie glanced over her shoulder as the man studied the monitors and made notes on his clipboard. She pushed Kathy's hair off her face. "I'll be back. And I'll bring you some clothes."

Kathy tugged her closer. "My papers," she whispered. "Don't say anything."

"I know, I know. All your work for Wingard Research is hush-hush. Don't worry."

Torie thought Kathy's obsession with confidentiality was a bit over the top, but she also knew if one of the big pharmaceutical companies got wind of what was going on at Wingard, they might try to grab the glory—and the money—for themselves. She winked. "I'll guard them with my life. See you this afternoon."

The man glared at her, then looked at the door.

"I get it, bloodsucker," she muttered, giving him her best withering glare. "I'm leaving."

In her hotel room, Torie nibbled room service toast and sipped ginger ale. No appetite might be a good thing, hip and thigh-wise, but she didn't like the lingering queasy feeling. She inserted her iPod earbuds and settled onto the bed with Kathy's notes.

And what was she looking for, anyway? Kathy was a medical researcher with the conviction that there were yet-to-be-discovered cures hidden in yet-to-be-discovered flora. Torie's knowledge of doing medical or botanical research was non-existent. Kathy never met a plant she didn't like. Torie, on the other hand, could barely keep silk plants alive. But she'd learned enough to be entrusted with the care and feeding of Kathy's personal houseplant collection when Kath had to leave town.

Polar opposites in every respect. Kathy, a willowy blonde, Torie a dumpy brunette. Kathy, who did serious, important work. Torie, who lived off her grandmother's trust fund. Kathy who loved the night life. A tease, a flirt, never short on male companionship. Torie who tagged along, seemingly invisible to the men surrounding Kathy. Yet, like the opposing poles on a magnet, Kathy and Torie's attraction had been instantaneous when they'd met two years ago, and a friendship had taken root, as firmly as any of Kathy's plants.

Torie stared at the sheaf of papers. Spreadsheets filled with numbers and pages written in Science-ese. Torie sighed. Not her idea of a beach read.

Kathy once said Torie could hold an entire book in her head. A major exaggeration, but for some reason, things she read stuck with Torie, whether or not she fully understood them. But right now, her head wouldn't hold onto ten words, much less ten pages. Her eyelids drooped. When the papers fell out of her hand, she admitted defeat and closed her eyes.

When she opened them, she checked the bedside clock. Two-thirty? How could she have slept over four hours? She crammed the notes into the night-table drawer and darted for the bathroom. After doing the bare minimum required not to frighten dogs and small children, she grabbed a cab to the hospital.

Pushing open the door to Kathy's room, she stopped short at the sight of a man in the chair beside the bed. Salt-and-pepper hair curled over the collar of his beige linen jacket. *Not a doctor* was her immediate reaction.

Torie inhaled a sharp breath and leaned against the jamb. He couldn't be here for her. But where had he come from? While Kathy drew men like wildflowers attracted butterflies, this one seemed older than her usual hangers-on. Sweat filmed her neck. Torie lifted her hair and let it float down, wishing she'd taken the time to clip it up.

She stepped backward. Before she could sneak out, Kathy's voice trapped her.

"Torie. Come in."

Ignoring Kathy's visitor, Torie edged around to the other side of the bed. Kathy was only a few shades darker than the stark

14

white hospital sheets. Her eyes glistened with fever. Red patches flushed her cheeks.

"Sorry I'm late. How are you doing?" Torie said.

"Don't think I'll make the Olympic track team." Kathy suppressed a fit of coughing, blinking tears away.

"They're trying to find the right course of antibiotics," the man said. "According to the doctors, she's picked up a bacterial infection that's resistant to the usual medications."

Torie's gaze snapped to the man. He stood and offered his hand across the bed.

"Derek Wingard." His pale-gray eyes peered through round, steel-rimmed glasses. Full lips curved in a friendly smile above a dimpled chin. Clean shaven, a hint of spicy cologne layering over the hospital antiseptic. In his late forties, she estimated from the creases around his eyes.

The name registered. "As in Wingard Research?"

"At your service."

"My rescuer," Kathy said.

Torie took him in. About five-ten. Lean, almost spindly. Definitely not a Tarzan type. She couldn't imagine him carrying Kathy out of the jungle.

"Not exactly," he said. "I was worried when I couldn't reach Katherine, especially after seeing the hurricane warnings."

"Hurricane?" How out of it had she been? "What are you talking about?"

Kathy's laugh turned into another coughing spell. "Derek always blows things out of proportion. Some rain, some wind, and he's calling it a hurricane."

"There were definitely storm warnings on the Weather Channel," he said.

"Storm. Not hurricane. Never made it to Tropical Storm status." Kathy coughed again.

Torie shifted her gaze to Derek. "So how did you find her?"

"When she didn't return my calls—"

"Cell phone fell in the water, not that it would have had a signal," Kathy interrupted.

"As I said, when she didn't return my calls, I found a Miami-based company that did search-and-rescue work, and they airlifted Katherine to safety. I came as soon as I got the word she was all right."

Torie shot a glance at Kathy, who didn't look very all right. She scooted a chair closer to the bed and perched on the edge of the padded vinyl seat. "Airlifted. Sounds exciting. Big macho hard bodies, right?"

"Don't remember. I was out." Kathy fingered the tie on her hospital gown.

"Damn it," Torie said. "I forgot your stuff. I'll go back to the hotel. Get you a nice nightgown, your toothbrush."

"No hurry." Kathy's eyes closed, and Torie stiffened with worry. The monitors beeped at a steady pace. She watched the numbers on the display. Although she didn't know what they meant, they weren't fluctuating. She took Kathy's hand. The returned grip said she wasn't really asleep. Torie breathed more easily.

"Did the doctors tell you what was wrong?" Torie asked Derek. "This morning they were going to run some tests."

He shook his head. "I offered the resources of my lab. They said they're used to these infections here. It's a matter of tweaking the medications and dosages."

"Kathy says your company researches treatments for obscure diseases," Torie said. "Or do you do tropical medicine, too?"

"Our primary concern is orphan diseases, yes. But research is research. If this bug spreads beyond this island, we can probably develop something."

"Count me in," Kathy said. "Faster treatment would be nice."

"The doctor said you'll be here at least a few more days,"

Derek continued. "Don't worry about your project. I'll assign it to Lonnie Freeman."

"Lonnie?" Kathy said. "How's he doing?"

"He's managing," Derek said. "It was his left hand he caught in the car door, not his right, which helps."

"First the broken leg, then the smashed hand. Poor guy is accident prone."

"Maybe he's a klutz, like me," Torie said.

"Or me, for falling the way I did," Kathy added.

Derek stepped back. "You need your rest. Let me know where to find your notes and I'll be gone."

"My office. Desk. File drawer. Bottom left."

Derek rose. "Do you need a ride?" he asked Torie.

"That would be nice," she said.

"Can you give us a minute, please?" Kathy asked. "I want to tell Torie what to bring me—girl stuff, you know."

Derek's face reddened. He ducked his chin in Torie's direction. "I'll meet you in the lobby."

"I won't be long," Torie said.

When he'd left, Kathy said, "My reports?"

"I can bring those, too. I didn't get very far. Fell asleep. Sorry."

A corner of Kathy's mouth curved up. "Pretty dry stuff."

"Maybe if you tell me what I'm looking for, I'll be able to pay more attention."

"I wish I knew. I planned to compare the two reports until"—she waved her hands—"all this happened. I thought you could look. I'd rather not say anything to Derek yet."

"Yeah, there's the minor detail that nobody's supposed to know you let anyone outside the company see the paperwork."

Kathy gave a wry grin. "That, too."

"Why not turn them over to your Lonnie Freeman guy? Wouldn't he be a better choice?"

"I trust you more. Lonnie can be a dweeb sometimes, and he can get lazy. If something looks funky, let me know."

Kathy's eyelids fluttered.

"Get some sleep," Torie said. "Derek and I will come back later, okay?"

"Ask the nurse for a pen and paper before you go. I need to make some notes about the plants I saw before I did the ass-over-teakettle thing."

"You are such a workaholic." Torie put the television remote next to Kathy's hand. "Why don't you relax? You're supposed to be on vacation, remember?"

"So are you. Go find a beach hunk. Maybe you'll find Mister Right and settle down."

Torie's stomach twisted. Settling down wasn't in the cards for her. Kathy's plants set roots. Torie didn't. She'd accepted the invitation to the island because she suspected her father had picked up her trail. She'd pushed things by staying in one place as long as she already had.

"Maybe someday. Don't worry about my life, just rest. I'll be back," she said, in a very bad Arnold imitation. She hastened to the lobby where Derek waited. He stood at her approach and flashed a friendly smile. The sensation in her belly was completely different now.

CHAPTER TWO

"Why the long face, Fozz? No redheads in here?"

Fozzie scowled at Grinch. "I'm merely in a contemplative mood."

"Whoa, something's got someone's shorts in a wad," Manny said. "Must need another round." He motioned to the waiter.

"Tonic for me," Grinch said when the man shuffled over. "I'm flying in the morning."

"I'm gone," Fozzie said. "Man like me needs his beauty sleep."

"As if anything would help your ugly puss," Manny said.

Hotshot waggled his eyebrows. "My money says sleep's not what Fozzie has in mind. He's going walkabout again."

"With an eye out for redheaded pulchritude, I'm sure," Manny added.

Tossing a bunch of colorful currency onto the table, Fozzie accepted the usual post-mission banter. "Get stuffed, the lot of you." He wove through the bar, eyes burning and throat scratching from the cigars and cigarettes. The concept of smoke-free hadn't hit this island. He pushed open the door.

Outside, the tropical air smothered him. Car exhaust combined with more cigarette smoke from people seated at the outside tables. His stomach churned.

He stuffed his hands in his pockets and wandered in the general direction of their hotel, trying to ignore the knots in his belly and the voices in his head.

Post-mission buzz. Get over it.

They'd done all they could. Whether she lived or died was out of their hands. Why couldn't he put it out of his mind?

Because you hate not knowing.

But would knowing they'd failed be worse?

You didn't fail. You did exactly what you were sent to do.

The smell of brine and seaweed grew stronger. Steel band music wafted from the distance. He realized he'd wandered to the waterfront with its nightclubs, restaurants and shops targeting tourist dollars. He followed his ears toward the music, discovering it came from a higher-end version of the bar he'd left. He glanced at his watch. An hour ago?

You've got it bad, my man.

Shrugging tension out of his shoulders, he passed through the opening in the low iron grillwork dividing the outdoor seating from the sidewalk, and found a table near the restaurant wall. Ingrained habit. Back to the wall, face the entrance, even when he was on personal time. Or was there personal time in his line of work?

Get a grip. You've got a new assignment. Move on.

He fished in his pocket for the file Blackthorne had sent to the hotel. A waitress, long dark hair blowing in the sea breeze, flashed him a white-toothed smile.

"Red Stripe," he said. "Skip the glass."

"Right away." She disappeared, hips swaying in counterpoint to her hair.

He turned the paper over and over in his hands. When the waitress returned and deposited the brown bottle in front of him, he took a long pull, quenching a thirst he wasn't aware he'd built up on his walk. He wiped the condensation from his hand and shifted the candle on the table closer. He unfolded the note and read the instructions for the tenth time. As expected, they were exactly the same as when the hotel desk clerk had handed him the papers.

Robert Stoker Hamilton, head of Epicurean Unlimited, a restaurant-supply company selling everything for the trade, including the kitchen sink. Bread, burger, or brazier, if a restaurant used it, Epicurean sold it. The man had hired Blackthorne, Inc. to find his daughter, and Horace Blackthorne had saddled Fozzie with the chore.

Locate Victoria Hamilton, age twenty-nine. Tell her Daddy wants to make amends. Last suspected location, Florida.

He looked at the next page. It hadn't changed either. An only child. Daddy thought she liked to read. Shipped off to a Swiss boarding school at age thirteen.

Fozzie couldn't imagine Victoria's childhood. His family's sheep station had been miles away from civilization, and he may have grumbled about the work, but there were always people around. Two sisters, a brother. Mom, Dad, his grandparents. Aunts, uncles, cousins. Station hands. A constant flow of people. Loud, loving people.

Bloody hell.

Find a grown woman, one who obviously had no desire to keep in touch with her old man. Then again, this could be a quick-and-easy. Find the woman, tell her Daddy wants her to come home. Mission accomplished. Much as he hated the way Horace Blackthorne required all his operatives to delve into the public side of Blackthorne, Inc., it came with the territory. Pulling a seek-and-find investigation was a hell of a lot better than babysitting some rich client's too-wild offspring so they didn't embarrass the parental units.

He flipped the paper. A high-school yearbook picture at least ten years out of date. Not much to go on. But that was why people hired Blackthorne, Inc.

With his mood lightened, Fozzie studied the low-quality faxed picture. A perfectly average face. He tried to add ten years and frowned. Women changed their appearances hourly. Hoping the

21

"more to follow" notation under the picture meant a thick dossier would be waiting in Miami, he surveyed the patrons, spotting at least five women who bore a vague resemblance to his quarry.

If one restaurant in a tiny resort town yielded five possibles, he could only imagine what it would be like searching an entire state. Even as he watched, a couple entered the restaurant. Another woman who touched at the nondescript image in the photo. Her eyes darted around the outdoor tables. He watched as a hostess began leading them across the patio, but the woman shook her head and said something to her companion. Older, Fozzie noted. Significantly. Her father? Normally, when men opted for younger women, they went for arm candy, and this woman was more like white bread.

The couple followed the hostess into the darkened cavern of the restaurant proper. He hoped Blackthorne's computer geeks were working on narrowing the field. Big time.

Torie ignored the butterflies swirling through her insides. Automatically, she scoped out the restaurant, trying to see if anyone took interest in her. In the five years since she'd learned of her grandfather's plans, she'd stopped trusting anyone.

If she was alone, she knew nobody would look twice at her, so lingering gazes or flirtatious smiles meant someone had ulterior motives. Likewise, she tuned into quickly averted glances. Or to people sitting alone. She took in the man in the shadowed rear of the patio who'd looked up when they'd arrived. Thick, curly brown hair and bushy eyebrows. Teddy bear came to mind. After giving her a casual appraisal, he returned to whatever papers he was reading. Probably waiting for someone. She tried to relax.

"Is this all right?" the hostess asked, waving her arms toward a table near the boundary of the outdoor patio seating.

Torie lifted her face to Derek's. "Um . . . I'd rather sit inside.

Is that okay with you? I . . . um . . . it's quieter. I'm kind of tired of steel drums."

He nodded, and they followed the hostess through the darkened interior of the restaurant. His hand at her back was simple courtesy. His behavior was strictly fatherly. *Yeah, right.* As if she'd had a normal father.

"Are you avoiding someone?" Derek asked when they'd been seated. "You've been looking over your shoulder since we left the hotel. You don't have some bruiser of a jealous boyfriend, I hope. Nobody who would get the wrong impression. My intentions are purely honorable, I assure you."

She laughed nervously. "A bruiser? Not hardly. Or a ninety-pound weakling, either. I guess I'm an inveterate people watcher." She hid behind the menu waiting for the heat to leave her face. Was she that obvious?

Change the subject.

"It was very nice of you to come all this way for Kathy," she said.

"I wanted to make sure she got the best possible treatment. Sometimes medical care in other countries isn't up to our standards."

"But didn't the doctors say they had more experience with these infections?"

He smiled. "I'll admit to a case of American ego. And a bit of selfish entrepreneurism. We're on the verge of a breakthrough, and Katherine's the best researcher I have. I need her healthy and on the job."

Over dinner, she parried his questions about her background, turning the conversation toward him. "How did you get involved in your line of work?"

His smile faded. "I lost my grandfather to one of those diseases nobody's heard of. I didn't know until I was much older that a viable treatment was within reach. But all the money goes into the high-profile diseases. The big companies would rather spend what they have in pursuit of the diseases that afflict millions, not hundreds." Bitterness edged his tone.

"Like AIDS and cancer?"

"Exactly. When my grandfather died, I made up my mind to use my inheritance to help others in his situation. I made some wise investments and founded Wingard Research."

"That's very impressive."

He spread his hands in a gesture of nonchalance. "I figure someone needs to stick up for the underdog."

"You must be doing a good job. Kathy enjoys her work." Torie tensed, realizing she was approaching questionable territory. Keeping the conversation away from herself was one thing, but she couldn't let Derek know that Kathy shared her confidential notes.

Derek didn't seem to notice. "Have you known Katherine long?"

"Not really. I volunteer at the library, and she was looking for reference books. We connected."

"And what do you do?"

She hesitated, sipping her wine while she collected her thoughts. "I guess we have something in common. I also inherited from one of my grandparents. Call me selfish, but I've never felt the urge to get a job or climb the corporate ladder. I move around a lot. Haven't really found anything I want to settle down and do."

Maybe it was the wine, maybe it was because Derek posed no threat, but Torie found herself enjoying the evening. Someone brushed by their table, bumping her elbow. Wine sloshed in her glass.

"Sorry," the man said.

"No problem," she mumbled into her drink. She felt his gaze ripple over her, and she gripped the stem of the glass.

He said nothing more, simply continued on his way. Once he passed, she twisted her head. Teddy Bear. On his way to the restroom. Or an excuse to get a closer look at her?

"I think we should leave," she said to Derek. "I want to get to the hospital once more tonight and see how Kathy's doing."

Derek checked his watch. "I need to touch base with my office."

"So late?" Torie asked.

"Experiments can run round the clock for days, and I'm expecting some significant results. I'll get you a cab. If I finish before visiting hours are over, I'll join you there. Give my good thoughts to Katherine."

Twenty minutes later, Torie pushed open the door to Kathy's hospital room. A stout woman in a white uniform bundled the linens from the bed. Torie's heart leaped to her throat as her stomach plunged to her toes.

"Excuse me?" Torie said.

The woman turned. "Yes?"

"The woman. In this room. Kathy. Katherine Townsend. Where is she?"

The expression on the woman's face confirmed Torie's fears.

"I'm sorry—"

"When? How? Why?" Torie fought to push the words past her tightening throat.

"I will get the doctor," the woman said. Sheets in hand, she bustled away.

Torie stared at the empty bed. On quaking knees, she backed out of the room. She couldn't stay in here, not one second longer. In the hall, she gripped the handrail on the wall while the world phased in and out around her.

A hand rested on her shoulder. She blinked away hot tears and stared up into deep-brown eyes. A caramel-colored face sharpened into focus. "I am Doctor Cardenas. You are . . . ?"

The words reverberated from the distance, echoing in her ears.

She was aware of her mouth opening, but no words came.

"Please. Come with me and we can speak in more comfortable surroundings."

A hand at her elbow. Walking on numb legs. Waiting for an elevator. Sitting in a padded chair. A cold glass pressed into her hand.

"Drink."

Torie blinked, and found herself seated at a wooden desk, a glass of water in her hand. With effort, she controlled her trembling and raised the glass to her lips. Cool liquid soothed her desert-dry mouth but did nothing for the emptiness in her heart.

She struggled for composure. Dr. Cardenas—that was his name, she recalled—stood at her side. His eyes held compassion and sorrow.

"Please. Before we continue, I need to confirm your identity," he said.

Numb, she pulled her passport out of her purse. He perused it, then handed it back. "Thank you, Miss Stoker. Would you like more water?"

"I'm—" she coughed, cleared her throat. "I'm all right. What happened to Kathy?"

"I'm afraid the infection spread too rapidly. Her respiratory system couldn't handle it and shut down." He crossed to the desk and removed a sealed envelope. "She left this for you."

He passed it across the desk, and she saw her name printed in Kathy's distinctive hand.

"Thank you." She put it in her purse, something to deal with later. What should she do now?

She should see the . . . body. Say good-bye. Somewhere deep inside she found the courage to ask.

"Are you sure?" the doctor asked.

No! If I don't see her, she won't be dead. "Yes."

"Very well."

The world shrank to the clicking of her sandals on the tile as they wound their way through a maze of corridors. The doctor pushed open a glass-paned door and motioned her inside. She held her breath, bracing herself for the sight of Kathy.

"Please wait here," Dr. Cardenas said, stepping into a small anteroom. He indicated two chairs beside a wooden desk and disappeared behind a pair of double doors. Moments—or an eternity—later, he returned. "This way." He held the doors open, and once again she held her breath. The doctor remained close enough to catch her if she faltered. Torie steeled herself. She was *not* going to pass out. Or get sick.

The room looked very much like what she'd seen on television. A steel door stood open and a long metal shelf extended from the depths of the compartment it guarded. A chill, not just from the refrigeration, cut through to her bones. A gray plastic bag, like an oversized sleeping bag, was unzipped enough to reveal Kathy's face.

"Did . . . did she . . . suffer?" Torie asked. Kathy's face, reposed in death, looked almost peaceful. Almost. The bluish-gray pallor made it impossible to deny she was dead.

"No. Her medications prevented that."

She stepped forward. "You're in a good place, Kath. I'll bet you're surrounded by plants—beautiful, flowering, colorful plants. I'll miss you."

She turned and pushed past the doctor and out the double doors. As she exited she heard the rasp of the zipper. She clenched her jaw and waited in the anteroom. Dr. Cardenas joined her.

"Is there anything else I can do?" she asked.

"We've contacted her parents. They're flying in from Michigan tomorrow."

"Her boss. Derek Wingard. He should know about . . . what happened. He's staying at the same hotel we—I am. The Royale."

"Yes, I remember. We spoke earlier today. Would you like me to notify him?"

Something told her she should deliver the news in person, but this time, she took the coward's way out. "Yes, please."

Clutching her purse, she stood. "Thank you, doctor. If there's anything I can do, you can reach me at the hotel."

"Do you need transportation?" he asked. "I can have reception call a cab for you."

"Thank you." Chin held high, spine stiff, she strode through the lobby to the street where the hospital smells disappeared behind the blend of ocean and car exhaust. A cab pulled to a stop.

"Miss Stoker?" The driver jumped out to open the rear door.

Torie slid into the seat. "Hotel Royale." She stared into nothingness, her eyes refusing to focus, as if by denying the world existed, Kathy would be alive again.

She navigated the hotel lobby, survived the elevator ride to her floor, thinking of Kathy entrapped in a body bag. As if watching someone else, she trudged along the hallway and fumbled her key card into the lock. She went straight to the minibar and pulled out the bottle of Bacardi, Kathy's favorite, and skipped the usual Coke mixer. "Here's to you, friend." She tipped the bottle to her lips, letting the fire burn all the way to her belly.

CHAPTER THREE

Torie shifted her armload of firewood and kicked open the door. Stomping her feet on the porch before stepping over the threshold, she gazed at the billowing gray clouds rolling across the sky. She hurried inside, dropping the wood into the box next to the stone fireplace before shrugging off her backpack.

Arranging the kindling and the logs precisely the way the books had demonstrated, she laid a fire. Within moments, warm orange and yellow flames shot up like dragons' tongues. She stared into the blaze for several heartbeats, proud at how quickly she'd handled the transition from the subtropics of sea-level Miami to the high-altitude temperatures of Aspen Corners, Oregon.

Unwrapping the long wool scarf from her neck, she hung it neatly on a peg by the door, along with her jacket. She flopped down onto the threadbare sofa and unlaced her boots, then yanked them off and wiggled her toes in their thick socks. Socks. Boots. Not sandals. She stretched her legs onto the hearth and let the warmth permeate her feet. She sat there, watching the flames, listening to the quiet music of the fire, sniffing the faint smoky aroma.

All in all, not a bad day. She'd found a few promising lichens, and had only landed on her backside once navigating a tricky hiking trail. She swore tree roots and rocks moved intentionally—just enough to trip you when you weren't looking.

Her stomach growled. She groaned. Reality beckoned. Lighting a fire was one thing. Cooking on the two-burner propane stove was something else. For that matter, cooking was something else. In Miami, she was the master of the microwave. Terrific at takeout. Absolutely regal at room service. Here, she settled for superlative at soup. Instant soup. Canned soup. Sometimes canned stew. Once in a while, the princess of peanut butter.

The wind picked up, howling like a not-so-distant wolf. Her pulse tripped. What if it *was* a wolf?

She chided herself for worrying. Even if it was a wolf, she was inside and it was outside. She went to the window and wiped a circle on the fogged pane. Tree branches waved along with the howling, adding creaks and groans to the fire's popping and crackling.

Dinnertime. She pondered the choices in the cupboard. Not exactly the menu at the Ritz Carlton.

"And what will Madame be having tonight? We have a delightful chicken with barley *à la* Campbell. Or perhaps she would prefer our delectable tomato basil *à la* Progresso?"

She reached for a can. "Madame will have the minestrone. And perhaps a loaf of your crusty French bread."

Although she was hungry enough to eat the soup cold, straight from the can, Torie put a pot on the stove. She popped the lid, scraping the last bit of soup into the pot, and lit the burner. She set a place at the round wooden table. Pulled a wine glass from the cabinet. Okay, so maybe it was really a wine *plastic,* like most of the kitchenware that had come with the cottage, but the overall effect was what mattered. She would sit at the table and have her dinner like a lady. Aspen Corners might not be the height of civilization, but that was no excuse for not being civilized.

She took a moment to check the plant on the windowsill. The one she'd salvaged from Kathy's apartment, the only living memory of her friend. Had it been only two weeks ago that she'd stopped by to water Kathy's collection and discovered the break-in? One more in a string of similar vandalisms in the neighborhood, the cops had said. Kids, probably bored with nothing more productive to do. Fifth one in three weeks.

Along with the scattered CDs, the strewn clothing, and the overturned desk drawers, all of Kathy's plants had been knocked over, uprooted, and trampled, apparently while she and Torie were still on Isla Caribe. One poor philodendron had struggled to hold onto life, and Torie had rescued it, nurtured it, and brought it along. She poked a finger into the soil, checking the moisture level before drizzling some water into the clay pot.

"Here you go, Phil. Drink up."

Outside, the howling grew louder. A loud crack split the air. She jumped, heart pounding. Gunfire? Here? Was it hunting season? Even if it was, who'd be stupid enough to go hunting in this weather? Something thudded across the porch. She picked up the unopened wine bottle and crept to the window. Pulling the curtain aside, she peered into the yellow glow cast by the porch light.

Wuss.

A tree branch—a large tree branch—skidded along the wooden planks. A louder crack, rustling branches, then a thunk. Somewhere, a tree had fallen.

Storms were commonplace enough in Miami, occurring almost every afternoon for half the year. Why should a little rain and wind bother her now?

Head high, she strode to the table and applied corkscrew to wine bottle so the wine could breathe. Given the selection at the Aspen Corners general store, resuscitation was more like it, but she'd make do.

Now, who would her dining companion be tonight? She'd

exhausted the small collection of paperbacks she'd found in the cottage.

She went into the bedroom closet and dragged the cardboard carton she'd brought with her to the bedside. No matter how many times she'd moved, these friends accompanied her. After clicking on the lamp, she pulled open the flaps and inhaled. To her, the musty smell was like fine perfume. Childhood memories flooded her. Sitting on Nana's lap, listening to her transform marks on a page into a magic carpet. Later, when she learned what all those marks meant, finding her own escape. Curled up in a chair, on a sofa, a window seat, or under the covers with a flashlight.

If she'd regret one thing about life in Aspen Corners, it wouldn't be the lack of fine wine. It would be the lack of a library. Or even a bookstore. Then again, she didn't plan to stay here very long. While cleaning the mess in Kathy's apartment, she'd found the notes reflecting Kathy's hopes that there might be a new cure in an obscure species of lichen, one that grew in this part of the country.

So here she was, in a cabin in the middle of nowhere. Correction. About five miles outside the middle of nowhere. And, if working on Kathy's project happened to coincide with Torie's personal agenda, so be it. With the approach of her thirtieth birthday, her father must be looking for her in earnest. When paranoia had her imagining Teddy Bear Man from Isla Caribe at a South Beach club, she knew it was time to go.

Aspen Corners, Oregon, population 897, was the last place anyone would look for Victoria Hamilton, conservative daughter of the proper and altogether stifling Robert Stoker Hamilton. Or Torie Stoker, library volunteer. Or, when she'd been with Kathy, simply Torie, South Beach party girl. And those identities didn't scratch the surface of who she really was. Maybe someday, she'd figure that one out for herself. Meanwhile, her lichen quest might actually do some good.

The aroma of soup filled the cottage. Her stomach rumbled again. The plants she'd collected would have to wait. She selected a thick volume at random.

"All right, Hercule Poirot. Dinner beckons."

She attributed her appetite to hours tromping along trails that meandered up and down as well as left and right, unlike the flat Miami landscape. Treadmills and ellipticals couldn't compare to mountain terrain. The first few days, her shins and quads had screamed in protest. Now, they merely whimpered. Then there was the cold, crisp air. Miami drained. Mountains invigorated.

She ladled a bowl of soup, took her seat, and tore off a hunk of bread. Absorbed in vintage Christie, with the storm fading to the far edge of consciousness, Torie worked her way through two bowls of soup. She mopped up the last remnants with another chunk of bread.

"My compliments to the chef, Antonio."

She cleared the table and ran the water, waiting impatiently for it to get hot. The front door slammed open. A blast of cold, damp air swooped into the room, followed by the stomping of booted feet.

Fozzie peered through the windshield wipers, trying to stay on the muddy dirt road. Didn't the engineers understand the shortest distance between two points was a *straight* line? He yanked the wheel and slammed his foot against the brake pedal as a fallen tree appeared in his headlights, half-blocking his side of the road. A crunch from under his rented compact coupled with a sharp pull to the right didn't bode well. He wrestled the vehicle to the shoulder.

Shit.

He grabbed his torch, smashed his battered Akubra onto his

head, and went out to inspect the damages. Flat. Of course. And why should he stand out in the pelting rain to fix it? That's what all that pricey rental-car insurance was supposed to cover, right?

He flipped on his cell phone. No signal? It took a moment to remember this was *his* phone, not a Blackthorne satellite unit. Besides, even if he could call, odds were it would be hours before a tow truck would get to Back of Beyond Bumfuck, Oregon. He reconsidered fixing it himself, but the repair folks could bring a real tire, not the stupid toy donut in the car. A fifteen-minute quick march should have him at his destination. He clicked the remote to lock the car and put his arse in gear.

Crossing his arms and burrowing into his tropical-weight jacket, he plunged ahead. This howling rain was nothing like the Miami thunderstorms he'd lived with lately. After countless false trails, he'd caught a break two days ago, and damn it, he was going to march up to her door, deliver his message and get the hell back to civilization. Better yet, back on an op with his team.

Marching, quick or otherwise, might be optimistic. He'd slog his way to her door. Head bowed, rain dripping off the wide brim of his hat, slog he did, keeping to the left-hand shoulder where he was less likely to break an ankle on the rut-filled road and could see approaching traffic, should anyone else be idiotic enough to be out in this weather. Little Miss Vickie had better offer him a nice, stiff drink while he delivered his message.

His estimate of fifteen minutes stretched closer to half an hour before he came to a narrow roadway branching off to the right. Scouting with his torch, he found a small sign nailed to a tree at the edge of the drive. At last. Lights in the distance gave him the final target.

Between his torch and the lights from the house, he could see well enough to move at a slow jog. He increased his speed along the tree-lined path as he got closer. His heart thudded, as much from the exhilaration that this mess would soon be over as from exertion. A compact SUV and a generic sedan sat at the end of the drive in a small clearing about forty feet to the left of the cottage. Giving them a cursory wave of his light, he noted both had Oregon plates.

The first doubts niggled. He reminded himself there was no reason to assume the elusive Little Miss Vickie, whom he'd discovered was using the name Torie Stoker, would have driven from Florida.

He vaulted a fallen log, but stopped short when the cottage's door opened. A man and a woman exited. The man had one hand on the woman's shoulder, the other at her waist. A date? In this storm?

Something about the woman's posture raised Fozzie's hackles. Not a willing partner, his instincts screamed. He doused his torch and ducked behind a tree, catching his breath. It had been a long time since he'd had to deal with altitude, and his body was letting him know it wasn't happy about the oxygen deficit.

Although he couldn't be certain, he'd bet his next paycheck the man had her at gunpoint. Fozzie's hand went for his sidearm, which of course wasn't there. This was a simple domestic seek and find, and flying commercial didn't jibe with firearms.

Crap. What was he doing? First, there were no guarantees the woman *was* Little Miss Vickie. Second, even if she was, for all he knew, she could have done something illegal and the guy was arresting her, not kidnapping her.

Shit, shit, shit.

He pasted on a smile, flicked on his torch, and stepped out of the trees. "Well, g'day. Am I glad to see you. My piece of crap rental car got a flat about a mile down the road. Any chance you can let me use a phone?"

The man's head snapped around. The woman took advantage of the distraction and stepped away. Fozzie extended his arms in an "I'm unarmed" gesture and strode toward the couple. Before he'd moved three feet, the woman yanked herself free of the man's grasp, and even through rain and darkness, Fozzie saw the shadowy blurred motion of knee to jubblies that had him protecting his own package in an unconscious gesture of masculine sympathy. The man went down. Hard.

The woman leaned over, picked up something and pointed it at him. He aimed his torch at her. He'd been right. A gun.

Still holding the light, he raised his arms above his head. "Don't shoot, ma'am. I only need a phone, but I'm sure there's someone else somewhere on this stretch of road who's not quite so hostile to poor unsuspecting stranded motorists."

"Get your light out of my eyes, buster, and maybe we can talk about it."

Fozzie complied. The man on the ground groaned and tried to get to his knees. The woman, who Fozzie decided definitely was his target, and even more definitely, was not someone he would continue to think of as the prim and proper Little Miss Vickie, kicked her assailant in the ribs.

"You can get out of here, whoever you are." She kicked him again. "Go. Tell my good-for-nothing father that I'll never go back. No matter what. Never. You got that?"

"I don't know what—" The man retched.

"Say it. Never."

"Never," he croaked.

"Good. Now I suggest you crawl into your car and get out of here before you drown."

He gazed up at her as if to ask for his weapon, then apparently thought better of it. He half-staggered, half-crawled to the SUV. He leaned against the door, head lowered, wheezing.

So much for thinking this Queen Victoria would give him a warm welcome if he told her who'd sent him. And why had Robert Hamilton sent someone else? Had Fozzie missed a communication from Blackthorne cancelling the assignment? If he'd schlepped out here, freezing his arse off when he didn't have to . . .

He lowered the torch and let the beam dance along the gun barrel. Semiautomatic. Shaking wildly in her hand. Her finger on the trigger. "Umm . . . you can put the gun down now. Please?"

The shaking grew more pronounced. Getting hit by a stray bullet would hurt as bad as getting hit by one aimed at him. Compared to that, hiking another mile in the rain, changing a tire, and driving to the nearest motel didn't seem like a bad idea. "I'll be on my way, ma'am. Sorry for the trouble."

All he needed to do was report that he'd found Hamilton's daughter, send the boss her address, and Bob's your uncle, mission accomplished.

He waited, watching, hoping she'd lower the weapon before he turned to leave.

He swore she shrank before his eyes. Damn. With his hands above his head, he approached. Slowly. "I'm not going to hurt you. Put the gun down, okay? Let's get you inside. It's cold and wet out here."

"Stop," she said. Her voice shook. "Don't come any closer."

It was obvious she'd used up all her anger when she'd escaped from Mr. Temporarily Singing Soprano. All that was left was fear. Fozzie sidled two steps to the left, then rushed toward her.

CHAPTER FOUR

Torie clenched her jaw. She was *not* going to fall apart. Not now. Not after she'd handled herself so well with that creep. She couldn't believe she'd actually kicked him *there*. And that it was so effective. He'd dropped like a rock.

The gun weighed heavy in her hand. Her shaking hand. She lifted her other arm to steady it. Something was wrong. Her hand. When had it gotten so big? So strong? So calloused?

She blinked. Her hand was empty. An arm wrapped around her waist. A new surge of anger flooded her. "No!" She wriggled, trying to free herself. To get into a position where her knee would do some good again.

"No you don't," the new stranger said, jumping aside. "We're going inside where we can talk. Out of the rain."

She tried to place his accent. British? Australian? More likely. Matched the Crocodile Dundee hat. They squished across the distance to the porch, her knees less quivery with every step. By the time they were at her door, she felt in control. Except for the gun. He had it; she didn't. But he didn't have it pressed into her ribs the way the other guy had. Maybe he was telling the truth.

Under the porch eaves, he removed his hat and slapped it against his thigh. "After you."

She opened the door and stepped inside. The fire had burned low, but compared to outside, the cottage was toasty warm. The aroma of soup lingered. Aussie-man followed, stopping right

38

inside the door. He lifted the gun. She froze. He pushed something, pulled something, and a chunk of the gun dropped from the handle. A bullet sat in his hand.

She'd never read a Guns for Dummies book, but she'd watched enough television to know he'd unloaded it. He extended the gun toward her, minus the other parts, which he slipped into the pocket of his jacket.

"Here. I think we'll both feel safer with it this way."

Gingerly, she accepted it. Stared at it, transfixed. Had she actually pointed it, fully loaded, at another human being? Her hands shook again.

The man's soothing tone penetrated her fog. He didn't try to take the gun away, but he walked her to the kitchen and, guiding her hand with his, opened a cabinet.

"How about in here?" he asked, his tone soothing. "Or shall we toss it down the dunny?"

Finally, his words registered. "Dunny?"

"Loo. Head. WC. Toilet. Although that was more of a figure-of-speech question because it would ruin your plumbing. The gun might survive, though."

In the stronger light of the kitchen, she got her first close look at the man. There was something disturbingly familiar about him. She tried to imagine what he'd look like dry, with his dripping wet tendrils of hair restored to their normal state. He stood there, waiting, his questioning brown eyes peeking from under bushy eyebrows.

Her grip on the gun tightened and she wrenched it free. "You! What's the deal? My father's double-teaming me now? Sends Mr. Nasty to scare me, and then you're supposed to come to my rescue? Is that it? How *dare* he? How dare *you?*"

"I don't know what you're talking about. I never saw that bloke before. I told you, my car broke down. Have a heart. It's bloody cold and wet out there. You wouldn't want me to catch my death, would you?" One corner of his mouth turned up.

"Why should I care?" she shouted. Leftover grief, full-blown fury, or demonic possession, she couldn't tell. But, totally out of control, she swung the gun at his head.

His reflexes were a lot better than his nasty partner's, and his hand corralled her wrist, then pried the weapon from her hand.

"I don't think so, Sunshine. I say we sit down, get warm, and discuss this like two civilized adults."

He hadn't hurt her, and he'd certainly had the chance. Little as she wanted anything to do with anyone her father sent, she figured she had more to gain by listening at this point. "All right."

"That's more like it." He flashed a cocky grin. She couldn't decide if she found it endearing, disarming, or if she wanted to wipe it off his face with coarse-grain sandpaper.

She *was* civilized, she reminded herself. She pointed to the catchall basket on the kitchen counter. "The gun stays there. We'll go into the living room."

He glanced over his shoulder toward the couch. His bushy eyebrows twitched. Aside from the bedroom and bathroom, the cottage was open space.

"Okay, living *area*," she said.

He did that grin thing again. Far too endearing, she thought. Undoubtedly used to getting his way, especially with women. Sort of a Kathy in reverse. Thinking of her friend brought her back to the present.

She shrugged off her jacket, gave it a shake, and hung it by the front door, motioning him to do the same with his. When he did, she saw his shirt was soaked through. More relaxed now, she studied the rest of him. Somewhere around six feet tall, muddy hiking boots, wet black denims. He turned to the row of pegs, and she couldn't help notice how that wet denim hugged his posterior.

"You're drenched," she said. "Let me get you a towel."

He pivoted, his eyes narrowed.

"There's no back door," she said, crouching and unlacing her boots. "You can follow if you think I'll run, but I'll expect you to clean the floors after you track mud all over them."

He knelt to remove his boots. "I trust you, Sunshine." A howling gust of wind shook the windows. "Neither of us wants to go out into that mess. According to reports, it's going to last all night."

His tone said he was willing to take her word. This time. If she wanted to, she could have crawled out the bedroom window, but he was right about one thing. She had no desire to go out in the rain.

She stood in the closet. When she'd arrived, Torie had found a box of clothes, which she assumed comprised an accumulation of items forgotten by other renters. She surveyed the contents, trying to find something suitable.

Just get him something dry to wear. He's out there, soaking wet, and is probably going to be there all night.

All night. The realization hit her, and she quickly found a pair of sweatpants that looked big enough. She almost smiled at a Tasmanian Devil sweatshirt and grabbed it, along with a pair of thick socks.

She ducked into the bathroom, added a couple of towels to her load and went to the living room. Area. She hung back at the doorway. The man had stoked the fire and was leaning over, warming his hands. Displaying some decidedly nice assets.

Sheesh. Get a grip.

Maybe that's why her father had sent him. Because he was a natural-born charmer and would work his way into her heart. And Dear Old Dad would have what he wanted.

Like hell. This was about what *she* wanted.

She popped into the bedroom, tossed her bundle on the bed

and stripped out of her wet clothes. A hot shower would be nice, but no way. Not while *he* was here. She dried off, climbed into some very sensible cotton underwear, a sports bra, and her own sweatpants. She reached for the matching top, hesitated, pulled a turtleneck over her head first, then the sweatshirt.

She gave her hair a quick rub with the towel, finger-combed it, glad she'd taken the time to get it cut short. Hadn't done much good as a disguise, obviously, but it was sure easier to deal with.

She gathered the clothes and towels again, marched to where *he* waited. Tossed everything on the couch. "Here. I found some dry things. Bathroom's through there." She hooked a thumb over her shoulder.

"Mind if I take a quick shower? I'll admit to being froze near through."

She refused to meet his gaze. "Suit yourself."

He shot her a curt nod, not another grin, as he took everything to the bedroom.

Good riddance. Then it hit her like the headmistress' ruler. She'd been found. She'd have to leave.

But what about the life-saving plants Kathy was so sure were here? Her chance to do good.

One thing at a time. First, she had to figure out how to get through the night with *him* in the house.

Fozzie stood under the shower spray, waiting for the warmth to penetrate his bones. He scrubbed himself clean with some girlie-smelling soap, and lathered some equally girlie-smelling shampoo into his hair.

For whatever reason, this Vickie-Torie woman had serious issues with her father. He rinsed, turned off the taps and yanked the curtain on the tiny shower stall. Wrapping himself in the towel she'd provided, he wondered what had happened to estrange father and daughter.

He'd grumbled plenty about the work on his family's sheep station, got into enough mischief over the years, but punishment had been meted out fairly, and never did he doubt his father's love. Not even from the wrong end of a switch.

He scraped his knuckles along his jaw. Shave? A nanosecond was all he needed to pass on that idea. No way would Vickie-Torie let him near enough for it to matter, and no way would he use that pink girlie-razor. Bad enough he smelled like a bowl of fruit.

He grabbed the definitely masculine-sized sweats she'd given him and wondered why she had them. What did he care? As long as their owner didn't come barging in with the wrong idea about why he was spending the night with Vickie-Torie. Pulling the shirt over his head, he caught the aroma of coffee wafting through the air. He swiped his hair once more with the towel before following his nose.

Torie sat on the couch, legs tucked under her, a flowery blue mug in her hand. She looked up when he approached. She jerked her chin toward the kitchen counter toward a yellow smiley-face mug. "Help yourself."

"Thanks." The wood floor was slippery beneath his sock-covered feet. He quickly poured coffee into his mug, feeling her eyes boring into the back of his head.

"Frank said he can't get here tonight," she said.

"Frank?" He brought his coffee to the couch. Torie stiffened. Skittish as a kangaroo in a roomful of pickpockets. He settled as far away from her as possible and flashed a quick grin. "Who's Frank?" The owner of the clothes he was wearing?

"He's got a tow truck," she said. "But he said he's not leaving his wife and baby unless it's a life-or-death emergency. His wife has the flu and the baby's running a fever."

"I'm sorry to hear that," he said. "About the wife and baby, I mean. But thanks for calling. I don't really need a tow, only someone to change a flat."

She eyed him as if he were a child. "I could loan you my car's owner's manual. It explains exactly how to do it. With pictures."

He cupped his hands around his mug and sat up straighter. "I'm perfectly capable of changing a tire. It was a matter of not wanting to do it in the rain when the rental-car-company contract covers it. Not that I didn't get just as wet and dirty hiking to this place. Any chance we can get my things dry? Don't get me wrong. I'm most appreciative of the loaners."

"No washer or dryer here, sorry. Have to go to town."

"No worries, then."

She buried her face behind her mug. Even though fireplace sounds and the noise of pounding rain filled the room, it was as if they sat in total silence. He took a sip of coffee. "We should talk," he said.

"I guess so."

"First, what should I call you?"

"Torie's fine."

"Torie it is. I'm Foster Mayhew, but people call me Fozzie."

Her lips twitched. Almost the beginnings of a smile. Almost. They flattened an instant later. "My father sent you, didn't he?"

Fozzie knew a lie wouldn't work. "More or less."

"What's that supposed to mean? He either did or he didn't."

"Technically, he hired my boss, and my boss sent me. Your father wanted to make amends, he said."

"That's a total load of . . . that's not true." Her hands clutched her mug until her knuckles went white. "I can pay you whatever my father paid if you'll say you couldn't find me. More, even."

"No worries about that. You're well past the age of majority, and if you don't want to go home, that's your business. But

44

your father did say he wanted to see you." Fozzie went for the guilt-inducing lie. "He mentioned . . . health issues."

"That's an even bigger load of . . . well, it's a truckload. A huge truckload. Did you see him?"

Fozzie shook his head. "Nope. We spoke on the phone once. That's all."

"Well, he's undoubtedly healthy as a horse. And even if he was on his deathbed, I wouldn't go. And his house hasn't been my home in over a decade." She raised her gaze, meeting his for the first time. "I saw you in Isla Caribe. At the restaurant. Why didn't you grab me then?"

He searched his memory, trying to match the woman in front of him to the possibles he'd seen, and couldn't place her. Chalk it up to his post-mission funk. Or to the fact that the woman in front of him didn't look much like the yearbook photo he was trying to match. "I wasn't looking for you there. I was on another job."

"You almost had me once," she said. "At a club on South Beach."

He remembered that night. He thought he'd seen her, but she was gone before he could confirm it.

"You're very good at hiding," he said.

She gave a wry laugh. "Not as good as you are at finding, it appears."

He shrugged. "What can I say? When you're good, you're good. But if it'll make you feel any better, you were a tough one to find."

"What did I do wrong?"

He heard the unspoken follow-up, *Because I'm going to have to run again, and I don't want to screw it up twice.* Leaning forward, he set his coffee on the hearth. "First, tell me why you're hiding."

CHAPTER FIVE

Avoiding his question, Torie clutched the coffee mug close to her chest. Although several feet separated them, Fozzie seemed to fill the couch.

Relax. He seems nice enough. But didn't they say that about Ted Bundy?

"I don't bite." He smiled again.

Not just the couch. His presence dominated the entire room. Careful not to spill her coffee, she got up. "Are you hungry? I have soup."

Another one of those grins. "If it's not too much trouble."

"Heating a can of soup? No trouble at all." Especially if it kept her in the kitchen. She hurried to the kitchen cabinet and reviewed the selections, calling out the choices. "What's your pleasure?" Her face grew warm as her own words clicked into her brain. His hesitation before answering added a few more degrees.

This was ridiculous. He was practically a bounty hunter, she was his prey, and if he saw anything in her, it was a price tag.

"Chicken noodle or rice?"

He chuckled. She knew she'd see that cockeyed grin if she looked his way.

"Surprise me."

Well, if he expected anything more than soup, he had a bigger surprise coming. Except maybe some bread. She wrapped the rest of the loaf in foil and popped it in the toaster oven while she took care of heating the soup. Unable to resist, she sneaked a peek in his direction. He thumbed through a book she'd left on the coffee table.

She debated offering wine. Would getting him passed-out drunk help? It was a long way from a glass of wine to passing out. Too many unpredictable variations along the way. Besides, all she had left was the bottle she'd opened for dinner. Not enough for passing-out drunk.

Maybe *she* should be the one drinking. She figured a drink might relax both of them. "Wine?" she said. "It's red, it's cheap, but it's all I have."

"Sounds perfect."

She poured two glasses. Stalling, she checked the soup, the bread, then the soup again. Stirred it. Got out a clean bowl. A spoon. Napkins. Carried them to the table. Went back. Butter for his bread. Guys didn't usually do that no-fat thing, did they? A knife to spread the butter.

Another trip to the table. Her heart skittered around in her chest.

"Smells good," came from the couch.

Just do it. It's a bowl of soup.

"Almost ready." She ladled the soup into a bowl. Tray? She unwrapped the bread from the foil and centered it on a dinner plate. He set the book down, crossed the room, and took the plate from her hands. "Thanks."

His fingers brushed hers. She sucked in a breath. Her gaze met his for an instant. She quickly lowered hers, past his broad shoulders, concentrating on the picture of Taz on the sweatshirt. Which hugged his torso. Very nicely.

He grinned.

She dashed to the kitchen for the wine. Returning, she put his glass on the table and sat across from him with hers. He slathered butter on a chunk of bread. Alternating bites of bread and spoonfuls of soup, he made short work of the makeshift meal.

"Excellent," he said, picking up his wine in salute. "I was hungrier than I thought."

"No problem." She swirled the wine in her glass.

"So, backing up . . . why does your father want you back, and why don't you want to honor his wishes? What's so tough about popping in, chewing the breeze, make the old man happy?"

"If I believed, even for a minute, that he wanted to apologize for ignoring me my entire life, I'd consider it. But that's not why he wants me. It's all about him. It always has been. Always will be."

She grabbed Fozzie's dishes and went to the kitchen. She filled the sink with soapy water, remembering what had happened the last time she'd done this tonight. Even though she knew it was silly, she kept an eye on the front door.

When she felt a hand on her shoulder, she shrieked.

Fozzie dodged a near collision between Torie's elbow and his breadbasket. "Relax, Sunshine. It's me."

She grabbed the edge of the sink and leaned forward. "You shouldn't sneak up on someone like that."

"I didn't think I was sneaking. Let me help. Payment for my dinner and all." He nudged her aside and took over dish duty. "Tell me about your father."

"Why should I?" She picked up a towel and started drying.

"Because I think I'm on your side. But I've got a job to do, and before I call my boss and tell him I've blown the assignment, I'd like to know it was worth it."

"You'd do that?"

He shrugged. Horace Blackthorne had chewed his arse before. "Tell me and I'll decide."

She turned her gaze to him. Funny, he hadn't noticed how

her brown eyes weren't plain brown. Streaks of gold, like miniature lightning bolts, radiated from her pupils.

The tug in his loins surprised him. As a woman, she was about as far from his type as they came. And as an assignment—well, he didn't mix business with pleasure.

Maybe it was because he hadn't had much time for pleasure lately. More likely, she seemed so filled with despair, he couldn't help but want to offer comfort. Grab her, give her a big hug, tell her not to worry.

He shook it off. He'd be out of here tomorrow. What he was going to report to the boss remained to be seen. He finished the remaining dishes, then ambled to the couch. Torie followed, still sitting as far away as she could. As she fidgeted, he finally figured her out. Normally, he rescued people. They were glad to see him. Grateful. Overjoyed, even. But this wasn't his usual assignment, and Torie wasn't a hostage to be rescued. Why should he expect her to warm to him? If anything, he was the enemy.

He should tell her thanks for the soup, change into his own duds, and deal with the weather and his flat. They both had lives to live.

Like some kind of cosmic dare, a howling gust of wind rattled the windows. The rain fell harder. So much for leaving. He knew Torie was safe with him. All he had to do was convince her so she'd relax. Keep things friendly. But business-friendly.

He smiled. She jumped up and poked at the fire.

"Maybe this needs another log," she said.

He forced his gaze away from her well-rounded arse. "Torie, sit. Relax. If you don't want to talk about your father yet, fine." He hoisted one of the books from the end table. "You like Dame Aggie?"

She swiveled to face him. She hadn't put down the poker. If she felt better holding it, so be it. It wasn't like she would thwack him with it. Would she?

"You read Christie?" she said, her eyes widening.

"Me mum loved Miss Marple. Saint Mary Mead seemed like a big city compared to where we lived."

"Where was that?"

"On a sheep station out in the middle of nowhere. South Australia."

She cocked her head. "Sheep station?"

"You'd call it a ranch."

She nodded. He could almost see her filing away a new fact.

He took the tiny opening she'd created. "What about you? Where did you grow up?" He already had a lot of the answers but didn't think it would help matters to let her know.

"Sometimes I think I'm still waiting to grow up. But if you mean where did I live, it was all over. Or nowhere. Or in my head. My parents weren't really into the child-rearing thing. And they moved around a lot."

"And I never got to go anywhere."

"As a shy kid, it's not that great, trust me."

He laughed. "Shy didn't work where I lived. The station was a family-run operation. Three generations. My parents, grand-parents. My brother, two sisters. Aunts, uncles, cousins. You needed something, you made it known. At high volume, usu-ally."

She breathed out a quiet sigh and smoothed her hair. "Young ladies *never* raise their voices. Young ladies *never* lose their tempers. Young ladies *never* disagree with their elders."

"You seem to have overcome that handicap."

She balanced the tip of the poker on the floor and juggled the handle from hand to hand. "I think I had an out-of-body experience. I still can't believe I did what I did."

"You did what had to be done. Fear and anger can let loose things we keep buried deep inside." He grinned. "Don't tell me you never *wanted* to do what you did tonight."

She scraped her top teeth over her bottom lip. "Not really. I mean I wanted to be *able* to do those things, but I never really wanted to *do* them. Does that make any sense?"

"Absolutely. Finding out you've got the balls—sorry—the strength to come through when you need to? That's empowering."

For several heartbeats, she didn't look convinced. "Power. Who'd have thought it? Me. Having power." Then she smiled. The first full-fledged, all-the-way-to-the-eyes one he'd seen. Dimples appeared. Backlit by the fire, she glowed.

He shifted his position. Oh, if she only knew what power she had.

He moved Agatha Christie to the coffee table and picked up second book. Glancing at the title, he said, "Are you into botany?"

"Not really. But Kathy was. She's why I'm here. Part of the reason, anyway."

"Kathy?"

"My friend in Miami." Sadness erased her smile. "She loved plants. We were in Isla Caribe together."

Loved plants? Past tense? Kathy? Isla Caribe? "Where is she now?" *Please tell me she's coming home tomorrow. Or that it's a different Kathy.*

"She died."

"When?" He sounded like a frog. He'd never confirmed her name. Yet somehow he knew. Torie's Kathy had been his. His palms sweated. Blood whooshed in his ears. But he had to hear it. "How?"

"There was an accident. She was collecting plants and fell. Her boss sent a search party, and they got her out, airlifted her to the hospital, but she picked up some nasty respiratory bug and . . . she didn't make it. The doctors said it was a drug-resistant strain."

As much as his failure, the sorrow in her voice devastated him. He lowered his head into his hands. They'd rescued their target, but she never made it off the island. Never made it out of the hospital.

Your mission was to get her out. You did it. Not your fault. The doctors should have had better drugs. Not your fault.

"Are you all right?" Torie's voice was distant, echoing. "Fozzie?"

He straightened, balling his hands. Damn, it was all his fault. He slammed his fist into his thigh. Getting a bead on Kathy had taken too long. Too many places to look. Grounded by bad weather.

And she was dead.

The walls closed in. He got up and paced. How long had Kathy been there, alone, in pain, before he'd located her? He crossed the room and opened the door. He stood there, hand on thighs, sucking in the cold, damp air for several long moments, waiting for his heart to stop jackhammering.

In the distance, lights moved like low-flying UFOs, reflecting off the raindrops. They shifted in direction, heading toward him. They disappeared, leaving only a gold after-image. He heard nothing but the wind and rain, but he didn't need to see or hear a car to know one was out there. A narrow beam of light flickered on, roaming from side to side along the ground.

He backed inside, closing the door. Torie sat on the couch, curled into a tight package, eyeing him the way a mouse might regard a cat. He reached for his jacket and dipped his hand into the pocket. "You expecting company?"

CHAPTER SIX

Torie tried to unearth the power Fozzie claimed she had. Apparently it had burrowed too deep to find. She watched him reach for his jacket. With the bullets. Not until he looked over his shoulder at her did she realize he'd spoken.

"What did you say?" she said.

"I asked if you were expecting company? Any folks prone to pop in without calling, especially on a night like tonight? Someone making sure you're all right?"

She gave her head a shake. "I haven't been here long enough for anyone to worry about me. Nobody's ever dropped by—until tonight."

The grim expression on his face frightened and comforted her at the same time. He strode to the kitchen and went straight to the basket. Loud clacking noises told her the gun was a deadly weapon again.

How far had her father taken this mission? If he was sending people who used guns, maybe she should do what he wanted.

"Sunshine, why don't you go to the bedroom? And close the door." His matter-of-fact tone, which she knew was meant to keep from alarming her, did the opposite. Someone approached, and the first thing he did was go for a gun.

She reminded herself that the last person she'd encountered was the owner of that gun. Fozzie hadn't arrived displaying one. But it was clear enough he was comfortable with it.

"Get a wriggle on, darlin'," he said.

Right. She scurried to the bedroom. Closed the door. There was no lock. No chair to jam under the knob. She crossed the room and went into the bathroom, where the door *did* have a lock. She tried to think logically.

How could she know someone was really coming? Or what he wanted? He might be meeting Fozzie. Another one of her father's minions. Fozzie might even be working with him. Playing savior again.

She couldn't do this. She had to leave.

The sound of her ragged wheezing surrounded her. She held her breath, counted to ten. She had to calm down.

She stared at her wool-clad feet. Her boots were still by the door. As was her jacket. She grabbed her nylon shell from the closet and slipped it on over her sweatshirt. It had a hood, and should keep her dry for a while. Fingers trembling, she laced on her sneakers.

Darn. Her new fancy backpack with the kazillion compartments was by the door. She found her hobo bag and zipped it open.

From the bathroom, she grabbed her travel toiletry kit and stuck it in the bag. From the dresser, she added another pair of socks, a turtleneck and some clean underwear.

Her nightstand drawer held her wallet, driver's license, and passport, along with her other vital papers. She added them, hooking her key ring around her finger and sticking her flashlight into her pocket. As she stood, zipping her bag shut, her feet bumped the carton by the bed. Her books. All she had left of Nana.

"I'll be back," she whispered.

She checked her watch. Barely five minutes had passed. Still no sounds from out front. Was she better off staying?

No. Despite what Fozzie had said, he'd try to talk her into seeing her father. And no matter how many times she'd told herself she wasn't a child anymore, deep inside she feared after one step inside his door, she'd immediately revert to that cowering and oh-so-obedient Victoria.

She'd rather live on the run.

She climbed onto the bed, struggling to maintain her balance as the mattress sank beneath her feet. Carefully, she opened the window. Cold rain pelted her face. She fastened the drawstring on the shell's hood and fumbled with the window screen. The odor of wet dust and earth filled her nostrils. The screen probably hadn't been cleaned in years. After some wrenching and wrestling, it popped free. She shoved it to the ground, off to the side, where it landed with a splash.

Swallowing her doubts, she tucked her bag under her shell, zipped it, then drew the waist string tight. She swung her right foot onto the window sill. Holding the frame, she hoisted herself up. She flashed on standing on the brick of a planter box when she was about five. She'd clambered up, wanting to get a closer look at the daffodils and snapdragons. But when it came time to jump down, she panicked and begged Nana to lower her.

"You're a big girl, Victoria. Your eyes are much higher than your feet. The ground looks farther away than it is. Lie on the ledge and see how close you really are."

She'd done it. And the next time, she jumped from a standing position. Over and over, laughing and clapping her hands, until Grandfather had sent her inside. To be a proper young lady.

Now, she had only a vague idea of how far it was to the ground. Lowering herself to a seated position, she let her legs dangle over the sill, and she squirmed herself lower and lower, her toes stretching and seeking *terra firma*. When she reached the limit of her balance, she slipped to the ground.

Terra not so *firma,* as it turned out. Water splashed and mud covered her sneakers, but she was down. Familiar enough with the terrain, she used her flashlight sparingly as she hunched over and scuttled for the trees. Roots grabbed for her, but she maintained her footing. She'd work her way to the clearing where she kept her car. It would have to be the long way round, but she didn't want to risk crossing the front yard.

The rain had slowed to a fine mist. She reached the stand of pines she used as her landmark. From here, it was a matter of sneaking from tree to tree. With the beam of her flashlight, she scoped out the ground between herself and the next tree to make sure there were no surprises. On a deep exhale, she plunged toward her target, straining her ears for any indication of what might be going on inside the cottage. When she reached the tree, she hugged its rough bark, inhaling the wet, pine smell.

More confident, she selected her next goal and moved onward. Halfway to the third tree on her route, she succumbed to a nasty root and landed firmly on her butt. When she stood, a golden glow registered in her peripheral vision.

The smell of smoke drifted over the forest aromas. She stopped. Stared at the cottage. Stood, slack-jawed, as red, yellow, and orange light flickered from the windows.

Fire. *Her books.*

She lowered her head and churned her legs toward the window she'd left open. It seemed so much higher from outside, without the bed to stand on. She jumped, clawing at the sill, bracing her feet on the cottage wall, straining to find enough upper body strength to hoist herself up and over. Hands gripped her wrists. Pried her fingers loose. Shoved her so she fell to the ground.

Before she could regain her footing, a large, heavy body dropped to the ground beside her.

Fozzie grabbed Torie's arm and tugged her to her feet. He didn't know which had frightened him more, finding her gone, or finding she'd come back to an impending disaster area. "You have car keys?"

She wrenched away. "Let go. I have to save my books."

"Sunshine, your house could blow. Books can be replaced."

"Not these." Damn. She was trying to climb the wall again. "They're all I have left of Nana."

Shit. Making sure he was out of kicking range, he put his hands around her waist and lowered her to the ground. "Where are they?"

Her eyes widened as if she couldn't believe he'd give in. "I can do it."

"So can I. Now tell me where they are."

"Box. Next to my bed."

He cursed under his breath, trying to remember the finer points of propane tanks exploding. A leaky pipe, valve, or too-rapid expansion of the gas might take out most of the cottage and everything in it. Or around it, which at the moment included himself and Torie. Distance was the better part of valor. "Fine. Now, get the car out to the main road. I'll catch up."

"But—"

"Don't argue. Run. Now. Fast."

Without waiting to see if she'd obeyed, he took three deep breaths, held the fourth and scrambled through the window. He dropped to the bed below, senses tuned to any unwanted presence. Damn, without any of his Blackthorne equipment, he might as well be deaf and blind.

He'd never spotted the guy. No clue he'd been flanked until he smelled smoke and found a flare the jerk had tossed through a window, along with an open container of what smelled like kerosene, and the couch was fully engaged. By the time Fozzie gave up on finding a fire extinguisher, a second flare ignited the curtains on the other side of the house. Torie hadn't answered his shouts, and he panicked that she'd either been grabbed or overcome by smoke.

He jumped from the bed and grabbed the damn carton. Saving Torie was his priority, and if she wouldn't leave without the damn books, he'd bring the damn books. Eyes burning, tears streaming down his face, he stood on the bed and balanced the carton on the narrow ledge.

"Lower them to me," Torie said.

Fozzie craned his neck around the box to find her standing below the window, arms outstretched.

Once the box was in her hands, he jumped out and snatched it from her. "I thought I told you to get to the car."

She shrugged. "Didn't seem right to leave you. They're my books."

"I told you I'd get them." This wasn't the time to argue about who was in command. "We need to call this in. Where's the nearest decent cell-phone signal?"

"In town. But that's five miles away. You don't think we could risk a call from the land line inside? It would only take a minute. The fire's not near the tank yet."

"Not safe. The house is full of smoke. What about neighbors?"

"I don't know anyone. I didn't exactly come here to settle down and make friends."

He took off toward the clearing where he'd seen the cars. Torie lingered, gazing toward the cottage. "Come on, Sunshine. Move it." He needed both hands to hold the carton, or he would have dragged her along. "Give us some light."

She played her flashlight on the muddy ground in front of them, the light bouncing as she picked up her pace to match his. "Why can't we just shut off the valve on the tank?"

"It could explode anyway. I don't want to risk it."

By now, they were far enough from the cottage that Fozzie

felt they weren't in immediate danger should the propane tank blow.

Ten feet from the car, Torie clicked the remote, and the boot popped open. He lengthened his stride and dropped the carton inside as Torie slid into the driver's seat. She slotted the key, and the engine sputtered, then sprang to life.

At least one thing was going right. He clicked his seat belt on. They left the clearing and headed along the narrow, muddy drive toward the main road.

"Which way?" she asked when they reached the turnoff. "Toward town?"

He checked his watch. After nine. Kind of late to be knocking on doors, especially if Torie didn't know her neighbors. "Good enough."

"Nothing will be open, you know. Aspen Corners isn't exactly a night spot."

"But if there's a cell signal, we can make calls. Don't suppose there's a motel."

She laughed. "Motel? No. There's a lodge about five miles the other side of town, though. They might have a room for you."

"Us, I think. You can't go back to your place. Not for a while, anyway."

She exhaled sharply. After a pause, she said, "Right. It hasn't registered, I guess. That everything could be gone. It's not my place, but it's my fault. I still can't believe my father would do something that terrible." Her voice cracked.

"Let's not jump to conclusions. I think we'll both do better after some sleep. In the morning, I'll check in with my boss and see if I can't find out more about your unwelcome visitors."

Nothing in the client information indicated Hamilton would resort to violence, but Fozzie'd been around long enough to know you couldn't jump to any conclusions when it came to why people did what they did.

In the shadows, Torie's hand brushed her face. Damn, was she crying?

"You want me to drive?"

She sniffed. "No, I'm fine."

"It's all right to be upset. You've had quite the night."

"I said I'm fine."

Right. "Sure. You know the road better than I do. Keep an eye out for my car. And a tree blocking half the road."

Another sniff, and a shadowy nod of her head. She seemed in control, so he tried to relax. For the next five minutes or so, with the exception of an occasional shaky breath from Torie, nothing but the gentle rain on the car's roof and the rhythmic swish of the windshield wipers broke the silence. Her hands remained firmly on the wheel. Fozzie stared out the window.

"There it is. Up ahead," he said. "On the left. Pull over."

She did as he asked. He flipped on his torch and hopped out. "Back in a tick."

He gave the car a quick survey. Nope. No good Samaritan had changed his flat. He checked his phone. No one had built a cell tower, either. He grabbed his carryall from the backseat, re-locked the car and transferred the bag to Torie's backseat. With the interior light on, he took in the tear trails lining the dirt smudges on Torie's cheeks. He climbed in and kept his gaze straight ahead. "Drive on."

After a few minutes, the misty rain escalated to major deluge. Torie flipped the wipers to high, and his heart rate seemed to accelerate to match. The road sounds shifted and he realized they'd hit a paved road. He held his phone, watching the signal strength. Finally, he got two bars and decided it was worth a shot.

"Should I call nine-one-one, or is there a local fire department?"

There was another long pause. "I don't know. I suppose it would have been smart to make a list of emergency contact numbers, but when I moved in, I wasn't really all together." She sniffled again. "I guess I'm still not. Sorry."

"Hey, no worries. Besides, if you did have the numbers, my guess is they'd be pinned up somewhere near the phone in the cottage, right?" He jabbed 9-1-1 into the cell.

The dispatcher's calm voice reminded him of Jinx, Blackthorne's unflappable coordinator. He gave the dispatcher Torie's address, stressed the propane tank's proximity to the house, and that there was no one in residence at the moment.

"We'll coordinate with the local volunteers," the man said.

"Anything I can do?" Fozzie asked.

"No, sir. We'll have someone out there as soon as we can."

Fozzie knew better than to keep the man from his job by asking unnecessary questions. "Thanks." He snapped the phone shut and glanced at Torie. "It's being handled."

"Good."

He made one more call to the rental-car folks and told them where they could find his car. Working for Blackthorne had a few perks, and he got no arguments once the clerk checked the rental agreement.

They continued without speaking until they rolled into the small stretch of buildings that comprised Aspen Corners. Looking like sets from an old western, all but one of the wooden structures was dark. A flashing neon sign proclaimed the one open establishment to be "Pete's."

If the sleazebucket he'd chased away earlier was hanging around for another crack at Torie, this might be where he'd wait. Fozzie hadn't seen the firebug's car, but it was possible firebug and sleazebucket were one and the same.

"Is there a car park? Um . . . parking lot?" he asked.

"Around the back, on the next block. Why? There's plenty of

room on the street if you need to go in, and it's closer."

"I want to take a quick gander."

She drove to the corner, made the turn and slowed to a crawl. "You want me to drive in?"

"If you would, please. One trip through the lot."

The lights in the parking lot let him see her face. From the way her mouth tightened, he knew the exact instant she understood what he was doing.

CHAPTER SEVEN

Torie tried to subdue the writhing sensation in her belly as she steered her Fusion through the half-full lot. Fozzie had to be looking for the car the creep with the gun had been driving. And what if they found it? Was he planning to go inside Pete's and start a fight? The thought he might be meeting the gunman, that he'd turn her over, flickered through her brain, but she dismissed it. If they'd been in cahoots, they'd already have a meeting place, with none of this search-the-parking-lot stuff.

And who'd started the fire? Was there a third player? Her gaze darted back and forth, searching for the silver SUV. The number of cars on such a miserable night surprised her, but Pete's was the only eatery and bar in Aspen Corners. Anyone working in town might be riding out the storm over pizza and burgers.

Thinking of Pete's greasy food didn't help the twisting in her gut. She rounded the last row. "I don't see his car."

"I didn't expect to. Still, better to know as much as possible. You want to go in? Tell someone to alert any neighbors about the fire?"

All she wanted to do was get away. "The nearest neighbor is a mile away from me. The rain should keep the fire from spreading."

"Then we'll trust the firemen to do their job and be off. You said there's a lodge about five miles from here?"

She nodded. "Little rental cabins—not much different from

my place, and a few rooms in the lodge building."

"Think they'll have rooms available?"

She hoped so. At least two of them. Was it peak season? How would she know? This move to Oregon hadn't been on her list until Kath's death rewrote it.

"Guess we'll find out when we get there," she said.

"You're sure you're okay with driving?"

Of course not. What she wanted was to curl up in the back-seat—maybe even the trunk, where it would be dark and cozy—and go to sleep so she could wake up from this nightmare, back in her Miami apartment, and spend the day at the library shelving books.

"No problem," she replied, trying to sound nonchalant.

As they drove, she sensed Fozzie was making a point of not looking at her. He certainly wasn't trying to make small talk. The silence hung between them like a scratchy wool blanket. Several times, she caught him pulling his cell phone from his pocket, staring at it, then putting it away. They'd passed the dead zone, so he could have made a call if he'd wanted to. Or was he waiting for someone to call him?

She gave up on thinking and watched the road for the turnoff to the lodge. There. A cutout fish jumped above a faded billboard announcing O'Neill's Lake Lodge, two miles ahead. She nudged her foot a smidge harder against the accelerator. Fozzie slipped his phone into his pocket—again—and sat up straighter.

She reminded herself to breathe as she steered into the small dirt area in front of the lodge. Fozzie unclicked his seat belt.

"Wait here," he said, clamping his hat onto his head. "I'll see if they have anything available. No point in both of us being soaked."

Before she could protest, he was out of the car, dashing up the wooden steps to the entrance. A light came on in a small window. Through the silver curtain of rain, she saw a portly man stretch, scratch his chest and drag his hand across his chin before he disappeared.

She wondered it if might not have been smarter to go to Eugene. Or Bend. Or any real town where they wouldn't be so obvious. There weren't that many places to look for someone out in the boonies. This might rank high on someone's list.

Just get through the night.

Isn't that what she'd been trying to do ever since Fozzie showed up? Things would look better in the morning. They always did.

And then what would she do? She'd made a promise to find some special lichen, one Kathy believed held the key to a new drug.

You didn't make your promise to Kathy. She was already dead. She'd never know.

But Torie had made the promise to herself, and that's what mattered.

The lodge door opened, and Fozzie darted out. One second he was on the porch, the next sitting beside her in the car, brushing rain off his hat. "Cabin thirteen. The only one left. Manager says he keeps meaning to change the number, but I'd call it our lucky night."

She swallowed. "What about two rooms? In the lodge?"

"Full up. Some family reunion. It'll be all right. There's a pullout couch in the living room. You can have the bedroom." He flipped on the dome light and showed her the map. Pointing to an X in a circle, he said, "It's over there."

Just get through the night. Your cottage didn't have a pullout couch. This will be better.

She threw the car into reverse, backed out of the lot, and found the drive Fozzie indicated. She wound her way through the twisting, muddy route, past scattered cabins. No silver SUVs parked in front of any of them.

"Take a left," Fozzie said, pointing. "Should be off that trail."

She passed a cabin with a camper-topped pickup parked in front, then saw the turnoff Fozzie predicted. The lane seemed to be about a coat of paint wider than her Fusion, and she sucked in her breath as if it would make the car smaller.

She didn't exhale until she stopped the car, pulling in as close to the wooden steps in front of the cabin as possible. A yellow light glowed a warm welcome from a support post.

Her trembling fingers were still fumbling with the seat-belt release when her car door opened. Fozzie stood there, hand extended, that bone-melting grin on his face. "Not five-star accommodations, but the manager assures me it's clean and dry."

She glanced at the dash clock before she turned off the engine. Ten minutes to midnight. Almost tomorrow. Before she knew it, the sun would be up, and everything would be on its way to normal.

And there's a bridge in Brooklyn I can get for a pittance.

It was impossible to avoid his hand, so she accepted it long enough to swing herself out of the car. She made a mad dash for the steps and the shelter of the overhang. Turning, she saw Fozzie grab his bag from the backseat then lope to her side. Damn, she'd bet he never tripped over tree roots and landed on his bottom. Which was far too well-defined under his sweats as he knelt to unlace his boots.

She toed off her wet sneakers. "Um . . . key?"

He dangled a black metal key. The kind with the long stem and two prongs on the end. Like the sort that opened doors in a decrepit mansion in an old horror movie.

Stop. He's a nice enough guy, and it's only one night.

He wiggled the key in the lock, twisted the knob and pulled the door open. "After you."

She picked up her sneakers and stepped across the threshold, all of a sudden aware of her own too-ample posterior. Turning, she crouched and set her sneakers beside the door. She took off her wet shell and hung it on an old-fashioned coatrack standing inside the entry. Fozzie flicked the light switch, and a lamp beside the couch went on.

Tiny, was her first thought. But clean. No roaches scuttled across the floor, and the air smelled damp and piney, not musty and moldy. She studied the L-shaped space. The couch, which she hoped was the sleeper, sat along the right-hand wall, and a small kitchen area with an oval wooden table and four chairs filled the rest of that side of the cabin. Cozy.

To the right, on the short leg of the L, Fozzie was already lighting a wood-burning stove. She left him to the task and headed to a doorway beyond the stove, which she assumed would lead to the bedroom. Almost. She found herself in a narrow bathroom.

Switching on the light, she was pleased to find the room as clean as the main cabin area. Skimpy towels and a teeny bar of soap, but a full roll of toilet paper on the spindle. Stall shower. Sink with a mirrored medicine cabinet above. She glanced at her reflection and immediately ripped open the soap wrapper and washed her grimy, tear-stained face.

A second door opened into the bedroom, which held a queen-sized bed covered with a thin blue cotton spread. She sat on the edge and took in the rest of the room. Dresser, a low chest, and a door back to the kitchen. She checked it. No lock.

She wandered out to the living area, where Fozzie had the fire going. She scouted the room. "No phone?"

"Nope," he said. "And no television, either. No Internet. Not even a radio. Rustic living at its finest. But there is electricity."

"I noticed."

"I take it there's a bathroom somewhere. With running water?"

She nodded and gestured toward the door. He got up from the couch, carrying his bag with him into the room. "Won't be a minute."

Sitting in the spot he'd vacated, already warm from his body heat, she felt as if she was invading his private space. If he wanted to sleep, she was in his bed.

She peeled off her wet socks, then got up and padded barefoot along the kitchen route to the bedroom, peeking around the corner to make sure Fozzie had closed both bathroom doors before getting ready for bed.

The toilet flushed, water ran in the sink. The taps squeaked, followed by a gentle tapping on the door. Her mouth went dry, unlike her palms, which went damp.

When there was no answer to his knock, Fozzie hesitated. "You in there?" he asked as he twisted the knob. He cracked the door. "Torie?"

"Come in."

He pushed the door open. Torie sat on the edge of a queen-size bed, her hands gripping the spread. Her toes pushed up and down from the floor, but he didn't think she was doing calf presses for exercise.

"You doing all right?" Stupid question. Even in the dim light from the ceiling fixture, anyone could see she was a wreck. Adrenaline letdown. What she needed was a round-the-clock session with sleep.

She nodded but didn't meet his eyes.

"Sorry to bother you, but the manager said there were extra blankets and pillows in a chest. I didn't see one out front."

She tilted her head toward a wooden blanket chest that reminded him of the one his mother used to store her good linens. When the crisply ironed white tablecloth and napkins came out, there was Someone Important coming to dinner. Woe unto anyone who didn't follow the Company Manners rules, which meant trying to get through a meal without spilling anything. Putting on an uncomfortable shirt with a tight collar. And pinchy shoes.

He liked it much better when the red-and-green cloth came out, with its scenes of snow-covered pine trees and horse-drawn sleighs trotting over snow-covered fields. He always wondered why Mum used that cloth, since it was usually hot as the blazes on Christmas, but she'd said it was a family tradition. Since the rules were relaxed, and the food was good at Christmas dinner, he stopped questioning her.

He opened the chest. The wool blankets and pillow inside snapped him out of his reverie. He grabbed them. "You should get some sleep. See you in the morning."

"Right. G'night." Her voice was low, as if she didn't trust herself to speak above a whisper.

He left the way he came, closing the door behind him. He reminded himself that a typical day's work for him was way, way outside the realm of Torie's wildest imagination. He wished she'd accept comfort from him, but understood her hesitation. He positioned the pistol within reach on the end table.

A SIG SAUER P226, nine millimeter. A decent weapon, assuming its owner took care of it. He'd prefer to test it, but that was impossible here. Not to mention he'd checked the magazine and found only eight shots left. They probably didn't sell that kind of ammo in the lodge gift shop.

He swiped his hands over his face. He needed to take his own advice and get some shut-eye. He gave the couch a bounce test. Lumpy, and the corduroy upholstery would leave him indented with stripes. As long as the couch turned into a bed, why not take advantage of being able to stretch out? He had no illusions that the mattress would be comfortable, just bigger.

He pulled out the bed, which was already made up, and prodded the mattress. He slipped out of the sweats Torie had loaned him. He'd put on boxers when he'd cleaned up, figuring his normal sleep-in-the buff habit wouldn't be prudent.

Crawling under the covers, he found what he expected. The mattress dipped into a valley in the middle, right over the annoying metal support bar. But it was a bed, it was indoors, and it was warm. He couldn't say that about all his assignments. He folded his hands behind his head and stared at the ceiling. Pine planks, with knots scattered like so many constellations in a starry sky.

All along the drive from Torie's place, he'd debated calling Blackthorne. One thing he knew as well as he knew his own name was that Horace Blackthorne would not send an operative in, guns drawn, to grab anyone on a client's say so. Not unless it was a confirmed hostage situation.

What he wanted to do was simply report that he'd located the subject, that she was fine, and he'd delivered the message. But he needed to talk to Blackthorne first, because another thing Fozzie knew as well as his own name was that the boss reported to the client.

Somehow, Fozzie didn't think "I found her but I'm not saying where" would fly, either with the boss or Hamilton.

With a sigh, he leaned over and switched off the lamp. A gold ribbon of light shimmered under the door from Torie's room. "Go to sleep, Sunshine," he whispered. With three mind-clearing breaths, he shut out the world.

Some time later, muffled footfalls brought him instantly awake. A faint beam of light swept across the far side of the room. He sat upright. "Don't move."

The light dropped to the floor, spinning in wild circles across the oak planks. He flipped on the lamp.

"Torie?"

Her hands were in the air, her eyes wide with fear. He realized he held the pistol and immediately lowered it to the table. "Shit. Sunshine, I'm sorry. I was asleep. Didn't think."

She stood, rooted and quaking like one of the aspens outside the cabin.

"Sneaking around in the dark isn't a good idea," he said. He sounded gruff, even to his ears. He softened his tone. "I guess I still have bad guys on the brain."

She didn't say anything, simply pivoted and retreated to her room, leaving her flashlight where it had come to rest. Crap.

He kicked out from under the covers, crossed the room, and spoke to the closed door. "Torie, wait. Please. I'm sorry I scared you. I'm awake now. What did you need? Let me help. Please?"

"I'm . . . I'm . . . Just go back to sleep." Her voice quavered.

Oh, God, she was going to cry and it was his fault. He'd pointed a gun at her, for Chrissake. And he was standing here in his effing boxers. He grabbed his sweats and remedied that before he freaked her out again. Stumbling into them, he went back to the door.

"Torie, we should talk. Can I come in?"

There were some shuffling sounds, and some sniffling, but the door opened. She still wore the sweats she'd had on earlier, but he could tell she'd taken off whatever she'd worn underneath the top. He snapped his gaze back to her face.

You are such an asshole. Point a gun at her, then stare at her tits.

He raked his hands through his hair. "Want some rooibos tea?"

Her eyebrows lifted. "They have that here?"

"I doubt it, but I always carry some." At her quizzical glance, he shrugged. "Me mum drank it. No caffeine, so it was a 'grown up' drink we kids were allowed to have."

Her gaze pierced his, as if she saw his need for connection to home and family. Her expression saddened. "Nana used to drink chamomile. She'd put milk and honey in mine."

"She was special, wasn't she?" Of course she was. Torie'd been willing to risk her life for a box of books that connected her to her grandmother. If he wasn't inserting his size elevens into his mouth, he was saying something totally stupid. And why? He never had trouble talking to people. He decided to keep his mouth shut for a while.

By the time the water came to a boil and he'd brewed the tea, Torie was no longer a skittish lamb. He eyed the straight-back wooden chairs around the table. "Couch might be more comfortable."

She gazed in that direction and stiffened. *Right.* At the moment, it was a bed. He crossed the room and folded it back into lumpy couch mode. "Better?"

"Yes. I don't know why, but it feels funny sitting on a bed, even though it's not really that much different sitting on the sofa."

"You don't need to be afraid of me, Torie. Not about anything."

"Yeah. I know."

She didn't move, so he took a seat at one end of the couch. When she did sit, it was at the far end, her legs tucked under her. With her tea held in front of her, her body language screamed, "Don't come near me."

Might as well pick up where they'd left off before the fire sent them in a new direction. "I'm going to have to report in tomorrow."

"What will you say?"

"I haven't decided. I think we should talk about it."

"What do you need to know? My father wants me to come home. As if I'd ever think where he lives is my home."

"Why won't you go back? Just to show him you're all right?"

She set her tea on the end table and leaned forward, pressing the heels of her hands into her eyes. "It's not that easy."

"It shouldn't be that hard. Take a deep breath and tell me about it."

CHAPTER EIGHT

Torie tried Fozzie's deep-breath technique. It took three tries before she thought she might be able to talk without bursting into embarrassing tears. Concentrating on her tea helped, but she couldn't get the words past the thickness in her throat.

Fozzie touched her knee. Gently, a fleeting tap, but she looked up. Worry filled his eyes.

"Did your father . . . hurt you?" His voice barely broke a whisper, but she heard anger behind it.

She almost laughed. "You mean beat me? Or sexually abuse me?"

He nodded.

"No, nothing like that. He never laid a hand on me. Sometimes I wish he'd have spanked me. Just to show he was aware of my existence. But he was glad enough to be rid of me."

"He hired us to find you."

She met his gaze. "Exactly who did he hire you to find?"

"Victoria Hamilton." A pause. "He didn't know you'd changed your name."

"Right. I never meant to hide. I came back to the States and moved around a lot, but I changed my name legally. It's a matter of record if you know where to look."

"Yeah. But there are fifty bloody states in this country, you know."

She raised her eyebrows. "You searched them all?"

Fozzie shook his head, his curls bobbing. "Nope, although I'm sure Blackthorne would have found the paperwork eventually. I was digging through archives at a library in Coconut Grove. I had your old yearbook photo—the only one we had to go on—on the desk beside me. The librarian came over to tell me they were about to close, saw the picture and said, 'Why, that looks like Torie Stoker,' and the penny dropped."

"Of all the libraries in all the towns in all the world," she said, "he walks into mine. I volunteered there."

Fozzie grinned. "You like Bogie?"

"Nana loved old movies—although I suppose to her they weren't old, just reruns. We'd watch together."

He raised his tea mug. "Here's lookin' at you, kid."

She couldn't help but smile. "I suppose I should be glad you found me when you did." With that thought, she realized she'd switched him from bad guy to a man on her side. It was a new sensation, but it felt kind of nice.

"So, tell me more. Why does your father want you back so badly now, if he never cared before?"

"Long story."

"I can make more tea."

Oh, there was that smile again. "No, I'm fine." Tea-wise. Butterflies-in-the-belly-wise, she was far from fine. She took another three deep breaths, but not to control the tears. "You're familiar with the 'poor little rich girl' cliché? They have that in Australia?"

"I've heard of it, yes. Even on a sheep station, we do get our book-learning." His eyes twinkled.

She accepted his jibe. "Well, you're looking at one. In spades. You know what my father does?"

"Head of some restaurant company."

"Yes. Epicurean Unlimited. My grandfather started it. My father never wanted to work for a living and lived off Grandfather's wealth."

She paused. God, she didn't work for a living, either. Was she her father's daughter after all?

No, because she wasn't out to exploit anyone. She wasn't throwing away money on personal luxuries the way her father had. She had a reliable financial advisor, enough money for a comfortable life, but she wasn't extravagant, and she tried to do good works. Didn't she? She thought of all the libraries where she'd volunteered, all the literacy programs she'd supported. She was *not* her father's daughter. She was Nana's granddaughter.

"He seems to be doing all right," Fozzie said.

"Have you checked the financials of the company?"

He balanced his mug on his thigh. "No, can't say that I have."

"Well, last time I checked, things were on a downward spiral. And I'm the solution to his problem."

"Explain?"

"The abridged version?" She sighed. "Before I was born, my parents did the jet-set thing. I was undoubtedly a mistake. I was definitely an encumbrance, but my grandmother tried to be there for me. Sometimes they'd leave me with her when they did their gallivanting." She swallowed the lump that rose in her throat. "I think I liked those times the best."

"I can see why you might be bitter," Fozzie said softly.

She raised her gaze. God, he looked like he understood. And cared. She hurried to continue.

"Then, one day, Grandfather said it was time my father learned the business."

"Which was a good thing, right?"

She shook her head. "No. My father hated it. And he was still on the road a lot, but not to the same kind of places. Grandfather insisted he see how everything worked, from the bottom up. That's when my parents sent me to Switzerland."

"Did you like that? Being in one place—and a beautiful one, I've heard."

Fire burned behind her eyes as the memories returned. "I was a dumpy nothing surrounded by girls of noble birth or with scads of money. Old money. I was there so my parents could brag about having a daughter in the exclusive Lucerne Academy for Young Ladies. And under pressure not to disgrace the family name."

"And that was important?"

"To them." She swiped her eyes with the back of her hand. "I kept hoping that if I made them proud, they'd take me back. At least where I could be closer to Nana. They never wrote. They visited me the first Christmas I was there. After that, it was a card, and one on my birthday—if they remembered."

She tried to forget about those days, how she'd paste a smile on her face, trying not to let the hurt show as everyone milled about in the mail center and brandished cards and letters, displayed their gifts, or how she stayed behind when everyone else went home for long weekends and holidays. All the excuses she made up about why her parents didn't visit.

"When they didn't show up for graduation, I was past hurt. I was angry. I packed up my things, and a friend and I spent six months touring Europe. I started using Torie Stoker as my name. I wanted to cut all ties to my family, since it was clear they wanted nothing to do with me."

She sucked in a deep breath. "God, I sound so pathetic. My father didn't beat me or abuse me, and maybe I should be grateful he never interfered."

"What about your mother?"

"She's probably busy giving parties or trying to get invited to them. Making sure she's got the right things to wear. That the newspaper columnists spell her name right."

Fozzie touched her knee again, and this time he left his hand there. "Every child deserves a parent's love. Unconditionally. For what it's worth, I think you turned out fine."

"You've known me less than a day."

"I'm a great judge of character."

His smile warmed her. Heat rushed to her face.

The next thing she knew, he'd sprung up and almost floated across the room, standing next to the window. Somehow, the gun had appeared in his hand.

"What—?" She stood, grasping the arm of the couch.

He motioned her to be quiet. She listened. To nothing. The rain had stopped. Then she listened to her heart and the blood pounding in her ears.

More than an eternity later, he returned to her side. "Nothing."

"People don't jump up in the middle of a conversation for nothing. And they especially don't grab guns for nothing. Tell me."

"I thought I heard something, that's all."

"Heard what? Fozzie, please. If you don't tell me, I'll imagine the worst." Lord, why did she want him to grab her in his arms and tell her she was safe? Easy. Because he obviously had enough strength to share, and hers was in definite need of replenishment.

"A car," he said. "We're the last cabin on this spur, and there's no reason for any cars to come down here. Not at this hour."

"But I didn't hear anything."

"I must have imagined it."

His look said otherwise and she told him so.

"Okay, I heard what I thought was a car, but it didn't come this way. Sound carries at night, and it was probably on the perimeter road. A false alarm."

False alarms implied there was a reason for real alarms. "Are you my bodyguard now?"

"Would you feel better if I said yes?"

She had to laugh. Simone at school had a bodyguard for a semester. Rumor had it he did a lot more with her body than guard it. Torie's gaze met his soft brown eyes. Had he inched his face closer to hers? No way. But damn, he had gorgeous eyes. And such long, thick lashes. Three coats of Revlon's 3D Extreme Mascara wouldn't bring hers close.

Don't be ridiculous. She searched for her voice, which came out strangely husky. "If you think I need a bodyguard, I guess I'm glad it's you."

His smile, slow and lazy, jump-started her heart. He leaned forward. She held her breath. He rested his hands on her shoulders and kissed her forehead. Like she was a kid sister. A pathetic kid sister.

"Get some sleep, Sunshine. I'll hold down the fort out here, and we'll get an early start tomorrow."

Fozzie watched Torie rush to the bedroom and shut the door. Damn, had he almost kissed the client's daughter? His personal *assignment?* Technically, he supposed he *had* kissed her. At least he'd caught himself before he'd done anything more stupid.

Why had he even been tempted? She was absolutely not his type. She'd seemed so fragile, so vulnerable . . . and so . . . so what? Bad enough he was going to plead her case with the boss tomorrow. Crap. He'd also gotten sidetracked before she actually told him why her father wanted her.

You're losing it. Get some sleep.

Torie wasn't the only one who needed sleep. He'd deal with his off-the-wall reaction to her some other time.

He pulled the couch out to a bed again and flipped off the

lamp. It took a lot more than three mind-clearing breaths before he finally drifted off.

Birdsong brought him awake. He stumbled into the bathroom, and let the hot water reunite his soul with his body. Shaving helped him feel human. Coffee would help even more. After folding his borrowed sweats and putting on his own clothes, he wandered to the kitchen and found the coffeemaker, but O'Neill's Lake Lodge didn't include those mini-packs of caffeine most places stocked nowadays.

He glanced at the closed bedroom door and hoped Torie had slept more than he had. He'd had better nights on a rocky mountainside. He debated jogging up to the lodge to see if they had coffee in the lobby but wouldn't leave Torie.

He ignored the gnawing in his belly and flopped onto the couch. Thumbing the button on his cell phone, he called the Blackthorne command center. Jinx answered immediately.

"Need a favor, mate," Fozzie said.

"Don't you always?"

"Well, this one could be dicey. I need you to tap into the old man's files and pull any communication relating to the Hamilton case."

"Shit, Fozz—you still on that one? By now, I thought you'd be on R and R."

"Soon enough, mate."

"I'm sure the redheaded population is mourning your absence."

Fozzie looked toward the bedroom door, still closed, and thought of Torie's brown hair. Plain, ordinary, natural brown hair. Suddenly, the typical bought-and-paid-for red lost much of its appeal.

Still, he had a reputation to uphold. Unwarranted as it was, he never bothered to correct it. No reason to let anyone know his pickups rarely extended beyond conversation and a few drinks.

"They can wait," he said. "Back to business. The favor I need doesn't entail the research, it's the fact that I never made this call and you don't know where I am. Can you handle that?"

"You doubt me? For shame. And of course, Blackthorne's not supposed to know I've been looking, right?"

"Took that for granted." Fozzie stifled a yawn. "Look, I'm going to call in and report to the boss later this morning, but I'd like to have more intel before I decide what I'm going to say. It's—" What was it, exactly? Cheating? Lying? Stretching the truth? More like begging, he figured. "It's complicated."

"I don't see a problem. Any clue to what I'm looking for?"

"Wish I knew. For starters, I need to know if there's anyone here but me."

Jinx was already tapping keys. "Not one of us, I can tell you that right now."

"No, I mean was there anything to indicate the client wasn't happy with our service, that he was going to go elsewhere? I've run into at least one other bloke looking for our target, and subtlety isn't his game."

"I'll check."

Fozzie took a quick breath. "One more thing. Can you run a plate? Oregon."

"Run a plate, as in sneak into the Oregon DMV database?"

"That would be it."

"You're pushing."

Fozzie braced himself for Jinx's next reaction before he continued. "Yeah, and all I got was a partial. Silver, a small SUV. Suzuki maybe. Or a Toyota. I think there's a B in it, and it ends in seven. Maybe oh-seven. Or eight-seven."

"You don't ask for much, do you? Why can't you be a car person like Hotshot? He'd have known make, model and year."

"I already told you. It was pouring rain. Dark. Plates get muddy. And I was preoccupied."

"All right, but don't hold your breath."

"Breathing as normal."

"On it," Jinx said. "I'll let you know."

"Thanks, mate." As Fozzie ended the call, the bedroom door opened and Torie's sleep-disheveled head poked out.

"I didn't wake you, did I?" he asked. Lord, she was *cute*. He didn't do *cute*. So what was with all the tingling below the belt?

"No, I've been awake."

More than she'd been asleep, he thought, taking in her red-rimmed eyes. But he knew better than to say it. "I've already showered, so the bathroom's all yours. I thought we'd grab breakfast at the lodge."

Fozzie paused at the entrance to the restaurant. Coffee aromas mingled with bacon and sausage. His mouth watered and his stomach begged. Laughter and the clink of silverware on china rolled out from the room. He stepped aside to get a better view.

The family reunion the manager spoke of last night was out in full force. He figured at least three generations filled four tables pushed together like a castle banquet room. Beside him, Torie inhaled audibly.

"Um . . . are you sure we should eat here? It feels like we're intruding," she said. She'd washed away all external evidence of last night, but she projected tension like an electric field. "We could probably get something on the road."

"I doubt they'll notice us."

A young woman arrived, smiled, grabbed two menus, and led them to a small table at the far end of the room. "It might be a bit quieter here."

Behind them, a youngster shrieked, "Look Gramma, a fish. Did you see it jump? High up in the sky?"

Their server grinned. "Then again, maybe not."

"No worries," Fozzie said. "Feels like home to me." He gazed out the window. Sunlight sparkled off the water, glistening like diamonds on the breeze-ruffled surface. He walked around the table and took the seat facing into the room, leaving Torie with the view of the lake.

The server dropped the menus on the table. "Would you like some coffee while you decide?"

"Please," Fozzie and Torie said in unison.

"Back in a flash."

With steaming mugs of coffee in front of them and the cacophony of the reunion behind them, Fozzie closed his eyes and savored the first few sips. To his relief, the Spartan accommodations had no relation to the quality of the coffee. Or the quality of the food. Eggs done just right, crisp bacon, and blueberry pancakes. Real maple syrup. Lord, if he didn't hate the countryside so much, he could do two weeks of R and R here, easy.

Torie picked at her omelet and nibbled at her toast, wiping her mouth with her napkin between bites.

"Not feeling well?" he asked.

"Fine." Her gaze never left her plate.

"Sunshine, you need to eat. Keep your strength up. Might be a long stretch before lunch. At least finish your juice. It's fresh-squeezed."

She took a few sips and continued working daintily on her breakfast. Must come from being an only child, he guessed. When he was growing up, it was the quick and the hungry. If you weren't the former, you definitely stayed the latter.

He lingered over coffee while Torie ate. When his cell rang, he excused himself from the table. "Jinx. Whatcha got?" He wandered outside, hitching a hip onto the bonnet of Torie's car.

"I don't know if it's good news or bad news, but there's

nothing pointing to anything unusual. All communication between Blackthorne and Hamilton seems to have been initiated on our end, giving progress reports—or lack of progress reports." There was a hint of teasing sarcasm in Jinx's tone.

"Hey, no wisecracks. The guy gave us zip to start with."

"I noticed," Jinx said. "Nothing in the transcripts indicates Hamilton was upset. Disappointed maybe, but he seemed patient and understood it might take a while after all these years."

"Didn't threaten to call us off?"

"Negative."

"Thanks. I owe you one."

"You owe me *another* one. Someday, I'm calling in these favors, you know."

"Say the word."

"Oh, no, you conniving Aussie. I am going to plan, and strike when you least expect it."

"You take care, Jinx."

"Will do. I'll let you know if I find anything."

Fozzie hung up and moseyed around to where he could see the restaurant's window. Torie was still at the table, still working on her breakfast. The way she ate, she could probably starve to death while eating a five-course meal. She certainly didn't look like the kind of woman who starved herself. Plenty of generous curves.

Or was she mad at him for last night?

He leaned against a hemlock. As he entered the boss's number, he automatically stood at attention.

Relax, idiot. He can't see you.

"Mr. Mayhew." Horace Blackthorne's deep voice resounded in Fozzie's ear. "So thoughtful of you to check in."

He snapped erect again. "Sorry, sir. Things got a trifle dicey, and then there was no cellular coverage until very late last night.

This is the first chance I've had to check in—during office hours, that is."

"Very well. I trust you are in satisfactory condition, despite your . . . dicey . . . situation."

"Perfectly fine."

"Have you located our client's daughter?"

"See, sir, that's what I want to talk to you about."

CHAPTER NINE

Torie nursed her coffee, watching Fozzie. Was he talking to his boss? He alternated between standing tall and pacing a small circle around a tree. No sweats today. He wore black cargo pants stuffed into the tops of his hiking boots, and instead of the Taz sweatshirt, he wore a long-sleeved black T-shirt under his open jacket. She tried not to think about what he'd look like without it, with the shirt clinging to his broad chest.

Enough.

They'd be out of here soon. She'd take him to a car-rental place, or the airport, or wherever he wanted to go, and be rid of him. Then, she'd go back to the cottage—assuming there was a cottage left. She'd stay long enough to get the philodendron she'd forgotten about last night, pack anything that wasn't ruined, and decide where she'd go next. Idaho might be nice. There ought to be lots of places to hide in Idaho. Besides, it had a nice ring to it. Lying low in Idaho. It wouldn't have to be for long. After her birthday, there would be no point in her father looking for her, and she could continue the search for Kathy's elusive lichens.

"All finished? Or will your man be back?"

Startled, Torie gazed into the expectant face of the server. "No, we're through."

The woman cleared the table and dropped the check in the middle. "Whenever you're ready."

Her man. The words brought a rush of heat to Torie's face.

As if. How could she have thought, even for a second, that he'd be interested in her as a woman? She thought he was going to kiss her last night—a real kiss—and then he did that kid sister thing. She was lucky she hadn't burst into tears right then. No, she'd managed to make it back to the comforting embrace of her pillow.

The memory brought the humiliation back. How he'd been all business this morning, acting as if he hadn't noticed her stupid reaction to him last night. At least she hadn't wrapped her fingers in his thick, curly hair and yanked his lips to hers.

He had a job to do, and he said he'd try to convince his boss not to rat her out. Even if it meant getting in trouble. He was kind. But he cared about her *situation,* not about her. She was plain, dumpy Torie, and why she'd ever thought he'd make any sort of romantic advance—she dropped the thought. Why should she care? It wasn't like she wanted to settle down with anyone. If she did, she'd have gone back to her father a long time ago.

She snatched the check, fumbled through her bag for her wallet, and dumped enough cash on the table to cover the bill plus a generous tip. If Fozzie was willing to risk his boss' wrath, paying for his breakfast was a small price.

She dashed for the ladies' room before she lost it. Young ladies *never* showed their emotions in public.

Drawing on years of keeping her feelings hidden, Torie emerged from the restroom moments later, her face repaired and her chin high. She strode through the lobby, smiled at the desk clerk and went outside to find Fozzie.

The trees danced in the breeze. The lake sparkled. On the dock, two men were giving fishing lessons to children. Fathers and their kids, she assumed. Building family memories. Memories she didn't have.

Snap out of it!

She yanked herself away from the pity party and sucked in

the clean, woodsy air. Dodging mud puddles left from yester-day's rains, she forced a cheerful smile on her face as she rounded the building. Fozzie was still on the phone. He nodded as if someone on the other end could see him, then dragged his hand through his hair. She already recognized the gesture as one of those "things aren't going the way I hoped" signals. Displacement behavior, according to a psych book she'd read once.

Don't jump to conclusions.

Because he wasn't happy about something didn't mean it was bad news for her. Maybe he was getting chewed out for disobey-ing orders. Maybe her father would accept the fact that she wasn't going to come back, and he'd call off his dogs. Maybe the sun would set in the east tonight.

She stopped at a polite distance, letting him converse in private, wishing she could read lips. Or that he'd put the call on speaker with the volume turned to high. He glanced in her direction and flashed a smile.

Which still created the dancing butterfly effect. Why not? She might be dumpy and boring, and oh-so-very-proper, but she was human, wasn't she?

He snapped his phone shut and ambled in her direction. He never looked down, but he didn't step in a single puddle. Never seemed to adjust his stride to avoid roots and stones. She checked to make sure his feet actually touched the ground and didn't float above it.

She waited, convinced all the obstacles that rushed out of his way were plotting to get into hers. Her heart beat out a rhythm for the butterfly ballet. What had he found out?

"You're looking a bit more chipper," he said. "Told you a good meal would set things right."

If only. He continued walking, and she turned to keep up

with him. He headed toward the steps and reached for his wallet.

"I covered it," she said.

"How much do I owe you?"

"Nothing. You might have saved my life a couple of times yesterday. I think I'm the one in debt."

"No worries. All part of Blackthorne's service. We like to keep our clients alive." He stopped short and his hands balled into tight fists. His grin flattened to a thin line.

"What's wrong?" Was someone else coming? She spun around, trying to see behind trees, straining to hear anything unusual. No bodies skulking around. No sounds but birdsong and rustling tree branches.

"Nothing." His features relaxed, but his smile was empty.

He surged forward. She trotted to keep up.

In the car, he gripped the steering wheel for several heartbeats before he slotted the key and turned on the engine. She willed him to relay what he'd found out but wouldn't speak the question aloud. Until she heard it, it couldn't be bad news.

At their cabin, he beelined for the bathroom. The door slammed.

Was that his problem? Morning post-coffee syndrome? She suppressed a smile and went outside to enjoy the crisp fall day. She followed a trail around the cabin, looking for the telltale signs she'd learned. Things that meant there was a possibility the lichens might be around. They wouldn't be near the lake—too wet—so she headed into the trees.

The shadows deepened despite the rising sun. Damp, earthy smells replaced the piney ones. She scanned tree trunks and rocks, but didn't see anything she hadn't already learned to eliminate. Maybe the elusive species grew in Idaho, and she could kill two birds with one stone. A side trail looked more promising. Not as brightly lit, and—she squinted into the shadows—was that one of the plants that shared the same habitat as the lichens? She visualized the picture in Kathy's botany book. Broad, shiny, deep-green leaves. Triangular in shape, arranged individually, not in pairs.

She stepped off the trail. The plants looked right, but no nearby lichens. Maybe a little lower? She grabbed an overhanging branch for balance and sidestepped down a narrow embankment.

"Torie!"

She turned as she heard her name. Her sneakers slipped on the mud-coated slope, she lost her grip on the branch, and she squealed as she slid down the hillside on her bottom.

"Torie! Sunshine!"

She clambered to her feet, brushing off leaves and twigs. "Over here," she called. She'd only slid about six feet, but it was a steep drop. To her right, she spied an easier route and cut across, hoping to reach the trail before Fozzie found out what a klutz she was.

She'd almost made it, when she looked up and saw a pair of boots. Her gaze moved upward, over black cargo pants, onto an outstretched hand.

"Here you go, Sunshine."

She grabbed his hand. Calloused, warm, and strong. He tugged, and then she was on the main trail staring into his eyes.

He steadied her. "When you weren't in the cabin, it scared me half to death. What were you doing down there?"

She wiped her hands across her bottom, hoping the evidence of her slide wasn't too apparent. They came back mud-covered. So much for that. She rubbed the excess dirt off on her thighs, then brushed her hands together. She tried to look like her detour down the hillside was all part of her plan. "I was looking for specimens."

"Specimens?"

"Plants. Lichens, actually. Did you know they're really a symbiotic relationship between an algae and a fungus?"

"I'll take your word for it. I don't suppose you'd be willing to tell me why you were looking for these lichens."

"Kathy. She thought they might have drug potential. I promised to keep looking."

"Can I help?"

If he'd pulled his gun out, she wouldn't have been more surprised. No, she probably could have tolerated the gun. "You? Here? Now? But what about your job? Your boss? Me? My father?"

He shrugged. "The old man's going to make some calls."

Her heart jumped to her throat. "To my father? What's he going to say?"

Fozzie heard the panic in Torie's voice. "Relax. For the time being, you're safe. And so's my job."

"For the time being?"

He took her hand and led her to a fallen tree. He lowered himself onto the makeshift bench and tapped a spot beside him. "Sit for a minute."

She did, hugging her tote to her chest.

"I had to tell him I found you," Fozzie said.

Her shoulders slumped. If not for the bag on her lap, he thought she might have collapsed like a popped balloon. "I understand."

"Wait a second. I told him I didn't think your father needed the details, only that you were safe."

"I hear a 'but' in there."

"Look at it from the other side. Your father is a respected businessman who's asked nothing more than to find a long-lost daughter. Ostensibly to make amends for a less-than-stellar job of parenting. There's no good reason *not* to tell him. He is paying for Blackthorne's services. And the boss is very particular about the company's public image." Torie didn't need to hear about the private, covert ops side of the business, where Fozzie spent most of his time.

"I said I understood."

"But you're an adult. Nobody can force you to go back, and after I explained that there were a couple of blokes of the not-so-nice variety who also wanted to find you, Blackthorne agreed that he wouldn't tell your father we found you. Yet."

She sat up straighter. "Really?" She sounded like a kid who'd just been told she was going to Disneyland.

He found he liked the sound. A lot. "Yes, really."

"I don't suppose your boss could convince my father to call off those not-so-nice guys?" She mumbled the words more to her purse than him.

"It gets a tad sticky there. If my boss questions your father, that's a dead giveaway that we've found you. How else would we know about it?"

She deflated again. "I told you I understand. You did what you could, and I'm really grateful. Honest. But I think it would be best if I disappear, and you get on with your next assignment. I'll be happy to drop you somewhere you can get transportation."

Normally, he'd jump at the chance to be rid of an assignment like this one. So why weren't they already driving to the airport? Because as soon as he'd seen the man trying to manhandle her last night, she'd become his responsibility. Maybe not his assignment, but she was his nonetheless. And the personal responsibilities were harder to cut loose. After Isla Caribe, he couldn't walk away.

"That won't be necessary," he said.

She stood and brushed off the seat of her pants. "Then please give me the car keys. *My* car keys. I'm sure you can call a cab or one of those rental-car places that picks you up. I have to leave."

She marched away. He watched her hips swing for a moment, then dashed after her.

"Torie, wait!"

She didn't stop.

"Torie. Sunshine. Look, we can talk about this some more, but there's something you ought to know."

She stopped and gave him a glacial stare. "What might that be?"

He grinned and hooked a thumb over his shoulder. "The cabin's back that way."

She went crimson. "Of course it is." She took off at a dead run.

Damnation. He jogged after her, keeping distance between them until she'd run herself out. He fell into step beside her. "I'd like to be on your side, Torie. Will you tell me why your father's so anxious to have you come home? Because he didn't hire Blackthorne to drag you back."

"We can talk in the car. On the way to Kathy's place."

"I thought you wanted to look for specimens."

"That was just something to do while you were . . . busy . . . in the cabin."

Right. Where he'd hidden in the bathroom, dealing with the guilt. He'd been joking about keeping clients alive, and, wham, Kathy's death sucker punched him. He was the reason Torie had lost her best friend. Telling himself it wasn't his fault, that it was a team effort, that bad things happened no matter what you did, hadn't helped.

Then he couldn't find Torie and he'd gone cold as a witch's tit. When he saw her car parked where he'd left it, he panicked. Had someone grabbed her? Thank goodness for the muddy ground. Her sneakers had left him a trail to follow.

"I'm sorry," he said.

She narrowed her eyes. "For what?"

He shrugged and smiled. "I'm not exactly sure, but I must have done something to upset you. And if I didn't, I know I will eventually, so maybe you'll put it on my account?"

That earned him a tentative upcurve of Torie's lips.

"So," he continued. "You said you want to go back to your cottage?"

"Yes. All my stuff is there. Some of it might be salvageable. And won't there be an arson investigation? Shouldn't we give statements, or something?"

"Guess I didn't think about that. I wanted you safe." In his usual line of work, they rarely hung around after the fireworks. They left cleanup to locals.

"And you did your job very well, thanks. Again."

He opened the car's passenger door for her. "I'm going to grab my bag, and we can go." He cut her off before she could say anything. "Buckle up. I'm driving."

She shrugged and he watched as she withdrew into herself, shrinking before his eyes.

As they drove, she fidgeted with her bag. Stared out the window. Fidgeted some more.

"You need a pit stop?" he asked.

She shook her head.

"Then let's quit avoiding the subject. Why did your father hire Blackthorne to find you?"

"Because if I don't show up, Grandfather will sell the company out from under him. He doesn't want *me*. He doesn't want to make *amends*. He wants to save his precious lifestyle."

"I thought your father owned the company."

"No, Grandfather has controlling interest. He may have retired, but he's the majority shareholder."

"So why would he sell it out from under your father? And

what does you showing up have to do with it?"

Her sigh ripped a hole in his heart.

"I told you Nana was always there for me, right?"

"You did."

"Well, even though Grandfather could be pigheaded and stubborn, he loved her. Dearly. He was—still is—an old-fashioned, male chauvinist pig. He would have been happier a couple hundred years ago, when women were property."

"Go on."

"Anyway, for Nana, he bent his personal rules. She had her own money, and he never tried to control it. When she left it to me, I don't think he was all that happy about it, but he didn't interfere." She paused. "She died four years ago. Grandfather stopped paying attention to Epicurean, and without his input—interference, my father would have called it—things went downhill. Grandfather is a businessman. My father isn't. Period. Always trying new schemes, trying to take shortcuts, anything to get out of actually working, but Grandfather was always there to keep him in check."

"For someone who cut all family ties, you seem well connected."

"Not directly. Everything goes through my lawyer and financial advisors. Until she died, Nana kept me informed through them. And since I own some Epicurean stock, I'm aware of what's going on."

He cocked an eye at her. "I didn't peg you for a financial wizard."

"Oh, I'm hardly a wizard. My advisors take care of that. But they let me know what they're doing, and sometimes I actually pay attention." She turned to him and smiled. "After all, if I didn't, I might have to work for a living."

"*Touché.*" He waited, hoping she'd continue without prodding. He hated the idea of causing her pain, but he'd promised

95

Blackthorne he'd get the skinny. By noon. Which, according to the clock on the dash, was about three hours from now. He'd let her take things at her own pace.

She fussed around for a bit, putting on lip gloss. Berry scented. Fluffed her hair. She looked at her hands, frowned, and dug a nail file out of the depths of her bag. The rasping sound as she slid it back and forth over a nail didn't *quite* set his teeth on edge. She'd file, look at the nail, run her thumb over it, then file some more. Eventually, she seemed satisfied and zipped everything back in her bag.

He dragged a hand through his hair and tried not to look impatient. Although it seemed quite the lengthy process, by the clock she'd only spent five minutes on her rituals.

"I don't suppose you want to get married," she said.

CHAPTER TEN

Torie wasn't sure whether she felt like laughing or crying at Fozzie's reaction. He'd practically driven off the road, his mouth hanging open like his jaw had come unhinged. Was he thinking about how outrageous it would be to be married to *her?* Or just shocked at the question, period? It had certainly surprised her, spouting from her mouth with no connection whatsoever to her brain.

"Only kidding," she said. "Relax."

His jaw reconnected, although now he looked more like a fish than a teddy bear, the way his mouth opened and closed with no sound coming out.

"Besides," she went on, "if I was willing to play Grandfather's silly game, I could have done it already. Then again, waiting until the eleventh hour might serve my father right."

"Sunshine, back up. You've lost me. What are you talking about?" His gaze darted back and forth between her and the road. He adjusted the rearview mirror.

"Grandfather's games. He doesn't like the way my father is running the company, but he doesn't want to come out of retirement to fix it. He's trying to do something he thinks would have made Nana happy, which would be transferring the company to me. But his chauvinistic streak won't let him do that. He can't see me in that role." She frowned. "Actually, neither can I, which is beside the point. So, he decided that I should marry a good man, settle down, and probably have the requisite two-point-three children. This man, who Grandfather's supposed to approve of first, would actually manage the business, while I stayed home and played happy homemaker."

"Which you don't want?"

She mulled that over. She'd never wanted a career. Sure, she'd had the usual fantasies about a husband who loved her, children she could love. But could she live that life? She'd certainly never had appropriate role models. Could she put down roots? As a kid, every time she'd hoped a move was the last, she was yanked up and dragged somewhere else. She still never stayed in one place very long. Not to mention she wasn't the sort to attract the man of her fantasies, and she couldn't bear thinking who her father and grandfather might pluck from some newspaper gossip column if she didn't come up with one of her own.

"Not on his terms. Since the deadline is my thirtieth birthday, which is eight months from now, my father is panicking. Hence all the interest in finding me."

"And if you don't get married? Or he doesn't approve of your choice?"

"Then Grandfather switches to Plan B, which is to turn over the company to Nana's pet charity, and my father is stuck trying to live off whatever he's bothered to save over the years. Or get a real job. I don't imagine either option is appealing."

"I suppose not." He did the hair thing again. "I don't suppose you'd be willing to call your father, tell him to leave you alone, and wish him luck? Maybe put an end to this?"

She'd already thought about that. Regularly. "No. At first, I was afraid he'd find me if I called. Trace the phone, figure out where I was. Hire someone to ferret me out from the call records. Some people are good at that, you know." She grinned at him. "I guess it didn't matter, did it? I mean, you found me without any phone records."

"Some of us are good at what we do." He grinned back. "Or just plain lucky."

"Either way, I'm outed. But that doesn't change things. If he knows where I am, even if your boss doesn't tell him, he could still find me. And if he comes looking in person, if I have to see him, I'm . . . I'm not sure I can say no. He's very persuasive. And I'm afraid I'll revert to little Victoria, doing everything he asks, still trying to win his approval."

"I don't believe it. You're too strong for that."

"You have more faith than I do. I've never been willing to risk it."

"What if I told you I could hook you up with an untraceable call?"

She pondered that for a moment. The thought of standing up to her father sent sweat trickling down her neck.

"Not anymore. Not after he hired people to come get me. With guns. And fire. Let him learn to eat peanut butter sandwiches."

Uncertainty flashed across Fozzie's face.

"What?" she asked. "You're thinking something."

"No, nothing."

"Don't do this. I already told you, not knowing is worse."

He made a show of navigating a series of switchbacks before he answered. "Fair enough. What would happen if you weren't around?"

She swallowed. "You mean, not around like in . . . *dead* not around?"

"Sorry. You wanted to know what I was thinking."

"I never thought of it. But I guess I should have, after yesterday." Was it only yesterday? It seemed as if she'd been running from these creeps for weeks. "He couldn't get my money. He gets a token to prove I didn't *accidentally* forget to put him in my will. Not enough to kill for."

"Does he know that?"

"Oh, my God. I don't know." She lowered her head to her hands. Her father had been cold, rigid, and self-centered, but to want her dead? "I never thought about it from that angle. That he'd think he could inherit from me and would want to speed things up. He'd have no way of knowing about my will."

"Hey, Sunshine. It was only a thought. Just gathering facts. I don't believe he's the type."

She stared at him, trying to read his face. He looked . . . older. Sad? Like he was trying to be kind, even if it meant hiding the truth. A truth he kept from her.

"You don't know him. *I* hardly know him, and I lived with him for thirteen years."

"Gut feeling. If he'd have wanted you that far out of the picture, I doubt he'd have bothered to call Blackthorne. Too open and aboveboard."

"But maybe he was trying to create the illusion of being the doting daddy. Hire you up front, all worried and penitent. Then sneak around behind your backs by hiring those creeps."

His gaze danced from hers to the rearview mirror. He frowned. "Doesn't make sense. Too many complications that way."

All the possibilities and ramifications slammed through her brain like so many bumper cars. "So, how do you see it?"

"From my point of view, which is that of an outsider, your father can either drag you back and force you to marry his idea of Mr. Right. Not likely in this day and age."

"You've got that one right. You said 'either.' What's the 'or'?"

"Or, he can drag you back and beg you to do what he asks, hoping you'll agree."

"Which I won't."

Fozzie paused, as if considering other options. "Or, he can drag you back, beg you to do what he asks, and hold something over your head. Blackmail. Any secrets?"

She snorted at that one. "Me? No way."

"What about bribery? A heap of money if you'd take his deal?"

"I don't need money."

"Anything else he could offer? Any threats to anyone, anything you care about?"

She'd spent her adult life avoiding attachments, not making them. "No," she said on a sad exhale.

He hesitated a moment, staring into the rearview mirror again. "How well do you know these roads?"

"Only that this one gets us back to Aspen Corners."

"Be a love and grab my bag, would you?"

His tone was even, but it was a forced evenness, if such a thing existed. She gave him a questioning look, but all he did was smile. The smile was forced, too. Her breath caught. She unclicked her belt and leaned between the seats to snag the bag's handle. "What do you need?"

"Outside compartment. Black case. There's a GPS in there."

She didn't want to ask why he needed it now. They weren't lost. She glanced in the side mirror, afraid she'd see a silver SUV. No, the sun glinted off of an old blue pickup truck, well behind them. Around here, every second vehicle was a pickup. Nothing to worry about. So why was her heart pounding?

Seeing him adjust his jacket so it wasn't confined by the seat belt didn't help. When he tapped the pocket, where she'd last seen him put the gun, her heart raced until she thought it would burst out of her ribcage.

She pulled out the GPS. "Okay, I have it."

"Power button is on the left."

Following his instructions, she turned on the unit and watched as it acquired satellites and then displayed a map.

"There's a plus and a minus sign to zoom. I need to know

the side roads around here, where they go."

"We're the blue triangle, right?"

"That's it."

She tapped the icons until the map showed their immediate surroundings. "Okay."

"Let me look, please." He held out a hand.

She put the unit in his palm. Multitasking didn't seem to pose a problem for him as he checked the display and kept the car where it belonged.

"All right, Sunshine. Thanks."

"Fozzie. What's going on? I'm in this car, and I think I have a right to know."

"Later." He sped up, and the truck shrank in the mirror. Without warning, he yanked the wheel. They made a sharp turn down a side road. He drove about twenty yards, then pulled onto the shoulder, next to a stand of trees. "Get in the backseat, Sunshine." He opened his door.

Fozzie ignored Torie's protests and questions and jogged up the lane behind the trees. From here, he had a sightline to the road.

There was every reason a pickup truck would be there. Pickups were the norm in this part of the country. This road was virtually the only route available. But something raised the hairs on the back of his neck, and he never ignored his early warning system. His arse had been saved enough times by paying attention to feelings he couldn't explain rationally.

According to the GPS, this turnoff wound around for about a mile, with no outlet. There had been a row of three rural mailboxes at the intersection with the road, so he figured three dwellings. Not impossible that an occupant of one of those dwellings was coming home. A full minute ticked away. He should have seen the faded blue pickup.

He eased around a tree, giving him a clearer view of approaching traffic. So, where was the damn truck? He couldn't have missed it. He'd had his eyes on the rearview mirror the whole time.

There. Engine and tire sounds drowned out the birds. His hand gripped the SIG in his pocket.

Chill. Shooting someone on a quiet country lane without a damn good reason would create more problems than it solved.

The truck appeared at the intersection, moving at a crawl. Pulled over at the mailboxes.

Fozzie watched. Waited. Nobody got out of the truck to open a mailbox. Was the guy one of the few blokes on the planet who believed in not talking and driving? Pulled off for a call? Did he have a decent signal?

Then the truck turned down the lane. Fozzie ducked through the trees and raced to the car. He yanked the back door open and fell on top of Torie, pushing her flat onto the seat. He shoved the SIG under the front seat, within reach. He ignored the panic in her eyes. Listened. No approaching truck. Yet.

"Trust me." He cradled her face in his hands. Gently, he pressed his lips to hers. She tasted like berries. She smelled like cheap hotel soap. And girly shampoo. Dumb move. This was supposed to be a diversion. He eased off.

But she didn't. Her tongue teased the seam of his mouth. He parted his lips a fraction. His tongue met hers. Lord, what was he doing?

But she kissed him back. For real. Her tongue delved after his. Teased. Danced.

"Torie," he gasped. Tried to pull away. She tangled her fingers in his hair and wouldn't release him. Her breasts pressed against his chest. Her tongue explored.

Automatically, he deepened the kiss. Probed. Relished. She tilted her head, giving him better access. Sweet Lord. This was no shy, insecure woman beneath him. Her tongue plunged deeper. Blood pounded in his ears.

He heard the tapping. Not his heart. On the window.

"You all right in there?" Deep male voice. Raspy, like a heavy smoker.

"Stay down," he whispered on a parting kiss. "Out of sight." He twisted around, positioning himself to keep himself between the man and Torie. "Yes, sir," he said, in his best American accent. "Everything's fine."

"Thought you might need help."

It didn't take much acting to look embarrassed. He'd switched plans on the fly, ditching the breakdown scenario, and his alternative could have gotten them both killed. At the time, it had seemed worth the risk. He prayed he'd been right. He lowered the window a few inches. Glanced at the SIG.

He winked at the man. "I just got home. It's been six months. We . . . well, we couldn't wait."

"Sugar, what's the problem?" A slow, breathy Southern drawl filled his ears. Fingers tugged at the zipper on his jacket. "I've missed y'all so much." Every syllable stretched to three.

"Got it. I'll be on my way, then," the man said. Fozzie studied him as he turned to go. Six feet tall. Skinny. Probably not more than one-sixty. Mid to late forties. Streaky blond hair curled out from under a ball cap. Stubble on a sun-bronzed face. Jeans, faded gray sweatshirt. An innocent would-be Samaritan? Or someone else looking for Torie?

Torie squirmed below him. "Is he gone?" she whispered.

"Not yet. Walking away." He watched the man amble back to his truck, which he'd left by the side of the lane, but close to the main road. The man stopped, glanced over his shoulder. Waited.

"Help me out here," Fozzie said. He pressed his feet against the side panel and braced his hands on either side of Torie. He moved back and forth, setting the car rocking. Torie gave him an impish grin and added her weight to the motion.

"You want me to scream your name?" she asked. "Or moan a lot?"

He snorted, trying to stifle a laugh. "I think he's out of earshot. But thanks for the offer."

Maybe another time. For real.

Right. Him and Torie. What was he thinking? Easy. He wasn't thinking. Not with the right brain, anyway. Sweet Lord, a pretend kiss designed to keep Torie's face out of sight had turned into a burst of passion. If he hadn't guessed right, if the man had wanted them dead, he'd have caused a traffic accident out on the road. So maybe his orders were to bring them back alive. But in what condition?

He forced his mind back to *their* immediate problem, and away from *his* immediate problem, which was nagging from below his belt line. From this point on, Torie was strictly someone to protect. And that meant using the brain above his neck.

He heard an engine start up in the distance. He twisted around and saw the truck turn, then head onto the road, continuing in the same direction they'd been going. Once his breathing approached normal, he hoisted himself to a sitting position. "I think we're clear."

Torie squirmed to the other end of the seat and leaned against the door. She finger-combed her hair. Her face looked like sunrise on Ayers Rock. "Was it good for you, too?" she mumbled, ducking her head. Even her quiet tone didn't hide the sarcasm.

"Hey, thanks for being a good sport," he said. "I didn't mean to scare you. It seemed like the best idea at the time. Nothing personal."

"No, no. Of course not. For me, either." If anything, her color heightened. "When your accent disappeared, I figured we were putting on a show."

Of course. Why else would well-mannered Torie have come on that way? "Right. You were ripper. Loved that Southern drawl."

She dipped into her purse and reapplied her lip gloss. "So, you think the guy bought it?"

Maybe. If he was who he'd appeared to be. Probably not, if he was one of the bad guys. No point worrying Torie.

He shrugged. "Don't see why not." The berry scent wafted through the car. He rubbed the back of his neck, trying to ward off an impeding headache.

She capped the tube and zipped it into a flowered pouch. "Who do you think he was? I'd say he wasn't from around here."

"What makes you say that?" He swung around so he mirrored her position.

"Beach boy hair. Too tan. This place doesn't get much sun."

Concern squiggled through him. If she'd gotten a good view of the man, he'd probably had a fair peek at her.

"Can we please get going?" she said. "I'd like to see the aftermath of the fire."

"Fire. Of course." He moved to the front seat and started the car. Torie slid into the passenger seat, looking out the windows, brow furrowed, pursing her lips in and out. He ran his tongue along his lips, tasting the remnants of a berry-flavored kiss.

"Wait. Stop for a minute," she said when they reached the place where the lane joined the road. "Can you back around, like you've stopped to get your mail?" There was more concern than curiosity in her expression.

"I don't think that'll be necessary," he said. "You're right. He couldn't have seen us from this spot. The main road is straight for quite a distance ahead, so if he didn't see our car out in front of him, this would have been a logical place to look."

She gazed into his eyes. Held him captive. "When are you going to start trusting me?"

"I trust you."

She shook her head. "Not enough. I want to be in on your thoughts. You're obviously more experienced in things like people coming after you with guns, but you have to remember, it's *me* they're coming after. I deserve to be in the loop."

He squeezed the bridge of his nose.

"Okay, then answer this," she said. "Have you considered the possibility that Mister Oregon Beach Boy knew where to look because someone told him?"

"It occurred to me."

"And you were going to mention it when?"

"I didn't want to worry you."

She sucked in a breath so deep he was afraid there wouldn't be any air left for him.

"I will say this once more. Tell me if it doesn't translate into Australian, and I'll try to use words you can understand. All right?"

"Yes'm."

She locked him with her gaze again. Spit the words out, clear and distinct. "I worry more when I don't know something."

"Got it. Sorry."

"Consider yourself on probation." A corner of her mouth turned up. "Now, I have a few more questions. But I'll ask them on the way." She waved her hand toward the road.

"In a minute. I need to check something. One tick." He hopped out of the car. He should have checked before they ever left.

CHAPTER ELEVEN

"Fozzie! Where are you going?"

How thick could one man's head be? Torie watched Fozzie circle the car, running his hands along the front grill, the wheel wells, almost tenderly, like he'd stroke a lover.

A lover. Her face flamed. She'd kissed him. Long, hard, and deep, the way she'd fantasized last night, until he'd given her that brotherly peck. But minutes ago, he'd covered her with his tight, strong body. "Trust me," he'd said. And she had. Something had possessed her, had her acting out her fantasy. With him. In the back of the car. With goodness knows what danger lurking.

Why? Because if she was going to die, it might as well be during a kiss like she'd never had before. For a moment, she thought it had meant something to him. But even as she'd kissed him, she knew it wasn't real. She'd let her dreams, her emotions rule the moment. And where had it gotten her? Humiliated. She was, to quote him, "a good sport." The story of her life.

Count on Victoria. She'll do it. Smuggle forbidden food into your room if you're on detention. Make sure your uniforms are cleaned and pressed after you've shimmied down the trellis to meet your boyfriend. Swear to the headmistress that you were with her all night.

Well, maybe once in a while a good sport deserved a good kiss, even if it was half-pretend. His half, but she'd die before she'd tell him.

She heard her name. Maybe several times before it actually

registered. She blinked. "What?"

"I said, will you hand me the torch from my bag, please? Outside pocket, where you found the GPS."

"Right." Torch. She fumbled through the bag, found a flashlight. He held out his hand. She lowered the window and passed it through. "What are you looking for?"

"Not sure, exactly."

She didn't release her grip on the light when he tugged. "I said, what are you looking for?"

He sighed. "Anything that doesn't belong."

"Like a bomb?" Her grip grew slack, and the light would have fallen if Fozzie hadn't had a firm hold on it.

He smiled. "More like a tracking mechanism. If I thought there was an explosive device, we'd be far, far away."

He dropped to the ground, flipped over and scooted himself under the car. She tried not to move, even held her breath, as if it would make her lighter, envisioning him crushed if she so much as shifted her weight on the seat.

After a moment, she heard a low whistle from under the car. When Fozzie emerged seconds later, he had a smile on his face and something in his hand. He lowered himself into the car.

"What is it?" she asked.

"Tracker. Not top of the line, but damn fine." He made an appreciative clucking sound as he tossed it up and down. "All anyone has to do is log onto a Web site and Bob's your uncle. They know where we are, and we don't see anyone following us."

"But if he has to log onto the Internet to find us, how can he do it from his truck? Heck, I couldn't even log on from the cottage."

"My guess is there's a home base. Someone calling the shots. But even so, the spotty cell-phone coverage can work to our advantage. The satellite system tells the GPS where we are, but it needs a cell signal to transmit that information back to the base. So, he's not tracking us every step of the way."

"So, that's good, right?"

"It helps, but not a lot. There aren't many choices for roads around here. All he has to do is wait until we get out of the dead zone and he'll have us again."

"But if they put that thing on the car, then they found us. Why not just grab us, or do whatever they were going to do then?"

"Sunshine, I don't know their agenda. Maybe it's been on your car a lot longer than we think. That might be how they found you at the cabin. Or maybe the guy at your cabin stuck it on after you told him to leave. I confess I wasn't doing a bang-up job, given I was distracted by the way you were pointing a gun at me, so he could have slipped it on then. Or maybe whoever is calling the shots is waiting for reinforcements and needs to keep an eye on you. But we know it's here, which gives us another card to play."

"Why don't you break it? Disable it? Throw it in the lake?"

"I could, but we'll let it ride along with us for a bit longer."

"Why?"

"So they don't get suspicious." He set the gizmo in a cup holder and faced her. Steely determination burned in his eyes. "I should have checked sooner. I got lazy. It won't happen again."

"It's okay. I mean, how were you supposed to know?"

Dragging a hand through his hair, he frowned. "Is there anyone else who might want you? We've assumed your father sent everyone. But let's think about it. I want you to remember last night. What were you doing before the first bloke showed up?"

"Washing dishes. Then the door opened, and this man was there, stomping his muddy feet. I tried to grab a knife, but I

110

saw his gun." Her heart pounded almost as hard as it had when she'd seen the barrel aimed at her.

"Did he say anything?"

"Not really."

"But he said *something*?"

She pressed her fingertips to her temples, trying to remember and forget at the same time. "He said, 'You're coming with me, bitch,' and I couldn't talk. Then he grabbed me, poked a gun in my ribs, and we were walking outside, and then you got there."

She still couldn't believe her father wanted to harm her. But if he hadn't sent all those other creeps, then who had? Why?

She shuddered. "Let me think. My father wants me to take care of his upcoming business problem. He hires you to find me. At the same time, someone else is coming after me for an entirely different reason? And he's not being nice about it?"

"More or less. There's always the possibility I'm wrong about your father, but it doesn't fit the facts. And there's another possibility to consider."

More? This could *not* be happening. "Which is?"

"The guy with the gun and the guy who torched the cabin aren't connected, either."

"*Three* people?" Her voice squeaked.

"My money's on two people who want you. Your father and someone else. But person number two might have hired out, the way your father did."

Her stomach lurched. She thought she might throw up. "And if he did, who's to say he's going to stop at two?"

He reached across the car and squeezed her hand. "Doesn't make sense. First, plain and simple it's expensive. Second, too many different mishaps will send up red flags."

"You think?"

He took her hand in both of his. His gaze sucked her in, like drowning in a sea of molten chocolate. "I'm not going to let anything happen to you."

She hoped she could believe him. But Idaho was looking better and better. "Can we get going?"

He released her hands. Smiled that cocksure grin. Damn. Bad enough it shot electric sparks through her insides the first time she'd seen it. Now, all she could think of was the way that mouth, those lips, felt on hers. Telling herself there was nothing personal behind the kiss didn't cut off the fireworks.

"In a tick. Have to check the traffic." He jumped out of the car.

Traffic? She hadn't seen a single car or truck drive by the entire time they'd been sitting here. Seconds later, he jogged back and leaned in the window. "Pop on out. Could use your help."

When he grinned again, there was no refusing him. "What should I do?"

"Shake a leg. Get across the road and flag down that van. Ask him which way to Aspen Corners, or Bend, or anywhere. Keep him occupied for about fifteen seconds."

"But—"

"No buts. Flirt. Do whatever women do to distract men."

She tried to protest that she couldn't possibly flirt, that no driver would even stop, but he gave her a gentle shove. She checked for traffic—none—and trotted across the road. Glancing over her shoulder, she saw Fozzie reach into the car.

From the distance, a green van approached. Flirt? She took a deep breath, fluffed her hair, licked her lips. Her heart pounded and her mouth dried up. Nope.

Relax. Nobody at school ever thought you could lie, which is why they always believed you. Think of making excuses to Sister Marguerite.

She could do that. She stood in the middle of the road and waved her arms above her head. The van slowed. She caught a glimpse of Fozzie scuttling across the road behind it.

The van rolled to a stop. A grandfatherly-looking man leaned out the window, peering at her from behind aviator-style sunglasses. A John Deere ball cap sat on his head. So much for Sister Marguerite.

"Can I help you, miss?" He lifted his sunglasses, revealing watery blue eyes. The smell of stale cigarette smoked filled her nostrils.

"Please. I think I'm lost." She sounded desperate. Not much of a stretch. She took a deep breath. "My sister-in-law's going to have a baby, and she said she was going to the hospital in Bend, and I'm not from around here, and I've been driving on this road and haven't seen any signs for Bend in ages. I'm afraid I missed a turnoff or something."

"You surely did, young lady. What you need to do is backtrack, then look for Crescent Cutoff. That'll take you acrost to Ninety-seven, and on up to Bend."

"Thanks. Do you think you could write that down? I'm so bubble-headed when I'm nervous, and it's Mary Jane's first, and I promised I'd be there."

He scrabbled through a pile of papers on the other seat, found a pencil and started writing. She braved a glance toward the back of the van. Fozzie gave her a thumbs-up and zipped back toward her car. She heard paper tearing. She smiled at the driver. He handed her a half sheet of paper with directions and a sketched map.

"There you go," he said. "And best of luck to your sister-in-law."

"Thank you. Thanks so much." She waited until the van drove off before crossing back to her car. Her knees shook, but it was a good kind of shaking. Exciting. Exhilarating. Empowering.

"You put that bug on his van, didn't you?" she said.

"That I did. Those blokes will be following him now, not us.

Should lead them on a merry chase."

"Where do you think he's going?"

"All over, I hope. The sign on the van said 'Central Oregon Electrical Repairs'."

She leaned against the car. "I can't believe I did that." Then again, in the last two days, she'd done a heck of a lot of things she'd never believed she could.

"Told you it would be a piece of piss."

"What?"

"I think you'd call it a piece of cake."

"I definitely like that better."

"Whatever you call it, you did it." He grabbed her in a bear hug. Just as quickly, he released her and stepped back, as if she'd burned him. "Sorry. Heat of the moment."

"No need to apologize. I understand." She forced herself to meet his eyes. "My fault. I got carried away myself. It was exciting, in a scary sort of way."

"Nothing to be afraid of. Worst that could have happened, he wouldn't stop."

"I was afraid I wasn't going to give you the time you needed. Or that he'd see you and"—she flapped her arms in the air—"I don't know. Get out and beat you up, or call the cops."

"Catch me? No way, Sunshine. No way." He grinned again. Slow, lazy, and confident as hell.

Bone-melting. That's what it was. She grabbed the door handle.

Fozzie felt Torie's tension roll over him as they drove toward Aspen Corners. Her knuckles turned white as she clenched the dash. She strained against the seat belt.

"Easy," he said gently. "We'll get there."

"You're so calm. Do you do stuff like this all the time in your job?"

"Not exactly." Most of the time he was doing the tracking, hovering in a helo.

"I'm sorry to be so much trouble," she said.

"No trouble at all, Sunshine." He'd foolishly thought this assignment was Blackthorne's idea of downtime, but he had a target to protect and damned if he wasn't going to protect her, with or without his technology. "I think our little diversion worked."

She seemed to relax. At least the foot tapping and dash clenching stopped. She stared straight ahead, her gaze fixed into the distance.

"Any back roads to your cottage?" he asked as they grew closer. What he wouldn't give for his infrared display.

She shook her head. "Only way in or out is off this road." She paused. "By car, that is."

"I'm sure these guys aren't hoofing it." They approached the final curve, and he realized he was holding his breath. He bunched his shoulders, then forcibly relaxed them on a deep exhale. He resisted the temptation to stomp on the accelerator and get it over with. While he doubted any visitors awaited their arrival, he dreaded what the fire might have done.

No cabin bits and pieces strewn over the road. Good sign. He sniffed the air. Faint traces of smoke, stronger wet forest smells. Another good sign. As he rounded the turn, the first glimpse of the cabin came into view. He reckoned he was as relieved as Torie to see it standing. Charring on the front, but didn't look bad.

"Let me out here," Torie said. "I'll go check."

"No can do. We'll go in together."

"Why? I thought we sent everyone on a wild-goose chase."

"Simple safety precaution. No way to tell what it looks like inside. Could be dangerous—walls or beams ready to take a tumble. Holes in the flooring."

She seemed willing to accept that. But as soon as he pulled into the clearing and stopped the car, she hopped out. Started for the cabin.

"Hurry up," she called.

"Stop for a sec. I said we're going together."

Hands on her hips, she waited for him. He opened the rear door and got the SIG. Her frown said she'd noticed.

"I thought you said the bad guys were somewhere else," she said. "You think those walls and beams might shoot us?"

He put it in his pocket. "I don't like leaving loaded weapons lying around."

She seemed willing to accept that, too.

Several yards from the porch, he veered to the left. "I want to walk the perimeter first." He stepped ahead, keeping her to the outside, half a pace behind him. Her anxiety to get inside was gone. Instead, her movements were tentative. Hesitant. Definitely submissive. He felt a twinge of remorse for sending her scurrying back inside her shell, but there was always a command hierarchy on an op, and right now, he was the alpha dog. He paused at each corner, making sure there were no surprises. His right hand gripped the SIG in his pocket.

"Doesn't look too bad," Torie said. "I was afraid it was blown to smithereens."

"Not even a single smither."

Not many clear footprints outside, either. Water had obliterated any obvious evidence of the flare-thrower's tracks. Continuing on, they approached the window where the first flare had come in. He moved in for a closer look. He could see the scorch marks where the fire had spread along the trail of accelerant, the charred sofa. Smelled the smoke.

"What do you see?" Torie asked. She held back, even though he hadn't told her to wait.

"Looks like the firefighters got here in time. Your couch is toast, the floors are a mess."

"Can we go inside?"

"Looks safe enough."

They finished the circuit of the cabin. He stopped at the base of the porch steps. She stood alongside him, close enough for her scent to override the smoke. Muddy boots had tramped up and down the steps, back and forth on the porch. He trotted up and pushed open the door. "I don't think they followed your rule about not tracking mud into the house."

"Firefighters are exempt from that rule."

He stepped inside, then motioned her to follow. "Why don't you grab what you need. This place isn't livable, and even if it was, it's not smart to stay here."

She stood in the doorway a moment, gazed around the room as if she were panning a wide video shot. Then she darted toward the kitchen area. He strolled toward the barbequed sofa.

"Phil. Thank goodness. I'm so glad you're all right," she said.

He snapped around. Who the hell was Phil? Torie bounded toward him and thrust a scraggly potted plant in his hand. "Here. Hold this."

"Who's Phil?" he asked.

A sheepish grin crossed her face. "A philodendron. I rescued it from Kathy's apartment. All her other plants were dead, but this one hung on. I couldn't bear to leave it behind." She stroked one of its heart-shaped leaves in a loving caress that had him imagining what it would feel like if she touched him that way. Suddenly wanting her to touch him that way.

He swallowed. "Uh, nice to meet you, Phil." He took a leaf between thumb and forefinger and gave it an up-and-down shake.

She giggled. Actually giggled. The sound warmed him as much as thoughts of her touch. Their eyes met. Held.

"Well. I guess I should get packing," she said.

"Right."

She backed away for several paces before breaking eye contact and turning for the bedroom. He followed, leaning against the jamb as she dragged a suitcase from the closet. The clay pot felt cool and moist in his palms.

Well, Phil. I might not have been able to save Kathy, but I'm damn well not going to lose you, too.

Torie stripped all the muddy bedcovers off the bed. "They're dry. I figured everything would be soaked."

"If the fire didn't reach this room, they probably didn't need to wet it down. Or maybe a fire extinguisher was enough."

She started to fold the dirty bedding. He set the plant down and stepped forward. "Let me do that."

While he folded, she went to the closet and brought out an armload of clothes, still on their hangers. She held them to her face. "They'll all need to be cleaned. They smell like smoke."

He stacked the bedcovers on a chair. "What next?"

She went to the chest of drawers and slid the top one open, giving him a glimpse of delicate lingerie. She shrugged. "Nothing. Packing's kind of a . . . private thing, I guess."

He spied a lacy scrap of peach-colored material as she scooped out the contents and dumped them beside the suitcase. She picked up a pair of silky panties and folded them carefully before putting them in the case. "Um . . . I guess Phil and I will hang out, then. Holler when you're done and I'll carry it to the car."

He wandered the living area, replaying the previous evening. Flares. Kerosene. But not a five-gallon jerry can. Not even a gallon. Merely an open plastic water bottle. Definitely disposable. Nothing left but a quarter-sized scar of melted plastic stuck to the floor planks. All in all, the place was surprisingly unscathed, considering firefighters would have had only one goal in mind. Put out the fire. Worrying about secondary damage wasn't on their agenda.

No phone book that he could find. He set the plant on the counter and dialed 9-1-1. "This isn't an emergency," he said as soon as the operator picked up. "I can hold if you're busy."

"Go ahead, sir."

"I called about a fire last night, near Aspen Corners, and I wanted to thank the firefighters."

"Let me see what I can do."

"Thanks." Fozzie glanced in the direction of the bedroom. No sign of Torie yet. He suspected she packed as deliberately as she ate.

After several moments, someone identifying himself as Jerry came on the line.

"I'm calling about the fire in the cottage near Aspen Corners last night," Fozzie said. "I wanted to thank you for the quick response."

"Actually, the fire was out when we got there. We figured you handled it. Looked like a fire extinguisher took care of the inside, and the rain took care of the outside."

"Someone threw flares and probably kerosene into the room. Will there be an investigation?"

"Sir, the state does all arson investigations. It can take weeks for them to get to minor damages. Do you have a suspect?"

"Only that he probably drives an old blue pickup truck. A Ford, I think."

"That's probably about a quarter of the population around here, but I'll pass the information along."

Fozzie sighed. "I know. Will you need us for anything? We hadn't planned to stay."

"No problem. We'll be dealing with the property owner."

"Thanks again for the fast response," Fozzie said and hung up.

Who the hell had put out the fire? Why had they started it? Had they been looking for something of Torie's?

He moseyed to the living area, turned a slow circle, checking to see if he noticed anything missing. He barely remembered the details from his brief visit. He examined it as an everyday living space. Compared it to his own apartment.

No television here, for starters, but there hadn't been one before. The whole place was a dearth of technical equipment. No computer. He stopped on the spot. *Everyone* had a computer. "Torie?"

Chapter Twelve

Torie repressed her upbringing and shouted from the bedroom when Fozzie called her name. "What?"

He appeared in the doorway. "Do you have a computer?"

"Laptop. But with no decent Internet access, I didn't bother to unpack it. It's in the car. In the box of books."

He seemed satisfied. She closed the suitcase and zipped it shut. Fozzie grabbed the handle and wrested it to the floor. "Let's go."

"One more thing," she said. "Where's Phil?"

"Coffee table."

She fetched the plant, carried it to the kitchen, and wiped down the sooty leaves. She slung her purse over her shoulder. "Okay. Ready."

Fozzie took one last look around. He gave a quick nod, then held the door. "After you."

"I've been thinking," she said as they strolled to the car.

"And?" Fozzie pressed the remote and popped the trunk.

"Maybe these people are looking for someone else. Someone tied to the cabin. Another renter. Maybe if they lose my trail, they'll start over and get whoever they're looking for. Or maybe we could call the owner and see if any of the renters seemed . . . suspicious."

She wondered why she hadn't thought of it sooner. Because she'd been sure it had been her father, and when Fozzie admitted that's who sent him, she never looked beyond that possibility. Her father had enough motive.

They'd reached the car, and Fozzie moved the carton aside to make room for the case. His mouth curled up. "How many mystery books do you have in that box?"

Her face heated. "You think it's too far-fetched?"

"Nothing's ever too far-fetched. But usually the answers are the simplest ones."

"Occam's razor. I know. But you have to look at all the possibilities, gather all the facts before you can draw your conclusions."

"True." He slammed the trunk, then glanced at his watch. "Let's hit the road. I need to check in with the boss at noon. Have to get out of this dead zone."

Check in. His boss. Right. She'd been busy thinking this whole thing was going to disappear when she'd decided she wasn't who the creeps were after. She'd forgotten Fozzie's job was to report her whereabouts to his boss. Who would tell her father.

Her chest tightened. She could hardly breathe. "What are you going to tell him?"

He didn't respond. Simply got into the car. She climbed in after him. "What? Tell me."

He sat with his hands on the wheel. "I'm going to tell him the truth. There's no alternative. I think once he hears the real reason your father wants you, he'll find a way to avoid having to tell him exactly where you are."

"You think?"

"No promises. But he's a fair man. And he doesn't like being hoodwinked. If your father wasn't aboveboard with him, he won't feel obliged to give away your secret."

She sighed with relief. "Thank you." She settled the plant on the floor between her feet. Fozzie started the car, headed toward the road. Could she ask him to help her disappear? Or should she wait until his boss gave the official word his job was over? Because one way or another, it was. He'd done what he'd been sent to do. All she needed to know was whether she had to keep hiding from her father, or if she could plunge back into the search for Kathy's elusive lichens. It would feel good to have a purpose again.

She glanced at Fozzie, who seemed lost in thought. She'd miss his slow, cockeyed grin. Definitely the taste of that one kiss. But he had a life, a job. She never set down roots. She was more like Phil than the pines and hemlocks that lined the drive. Her roots were more like the potted variety, easy to pick up and move. She clutched her midsection against the growing ache.

Trying to set roots never worked. All it brought was pain. Because sooner or later, someone would yank you up by the roots, and the new pot was never the right fit. Too big, too small, wrong soil. Not enough sun.

She whirred down her window, enjoying the crisp air, clean and fresh after the smoky interior of the cabin. Fozzie did the same. They exchanged an awkward glance.

Gripping Phil between her feet to steady it on the curving road, she stared at her lap and tried to compose a "We'll always have Aspen Corners" speech.

"Which way?"

She looked up, realizing he'd stopped the car. They'd reached the main road. Which way indeed? "I guess where you can make your phone call."

"Nowhere you need to be?"

She shook her head. Except for wanting to help Kathy, she couldn't remember when she'd needed to be somewhere. That meant going *toward*. She usually went *away*. Like now. She pointed away from Aspen Corners. "That way."

He glanced around. "Where did the GPS go?"

She found it in one of the cup holders. He turned it on,

studied it, frowned, dragged his fingers through his hair. "Definitely Back of Beyond," he muttered. He tapped the unit a few more times before he appeared satisfied, then reached for his seemingly bottomless carryall again. She watched him attach a suction cup device to the dash and settle the GPS into a cradle.

"Know anything about Suncrest?" he asked. "We could be there in plenty of time for lunch, and I can check in."

"Never heard of it."

"Looks like a small town this side of Bend."

Town. There'd be accommodations. Maybe one with an Internet connection, and she could plan for Idaho. Do laundry. Maybe she'd get another car, something less conspicuous in the mountains. "Sounds fine."

She studied Fozzie as he drove. He seemed to be one with the car, hands light on the wheel. Eyes checking mirrors. Avoiding glances in her direction. Which was fine. Yet she sensed an underlying tension in his demeanor. Worry lines furrowed his brow, his jaw muscle twitched. Every now and again, he'd shrug his shoulders to his ears, then drop them, as if trying to loosen tight muscles.

She resisted the urge to reach over and massage the base of his neck. She turned her attention to the window, watching the trees blur into a green-and-brown ribbon at the side of the road.

Anticipation rose as the miles rolled under the car. Turning the page on one chapter, starting a new one. After about twenty minutes, Fozzie's phone chirped. He looked at the GPS, then at her. "Voice message. We're about two miles from town. It can wait. What do you feel like eating?"

She didn't. "Anything. You pick." With a goal in sight, all she wanted was to get the next phase of her life underway.

"Welcome to Suncrest," the sign by the road said. They

entered a minuscule business district that bordered on the green expanse of a golf course. Storefronts surrounded a small park.

"Main Street, USA," she said.

"Golf and fishing seem to be the reasons for the town." Fozzie gestured toward the shops. Golf pro shops. Fishing tackle, bait, boat rentals. He cruised down the street. The next block was restaurant row. Fast food joints on one side. Chinese, Italian, a sandwich shop and a sports bar on the other. This place had nothing she needed. After lunch, they'd go to Bend so she could finish carrying out her plan.

"Parking's that way," she said, pointing toward a sign.

He found an empty space in the public lot, and they strolled around the corner to the sandwich shop. Inside, she excused herself to use the ladies' room while he checked his phone messages.

"Anything good?" she asked when she returned.

The worry lines had smoothed. "The boss agrees that your father doesn't need to know more than you're alive and safe. If you'd like, someone at Blackthorne will act as a go-between for any messages, should he want to reach you. They'd need an address, phone number, or an e-mail."

Her bones dissolved. She sank into the booth, gripping the edge of the table. Was it almost over? She resisted the urge to wrap her arms around Fozzie's neck. Instead, she sucked in a deep breath. "Sounds fair. I can give them my lawyer's contact information. He knows how to get in touch with me."

"Excellent," Fozzie said. "You ready?" He gestured to the menu.

A waitress hovered. Torie selected a salad at random. As she placed her order, the lights flickered. Went out, then on again. She shot a questioning look to the waitress.

"Nothing to worry about," the woman said. "We've had electrical problems off and on all week. There's a guy working on the wiring now. He should be done soon. Doesn't affect the kitchen, so your meals will be fine." She wrote their orders on her pad and bustled away.

By the time their food arrived, Torie was anxious to leave. She was ready to suggest they get it packed to go, but Fozzie was digging into his sandwich with such gusto that she didn't have the heart to pull him away. She poked at her salad and tried not to let her impatience show when he ordered dessert.

"Since you've taken care of your responsibility, and your tracking gizmo decoy bought me time to get away, I'm going to leave," she said.

"Where to?" he asked around a mouthful of cobbler.

"Probably better if you don't know. Once we get to Bend, I'll take it from there."

"What? You think I'd tell your father? After all I've done?" Creases at the edges of his eyes deepened with a widening smile.

"Of course not. But Nana always said a secret's not a secret if two people know it. Besides, I'm not sure where I'll end up."

"And what if I want to send you a Christmas card?"

Her heart skidded through the next few beats. Did he want to keep in touch? He raised his eyebrows and went back to his cobbler. No, he was teasing. She took a quick, steadying breath and matched his tone. "I guess you'll have to send it to my lawyer."

He frowned. "Give me your phone."

Puzzled, she fished it from her purse and handed it over. He pressed some buttons, then handed it back. "You've got my number now. Don't be afraid to use it."

Fozzie slipped his credit card back into his wallet. Throughout their meal, Torie'd seemed antsy to get moving again. To getting one step closer to cutting ties to him?

Why hadn't he told her the whole truth about his call to

Blackthorne? That his assignment was finished, that the old man insisted he take time off. That he wanted to spend it with her. Why? Because it nagged at him that she was likely still someone's target, he told himself. Not because he wanted to spend time with her. Period.

Impossible.

She needed protection. And he protected people. Rescued them. Simple as that. So why hadn't he mentioned the call to the fire department? Ask if she had something someone might find valuable. Because he didn't want to scare her?

Right. Now, if he mentioned it, she'd probably rival the old man in the arse-chewing department, for not telling her immediately.

He should suggest they travel together, wherever she decided to go. At least that way, he'd be able to keep an eye on her. But she'd made it clear she wanted to go it alone.

Reality check. She'd been his assignment, and now it was over. He'd help her disappear, and they'd get on with their lives. He figured as long as he was on this side of the country, Vegas might be his next stop. He thought about the lights, the noise, the constant action. Good-looking women.

"Let's go out the back," he said. "Closer to the parking lot." Torie wiggled out of the booth, and he followed her through the restaurant, enjoying the gentle sway of her hips. Definitely not Las Vegas showgirl hips. But definitely inviting.

Hell, maybe Torie'd like a side trip before she disappeared. Easy to get lost in the throngs. And after the last couple days, they could both use some quality R and R. He could keep an eye on her and maybe have some fun at the same time.

He shoved those thoughts away. Torie wasn't an R and R fling.

She pushed open the door and stepped toward the parking lot. Bright sunlight blinded him momentarily. He paused, trying

127

to remember where he'd left his sunglasses. An elderly couple shuffled toward the door, and he held it for them as Torie continued to the car.

"Thank you, young man," the old woman said. She half-stumbled over the threshold, and he steadied her.

"No worries, ma'am. Watch your step." He sought Torie, who was halfway to the car. She'd picked up her pace, and along with it, the sway in her hips. Reaching for the keys in his pocket, he paused a moment, allowing himself a brief smile.

A man in a John Deere ball cap strode toward him, listing under the weight of a metal tool case. He grunted something that sounded like "Excuse me" as he reached for the door. Fozzie stepped aside, his gaze automatically backtracking the man's path. To a green van parked about three slots away from Torie's Fusion. With "Central Oregon Electrical Repairs" emblazoned on its side. Fozzie's heart jumped to his throat.

"Torie!" He sped toward her.

She turned, smiled. Stood beside the passenger door of the car. Before he reached her, a man stepped out from behind her Fusion, put her in a choke hold and dragged her between the rows of cars toward a silver SUV. Damn, it had *not* been there when they'd driven in. He'd checked. He whirled his gaze across the lot. At least half a dozen pickups, but there was a faded blue one parked near the entrance, engine running. That hadn't been here before, either.

"Fuck."

"Such language. For shame." A man's gruff voice cut through the traffic noises from the street beyond the lot. Pickup Truck Man appeared from alongside the Fusion, the jacket draped over his arm not quite concealing a gun barrel. He stepped close enough to grab Fozzie's elbow and whisper in his ear. "You're going to take a little ride. But look on the bright side. At least you had a little fun with your girlfriend first."

Fozzie clenched his fists. "You wouldn't dare shoot me here. Not in a public place."

"You're probably right," the man said. His eyes narrowed to slits. "But my partner is holding a grudge against your girl. I don't check in every five minutes, she's going to be hurting. Try anything, make any quick moves, and I promise it'll hurt her more than it hurts you. A whole lot more. Now, let's make it look like two old buddies are strolling across the parking lot, shooting the breeze. You first." He motioned Fozzie toward the pickup.

Fozzie's brain shifted into overdrive. Disarming the guy wouldn't be a problem. Doing it so no harm came to Torie would. He strained to see where the SUV was going. Out of the parking lot. Left turn. And gone. He couldn't risk that the phone-call threat was an idle one.

The man raised the cover from the bed of the pickup and lowered the tailgate. "Up there. Face away from me. On your knees."

Fozzie looked into the cramped space. Sweat trickled down his neck. His heart slammed against his ribs. He struggled to breathe. "Can't I ride up with you? I'll be no trouble."

The man laughed. "Yeah, right. Time's a-wasting. Move it."

Fozzie hoisted himself onto the metal platform.

"Cross your legs at the ankles."

He did. He felt his boots yanked off, his ankles bound.

"Hands behind your back."

Fozzie clenched his fists, but the man secured his wrists with what felt like nylon flex cuffs. Available off the Internet for a pittance. The man patted him down, none too gently.

"Sorry, mate, I don't swing that way."

The man gave him a shove. Then he stripped him of his belt and emptied his pockets.

"I don't suppose there's any way we can talk about this?"

Fozzie asked. "It's not like I even know the woman."

"Didn't look that way to me," the man said.

Fozzie's internal clock ticked away the minutes, waiting for the man to make his call. Had he blown his chance to escape? To go after Torie? With a shove, the man forced him into the bed of the pickup. Fozzie blinked away the stars swimming in front of his eyes when his head hit the corrugated metal floor. When he heard the man's voice say, "All's okay. On schedule," he wasn't sure if he was more angry or relieved. He'd let himself be distracted. Had downplayed the danger to Torie. If her father hadn't sent these thugs, who had, and why?

Then there was a loud crash as the cover on the truck bed slammed closed. Everything went dark. He fought the panic.

You're in a truck. You're fine. Ride it out.

Several minutes passed before he heard another thunk as the truck door closed. He rolled as they started moving. He wriggled onto his arse, trying to find a way to brace himself against the bouncing. Not enough height to sit, but he managed to hunch himself along until his back was against the cab and his feet wedged against the wheel well. The truck bounced. Pain shot through his wrists, and his head banged into the bed cover. The truck turned. He teetered. He twisted until he lay on his side. Not a lot better, but the position let him adjust to the truck's motion more easily.

Within minutes, panic rose again. His breathing accelerated until wheezing gasps filled the space. Tremors rippled through his body. Traces of kerosene wafted through his nostrils. Was he running out of air?

He was back in the ravine, trapped by the rock slide, his arm broken, certain nobody would find him and he would die. All he could remember beyond the pain was telling himself eight-year-olds didn't die. Only old people died. His naivety had given him the strength to hang on. But the memories refused to leave him alone.

It's not the same. You're in a truck. Going somewhere. Moving. Concentrate on the motion. Someone knows where you are, even if he's a worthless piece of shit. You're not alone.

After what seemed days, his breathing slowed. Even in his hot, stuffy, confinement, a cold sweat filmed him. He clenched his muscles, willing the trembling to subside. The truck bed wasn't airtight. He wasn't going to suffocate. Cursing his weakness, he struggled to force his mind elsewhere.

Someone had found Torie. His brilliant switch of the GPS tracker had backfired. Of all the electrical problems in all of central Oregon, why had they happened in *that* sandwich shop? No way, no way on the planet the electrician was in on it. No, sometimes you got lucky, and sometimes you got screwed. In this case, it was the creeps who got lucky. They'd tracked the signal to the parking lot. Probably didn't even realize the GPS had been switched. Saw Torie's car, and Bob's your uncle. Sit back, relax, and wham, bam, thank you, ma'am. Almost as slick as a Blackthorne job.

The truck slowed. Turned again. Bumped. Jiggled. He braced his feet. A dirt road, he guessed. More twists and turns. More bruising bumps. And then they stopped. Fozzie held his breath, trying to stave off another panic attack. Would they leave him here? Wherever here was? The truck's door opened. The bed cover rose a few inches. Dappled light filtered through. Fozzie squinted, trying to avoid being blinded by the change from total darkness. His captor lowered the tailgate.

"Out. Now."

CHAPTER THIRTEEN

Torie squirmed in the backseat of the SUV, testing the bindings on her wrists and ankles. "What do you want with me? Who sent you? My father?"

"Shut up, bitch," the man said.

"What's he paying you? I can match it."

"Shut up, bitch," the man repeated. "You've caused me enough trouble already. Be glad this car doesn't have a trunk, because believe me, that's where you'd be."

"Can't you tell me why you want me?"

"The boss said to get you out of circulation for a while. I'm just following orders."

"Who's your boss?"

"You have trouble with plain English? I said, shut up, bitch. You keep your mouth shut until next Monday, and everything will be fine."

"Monday? What's Monday?" She searched her memory. Nothing came through.

"If you behave, it'll be the day I let you go." He twisted around and leered at her. "What happens between now and then is up to you. You're not exactly my type, but if I'm going to be stuck with you for over a week, I might as well get some personal satisfaction while I'm at it. For now, sit still and be quiet. Or I'll toss you in back."

Next Monday. Over a week. Today was Saturday.

Torie shuddered. She hadn't had a clear look at him, but her captor was definitely the same guy who'd grabbed her at Kathy's cottage. The one she'd kicked. Was he holding a grudge? Would he do something comparable to her? She clamped her mouth shut. Smarter to revert to proper young lady behavior. Much smarter. But being quiet left her alone with her thoughts, and they weren't pretty ones.

What *would* he be doing to her between now and next Monday? Visions from all the mysteries and thrillers she'd read tumbled through her brain. He'd let her see his face. She could identify him. Didn't that mean he planned to kill her? But he said he'd let her go. He'd said everything would be fine. He probably meant fine for *him*. Rape? Mutilation? Torture?

Her heart skidded around her ribcage until she thought he'd tell her to shut up again. A film of sweat coated her. She wiggled her wrists, hoping her bindings had loosened. Nothing. If anything, she was making things worse by chafing her skin, rubbing it raw.

She craned her neck, hoping to see her car behind them. Fozzie had seen her being captured. He'd promised to take care of her. He'd be following, wouldn't he?

No one had ever taken care of her before. Why should she expect it now? If she waited for Fozzie, she could be dead.

Torie tried to spot landmarks, to remember each turn. She strained to hear something that might help pinpoint her location. A train whistle putting her near a railroad, airplanes overhead putting an airport nearby—anything. With the windows rolled up, she heard the tires against the road, broken only by the man's cell phone. He'd had three calls already, answering each with a guttural "Yeah." He listened briefly, then said, "Roger" and hung up. His boss checking up on him?

The car turned onto a side road. Then another. She doubted she'd be able to find her way back to Suncrest, even if she miraculously overpowered her captor and got her hands and legs free. She inhaled, trying to calm herself, smelling greasy burgers and French fries.

How long had they been driving? She peeked at the clock on the dash. It blinked 12:00. She sighed and tried to get comfortable.

Another call. But this one was different. After his initial, "Yeah," he said, "No problems. We're good. Check in when you can."

A new caller? She looked up. He caught her gaze in the rearview mirror. She ducked her head. He had to know she could hear his side of the conversation. Apparently it wasn't that big a deal, or he'd have stopped and gone somewhere she couldn't overhear. Like he didn't care that she'd seen him.

The phone rang yet again. Another "Yeah." Then, "We're on schedule." The gruffness was gone. A pause. "It wasn't there. Must have fallen off." Another pause, longer this time. "Hell, you're the one who knows where it is. We got what you sent us for, what difference does it make?"

The car slowed. "All right, all right. Tell Chuck. Let him find it. He'll be free soon enough."

Chuck. Someone's name was Chuck. Other than that, it seemed clear enough why he hadn't bothered to get out of her earshot. His responses were too cryptic to comprehend.

"I told you, I'm on top of it." Another pause. A deep exhale. "All right." He set the phone down. Turned and glared at her, flat gray eyes beneath pinched eyebrows.

He accelerated for several minutes. His knuckles whitened on the wheel. Without her hands to steady her, she was almost thrown over when they took a turn. He slowed to a more reasonable speed for several more minutes.

The car stopped. She peered out the window. They were . . . nowhere. He'd just stopped. Barely pulled onto the shoulder.

Generic forest in all directions. Generic to her. Kathy would probably know each tree, each bush. Tears brimmed. She blinked them away. Whoever this creep was, she wasn't going to let him see her cry.

He got out of the car. Opened her door. Was he going to dump her here? They'd been driving for what seemed like forever. How far from civilization were they?

He waved his gun at her. "You're not going to do anything stupid, are you?"

She shook her head.

"Good." He went to the rear of the car, popped open the hatch and returned with a greasy-looking red rag. Holding an end in each hand, he twirled it into a narrower length. Raised it toward her face. If he put it in her mouth, she'd throw up for sure. "I've been quiet," she whispered. "Like you asked."

He yanked her head forward and tied the cloth around her eyes. A gasoline odor wafted down, not strong, but enough to dominate her sense of smell.

Why would he blindfold her now? As the car started moving again, she stiffened. Without being able to see, she couldn't anticipate any turns, and it was impossible to maintain her balance whenever they rounded a bend. And they rounded a lot of bends. Was he driving in circles to confuse her? She scooted over, trying to brace her feet against the back of the passenger seat. Carefully, afraid she'd incur her captor's wrath if she called attention to herself, she wiggled her nose, her chin, her neck, trying to dislodge the blindfold enough to see. No such luck. She had impressions of light and shadow as they drove through what had to be more forest. Her only indication of speed was how fast the lights and shadows flickered. The gasoline residue in the blindfold stung her eyes, and she closed them.

Had she dozed? Slowly, she became aware of a change in the background noises. Traffic sounds. Other cars. Had they reached a highway? For her, like the clock on the dash, time stopped. Finally, so did the car. A whirring sound. Garage door opening? The car moved forward again, then halted. The light level dropped. A repeat of the whirring sound. So, she was in a garage with an automatic opener. Suburbs? But where? Two weeks in Aspen Corners hadn't given her time to learn much about the geography.

Her door opened, and she almost tumbled out of the car. The man yanked her arm, then swung her over his shoulder like a sack of flour. When she tried to kick and pound, he simply gripped her tighter, once again telling her to shut up.

I didn't say anything.

She stopped struggling. What good would it do her to break free?

He shifted her slightly, removing one hand. She sensed a door opening. Rising, as if he climbed a step. Then a click, and it got lighter. Another door, then down a series of steps. Twelve, she counted. Another door. The air had a closed-in feeling, as if it hadn't been disturbed in a while. The rag across her face gave everything a gasoline scent.

He strode a few more paces, then swung her down. She landed on her side, on something that gave under her weight. The man flipped her facedown, pressing on her back. Felt more like a knee than a gun. He yanked off her blindfold.

"Don't move," he commanded.

"I won't." Her voice was little more than a squeaky whisper, which sent a surge of anger through her. She was being sensible, not cowardly. She cleared her throat but didn't speak.

The gasoline smell had left with the blindfold, replaced by a damp, earthy odor. She turned her head to the side. Coarse fabric pressed against her cheek. With a snap, her arms were free. She rubbed her wrists. He'd taken her watch.

136

"You're not going to kick me if I cut your feet loose, are you?"

"No. No, I won't move. Promise."

"Good." She felt him removing her sneakers. Another snap and she could wiggle her legs.

"Thank you," she whispered.

Before she could turn over, the door closed. A lock snicked. She raised herself on her elbows, blinking. She sat up, rubbing and rotating her ankles, trying to get the circulation back. Her eyes stung as the blood returned along with fiery pins and needles. Biting her lip, she surveyed her prison.

Fozzie lay where he was, waiting, testing his opponent, taking in oxygen.

The man pounded on the tailgate. "I said, come out of there. Or would you rather I shoot you?"

"Don't think you'll do that, mate." Fozzie kept his voice low enough so the man had to lean in to hear him. "Forensics is too damn good these days. You'll never get away with it."

"Didn't say I'd kill you. Just shoot you."

By now, Fozzie's eyes had adjusted to the light. "No need. But your hospitality and accommodations have been less than stellar. I can't feel my hands or legs."

"Get your ass out here, scumbag."

"Well, that portion of my anatomy's not feeling much at the moment, either. Maybe you could come in and give me a hand."

"Move it. Now."

"All right, mate. No need to get testy. I'm moving." Fozzie ignored the pain in his hands as he hunched forward. "You think you might raise the bed cover some more? Make it a might easier to do what you're asking. Don't have much room to maneuver."

"Don't see no reason to make it easy. Wasn't for you, I'd be enjoying a cold one with a babe at home."

"Well, don't let me stop you. What say we both go find a babe and a brew? I'll even buy the first round."

"Shut the fuck up and get out of the damn truck."

"No need to swear, mate." Fozzie stopped. "Gotta catch my breath. Wasn't much air back here, you know." He waited. Would the man take the bait?

"Christ on a crutch," the man muttered, leaning in. He grabbed for Fozzie's ankles to drag him out of the truck. "You are such a—"

Fozzie drew his legs close to his body. The man leaned farther in. Putting every bit of power he could muster into his legs, he kicked out, catching the man on the nose. The man's head shot backward, connecting with the edge of the bed cover.

"You should have raised it like I asked," Fozzie muttered as he scrambled out of the truck. The man lay motionless on the ground, blood gushing from his nose. Hunching along on his arse, Fozzie manipulated his wrists against the tailpipe of the truck. Every now and again the gods smiled. The truck was old, the exhaust pipe worn and ragged. Thankfully for his tender flesh, it didn't take much to work through the restraints. His wrists snapped apart, and he shook them to get the blood flowing. He'd deal with the burns later. On hands and knees, he lurched over the ground for the man's gun.

With the weapon in his possession, Fozzie relaxed and concerned himself with getting his feet released. The ankle binding didn't lend itself to a repeat of the tailpipe method. Not without some serious foot damage. He searched the man's pockets for a knife, or anything sharp. No such luck. The man stirred, groaning.

"Sorry, mate." Fozzie used the grip of the gun to deliver a knockout blow. Once he was confident he had a few minutes, Fozzie untied one of the man's sneakers and pulled out the lace. He threaded it around the plastic of the cuffs binding his ankles and seesawed his hands, creating enough friction heat to melt through the plastic. Free at last, he leaned forward and rubbed circulation back into his ankles. He sucked air, more out of relief than exertion. Standing, he twisted and stretched cramped muscles. They were on a dirt road, not much different from all the other roads he'd been on lately. A field on one side, forest on the other. Judging from the light, they'd been on the road for several hours.

Time to get out of here. Wherever here was. First, he dragged the man out of sight of any passing cars, not that he'd seen any. Next, he went through the man's pockets. A wallet with thirty bucks in cash. A Visa card and California driver's license both in the name of Charles Palmer. Picture on the license matched the man on the ground. The man traveled light. Fozzie hobbled to the truck, hoping to find his shoes along with everything Charles Palmer had taken from him. Fozzie stuffed the wallet in his back pocket.

In the cab, the sight of the man's cell phone on the passenger seat sent his heart pounding. Had he missed a check-in? Was whoever had Torie waiting?

Shit.

Too much time in the sweatbox had boiled his brain. He scrolled through the call log and found the last number. He was about to punch redial when he checked the display. He'd never been so happy to find no bars. Whoever the guy was calling had to know the cell reception sucked. Palmer had most likely checked in at the last decent signal. At least Fozzie hoped so.

He finished his search of the cab. Aside from a pack of cigarettes and a lighter connected by an elastic, an array of crumpled candy wrappers, and a well-worn zippered jacket, there was nothing.

"What did you do with my stuff, you bucket of pus?" He

popped open the glove box. An owner's manual in pristine condition. A handful of condoms. Two candy bars.

He pocketed the lighter, closed the glove box. Reconsidered. Put the condoms in his other pocket.

Now. What to do with Palmer? Tempted to leave him by the roadside, Fozzie abandoned the thought. He slipped off the man's shoes, replaced the lace, then shoved his feet into them. Not quite his size, but tight sneakers beat socks, hands down.

He hoisted the man over his shoulder and shoved him into the truck bed. Slamming the tailgate and the bed cover in place, he sneered. "See how you like the ride back there."

First order of business. Figure out where the hell you are, and where Torie is. He stomped to the cab, climbed in and cranked the ignition. Third of a tank of gas. Which way? Ahead, in the direction they'd been traveling, things seemed more and more remote. Better odds that a cell signal would be behind him.

He threw the truck into reverse, spun into a three-point turn, and drove, checking the cell signal every few seconds, hoping the battery would last. What kind of an idiot didn't have a charger in his vehicle? Or anything else, for that matter. From the looks of things, Palmer used this truck to get from point A to point B and nothing more.

After about five minutes, the dirt lane ended and Fozzie paused, deciding which way to turn. Seeing a tractor laboring to tow a hay wagon to the right, he turned left. The new road was paved, but barely. Pitted with potholes ranging from quarter-sized to virtual sinkholes, the road was no easier to navigate than the winding dirt lane had been.

The truck rocked in rhythm to a loud clunking noise. Guess his passenger had come around. Fozzie hit the accelerator, aiming directly for a pothole the size of a dinner plate. The truck bounced. A curse came from the back.

"What's the matter, mate?" he said under his breath. "Can't handle a taste of your own medicine? At least your hands and feet aren't tied."

He drove, counted to a hundred and checked the phone display. At last. A signal. He punched in Blackthorne's command center's number, hoping Jinx was on duty again. Or still.

"Blackthorne." Jinx's voice. Fozzie heard hesitation in his tone. Of course. The number wasn't available to just anyone, and Fozzie was using an unfamiliar phone.

"Jinx, it's Fozzie."

"Where the hell are you?"

"I was hoping you could tell me. Does this piece of shit cell phone I've borrowed have a GPS signal you can track? Or can you triangulate off cell towers?" Jinx was good, but could he do anything before the battery died?

"The great Foster Mayhew doesn't know where he is? That's one for the books. Care to explain? Is there a redhead involved?"

"Jinx, I promise to fill you in. Over beer. On me. But I'm running out of battery here, and the cell signals come and go." He checked the time on the cell phone, apparently one of its only features. Crap. Had it been that long? Jinx confirmed the time. Almost four. "If it helps, I'm within a three-hour radius, by pickup truck, of a town called Suncrest in central Oregon. Not far from Bend. From what I can tell, we were on back roads."

Jinx's tone turned serious. "On it."

Fozzie pulled onto the shoulder and stepped away from the truck. He had a better signal, and for all he knew, he was going in the wrong direction. Might as well wait. Maybe a car would come by, someone he could flag down, ask for directions.

You'll lose man points for that one.

He could handle it. However, wherever he was didn't seem to be a place anyone else wanted to be.

The waiting brought its own demons. On the job, there was a lot of waiting, but they never went in deaf, dumb and blind, which was how he felt now. He ignored the escalating shouts and kicks from the rear of the truck, trying to keep his mind clear. Away from Torie. Was she alone, frightened? Wondering if he'd find her? Hurt?

I'll find you. Promise.

He studied the terrain outside. Nothing like the sheep station of his childhood. He forced himself to remain in the here and now. Away from the memories. Memories of being alone, wondering if someone would find him. Waiting.

He almost hit his head on the roof of the cab when Jinx's voice came over the phone.

"You're about twenty miles from Suncrest as the crow flies. Head west."

Relief swamped him. "Thanks."

"Save it. I've got more."

"What?" His heart rate kicked into a higher gear.

"Your phone is in Suncrest, too."

Fozzie wasn't ready to admit he'd been blindsided. "Good to know. Hey, check another one for me, will yuh?"

"Pushing the envelope, are you?"

"Put it on my tab." Making contact with Jinx cleared a few more brain pathways. He gave Jinx Torie's number. Scrolled through Palmer's call log and added the number he'd been calling regularly. He jumped out of the truck and read off the license plate.

"Oh, and see what you can find out about this guy," he added. "Charles Palmer." He pulled out the man's wallet and relayed the information from his driver's license and his credit card.

"Aussie, you've pushed the envelope into another zip code." But there was understanding in his voice. "Back when I can."

Armed with a goal, and a direction to find it, Fozzie headed out. He pressed the accelerator and dodged potholes, paying no heed to the complaints from the rear. If only the roads went in the same direction as those crows.

Chapter Fourteen

Torie waited for her eyes to adjust to the dim light. The only source seemed to be a tiny, grime-covered window near the top of one wall. Above her, a single light bulb hung in the center of the ceiling. She scanned the room, but found no switches. No way to turn it on. Didn't those kinds of lights usually have pull cords?

The walls were rough concrete block, the floor a dingy concrete slab. She lay on a twin mattress. No sheets, no blankets, no pillow, no box spring. Only a musty smelling, blue-and-white, ticking-covered mattress.

She got up and paced. The room was a few feet longer and wider than the mattress. And no bathroom? Was she going to be here for a week?

No way she could squeeze out of that window. It couldn't be more than six inches high. And that assumed she could open it.

The overhead light came on. Someone pounded on the door. "Get on the bed. Sit on your hands."

"Okay," she said, following his instructions. No point in pissing him off before she knew what was going on.

She heard rattling, clunking from the door. He entered the room and closed it behind him. She avoided his gaze, on the infinitesimal chance he'd overlooked the fact she could identify him. Or could she? She'd never really gotten a clear look at him. Height, build, hair color. She'd know his voice. That was it. After she noticed he still carried a gun, she kept her eyes on her lap.

"Okay, bitch. Here are the rules. I control the light. You're quiet, I turn it on. You piss me off, you stay in the dark. I bring you food. You piss me off, you don't eat. I say when you can use the john. You piss me off—"

When he stopped, she braved an upward glance. His mouth twisted into a sardonic smile. "You piss me off, you piss yourself. So ask nice." He laughed at his feeble joke. Her gut clenched.

"Questions?" he asked.

"It's cold in here. May I have a blanket? Or some more of my clothes?"

He seemed to consider that for a moment. "Your clothes are long gone. You should be glad I'm leaving you the ones you've got on. I'll see about a blanket. Maybe."

"Thank you. And, if you don't mind, I'd really appreciate it if you'd let me use a bathroom."

He grunted as if he'd expected the question. After a moment, with her heartbeat pounding in her ears the only sound in the room, he grunted again. "You're not going to try anything silly, are you?"

"No, of course not." Her eyes flicked to the gun at his side.

"Hands on your head."

She obeyed.

"Stand up."

She rose.

He opened the door. Motioned her to exit. When she passed him, he grabbed the back of her jeans. "Upstairs."

She counted the twelve steps. Wooden. Rustic. She halted at the top.

"Open the door," he said.

She obeyed and found the door led to a garage, empty except for the Suzuki SUV. The door was recessed between two shelving units, and it clunked against one as she pushed it open wider.

"Careful," he snapped. "Over there." He gestured to another door along the adjacent wall.

She stepped into a kitchen. He pushed her across the space and into a small powder room. "Be quick."

She turned on the water in the sink and splashed her face. There was nothing in the room but the toilet and pedestal sink. And, thankfully, half a roll of toilet paper. No towels. Not even a mirror. Did anyone live in this house?

"Hurry up in there."

With him standing probably right outside the door, listening, the urge passed. But if she didn't go now, no telling when she'd get another chance. She concentrated on relaxing until she could do what she needed to.

She finished and rinsed her hands. Afraid to use up the toilet paper in case this was her entire week's supply, she wiped her hands on her jeans.

Taking a deep breath, she tapped on the door. "Finished."

"Hands on your head."

She sighed. "Ready."

He pulled the door open and they reversed their trek down to her hole. She managed a glimpse of the kitchen. Clean. Virtually empty. Nothing on the counters, no dishes in the sink. Nothing on the fridge. Definitely not the lived-in look.

At the bottom of the stairs, he nudged her into her prison. She checked the door as she entered. Not a standard lock. A padlock. She heard him click it shut, leaving her alone again.

She wandered from one side of the room to the other, trying to organize what few facts she had. She was being held in some sort of storage cellar. The Spartan appearance of the kitchen reinforced her hypothesis that nobody lived here. Would anyone notice activity in a house that was supposed to be empty? Would they call the police if they did? Then again, she had no clue if anyone else lived close enough to notice. She could be in some isolated farm house, or some vacation home, or in the servants' quarters of some luxury mansion for all she knew.

She heard thumping from above. Then down the stairs.

"On the bed. Hands on your head," he called from outside the door.

This was going to get old. Fast. "Okay."

The padlock released. The door opened. A blanket flew in. The door closed.

"Thank you," she called out. He might be a brute, but she'd been brought up to be a lady. Her laugh turned into a sob at the thought her father might have hired an ape like this, after all the lectures about proper behavior. She shoved her fist against her mouth so he couldn't hear her cry.

The overhead light went out. She wiped her eyes. Crying wasn't going to get her out of here, although at the moment, she couldn't figure out what would. She had the clothes on her back. A mattress and a blanket.

She paced again. Tried to think logically. Made a mental list of the facts at hand. Someone needed her out of the way. Not dead. Or not dead yet. Was that why they were holding her? She might be needed between now and next Monday, so they had to keep her alive? And after Monday, what?

So, she either had, or they thought she had, some piece of information that wouldn't be needed after Monday. She racked her brain, trying to think whether Epicurean had announced any new developments. A merger? She'd know about that. A hostile takeover? Her lawyer would have told her that, too. But she'd been hard to reach for a while. What did she know that might have an effect one way or the other? And if her father hadn't sent the man, then who had? What could she have that *anyone* could want? For the life of her, she couldn't think of anything. Tears welled again as she thought how true that might be. Her life could be ending soon, and she didn't have a clue why.

Dusk was fading to dark by the time Fozzie nosed the pickup into a slot in the Suncrest parking lot. A scattering of light poles cast a yellow glow over the area. He was surprised to see Torie's Fusion sitting right where they'd left it. He wasn't surprised when it was empty. He popped the trunk. Empty as well.

Fozzie scanned the parking lot. A green Dumpster sat at one end, about ten feet from a Salvation Army drop box. He rushed across the lot. Could it be that simple? The Salvation Army box had a swinging door like a trash receptacle. He pushed the door inward, but even though there was a light pole close by, he couldn't see inside. Besides, with his luck, his stuff would be in the smelly Dumpster. He abandoned the Salvation Army box and crossed to the Dumpster. He jumped, caught the edge and hoisted himself up.

"Hey, you got no call to be there. That's Wally's territory."

Fozzie looked down at the voice. A wizened beanpole of a man in a baggy sweater stared up at him from behind a pair of too-familiar looking sunglasses. And a battered Akubra. Fozzie dropped to the ground.

"And where's Wally, then?" Fozzie asked, giving the man a friendly smile.

"You're lookin' at him."

"Gotcha, mate. No problem. It's just that I lost some important stuff. Maybe you've seen it?" He ran his gaze over Wally, halting at his feet. "Nice boots. New?"

Wally gave him a wide grin. The guy's fingers probably outnumbered his teeth. "A bit on the roomy side, but nice."

"Tell you what, Wally. I've got some sneakers here that would probably fit you better. What say we trade?"

Wally pulled off the Akubra, then a knit cap and scratched his head through greasy, matted hair. The sleeve of his sweater fell back, revealing three wrist watches adorning his arm. Fozzie had no doubt one of them was his.

"Dunno." Wally scratched his head again. "Don't seem equal."

"Well, the way I see it, you did all right with the swag today, most of which used to be mine. I'm sure we can work something out."

"Once it hits the Dumpster, it ain't yours no more."

Fozzie gritted his teeth. "Aye, mate, but I wasn't the one to put it in the Dumpster. Seems you could cut me some slack. How about we look at what you got? I'm thinking you pulled a bit of ready cash out of the deal, too. Seems you're far enough ahead to do me a little favor."

Wally gazed heavenward, wrinkled his nose, and worked his mouth back and forth before answering. "This way."

Fozzie followed as Wally led him through the parking lot and down a narrow alley. The back side of a warehouse, he guessed. Security lights provided enough visibility. Wally stopped in front of a wooden packing crate about four feet square. A ratty blanket tacked to the top created a door. He ducked inside and pulled out Torie's suitcase and Fozzie's duffel.

"Got some good stuff in here. Worth some green, or goods in trade, it is. Miss Alice would like these frillies, and the other duds would do her well come wintertime."

Fozzie pictured Miss Alice as a female equivalent of Wally and tried not to think of what she'd look like in Torie's *frillies*. "What about cell phones?" he asked.

"Don't got no use for them gadgets. Had one once. Batteries died. And nobody to call." He disappeared into his shelter and came out with a plastic grocery bag. He held it open for Fozzie, displaying the two missing phones with chargers. And his GPS. "Might as well take 'em."

"I thank you, Wally. That's most noble."

"Seems wrong to keep everything if it's like you said. Wasn't your doin' that they're in my territory. And everyone knows Wally don't keep what he don't need. He spreads it out to them what does."

"A true gentleman," Fozzie said. "I don't suppose you'd consider returning purses, car keys, and wallets now. Of course, you can keep the cash inside for your trouble. And I'd be most obliged if you'd be willing to part with my torch—flashlight. I'm truly in need of that."

Wally did the rubber-lip thing again, then nodded his head solemnly. "Sounds fair enough. Flashlight's nice at night, but I got another one. No use for cars. Gas costs too much nowadays. Nowhere to go."

Wally pulled the blanket aside and disappeared into his box. Fozzie tried to get a glimpse inside, wondering if there was some hidden passage to a giant storage center. Like a circus clown car. Between Wally's body and the dim interior, he couldn't see much. Piles of clothing, mostly. But Wally seemed to know what he was doing as he moved things aside and plucked a variety of items, putting them in another plastic grocery bag. He backed out and extended the bag.

Fozzie accepted it as graciously as he could. He debated asking for Torie's tote, but figured Wally and his cohorts could use it. He and Torie could replace their clothing easily enough. He'd miss his hat, though.

"One more thing," Wally said. He scuttled behind the Dumpster and returned dragging a cardboard carton. "This wasn't inside the bin, so I ain't got no claim. Plus, I never was much good at reading."

Torie's books. He'd forgotten. He knew she wouldn't care about her clothes once she got her books back.

"Thanks, Wally. You're a right fine bastard."

"You got no call to say that about me," Wally said with a scowl.

"Sorry, mate. Where I come from, bastard means a damn good friend."

Wally gave a solemn nod. "I kinda figured you wasn't from around here. Texas maybe?"

Fozzie laughed. "A little farther away than that."

"You still wanna trade shoes?" Wally asked.

"Afraid so. These aren't working for me. Too small."

Wally sighed. Fozzie kept from backing away at the man's fetid breath.

"Too tight's no good, gotta give you that." Wally toed off the boots, bent and pulled a rolled up sock from each. Fozzie unlaced the sneakers he wore and they swapped footgear. Wally walked a few steps, bounced on the balls of his feet, then gave another gaping grin. "Too big's better than too tight, but just right is best of all."

"You got it. Take it easy. Sorry, but I've got to run."

"Nice doing business with you." Wally extended a hand. "You bastard."

Fozzie gripped the man's bony fingers. "You, too. Take care."

As he strode back to Torie's car, Fozzie remembered Palmer, still stuck in the back of his truck. He resisted the temptation to leave him there. He patted the truck's keys in his pocket. No need to make it easy, however. He'd keep the man's cell phone, too. After he put everything but the GPS into the Fusion, Fozzie jogged over to the truck and raised the cover. Palmer tried to jump out. Fozzie shoved him back.

"You want to tell me where the girl is, or you want to stay locked inside?" Fozzie moved his shirt aside enough to show the gun tucked into his waistband.

Palmer recited an address in a town Fozzie hadn't heard of. Fozzie fed it into the GPS, confirmed the town and address existed. "Why did you grab us? Who are you working for?"

Palmer shrugged. "I get paid. I don't ask questions."

"You set the fire to Torie's place, didn't you?"

Palmer crossed his arms across his chest. "I don't answer questions, either." The look gave Fozzie the answer he needed.

Much as he'd like to get in Palmer's face and grill him, worry for Torie took over. "I'm outta here," he said. "You're on your own." He doubted Palmer would call the cops.

Shit. But Palmer might call his partner. He couldn't leave the guy locked in the back of his truck. Or could he?

"Sorry, but you're going to have to hang tight a little longer." He motioned Palmer to slide back into the truck bed, then locked the cab. Palmer pounded.

Fozzie slapped the bed cover. "I have a few things to do. You stay quiet, and I'll let you out when I'm done. Make any noise and you can kiss ever having a brew with a babe good-bye."

He loped to where he'd left Wally and found him sitting on a sheet of plastic, leaning against his box.

"Hey, bastard," Wally said. "Back already?"

"I need a favor."

"Wally helps his friends." He struggled to his feet. "What do I have to do?"

Fozzie handed him the keys to the pickup. "There's a blue Ford pickup in the lot. I want you to wait until"—he did a quick calculation of the time he'd need—"ten o'clock, then unlock the cover from the back. Can you do that for me?"

Wally slid the sleeve of his sweater up his arm and inspected his watches. He tapped one. "Ten o'clock. Unlock the back of the blue truck. No problem."

"Right. And if I were you, I wouldn't hang around. The guy inside's probably going to be royally pissed. You might want to add those keys to your collection after you unlock the truck."

Wally grinned. He sat down again, studying his watches.

Fozzie trotted to the Fusion and had already started the engine when he paused. Better to be safe. He popped out of the car to make sure nobody had found and reattached the tracker to the Fusion.

You're finally thinking.

Time to find Torie. He set the GPS on the dash, punched Jinx's number into his phone and hit the road.

"Command Center," Jinx answered.

"Hey, it's me. Got anything?"

"Of course."

"Got anything good?"

"Well, that's another question. You'll have to be the judge of that."

Chapter Fifteen

Torie thought as she paced. Next Monday, the man had said. Next Monday was nine days from now. He'd taken her watch. That window would let her tell day from night and not much else. What little light filtered through the filthy window had a faint yellow cast. From a streetlight? Should she start scratching the days into the concrete walls?

Get real. You've only been here a few minutes, and you're acting like it's a life sentence.

Maybe it was. A chill snaked down her spine. She couldn't shake the all-pervading fear that this guy was going to get rid of her as soon as she wasn't needed, no matter what he'd said.

Keep calm. Pay attention. Be docile. Earn his trust. He'll drop his guard eventually. Be ready.

The dim room grew darker. She snapped her gaze to the window. Gone? A window couldn't disappear. He'd covered it with something. The sound of hammering filled the room.

She shuffled her feet as she walked, feeling for the mattress, and lowered herself. The thought of her face on the mattress turned her stomach. Finding the blanket, she wrapped herself in the scratchy wool before lying down. She stared into the darkness and listened to the silence.

Not total silence. Her breathing filled her ears. With conscious effort, she slowed it down. Wind rustled branches outside. She strained to hear any traffic sounds. Like maybe police sirens? Even dogs barking. Cats yowling. Anything to let her know she wasn't alone.

After a while, the light snapped on. She squinted against the sudden brightness. The man pounded on the door again, repeated his commands. She finger-combed her hair and sat up. "Okay."

The padlock released. The door opened. The man filled the doorway. He lowered an oblong plastic container to the floor. "Dinner. You have ten minutes." He backed away, locking the door behind him.

After listening to his footfalls climb the stairs, she brought the container to the bed. Inside, she found a slice of lukewarm pizza on a paper plate, and a bottle of water.

She wasn't hungry, but had no idea when—or if—he'd feed her again. She forced the pizza down. The spicy pepperoni made her thirsty, so she sipped at the water, afraid to drink too much. No telling when he'd take her to the bathroom. She wondered if he'd leave the plastic box, if she could use it as an emergency toilet.

It seemed like a lot longer than ten minutes before he pounded on the door again. This time, all he said was, "Leave everything by the door. Stay on the bed."

Not knowing when he'd be back, and knowing dehydration could be a problem, she kept the water bottle, hoping he'd allow it.

The door opened wide enough for him to grab the box. If he noticed the water bottle wasn't in it, he said nothing. His footsteps clunked on the stairs. She waited, but the light didn't go out.

She lay on her back, gazing at the cracks and water stains in the ceiling. When she was a little girl, she and Nana would sit on the grass and see pictures in the clouds. She let her mind wander, conjuring up memories of the blue sky, the puffy white clouds. Air that smelled of lilac and honeysuckle. The breeze that played through her hair. Birds singing in the maple tree.

When the room went dark, the memories remained.

She dozed until he came downstairs again. This time, the lock didn't open as readily. He hadn't turned on the light. He leaned against the doorway. "You need to go?"

"Please," she said.

"Hands up."

Hands on her head, she approached him. Smelled the beer on his breath. Was he drunk? Could she knock him over as they climbed the stairs? Did she dare try? What if she failed? He'd lock her back up. So far, he'd ignored her.

"Move it," he said. His hand gripped her jeans. His motor skills seemed fine as he marched her upstairs. She used the bathroom, splashed water on her face and rinsed her mouth out, wishing she had a toothbrush.

He escorted her downstairs when she finished. He left the door to her room open long enough for her to see her way to the bed.

"Sleep well," he said. Then he laughed, the sound chilling her to her bones. She curled up in a ball and closed her eyes.

The overhead light shattered the darkness. She blinked, then squeezed her eyes shut. How long had she been asleep?

The door opened without the usual preamble. The plastic container appeared. She rolled off the mattress and checked the contents. A bowl of Cheerios and a plastic cup of milk. A plastic spoon. And two wet-naps.

She had little appetite, but she poured half the milk over the cereal, then drank the rest. She finished her breakfast and replaced the bowl, cup and spoon in the container, then placed it by the door. Using one of the wet-naps, she wiped her hands, face and neck and added the used cloth and its wrapper to her dishes. She stuck the second wipe in her pocket to use on her next trip upstairs.

The cereal sat like a boulder on top of last night's pizza. She walked around the room, trying to loosen stiff muscles. She'd need to stay fit if she was going to be able to escape. She did a few half-hearted crunches, tried to remember some moves from the few Pilates classes she'd taken. Her lids drooped. Had he drugged the milk?

She lay back on the mattress. If he had drugged her, he probably wouldn't be taking her upstairs any time soon. Her head seemed clear enough, but she was sleepy. She dozed in fits and starts. The light went off for a while, then came on. Then went off. She counted away the seconds. Three thousand, two hundred and fifty-nine. Give or take. Of course, she couldn't do the math to convert it to minutes, not without a calculator. Why bother?

The man brought her upstairs again. His beer breath was gone. Stubble darkened his cheeks. He grabbed her butt instead of her waist this time. She jerked away. When he brought her down, he blocked the doorway to the room so she rubbed against him as he shoved her inside. He laughed his bone-chilling laugh.

"Please," she whispered. "Why am I here? Can't you tell me that much?"

"I told you to be quiet." He backhanded her cheek.

Tears sprang to her eyes, but she refused to react. She waited until he'd locked her in before she put her hand to her stinging cheek and cried.

Why was she so weak? Why couldn't she stand up to him? She'd kicked him in the balls once, hadn't she?

Slow down. You'll have your chance. You have to win his trust first.

Drowsy, she lay down again. The light stayed on. Wishing for a pillow to hide her eyes, she cocooned herself in the blanket.

157

She preferred the dark, where she could escape to a happier place. If he'd drugged her, he should have used more.

Where was Fozzie? Had he blown her off? He'd done his job when he talked to his boss. He had no obligation. She'd told him she didn't want him to know where she was going. Maybe he'd said good riddance when he'd seen her forced into the SUV.

No, he couldn't. Wouldn't. Yes, of course he could. Would. She was plain, dumpy Torie. "Just a friend" Torie. If she wasn't his job, he'd move on.

But it would be nice to have him around. He was funny. And cute. And warm. Like the teddy bear she'd had when she was three. She thought of their bodies pressed together in the car, pretending to be lovers. She pulled the blanket tighter around her.

Fozzie adjusted his cell phone to speaker and started Torie's car. "Talk to me." He rummaged through the plastic bags Wally had returned, checking his available assets.

"Your Palmer guy. Arrest record an inch thick. Done time. Mostly auto theft, a couple of assault charges and one for arson. Address listed in Chico, California. No current employment, at least none he's reporting."

"The truck?"

"Plate comes back to another blue pickup. Different year, registered to a construction worker in Klamath Falls, Oregon."

"Sounds like Palmer was bright enough to swap plates." Fozzie hadn't seen signs of vast intelligence in the man, but that didn't mean he hadn't picked up a few pointers from the sorts he likely kept company with. Going to prison taught you how to be a better criminal. "Get anything to connect the two trucks? And what about the SUV partial I gave you?"

"Sorry, no time. Wish I could get you more, but the boss has some priority cases coming down hot and heavy. He hasn't filled all the gaps created by opening the Miami office, and I'm doing triple duty here. He's got three teams deployed, and they all need the skinny yesterday."

"Hear you. Thanks for sneaking me in. I'm on my way to an address Palmer gave me." He repeated it for Jinx. "If you have spare time, any intel on the property would be greatly appreciated."

"No promises." Jinx's normally calm voice held undercurrents of tension.

"Understood."

If the workload had Jinx frazzled, Fozzie wondered why Blackthorne hadn't ordered him back. He ran through the call log on his phone. Nope. Nothing.

Did the boss think he'd burned out?

No matter. He was on vacation, per orders, and right now his vacation consisted of getting Torie away from whoever had her. Time to get his arse in gear.

Palmer carried a nine-millimeter Smith & Wesson. Fozzie dropped the magazine to check the ammo. Nine cartridges, plus another one in the chamber. He set it within reach. Checked the car's fuel gauge. Barely quarter of a tank. No point in being stranded. Wally had returned his wallet, and Torie's. He'd left only five dollars in each, but hadn't taken the credit or ATM cards.

He pulled into an open gas station and started to open the door before he remembered Oregon's law about self-service. Like, you couldn't do it. "Fill it. Regular," he said to the kid who ambled over.

While the kid babysat the hose, Fozzie plugged his cell into the charger, hit the restroom, and brought a large coffee, a package of beef jerky, and a couple of power bars to the counter.

Advance planning gave you the edge. Recklessness got you killed.

Of course, normally, he and his team had a little more information than an address. Floor plans, recon, surveillance equipment. He had his GPS, a cell phone. And a Smith & Wesson with ten rounds. Which meant the guy who had Torie had his SIG back. Probably reloaded, with backup ammo.

He followed the route his GPS gave him, planning. Darkness was on his side. He'd prefer night-vision goggles, but his torch would have to do.

Hang in there, Torie.

There was more traffic on the road now. Saturday night. Weekend congestion. Doing forty felt like a turtle's crawl. He checked the GPS for an alternate route, but this was it as far as roads went. The readout said fifty minutes to his destination. Even adding time for Palmer to get to a phone, this was cutting it close.

Not to mention he was working on the assumption Palmer had told him the truth about where they'd taken Torie. And that she'd still be there. He leaned forward, as if it would make the cars ahead move faster.

Twenty anxious minutes later, the road forked. Most cars peeled left. The GPS lady's voice told him to stay right. With a clearer road ahead of him, Fozzie pressed the accelerator.

When he was within ten minutes of the address, he slowed. His instincts said to storm the house and grab Torie. His training said to hold back. Survey the area. Plan. He let his training rule. From this point on, Torie was a hostage. A target. An assignment. He would do whatever it took to get her out, but he could *not* think of her on a personal level. Emotions had no business in his work.

Sounded good in his head. Something in his chest wasn't buying it.

He found the address in a residential neighborhood. Definitely middle-class. Cookie-cutter houses. Landscaping saying the development had been around a while. Streetlights illuminated the area. He turned off his headlights. Cruised toward the destination. Shut off the damn GPS lady's voice.

Address numbers were conveniently painted on the curb with luminous paint. Made it easy for cops and firefighters. And covert search-and-rescue operatives.

His pulse accelerated as he found the house. A "For Sale" sign was jammed into the lawn. No lights on in the front windows. He drove past, around the block, checking for an inconspicuous way to access the property.

From the street behind, he stopped where he could see between houses to the rear of his goal. Dark. But from the house next door, faint light glowed behind a curtained window. The rest of that house was dark. Night-light? Child's room?

Lights moved from room to room in homes along the block. At this hour, most folks would be finished with dinner, settled down to watch television. Kids probably busy doing their social networking, earbuds blasting music, oblivious to anything else.

He longed to be hovering above from the relative comfort of his helo. He visualized his instruments, felt his fingers running over dials, tapping keys. He'd have picked up heat signatures of anyone in Torie's house as well as the neighbors'. He'd be directing the action on the ground. Everyone would be safe.

A dog yipped from a nearby yard. Fozzie was glad he'd bought the jerky, although at the time he'd figured he'd be the one eating it. But if he was going to enter via an alternate route, he might need to bribe a sentry. Fozzie waited, making sure lights weren't coming on. The dog's yipping stopped, and the night's stillness returned.

He moved on. What he could see of Torie's backyard consisted of open space. He relegated sneaking in that way to

Plan C. On the one side, the neighbors with the child were likely to be light sleepers. And the dog on the other side didn't bode well. Now, all he needed were Plans A and B.

He parked the Fusion several houses down the street from his goal, in front of a house well-hidden by landscaping, and away from any streetlights. Final check. His black pants and shirt would provide suitable camouflage. He'd considered the shoe-polish-on-the-face routine, but decided if he happened to run into anyone, looking like a crook wasn't in his best interest. Cell phone on silent. He pulled his shirt free from his waistband. Weapon out of sight, but handy. He dragged a hand through his hair.

Let's do it.

Okay, this was no Blackthorne mission, but thinking the familiar go-ahead signal settled him.

He flipped off the dome light, then eased himself out of the car. As quietly as possible, he closed the door. Under ideal circumstances, he'd wait until four A.M. when the guy's body rhythms would be at their deepest ebb. But there was nothing ideal about this job. He'd debated waiting, even if it meant Palmer would call and warn the guy in the house. He saw two outcomes to that scenario. One, the guy would move Torie, in which case Fozzie could intervene. But the second option, that the guy would consider the situation a bust and take it out on Torie, perhaps killing her, wouldn't go away, and he wasn't going to gamble with her life. Near as he could figure, odds were even. And with Torie's life at stake, he didn't think even ninety-ten would be good enough.

Not because it was Torie, he told himself. He couldn't stand to lose, regardless of the target. A fleeting memory of his failure with Kathy whisked through his brain and he swept it away.

Focus.

He kept his stride casual as he approached the house. Four

wooden steps led to a small entry at the front door. He positioned himself out of peephole range, then pressed redial for the number Palmer had been calling into Palmer's cell, hoping there'd be enough battery for a short call.

The faint ringing inside alleviated some of the nagging fear that whoever Palmer had been calling wasn't the same guy who had Torie. That he'd have passed her off to someone else. The fewer players, the fewer chances for errors, and if there was a payoff, the fewer blokes to split it with. So far, everything had pointed to two people, three at the most. The big question—was number three inside as well?

"Where the hell have you been?" a gruff male voice answered.

Fozzie held the phone away from his mouth, draping his fingers over the phone to further muffle his voice. "Problem," he whispered. "Need help. Outside." He ended the call.

From inside, he heard Palmer's name being hollered a few times before the man figured out the call had ended. Fozzie kept his weight on the balls of his feet, listening as footfalls drew closer to the door. The Smith & Wesson was tucked into the waist of his pants, but he hoped to avoid using it. In and out like the wind. Which was why he hadn't called the cops for backup. Between time wasted explaining, and the fear they'd come in guns blazing, he opted to go solo, despite the drawbacks.

The door opened a crack. Fozzie kept his breathing slow and even. Then another inch. Although the streetlight was a house away, it gleamed off the metal of the man's pistol. Fozzie sprang, grabbed the man's wrist, and wrested the gun from his grasp. He shoved the guy back inside, coldcocked him, and kicked the door shut behind him.

Like the wind. He smiled.

Tucking the reconfiscated SIG into his pocket, Fozzie looked around. A small DVD player on the floor provided the only light. A beach chair. A couple of pizza boxes, a strewing of empty beer cans.

"Nice place you got here, mate," Fozzie said under his breath as he dragged the man farther into the room. "Has that lived-in look."

Since he had no real restraints, he bent down, unlaced the man's shoes and used the laces to bind his ankles, then his wrists behind him. That would have to do for the moment. Next, he appropriated his cell phone.

Once he was satisfied the man wasn't going anywhere, he took a deep breath. He resisted the urge to holler Torie's name. He'd been swift and silent, but there could be someone else in the house.

Rule number one. Clear the scene.

At least the curtains were all drawn. He cupped his hands over the flashlight and kept the beam low. Gun at the ready, he moved from room to room. Given the lack of living room furniture and the "For Sale" sign out front, Fozzie suspected nobody was supposed to be living here.

Three bedrooms, all but one completely empty. And the furnishing in that one consisted of a single air mattress and sleeping bag, and a small pile of clothes. The bathroom in the hall held one damp towel. Spoke to the guy being alone. Nobody hiding in the shower, nobody stuffed into the cabinet below the sink.

His pulse kicked up. So where was Torie?

Fozzie checked the kitchen. Beer in the fridge, half a gallon of milk, some cold cuts and a jar of peanut butter. A loaf of bread and a box of Cheerios sat on the counter, but the cupboards were as bare as Mrs. Hubbard's.

Off the kitchen were two doors. He opened the first. Bathroom with sink and toilet. Nothing under the sink here, either. The second door led to a garage, with the SUV parked inside. Could mystery man number three be here? Warily, he approached the vehicle. No stranger burst from behind the car. Fozzie checked the car. A Suzuki, he noted. He could report that to Jinx. A tool kit in the back, a crumpled Mickey D's bag on the floor on the passenger's side. Otherwise, empty. His heart pounded a rapid staccato. Had he made a mistake? Had Palmer conned him? Was Torie somewhere else after all?

From inside, the man groaned. Fozzie rushed back inside, ready to grill him. No, he was still out. Had he punched him that hard? Knowing how much fear and anger had backed his blow, he was afraid so. He emptied the man's pockets. Keys, pocket change, wallet. Some cash, credit cards, driver's license. No clues to Torie's whereabouts.

Had he missed something? "Torie? Are you in here?" Although he wanted to shout at the top of his lungs, he kept his voice low enough so neighbors wouldn't hear.

Silence.

He tried the kitchen again. Maybe there was some sort of clue. A plastic trash bag hung off one cabinet knob. He lifted it free and inspected the contents. Pizza crusts. A plastic spoon, some wadded up paper towels. Paper plates, cups, and a disposable bowl.

And, at the bottom, a glimmer of hope. A pair of women's sneakers. Same kind Torie'd been wearing. And flex cuffs, sliced open. He'd had a prisoner, and it had to be Torie. He grabbed the sneakers out of the bag.

"Torie," he called, louder, not caring if the neighbors heard. "Sunshine, where the hell are you?"

CHAPTER SIXTEEN

Noise from upstairs brought Torie alert. What next? Was it lunchtime? The aftertaste of her breakfast lingered. She sat up, rubbed her eyes.

He was walking around. From the rapid footsteps, he was upset. Torie tensed. Her stomach roiled.

He'd seemed calm before and he'd still hit her, merely because she spoke. What would he do if he was angry, even if it wasn't her fault? She listened, waiting for the sound on the stairs to signal his arrival.

Above, doors opened and closed. Footfalls grew louder, softer, and louder again. He must be storming through the house. Temper tantrum? Someone else around? She didn't hear any arguing, any shouting.

Don't second guess him. Be calm, be quiet, and be ready.

Was he calling her name? What could that mean? So far, he'd only called her bitch. She got off the bed and jogged in place, trying to warm stiff muscles in case she had a chance to make a run for it. A woman's strength was in her legs, not her upper body. She visualized kicking him again, the way she had the first time, but knew he'd be on guard. She'd been lucky that night. She did some calf lifts. Shoes would help.

Slow down.

Clattering on the stairs. He was running this time. God, what was happening? What was he going to do to her?

And he was definitely calling her name. But . . . she listened.

No. It wasn't the same voice.

"Sunshine? Sunshine, talk to me. Where are you?"

There was no mistaking that Aussie accent.

"Fozzie? Is that you?"

"Hang on. I'm right here."

She heard the lock jiggling, some muttered curses. Then the distinctive snick and click as the padlock released. The clunk as it was lifted from the hasp. And the soft creak as the door opened.

She hesitated, afraid she was hearing things. Even when she took in Fozzie's disheveled mop of curls, she looked again.

"Fozzie?"

"In the flesh, Sunshine. You gave me quite a scare."

They stood where they were for several heartbeats, as if someone had pushed a pause button. He, inside the doorway, she beside the mattress. And then, someone hit "resume."

"You came," she said and rushed toward him. To touch him, to make sure he was real. She splayed her hands across his chest, letting his heartbeat course through her. "It's really you." Her voice caught.

He gathered her in his arms. Pulled her head against him. Stroked her hair. Tucked a finger under her chin and lifted her face so she met his gaze. Hot tears burned behind her eyes.

"Of course it's me. I—" He cleared his throat. "Let's blow this joint, okay? Time to talk later."

"Right." She wiped her eyes. He took her hand and led her upstairs.

"What about him?" she asked as they passed the man's body on the living room floor. "You didn't . . . kill him?"

"No, just cleaned his clock."

"Are you going to leave him there. Tied up?"

Fozzie stopped, looked at the man, then her. "I've got his weapon, his keys, his wallet, and his cell phone. It's unlikely he'll be going anywhere. But if you like, we can put him downstairs."

It would serve him right, but she couldn't bring herself to do it. She shook her head. "I wish he'd told me why he wanted me."

The man groaned. Opened his eyes. Groaned again.

"You want to ask him?" Fozzie said. "Or should I?"

"Go to hell," the man said.

"Someday, maybe," Fozzie said. "But not today. Why did you take us?"

"Go to hell."

"I don't think he's going to talk," Fozzie said. "You're safe, that's what matters." He squeezed her hands, then bent and loosened the man's wrists. "He should be able to work himself free. We'll be long gone before he can do anything about it. I doubt he's going to be calling the cops."

"Shouldn't we?"

He straightened. "All that will do is create red tape. And advertise where you are."

It wasn't over. Not until she figured out who these people were, and what was going to happen next Monday. "Let's go." She gave one backward glance over her shoulder. The man groaned and shook his head as if trying to clear it, then grimaced and groaned again.

"Whopper of a headache, eh, mate?" Fozzie said. He dropped Torie's hand. "Wait. Almost forgot." He darted back to the kitchen and returned, his hands behind him. He grinned and brought them forward.

"My shoes!" She snatched them. Before she could put them on, he took her hand again and hurried her out the door.

"Time enough when we're out of here," he said, hustling her out the door.

She stepped onto the porch and took in the surroundings.

The dark surroundings.

"What time is it?" she asked. "What *day* is it?"

Without answering, Fozzie guided her down the block to her Fusion. He helped her in, started the engine and pulled away from the curb. Smoothly. Quietly. If she'd been driving, she'd definitely have burned rubber. But despite his calm driving, his knuckles were tense on the wheel. His jaw muscles twitched. Creases furrowed his forehead.

She slid her feet into her sneakers as they wove through the residential streets. The dash clock said it was ten-thirty . . . P.M.

"What day is it?"

"Still Saturday," he said.

"I don't get it. I thought I'd been in there for at least a full day."

"Hard to judge time when you're locked up."

"But he gave me dinner. Then breakfast." She thought about the darkened room, the way he'd controlled the lights. "He was playing mind games with me, wasn't he?"

"Most likely."

She finished lacing her shoes. Shivered. Fozzie flipped on the heat. He didn't speak again until they were well along the highway.

"Did he hurt you?"

She touched her cheek. "Not really."

"Torie, I'm—this was all my fault."

"No. You said to stay close, and I never realized how serious things were. I thought you were just being . . . you know . . . macho."

"I didn't want to scare you." He faced her. "And, yes, I remember. Not knowing scares you more. It's going to be tough to break that habit." He gave her that lazy grin. Her insides melted.

She smiled back. After all the fear, it felt good. "Well, maybe

you won't have to worry about it anymore. We're safe now."
When his grin disappeared, she tensed. "Are you saying there's
still more scary stuff out there?" She looked at him more carefully. Highway lights illuminated his face. Haggard, tense.

His continued silence spoke volumes.

"What happens next?" she asked.

CHAPTER SEVENTEEN

Fozzie ran his hand through his hair. She'd asked the question of the week. "We go someplace safe. Regroup. Any suggestions?"

"We?"

"We. As in you and me. Us. Together. Joined at the hip. Until we figure out what's going on."

She didn't argue, simply stared out the window. "Not back to Aspen Corners, I guess."

"Not anywhere you've been. I'm thinking we'll find someplace to spend the night. Do some shopping. Make plans."

She tilted her head and gave him a quizzical grin. "Shopping? You want to go shopping?"

Right. She didn't know. "Um . . . while you were . . . indisposed—"

"Kidnapped."

"Right. Actually, before that, while we were having lunch, they got rid of everything in your car. Thought we might need to get some new duds."

"Wait. They?"

"Gunman had you. Firebug got me."

Her eyes flew open. "Are you all right?"

"Right as rain, I believe is your expression." He reached into his pocket and pulled out the guy's wallet. "Take a gander. Maybe the name will ring a bell with you. Torch is in the console."

She switched on the light and held it over the wallet. "Alfred

B. Abbott? Never heard of him."

"What about where he's from?"

Torie read off a street address. Not the one where he'd found her. "This says Klamath Falls. Is that where we were? I'm clue-less about Oregon geography."

"No, we were in Oakdale."

"So I wasn't in his house?"

"He might own it. But he sure as hell doesn't live there."

Klamath Falls. Why did he know Klamath Falls? He searched his memory banks. Right. Palmer had switched pickup truck plates with someone in Klamath Falls. Could it have been Abbott? And if it was, what did it mean? That they knew each other. Nothing new. And who did the SUV belong to? "Anything else in there?"

"Couple of credit cards." She paused, leafed through the wal-let. "Triple-A membership, insurance card. Eighty-seven dol-lars."

"All in Abbott's name?"

"Yes. All but the cash, of course."

"What kind of car is on the insurance card?"

"Suzuki. And the car he kidnapped me with was a Suzuki SUV."

"Okay, then it's probably his. No other cards?"

She looked again. "No. That's all. You said they took all our clothes?"

" 'Fraid so."

"Do you think it's illegal, or unethical, to use his eighty-seven dollars toward buying new ones?"

He grinned. "I don't have a serious problem with it. Someone got our clothes and our cash, but we still have our credit cards. And cell phones."

"I thought you said they took everything." She gasped. "My

books. Nana's books. They were in the car." She sounded close to tears.

"Hey, it's all right. Those are safe."

"You have them?"

"In the trunk. I think they're all there."

"Okay, now I'm confused. They took our clothes and cash, but left our credit cards? And my books? What kind of crooks are they?"

"My guess is lazy. Or at least Palmer is. I found the stuff in a Dumpster."

"Who's Palmer?"

"The firebug. Have you ever heard of him? Charles Palmer."

"No, but Abbott talked to someone named Chuck on the phone. You think it's the same guy?"

"Absolutely."

She tugged on her hair. "Are you *sure* it's still Saturday? What went on while Abbott had me?"

"Later, Sunshine." He read the freeway sign. "Know anyone in Eugene?"

"No. Until two weeks ago, I'd never been to Oregon."

"Eugene, it is. We can overnight there, then decide where to go next. It's about an hour. You okay?"

"Um, can we make a pit stop first?"

"No problem."

"Fozzie?"

Lord, first her smile, now the way she said his name. He fought the tug in his loins. Post-mission buzz, he told himself. "Yes?"

"That thing you said before. About being joined at the hip. You didn't mean it about bathrooms, did you?"

"Not all the way," he said.

She furrowed her brow. He swung off at the next exit and found an open station. Torie opened her door.

"Hang for a sec," he said.

She glared at him. Tapped her foot.

He cursed the Oregon law about self-service again. Much harder to be inconspicuous if you had to talk to someone to fill up your tank. Keeping his head averted, he said, "Fill it—regular" to the geezer who shuffled over.

While the old man filled the tank, he walked inside the mini-mart, toward the restrooms with Torie.

"You are so *not* coming in," she said. She opened the door labeled Women and peeked inside. "Besides, it's a one-seater. I promise to keep the door locked."

"I'm going to use the gents," he said. "But if you're out first, wait right here." Not that any woman used a restroom faster than a man.

When he finished, the door to the ladies' room was closed. It took some effort, but he didn't pound on it to make sure she was still in there. The mini-mart was empty except for the woman behind the counter, who seemed engrossed in a magazine. He eyed the coffee machine at the other side of the store, but parked himself right outside the restroom doors until Torie emerged. The only way anyone would get her would be if they beamed her into space. And even then, he'd grab her before she dissolved, and stick with her all the way to wherever.

She smiled when she saw him. He almost forgot about wanting coffee. She'd washed her face and smelled like institutional soap. Damp tendrils of hair curled around her forehead. He stepped closer, took her hand. Despite the smile, the strain hadn't left her eyes. He brushed a stray lock of hair away from her face.

"Can I buy a toothbrush? Please?" she said. "My mouth is disgusting. Or mouthwash? Gum?"

He thought about stocking up on some basic essentials, but decided against it. They were still too close to Oakdale. Better to be unmemorable, not a couple doing their weekly shopping at a small-town petrol station mini-mart at eleven at night. "No problem."

· He walked with her while she picked out a travel toothbrush and mini tube of toothpaste. "Don't suppose you want to share?" he asked.

She lifted her eyebrows. He grinned. She blushed. He plucked a second toothbrush off the rack. "No worries." God, she was cute when she got flustered.

Chill, idiot. On task.

"Coffee?" he asked, already guiding her to the counter. He filled a cup for himself.

"No, thanks."

He added a pine-tree-shaped air freshener to their purchases. He didn't mind the smell of sweat. He was used to it, but he'd seen Torie wrinkle her nose and crack her window. He settled the bill and stuffed the bag with the toothbrushes into a pocket of his pants. When they were back in the car, he hung the freshener and checked the GPS to see if there were lodgings listed. Seemed to be plenty. He'd pick one later. For a moment he considered pushing on. Maybe to Portland. Bigger city, easier to disappear.

No, he was beat. Eugene would do. Another hour was enough driving, and tomorrow they'd have time to develop a plan. Torie had a laptop. With Internet access, he could do some digging. Not as deep as Jinx of course, but until things quieted down at Blackthorne, he'd have to do what he could on his own. Again.

"Let's do it," he said. They left the gas station and got back on the highway.

"Was it smart to use your credit card?" Torie asked. "Won't they be able to trace you?"

"It's not as easy as it looks on television. Credit-card companies don't give that information out without a warrant.

No way these guys are cops."

"What about hacking in?"

He shook his head. "Damn tough systems. I wouldn't worry about it. All that business about finding you from your cell phone, or using your ATM card? Plays well on TV, but your average Joe can't get into those records." He didn't think it was necessary to mention how Blackthorne, Inc. wasn't your average Joe. Not that Jinx or anyone else truly hacked. They had legal access to databases off-limits to civilians. With maybe a touch of creativity and some well-cultivated inside contacts. "And from what I've seen, our guys are a few rungs below average."

"You're not saying that to appease me, are you? So I won't worry about people tracking us?"

"Sunshine, if I thought there was any way on this earth those goons could find us because I stopped for gas, I'd never have used my card. And my card has extra protection. Anyone wants to trace a charge, I'll get notified. So will my boss."

She cocked her head, gave him a skeptical look. "Really? They do that?"

"Comes with my job."

"You know, you never told me what you do."

What he did. He lied about what he did, that's what he did. He adjusted the rearview mirror. "I work for Blackthorne, Inc. I told you that."

"Not really. All you said was my father hired your company to find me. So, is that what you do for Blackthorne? Find people?"

He didn't meet her eyes. "That's about it." He wasn't really lying, but he didn't think she needed to know what finding people normally entailed.

She was quiet for a moment. When she spoke, her voice was hesitant. "But you already found me. Why are you still here?

You said you weren't going to bring me back. Are you still on the job?"

"More or less."

"What's that supposed to mean?"

"Look, we've both had a rough couple of days. Let's discuss this later, all right?"

"But—"

"Torie, I'm tired. You're tired. We can talk tomorrow."

To his surprise, she didn't argue. "All right." She wrapped her arms around herself and looked away. "Sorry."

Shit. "Sunshine. Don't apologize. You didn't do anything wrong. It's just—complicated, okay?"

Double shit. Just tell her. You care.

Damnation, he *did* care, and telling himself that he cared about everyone he rescued wasn't cutting it. The realization scared him more than he was willing to admit. He was tired. She'd been in trouble. He'd found her. Rescued her. And he was stuck in post-mission chaos, when the adrenaline left, and body and mind needed time to catch up. He'd be fine tomorrow. Except he'd be in a hotel room with Torie. He wasn't ready to deal with it, and he'd bet Torie wasn't either.

"Is my father paying you?" she asked. "Under the table, if you're not working directly for Blackthorne now?"

"No. Definitely not."

"Then who is? I think I have a right to know. I mean, if someone's paying to find me, or kidnap me, or watch me, or whatever, I should know who."

"Look, not now, okay? I said it was complicated." Women. They always wanted to talk about stuff.

Christ, he'd practically snapped her head off. He didn't need to look at her. He could feel her cowering like a kicked puppy. They rode the next forty-five minutes in a cold, thick silence.

Once they hit the city limits, he queried the GPS for nearby

177

hotels. He glanced at Torie. Her eyes were closed, but her stiff posture said she wasn't asleep. The two of them looked like they'd been rode hard and put up wet. Smelled that way, too. But what he needed was the last place someone would look. Palmer and Abbott struck him as the low-budget type. He'd put money on them thinking he'd do exactly what they would.

He aimed the car toward the Plaza. Pulled up to the portico, and a bellman rushed to open Torie's door, then his. She got out of the car and gave him a puzzled look. He shook his head, hoping she'd take his cue and not speak.

"Checking in, sir?" the bellman said.

Fozzie pasted an apologetic expression on his face and an American accent into his voice. "I hope so." He dragged his fingers through his hair. "Damn airlines. Late flights, missed connections, and God only knows where our luggage is. I hope there's a room here. If not"—he tilted his head in Torie's direction—"she's going to come apart." He lowered his voice. "And it won't be pretty."

He tossed the man the keys and took the claim check. He went to the trunk and pulled out Torie's box, slipping the two weapons inside. Walking into the hotel with two pistols in his pants wasn't going to cut it. "This is all that made it. Damn airlines," he muttered, hefting the box and stalking toward the lobby.

Torie trotted alongside. "What?"

"Shh. Let me give this a go. If it doesn't work, how are you at meltdowns?"

Her eyes widened. "Like a public hissy fit? Me?" She shook her head. "I don't think so."

"Well, let's hope it doesn't come to that. Meanwhile, look disgusted with me." He didn't think it would be a stretch.

He approached the registration counter where a middle-aged woman looked up from her computer. He stayed half a pace away. No need for her to get a whiff of him.

"May I help you, sir?"

"I hope so. To make a long story short, this was supposed to be a special getaway. But so far, it's special in all the wrong ways. No luggage, no dinner, no sleep. Can we get a room? Not sure how many nights. Can we reserve for three?"

She tapped some keys. "Yes, sir. We'll need twenty-four hours notice if you're going to leave prior to that date."

"Not a problem," Fozzie said. "And we'd like a suite, if you've got one." Beside him, Torie inhaled a quick, audible breath. He turned to her. "Don't worry about it, dear. This is our time. Cost is no object."

The clerk gave him a polite smile. And Torie a knowing look. "Yes, I have a suite open. One or two bedrooms?"

"Two," Torie blurted.

"One," Fozzie said, staring at Torie, trying not to wither under her glare. "We can't very well work things out in separate rooms, you know. We did agree to give this a try."

"I can give you a one-bedroom, but with two queens," the clerk said. "And a pull-out couch in the living room."

Wasn't that how he'd spent last night? Seemed like a week ago. "That'll be fine," he said. He handed over his credit card, and the clerk busied herself at her computer. When she finished, she looked up.

She seemed to scrutinize both of them, but her gaze lingered on Torie. "We have a special getaway package. Champagne, breakfast in bed, two-for-one dinner in our rooftop restaurant. I can set it up for tomorrow if you'd like."

"Sounds like a good idea," he said.

"Here you go. I need you to sign here, and initial here, to confirm the room rate and the getaway package. Plus your car information here." She tapped each place on the form with her pen. Once he'd signed, she laid a folder with two key cards on the counter, pointed to the room number, then added a brochure. "Details are in there," she said. "The elevators are to your left. Is there anything else you'll need?"

Torie spoke up. "We don't have our luggage. Do you have toiletries? And maybe a gift shop where we can get some emergency clothes?"

"I'll get you each a complimentary amenity package," the clerk said. She stepped to a long console behind her, opened a drawer and returned with two small plastic bags. "His and hers. I'm afraid our gift shop is closed for the night, but there are robes in the room. And we can arrange to have your clothes laundered overnight. Call the bell desk when you're ready. There's a laundry bag in the room."

"Thank you *so* much," Torie said, accepting the bags.

"One other favor," Fozzie interjected. "We'd appreciate it if you'd put a do-not-disturb flag on the phone. We'd rather nobody knows we're here."

The clerk's eyebrows lifted.

"My parents," Torie said. "They're not too happy about the way things are between us." She looked at Fozzie and smiled— almost sincerely. "You were right. We should try to work things out."

"I'll note it on your registration. You'll have a full privacy block."

"I thank you very kindly, ma'am." Fozzie said.

He took the keys in one hand, balanced the carton on his hip with the other, and strolled toward the elevator. He looked at the envelope with the room number. Fourteen forty-two.

"We've been cooped up in the car a lot lately. And this elevator seems to be taking its sweet time. How about walking up?"

She looked at him in disbelief. "The stairs? It's *fourteen* flights. I don't think so."

The elevator dinged. The doors opened. Torie stepped in. He

took a step to follow. It was as if a force field hung across the entrance to the car. He swallowed.

It's an elevator. You ride in elevators. Fourteen floors. A minute, minute and a half, tops.

His feet didn't move. He made a show of adjusting the book box.

"Well? You coming?" she asked over her shoulder.

CHAPTER EIGHTEEN

Torie turned. Fozzie stood outside the elevator. "Well?" He couldn't be serious about climbing fourteen flights of stairs. The doors began to close. She slammed her hand against the rubber edge of the panel to keep them open. "What's the matter?"

His lips flattened. His chest rose on an inhale. He stomped into the car, clutching the box in front of him. When he didn't move, she punched the button for fourteen and leaned against the back rail. While Fozzie seemed intent on watching the floor numbers change, she read the hotel information posted in the car. "There's a gym on the third floor if you really want some exercise," she said. He didn't respond. She looked at him more closely. Sweat beaded his upper lip. His breathing was rapid and shallow.

"Hey, are you all right? You're not going to get sick in here, are you?" Not on her books.

He gave his head a quick shake.

"Fozzie? Did something happen to you with that firebug guy? Are you hurt?" He'd gone to some lengths to rescue her. She'd been so caught up in her own ordeal she hadn't considered he might have been in danger as well. No matter how aggravating he was when he refused to tell her anything, she shouldn't have assumed nothing had happened to him. She stepped forward, put her hand on his shoulder. It tensed beneath her touch.

The elevator chimed and Fozzie stepped out before the doors had finished opening. He grabbed her by the arm and charged down the hall.

Lord, maybe he *was* going to be sick. She trotted to keep up.

At their door, she took the envelope from him and removed a key card. Sliding it into the lock, she waited the interminable second for the light to turn green, then shoved on the latch. She stepped aside. "You first."

He strode into the room, laying the carton on the floor beside a small table in the entry. Instead of heading for the bathroom, he crossed the spacious living room and opened the sliders. He stepped out onto the balcony and leaned over the rail, head bowed. He wasn't throwing up over the balcony, was he? No, she heard him gasping long, deep breaths.

"Are you all right?" she asked again. Why she bothered was beyond her. The man wasn't going to say anything, or if he did, it would be to tell her he was fine. As if.

"I'm going to shower," she said. Or bathe, or both. She couldn't wait to scrub away the memories of her day. When he didn't respond, she left him to deal with whatever his problem was.

Men. They'd never talk to you.

Hotel toiletries in hand, she wandered past the kitchen, through the dining area, and into the bedroom. Two queen beds, as promised. A sitting area with two easy chairs. She glanced at the mirrored closet doors. God, she was a mess. Opening the door to avoid her reflection, she found four robes. Two terrycloth, two silk.

How much was this room costing? Who was paying? Fozzie had handed his credit card to the desk clerk without batting an eye. Never even asked the rate. And it had to be a small fortune. The suite was bigger than the entire cottage at Aspen Corners.

It was after midnight. Exhaustion washed over her. She took the women's toiletries and left the guy packet on one of the beds. Grabbing a terrycloth robe, she went into the bathroom.

Wow. Jacuzzi. Glass-enclosed shower. Marble counter. Brass fixtures. Separate enclosure for the toilet. High end shampoo, conditioner, bath crystals. She had a fleeting thought of the two of them in the Jacuzzi, jets on full. Sheesh. She must really be tired. A few minutes ago, she was cursing the fact that he was acting like a typical male. Now she was fantasizing about some of the other male traits.

She turned on the shower and stripped out of her clothes. If she had anything else to wear at all, she'd have trashed them. She adjusted the water as hot as she could stand it and stepped inside the spacious tile enclosure. She lathered and rinsed her hair twice with the fragrant herbal shampoo. Scrubbed her body with soap *and* the shower gel provided. Shaved. She watched the suds swirl down the drain, wishing they would take the memories with them.

There was a gentle tap on the door. She started. "Yes?"

"You okay in there?" Fozzie asked.

"Fine," she called. "I'll be out in a minute."

"No worries. Take your time."

She did one last rinse, letting the water sluice over her. She dried herself with an oversized plush bath towel, wrapped a smaller one around her head, and slipped into the robe. Belting it, she opened the door and peered into the bedroom. Fozzie wasn't there. Neither was the second pouch of toiletries.

She ducked back into the bathroom. Dried her hair. Used the hotel deodorant. Brushed her teeth. Used the mouthwash. Finally, she felt as though she'd rid herself of Alfred B. Abbott. She examined her cheek, where he had slapped her. No discernible mark, although her jaw was tender when she pressed it.

She padded into the living room and found Fozzie on the couch, a crystal glass of what she assumed was whiskey in his hand. Barefoot. Wearing a silk robe. She came to a dead halt.

His eyes moved up and down her body. Despite the long,

thick robe she wore, she felt suddenly naked. When his lips curved up into his lazy grin, heat spread through her. Apparently, he'd recovered from whatever had bothered him.

"Um . . . shower's free," she said.

"Thanks, but I used the other one."

She followed his gaze to where steam wafted from a door between the kitchen and living room. Two bathrooms. "Cool."

"Posh digs," He gestured to a white plastic bag sitting on top of her book box. "I called for someone to fetch our dirty duds."

There was a knock at the door. "That was quick," Fozzie said. "If you want your stuff washed, better get a wriggle on."

She hurried to the bathroom and scooped her clothes off the floor, carried them to the living room and stuffed them on top of Fozzie's. She ducked out of sight of the door while Fozzie answered.

"That'll be fine. Thank you kindly," Fozzie said. The door clicked shut. She heard him throw the latch.

"All taken care of." He gave her an apologetic smile. Or was it? There was a hint of mischief in his eyes. "They said they'd rush, but noon was probably the best they could do because it's so late."

It dawned on her that she'd put everything into the bag. Including her underwear. Which meant she'd have robes, period, to wear until their clothes were delivered.

No wonder his eyes had twinkled.

"Would you like a nightcap?" he asked. "Help you unwind." He headed toward the wet bar, his robe open at the top, revealing a fine mat of light-brown hair that formed a darker line down the center of his chest. Pointing downward.

"Um, I think maybe I'll go to bed."

"Suit yourself. I'll bunk out here." He faced her, the teasing twinkle gone. In its place was a softer look. "If you need anything—to talk, whatever—I'm here."

"I'm tired. I'll be fine."

"Sleep well." His voice sent another ripple of heat through her.

She went to the bedroom and pulled back the covers on the bed near the window. Talk? Since when did he want to *talk?* He undoubtedly meant if she talked, he'd *listen.* Well, what she wanted was answers, which meant he had to do the talking. And it was definitely too late to get into that now. With luck, she'd sleep until noon and her clothes would be back. She'd get dressed, go shopping, and then trash them.

She fluffed up the pillows, shrugged off the robe, and sank into the mattress, surrounded by the clean, fresh smell of freshly laundered sheets. Mega-thread-count sheets. Not filthy ticking. She lay back and waited for sleep.

But when she closed her eyes, she was back in that cell of a room. Instead of clean sheets, she smelled the beer on his breath. Felt the sting of his slap. Why? She'd been his captive, but not nearly as long as she'd thought. Hours, not days. She should be able to shake the aftereffects. Why should there even *be* any aftereffects? She'd been virtually on her own since she was thirteen.

She tiptoed to the door. Opened it. Crawled back into bed. Hugged a pillow to her chest. Threw it on the floor. Tossed. Turned. Tossed some more.

Maybe she should have had that nightcap. Calm her nerves. Better yet, she should have brought one of her books with her.

That would do it. She put the robe on and pulled the door open a crack. A golden glow gave her enough light to see. She crept through the suite. Fozzie lay on his back on the couch. His empty glass lay on the coffee table, the end table lamp still on. He, apparently, could fall asleep no matter what. He hadn't even bothered to open the bed. Or get blankets. Thank goodness he'd left his robe on.

She knelt beside the box and tugged on the flaps, which Fozzie had interlocked. The sound of cardboard on cardboard blasted through the silence. The flaps finally parted and she reached inside. Instead of the comfort of a well-worn book cover, she felt cold, hard metal. She gasped.

Fozzie jerked awake, heart pounding. Torie crouched near the door. He raced to her side, put a hand on her trembling shoulder. "What's wrong?"

"Sorry," she said. "I didn't mean to wake you. I tried to be quiet, but I wanted something to read, and—" She hiccupped, sniffed. Her entire body shook.

"Aw, Torie. Sunshine. Please don't cry. It's all right. It's normal." He grasped her shoulders and turned her to face him.

Her fingers explored her cheeks. Her eyes widened, as if she was surprised to find them wet. "Sorry," she whispered.

He pulled her close. She smelled like a garden. He buried his face in her hair and inhaled her scent. Caressed her back. Absorbed her warmth.

"First, quit apologizing. If anyone apologizes, it should be me. I should have taken the guns out of the box and locked them up as soon as we got in."

She exhaled a shaky breath and spoke into his chest. The vibrations quivered his insides like a plucked guitar string. "It's okay. I know you took them from those creeps. I wasn't expecting them, and I'd been thinking about . . . you know . . . people trying to kill me." Her head tilted back, her palms splayed on his chest. "It's not like you walk around with a gun."

True enough. He only carried on ops.

She nudged against him. Smiled. "Or do you?"

He backed off. Damn, he should have worn the terrycloth robe.

"Don't go." She threaded her fingers into his hair and pulled him into a kiss. Nothing tentative about it. No hesitation. Just pried his lips open with her tongue and went straight for the tonsils. His mind screamed for him to break the kiss. To send her back to bed. To explain what she was feeling wasn't real— not in a personal sense. That it was all triggered by what she'd gone through. But his lips weren't listening. The rest of him was having a damn hard time ignoring her, too. One short kiss. That's all. He didn't want to hurt her feelings, did he?

His tongue found hers. He explored the warm depths of her mouth. Returned the kiss. Savored the taste of her. The smell of her. One more minute. Then he'd stop.

Her kiss grew more frantic, desperate, demanding. "I want you," she said, barely moving her mouth from his. "Make everything go away. Make me forget."

Crap. Gasping, he cradled her head in his hands. Forced himself to step back. "Torie, you don't really want this. Not the way you think you do."

She pulled his hands away, confusion and hurt telegraphed in her face. "But—?"

"You've had some very scary times. It's normal to get . . . aroused . . . when you know you're safe."

She lifted her chin. "So, what's wrong with doing this if it's normal? Being normal feels pretty good right now."

He tried to smile. "I don't want you to want me only for my body."

"Will you be honest with me if I ask you a question?"

Was she going to demand to know who he was working for? Would he admit the truth if she asked? "I'll try."

"Remember when we were in the car, on the side road? And the man from the pickup came over and you pretended we were making love?"

How could he forget? How soft she was, how well she played the game. "I remember."

"Can you look me in the eye right now and tell me you were really acting?"

He kept his gaze locked with hers. "I wasn't acting."

"Neither was I. And I don't care about tomorrow, or the next day, or next week. I don't care if it's nothing but a physical release. I want it. I need it. I want to feel *now*. I want you to hold me. I want to be in your arms. I want to feel your strength. I want to forget that horrible basement and the mind games." She unbelted her robe. "I want you to take me into the bedroom and make love until the world goes away."

"Torie, I—" Sweet Lord, she stood there, bathed in soft lamplight, her breasts round and firm, her nipples puckered into tight peaks. "I'm a man. Are you sure this is really what you want? Because in about thirty seconds, I'm not going to be able to say no."

"Say yes." She let the robe fall from her shoulders. With her soft curves, her lush figure, she looked like the goddess standing on the seashell. Whatever her name was. Right now, he was hard-pressed to remember his own.

"Yes." It was more of a croak than a word. "Give me five secs." He dashed for the bathroom, thanking the gods that he'd emptied his pockets before tossing his clothes into that laundry bag. He yanked open the drawer and snatched the condoms he'd taken from Palmer's truck, hoping the guy had an active enough sex life so he replaced them regularly.

Torie was strolling to the bedroom. He watched her walk, her hips swaying with each leisurely step. Thoughts of being inside her, feeling her squeezed tight around him, kept his blood cascading south.

Sweet Lord, he'd had post-mission sex before. He knew what it meant to have nothing more than release as your goal. But no matter what Torie said she wanted, she deserved more. Because no matter what, tomorrow always rolled around, and they would both have to face the awkwardness that came with it.

Damn, he should let her go. She'd be upset for a while. But in the long run, she'd be better off without the regrets.

She gazed over her shoulder, beckoning with her eyes. Needy eyes. She crooked her finger. She might as well have grabbed him by the cock. "Coming?"

Not too soon, he hoped. He dropped his robe and followed.

He caught up at the doorway. She stopped, gazed at him with eyes that sucked him in. Trapped him, the way he'd been caught in the rock slide when he was eight. He couldn't escape then, he didn't want to escape now. "You're sure about this? Because once I go through the doorway, I don't think I'll be able to leave."

In response, she tugged him down for another kiss. There were no barriers between her warm, soft skin and his body. His chest ached. His cock throbbed. Without breaking the kiss, he backed her into the room, aware only that there was a bed in here somewhere. Two of them, actually. They shouldn't be that hard to find.

Did he even want to? He could kiss her forever. Her body against his. Every point of contact a mixture of torment and delight. He felt the wetness where his cock rubbed against her. Her hands moved to his chest, rubbing circles over his pecs. Kneading. One hand toyed with a nipple. The other, fingers dancing, moved lower.

He grasped her wrist with his free hand. Staggered the last few feet to the bedside. Tossed the condoms onto the night-stand. Practically threw her against the bed. She half-stumbled, and he wrapped an arm around her to steady her. He gasped for breath. "God, Torie."

She clung to him. "Don't let go."

As if he could. She lay back, pulling him with her. She wrapped her arms around his back. Pulled tighter. Skin to skin, they lay there, still kissing, barely breathing. Her body shifted under his. She squirmed against his cock. Her breasts were soft pillows under his chest. Too good. Much too good. Control slid away.

He got on his knees, caging her body with his. She whimpered, reaching for him. "Don't stop touching me."

"I'm right here." God, could he get any harder? She wrapped her fingers in his hair, pulled him tighter against her. Arched her back, bringing her breasts closer to his mouth. He swirled his tongue around her nipple. Tugged it with his lips. Scraped it with his teeth. She reached for him again. Her fingers cupped his balls. Fondled him.

So good. Such exquisite pleasure. There was nothing but her touch. Pressure built. He fought to tamp it back.

"Slow down," he moaned, stilling her hand. Lord, he'd lasted longer when he was seventeen. And they were barely into foreplay. He found some hidden reserve of control and rolled onto his side next to her.

"No," she cried.

CHAPTER NINETEEN

Torie grabbed for Fozzie, desperate to regain contact. Why had he moved away? She flung her leg over him, pressed herself against him. There was no mistaking his desire. A crazed hunger filled her. She flipped him onto his back, straddled him. Parting her legs, she slid along his hot, slick length. She was wet. So was he. She grabbed his hands, placed them on her breasts. Pressed them tight against her. Pleasure shot to her groin. She rubbed against him, driving herself higher and higher, closer and closer to that pinnacle she craved.

Somewhere, deep inside her head, a tiny voice of reason asked if she knew what she was doing. Darn right she did. She was doing what *she* wanted, what made *her* feel good. She told the little voice to get the heck out of her head.

She concentrated on her pleasure. "Touch me. Don't stop touching me," she demanded.

Fozzie's lips were parted, eyes squinted shut. "Condom," he said.

"Don't talk. Touch."

"Condom," he said, louder.

The word finally registered. She almost dismissed it. Almost. But she leaned over as far as she could, groping for one of the packets on the nightstand with one hand, keeping his hand on her breast with the other.

Her fingers found the foil square.

"You're going to have to stop while I put it on," he said.

She tore the packet open, plucked out the contents and flung the wrapper aside. Her hands shook. "Do it." She handed him the condom, sliding along his thick length one more time. She perched on his thighs, pressing against them, not wanting to lose the connection as she waited impatiently for him to sheath himself.

"Don't you think you're taking this a tad fast?" Fozzie asked.

"Not fast enough. I want you. Inside. Now." She took his penis in her hands and lifted her hips, positioning herself above him. She lowered herself slowly, letting the pleasure build again, then took him to the hilt. He gasped.

She rocked against him, needed his touch. Needed to touch him. She spread her fingers over his chest. Stroked. Pressed. Kneaded. She leaned forward, nibbling at the tight nubs of his nipples. She tightened her muscles around his length, squeezing him inside her.

"Torie," he gasped. "God." His hips bucked. She reached behind her, fondled his tight balls. "I can't . . . You're making me . . . I'm going to . . ." His hips pistoned faster. His breath came in short, explosive gasps. His eyes closed. His grip tightened. He grabbed her waist. She matched his pace, her own release shattering through her. She collapsed onto his chest.

Her head rose with each breath Fozzie took. His heart galloped beneath her ear. She lay there as the universe reformed around them.

"I feel so used," he said. He caressed her sweat-filmed back. "So cheap. How will you ever respect me in the morning?"

"I'm sorry. I don't know what came over me."

"Sunshine, didn't I tell you to stop apologizing? You've got nothing to be sorry for."

"I don't usually do stuff like that." She buried her face in his chest. His hair tickled her nose. "I never do stuff like that," she whispered.

"Like what? Enjoy yourself?" He ruffled her hair. "If you don't, you should."

"You didn't mind? I was kind of . . . I sort of . . . took over." She turned her head, resting her cheek on his torso.

"Mind?" He laughed, the sound rumbling up from his chest. "You can take over any time you want."

"I thought guys always wanted to be in charge." The guys she'd known that way certainly had.

He ran his finger along her jaw. "Tell me. Did you enjoy yourself?"

Heat rose to her face. Would he think she was brazen? A slut? "Yes," she admitted softly.

"Well, so did I. I hereby give you permission to have your way with me any time the fancy strikes." He tapped her on the nose. "I'll be right back."

He'd softened inside her. She rolled off and curled up while he went into the bathroom. Water ran, the toilet flushed. He came back a moment later and crawled in beside her. "It's two in the mornin'. Sleep, Sunshine."

"Hold me?" she whispered.

He turned onto his side and pulled her against him, draping one arm over her waist. She took his hand and nestled it onto her chest. His warm breath fanned her back. Her breathing slowed to match his, and the world disappeared.

Torie drifted awake, slowly aware she wasn't alone in bed. She shifted. Fozzie's arm tightened around her waist. She blinked the bedside clock into focus. Seven-thirty. He'd held her all night. She grasped his hand and worked her way out from under, trying not to disturb him. She crept into the bathroom and attended to her immediate needs. The Jacuzzi seemed like a perfect way to start the day. She was about to turn on the taps when she heard him call.

"Torie?"

Was there a hint of panic in his voice? She poked her head around the doorway. "Yes?"

"Mornin'," he mumbled. "Timezit?"

She smiled. "Seven-thirty. You can sleep a little longer. I'm going to clean up."

He leaned up on an elbow. "You okay?"

How should she know? A few weeks ago, okay meant following a comfortable, somewhat boring, routine. Now she was in the middle of some . . . what? Some strange mystery that required her absence until next Monday? Monday. She'd totally forgotten.

"I'm fine. But do you know of anything happening next Monday?"

"Monday?" He sat up, scratching his head, the rumpled sheet not disguising a significant hard-on. "What about Monday?"

She glanced at the unused condoms. Monday was a good week away. She was enjoying the liberated Torie. "Never mind. It can wait. I just remembered something else I wanted to try last night." She pounced onto the bed and whisked the sheet away. "You did mean what you said, didn't you?"

"About?"

She hovered her mouth over his erection, teasing. "About having my way with you any time I wanted?"

He folded his hands behind his head. "I'm a man of my word."

Was she really doing this? Shouldn't she think things through? One thought flashed through her mind. Condoms were for more than preventing pregnancy. She trusted he'd have stopped her, but asking was more responsible. "Can I do this without a condom? You're . . . safe?"

He smiled. "No worries."

She took a breath. Kissed him there. Smooth. Warm.

Tentatively, she flicked her tongue. He tasted salty. Musky. His penis twitched.

She looked up at him, trying to read his expression. Was he bored? Did he think she was being silly? Was he trying not to laugh? "Is it okay? I've . . . I've never done this before."

He cupped her face in his hands. "Sunshine, I'm honored. But if you're not sure, we can wait."

"No. If I learned anything in that basement, it was that waiting for the right moment might mean you never get to do things you've always wanted to do."

"And you've always wanted to do this?"

She felt herself blushing. "Well, not always. But I've been curious."

He chuckled. "Then satisfy your curiosity."

"You'll tell me if I'm hurting you? Or doing it wrong?"

"Mind the teeth." He lay back, eyes closed.

Fozzie sat in the leather easy chair, his feet on the padded ottoman. He checked their decimated breakfast tray. "The last strawberry." He dangled it just beyond her grasp.

When she reached for it, her robe opened, revealing the curve of her luscious breasts. He couldn't resist brushing his toes against the silk.

"Stop that." She gave him a playful slap. "Haven't you had enough?"

"Never. And we've still got a couple of condoms left," he said. "You sure there's nothing else you want to try?" She'd proved to be a very quick study. And after an interlude in the Jacuzzi followed by an invigorating room service breakfast, he was recharging. Surprisingly fast. For a moment, he wondered if he was dreaming. If he was still back in Palmer's truck, fantasizing to keep his sanity. Or would he be insane if he believed his fantasies? This Torie was miles away from the Torie he'd met a few days ago.

"You're terrible." She giggled. And blushed.

Miles? No, light years away. His chest bonged. "Is that a no?" He smiled. "There are things I'd like to try, you know."

"For now, yes, it's a no."

"Then I guess it's a matter of finding one of your girly American football games on the telly. Isn't that what guys here do on Sundays?"

"Suit yourself. But there are two televisions in the suite, so if you think you're going to force me to sit and watch football with you, forget it. I'll work on our shopping list."

"List? You're making a list?"

"Don't you think that's a good idea? We've got almost nothing."

"I figured we'd go to some mega-store and browse the aisles. Pick up what looks good. Tomorrow. Or the next day. I'm happy enough to sit around in these posh robes and order room service."

"Men." She stood, adjusted her robe, and seemed to float to her box of books. Who needed television? He could watch her all day. She removed two or three, running her hands along the covers before setting them onto the table. Once she seemed satisfied with her selection, she brought it over to the couch and curled up in the corner, tucking her legs under her. This time it was the lower half of her robe that gaped. Lord, he was ready to pay her back for what she'd done to him this morning. She'd smell like the bath salts, like the perfumed soap. Taste like Torie. He'd drive her to the brink, the way she'd taken him to the edge, then he'd back off until she begged. The way he had.

His fingers went to the pocket of his robe and found the condoms he'd put there. Spontaneity was good. Being prepared was better.

When he looked at her and grinned, she rolled her eyes. But she put the book aside.

Later, they ended up in bed. She was curled on her side, her head tucked into the hollow of his shoulder. Her fingers toyed with his chest hair. She was warm against him. He ran his finger along her curves, letting them come to rest on her round arse. Such smooth skin.

"Why Fozzie?" she said.

"Hmm? Why what?"

"Why do they call you that? After the Muppets?"

He shook his head. "Nope. Me little sister Meg. She couldn't say Foster. It came out Fozzie, and it stuck. She'd never seen the Muppets."

"The first time I saw you, I thought you looked like a teddy bear. So the name made sense."

"Teddy bear?"

"I had a teddy bear once. Until I was three. I used to sleep with it until my father said only babies slept with teddy bears." Her voice trembled. "He threw it away."

"Aw, Sunshine. That was cruel. I had a stuffed koala. I think it's still back home. Not much fur left. I slept with it until I was . . . well, a lot older than three."

"Really?"

"God's honest truth. I promise, I won't lie to you."

"So if I ask you something personal, you'll give me an honest answer?"

"Go for it."

"What happened in the elevator last night?"

He hesitated. She waited. And he knew, with Torie, he couldn't brush it off. She'd worked her way inside him. Deep. Too deep to dismiss with a flip reply. And with her snuggled beside him, sated with lovemaking, he found that the words came. Words he'd never told any of his teammates, and they put their lives on the line for each other.

"When I was eight," he began. Took a shaky breath. "Me mum and dad took Tony and Meg—Abby wasn't born yet—to town. I'd begged off. My aunt and uncle were about, they'd tend to me. But they thought I was in town with Mum and Dad, and they left on their own errands. I didn't mind. Kind of enjoyed being alone for a change, and it made me feel important. I was feeding the poddy lambs—"

"The what?"

"Orphans. Anyway, one's missing. You know, sheep are the dumbest creatures on God's green earth. They can't survive on their own. So I have to find it. I saddle up and ride out. I hear bleating, so I'm going to be the hero, save the baby lamb. Only General—the horse—spooks, and I go flying."

"Were you hurt bad?"

"Nah, but General hightailed it elsewhere. I found the poddy, stuck in the bottom of a dry creek bed. Dumb critter had backed into an outcropping of rocks and boulders. Got its foot stuck. I tried to pull it loose, and half the creek bed slid down on top of us."

"Oh, my God. How did you get out?"

He'd always tried to keep the memories in their own special compartment in his brain. But he'd promised Torie the truth. Even if he had to open the box. His heart rate kicked up. A ribbon of sweat trickled down his neck. "My folks finally found me. I had a busted arm. When you can't move for two days—"

"Two *days?*"

He shrugged. "Nobody realized I was missing until the next morning. One of the station hands found General and wondered why he was outside with all his tack on. Took 'em a while to find me."

"You must have been terrified." She snuggled closer. "I can

see why you might be claustrophobic."

"It's not usually quite so bad, but after Palmer—well, it brought things to the surface."

"After Palmer what?"

He tried to keep his tone nonchalant. Not to think about being trapped. "He grabbed me after Abbott snatched you. Tied me up, tossed me in the bed of his truck, and closed the lid."

She sat up. "Why didn't you tell me? I feel like an idiot, thinking I was the only victim of those two jerks. Most of the time, Abbott left me alone. You were in worse shape."

"Hey, I got away, and I found you. It's over and done. And we're here now, safe, so let's forget about it." He pulled her against him. Having her close sent the memories back where they belonged.

Was this what it would be like to have someone you loved waiting when you finished an op? Someone to take away the post-mission heebie-jeebies?

Loved? What was he thinking? No way. He couldn't love Torie. Not after a few days. It was all a side effect of what they'd been through. Maybe someday, years from now, he'd quit the ops work. Then he could think about falling in love.

So why did he feel like he'd jumped off the edge of a cliff and found out he could fly?

CHAPTER TWENTY

Torie readjusted the shopping bags in her arms and slipped the key into the hotel room lock. Fozzie had begun to fade somewhere around hour two, but had reluctantly agreed it was better to get as much as they could in one trip. Not to mention he still took that "joined at the hip" thing seriously, hovering outside dressing rooms, fidgeting at the makeup counter. He'd even demanded they use the family restrooms. So much for her suggestion that he go to the movies while she shopped. And she *shopped.* Unlike Fozzie, who had marched into the men's department at JCPenney and spent all of fifteen minutes grabbing an assortment of jeans, T-shirts, and other nondescript ultracasual guy-wear. One three-pack of cotton briefs. And, after she'd pushed, one dress shirt and a nice pullover.

He rolled their new luggage set behind him as he followed her into the room. She dropped her packages on the aircraft-carrier-sized dining table. Fozzie added his armload of bags to the pile. He dangled a pink-and-white-striped bag from his finger. "Some haul."

She snatched the bag. A warm flush coursed through her as she thought about what he'd added to her more sensible purchases. He'd had way too much fun helping her shop for lingerie. Well, she didn't think he'd noticed the silk boxers she'd added. He'd had his back to the counter until everything was rung up and bagged. He obviously wasn't embarrassed, not after the way he'd teased and cajoled her about some of the more—risqué?—items.

It hit her then, as she replayed the afternoon. What she'd chalked up to boredom and impatience was anything but. He'd been watching. Everyone. Everywhere. Making sure they weren't being followed. Making sure nobody was going to pop out from behind a display and drag her off. Her mouth went dry.

She opened a bag. "I'll put your rooibos tea in the kitchen."

"It's after five. I'm ready for a real drink," he said. "You want one?"

She kept her voice steady. "Please. A glass of wine sounds nice."

"Here or upstairs? There's a rooftop lounge."

She looked at him. He'd survived the trip down in the elevator and back up, but it had obviously required a concerted effort. On the way down, she'd stood close and held his hand, but they'd met with a packed car on the return trip and couldn't even set their packages down. He'd zoned on the floor numbers through a half dozen stops, and was breathing heavily by the time they got to their floor.

Then again, they were on fourteen and the lounge was on eighteen. "Here is fine," she said. "White wine, please."

Fozzie stood at the wet bar, peering into the minibar's offerings. He wore the same black shirt and cargo pants he'd worn yesterday. Even though her clothes had been laundered, she'd ditched them in a trash receptacle in the food court. She'd never be able to wear them without thinking of what had happened.

Fozzie couldn't seem to understand that although she'd bought new jeans, sneakers and sweats, she needed to wear something at least a *little* different. Nothing fancy, just slacks and a striped turtleneck. She'd restrained herself once she found out he was adamant about putting everything on his card. She shrugged out of her new blazer and draped it over the back of a dining room chair and kicked off her loafers.

She heard a soft *pop* and the gurgle of wine being poured. Fozzie walked over and handed her a chilled drink. In his other hand, he held a beer. He tapped his bottle against her glass. "To fresh beginnings. Wherever they take you."

He hadn't said "us." Did that mean he was getting over this bodyguard stuff? Or had he had his fill of her?

No matter. She'd already gotten what she'd asked for—a night to remember. No strings, no regrets. "Fresh beginnings," she echoed.

"Suppose we should catch the news. Find out what's going on," he said. He strolled over to the coffee table and picked up the remote.

Reality slammed into her like a freight train. She'd tried to bury the memories of what had happened, but there was more going on than the trauma of being grabbed and locked in a room. There'd been a reason for it. Something about Monday.

Forgetting her purchases, she crossed the room and sat next to Fozzie. "Do you know of anything going on next Monday? I started to ask before, but we got . . . distracted."

"I'm sure there's lots going on next Monday. Why do you ask?"

"Because when Abbott had me, he said if I behaved myself, he'd let me go next Monday. So something must be happening, and they think I have information."

He lowered the remote. "Do you?"

"I have no clue. I thought it might be about Epicurean, not that I have any influence one way or another. I couldn't think of anything else. But I wasn't thinking all that clearly," she admitted.

He took a swig of beer, then put the bottle next to the remote and strode to her book box. "Your laptop's in here, right?"

"It was."

He pulled the books out and she stacked them on the table as he handed them to her. Her entire past shrank to a pile of books.

"Here we go." He extracted the laptop along with the power adapter and carried them to the workspace off the dining area.

She left her books to follow him and picked up the tent card on the desk. "Internet access is free in the suites."

"Very noble of them." He plugged the power cord into an outlet on the lamp, the Ethernet cord into the port, turned on the machine, and retrieved his beer while it started. He stood behind the desk chair until the log-in screen popped up. "You want to enter your password?"

"Hit enter. No password."

He frowned and shook his head. "Not smart. If there's something on this machine, and Palmer hadn't been so lazy, they'd have found it in a heartbeat."

"I can't imagine what anyone would want. I hardly use the thing, except for e-mail and surfing. I hit a blog once in a while, check out author sites. I do my banking online." She gave him an "I'm not totally stupid" look. "And you have to have a password for that one. I play Solitaire. That's about it."

He looked at her as if she were crazy. "No chat rooms? No MySpace or Facebook or whatever? Don't tell me you don't spend hours on YouTube."

She shook her head. "I'm not into the Internet. Is that a crime?"

"No, just unusual."

"I'd rather read. You going to tell me you have a MySpace page? A blog? A Web site?"

He laughed. "No, but I do have passwords on my computers." He called up a browser and opened Google. She watched him type "Epicurean Unlimited" into the search window.

"I'll be surprised if you find anything there. My financial

advisor would have let me know if there was something big enough to affect stock prices."

"We've got to start somewhere. I'll poke through the financial pages and see if there are any rumblings. Do some searches. You don't have to hang. It's boring."

She agreed with that. "I could call my advisor."

"It's Sunday."

"Right. Okay. I'll read." She grinned. "If you need me, just whistle. You know how to whistle, don't you?"

"Put my lips together and blow." He gave an exaggerated pucker.

She punched his shoulder, then retreated to the corner of the couch with her wine and Jane Austen. Her glass was almost empty when Fozzie's voice interrupted. She closed the book around her index finger. "What?"

"I said, Epicurean sells products from here to the moon, and it could take weeks to find anything. What about some of the players? Anyone who might be involved in a scandal? Invented a new pot scrubber? Come up with a formula for a calorie-free chocolate cake?"

She noted her page and set the book aside before joining him at the computer. She put her hands on the back of his chair and leaned over to see the screen. His curly hair brushed her chin. "My grandfather's the main player. But I can't see why he'd do anything now. He's said he'll give the company away if I don't come home, but there's eight months left for that. Then there's my father, of course. I suppose if there was some sort of a scandal, the value of the company would drop, but he's likely to be out on his ear anyway. Unless he has some get-rich-quick deal that he thinks he can pull off so he's got a cushion to keep him going."

"Let me try it from the other direction, then." Fozzie carried his empty beer bottle to the kitchen, threw it in the trash and grabbed another from the bar. "More wine?"

She retrieved her glass and joined him. "Okay, but I should eat something." She looked at the assortment of cheeses and crackers. Then she looked at the price list. "Sheesh. This is highway robbery."

"Don't sweat it. If you're hungry, eat. Or call room service."

"I can't let you pay for all this."

He narrowed his eyes. "It's covered. I'll let you know when it's your turn to start paying."

That nagging doubt twirled around in her belly. "Covered by whom?" She'd backed off before, but as long as she was making new rules, she wasn't going to back off now. "You've avoided answering long enough."

He pushed past her, went back to the computer.

"Fozzie, I'm serious. Who's footing the bill for this? Paying you to be joined at the hip?"

He didn't turn around. Mumbled something. Tapped some keys. With vigor. She skirted the package-laden table and went to the desk. "I didn't hear you," she said.

When he didn't respond, she simply slammed the laptop cover onto his fingers, smiled sweetly and repeated her question.

Fozzie yanked his hands free and gave them a shake. "Hey. Easy does it. I think I'm missing some skin."

"So, answer my question."

He stared straight ahead, as if the computer screen was still in front of him.

"Fozzie. I mean it."

"Me," he said on a sigh.

Fozzie forced himself to face Torie. Her mouth hung open. Her eyes held countless questions. He waited. Ten breaths later, she shook her head in puzzlement and grabbed her books, then disappeared into the bedroom. The door closed short of a slam, but he didn't hear the click of the dead bolt. Did that mean she wanted him to follow?

Bloody hell. Women.

Okay, so he should have been honest with her from the get-go. He hadn't actually *lied*. Merely left off some bits and pieces. But, hell, he'd as much as admitted he cared about her. Why had she stormed off? She could have thrown her arms around him and thanked him, right? After all, he *was* using his vacation time to watch her arse. She didn't have to know he was doing it because he cared about more than her curvy arse, nice as it was. He was definitely *not* going into that L-word territory again. What difference should it make? She'd been in trouble, and he wanted to make sure she was all right. That's what he did and not only on the job.

Crap.

He flipped the laptop open and swigged his beer while he waited for the search engine to reappear.

Might as well drain the results of the first bottle. He set the beer down and went to the small bathroom off the kitchen. On his way back, he noticed a scrap of paper on the floor. Must have fallen out of Torie's books. He bent and picked it up. A sealed envelope with Torie's name on it. He looked at the closed door. Maybe he'd give her a little more time to herself. He laid it on the desk and entered Abbott's name into one of the databases Blackthorne subscribed to. And waited. This was what Jinx loved to do. Fozzie wondered if things at Blackthorne had calmed down enough so he could grovel and get Jinx to do some of this research.

No way. The boss would never approve, and getting Jinx in trouble wasn't going to do either of them any good.

The screen flickered, and he turned his attention to his search results. He grabbed the pen from the desk and searched for a notepad. When he couldn't locate one nearby, he jotted notes on the back of the envelope he'd found. Abbott had done time. He'd have to check to see if that connected him to Palmer. He tried to ferret anything out of the man's employment history that was food-related. Although the jerk could be a truck driver who delivered stuff to restaurants anywhere in the country.

This was getting him nowhere, unless down the road to a nagging headache counted. He glanced at the closed bedroom door again. Then at the sleeper sofa. So, he'd have a headache *and* a backache. Unless he apologized. Women expected that. Even when you hadn't done anything you thought was wrong. They'd pick up on something. Hell, Torie apologized for everything. She probably expected it.

He logged out of the search, pushed his chair back and crossed the room. He hesitated at the door. From inside, he thought he heard soft sniffling noises. Bloody hell. He tapped on the door. "Torie? Can I come in?"

She didn't answer. Well, that wasn't a "no," was it? He opened the door and peeked in. Torie sat, cross-legged on the bed, staring at some papers. She looked up, wiping her eyes when he entered.

"What's wrong?" he asked.

She shrugged.

He sat down beside her. "Something in there? Bad news?" He gestured to the pages she held.

"Bad memories," she said. "I'd forgotten all about these. They were Kathy's." She stuffed them into an oversized envelope and tossed them aside. "I keep wondering if she died because of me."

"Why would you say that?" He took her hand in his. Ice cold. He reached for the other one, clasped them both to warm them.

"If I hadn't gotten food poisoning, I'd have been with her. Even if I hadn't kept her from falling, I could have gotten help.

She was there for days. All alone. Maybe she wouldn't have gotten whatever infection killed her, or it wouldn't have been so bad, and the treatment would have worked."

He tensed. "I'm sorry," he said. "It was my fault as much as yours."

She wrested her hands from his grasp. "What do you mean? You didn't even know her."

He hung his head and stared at the stitching on the quilted bed cover. "I'm not a detective, or even an investigator. Not really, although I work for a company that does things like that. Mostly, I do search and rescue."

He waited for her to make the connection. A heartbeat later, her eyes told him she had.

"In Isla Caribe. You . . . you were there because . . . her boss called in a rescue team . . . that was you? You airlifted her out?"

"I'm part of the team—the intel specialist. The one who was responsible for locating her in the jungle. We didn't have a lot to go on, and there were weather delays. It took longer than it should have. We got her out, but like you said, she died. I've been asking myself the same question. If we'd found her a day earlier, would she still be alive?"

"You never said anything."

"When we rescued her, I didn't know who she was. I keep our targets as anonymous as I can. It's the way I deal with the job. And when you started talking about Kathy and Isla Caribe, I realized I knew who you were talking about." The words stuck behind the wedge in his throat. "I saw how much you cared about her. I couldn't bring myself to tell you I played a part in her death."

He barely breathed until she answered.

"If I'd been there, there probably wouldn't have been any reason to call you. So it's not your fault."

"It's not yours, either. You don't know what happened. If you were there, you might have ended up the same way Kathy did. We can't go back and undo what's done. We do our best, and have to move on."

"Can you do that?"

"If you can't, you'll be eaten alive."

"How do you forget?"

"I don't forget." He knew every single target he hadn't saved. Not always by name, not always with a face, but he remembered every detail of every op gone south. More than he remembered the successes.

"That's why I was in Aspen Corners. To make something good come out of Kathy's death. To carry on what she wanted. Even though I'm lousy at that stuff."

"First, I think you can be good at anything you set your mind to. Second, living on in the memory of those you leave behind is the best memorial anyone can ask for. What say we take a moment and celebrate Kathy's life?"

"That would be nice." She leaned into him, and he wrapped his arms around her. They sat in silence for a moment. "Is this what you usually do?" she asked.

He gave a quiet snort. "Don't think a group hug would work with the lads. No, we usually get shit-faced."

"More like a wake than meditation, then?"

"Definitely."

"I don't drink much. Wouldn't take much to get me . . . shit-faced. I've got a better idea. How about if we plant a tree in her memory? Since I couldn't even manage to hang on to Phil."

"Sounds good. Where? What kind?"

"I don't know. Her parents live in Michigan. She's buried there."

"I don't think we can drive to Michigan to plant a tree."

"What about online?" she asked. "I'm sure they have things like that."

"I'll bet they do. Let's take a gander." He helped her off the bed. She snaked her arm around his waist as they strolled to the computer. He gave himself points for his admirable restraint in not suggesting another way to celebrate life.

Torie browsed several sites before choosing one that suited her fancy. "Darn," she said as she entered the data. "I don't know Kathy's parents' address. To send the certificate."

"Have it sent to you," he said. "You can forward it."

She looked at him. "As if I have a home now?" She turned back to the keyboard. "I'll have them send it to my lawyer." When she got to the payment screen, she stopped again. "I'm paying for this," she said, only a touch of anger in her tone. "But can I use my credit card online? Or do I have to let you pay, and then reimburse you?"

From what he'd seen of Palmer and Abbott, he was more convinced they were two-bit thugs who wouldn't have access to that sort of information. But he also knew the best way to hack wasn't to hack at all. It was to have someone on the inside, and he was convinced that there was a player number three in the mix, and he didn't know how savvy that fellow might be. Odds might be a thousand to one, but he wasn't going to risk Torie as that one in a thousand.

"I'd feel better if you'd let me use mine. Until I get a handle on who these blokes are." He raised his hands in mock surrender. "And I promise, you can pay me back."

"All right." She relinquished her seat so he could fill out the forms. "Can I use my ATM? Or do I have to have money transferred to your account?"

"This will be behind us in a few days. I can cover it. We'll tally up at the end."

"Well, I'm keeping track. Down to the penny."

He knew better than to argue. "Fine. Tally away."

She went to her new purse and pulled out a stack of receipts.

"Is there an envelope around here I can put these in?" She lifted the one he'd been jotting notes on. After glancing at it, she waved it in front of his face. "That's Kathy's writing. Where did you get this?"

CHAPTER TWENTY-ONE

Torie stared at the paper. Her name in Kathy's distinctive print-
ing stared back at her.

"I found it on the floor," Fozzie said. "I was going to bring it
to you, but I got busy with a search."

She remembered the doctor giving it to her at the hospital in
Isla Caribe. She'd been too upset to deal with it, had shoved it
into one of her books, along with Kathy's notes, before she
packed to leave Miami.

"Kathy left this with the doctor. She must have written it
shortly before she died." With shaky fingers, she started to rip
open the flap.

"Wait," Fozzie said. "I need those notes on the back." He
strode to the kitchen and came back with a knife. "Let me."

As he slit the envelope, a million thoughts ran through her
head. Had Kathy known she was dying? Were these Kathy's last
wishes? Had Torie dropped the ball by not remembering she
had the envelope? What if Kathy had said she wanted to be
cremated and her ashes scattered on South Beach? Would she
be looking down from wherever she was, hating Torie for letting
her parents bury her in Michigan? Would she come back and
haunt her? Was that why bad things were happening?

Fozzie extracted a single sheet of paper. Without looking at it,
he held it out to her. On wobbly legs, she stumbled to the couch
and sat down before reading it.

Torie stared at the words.

Fozzie sat beside her. "What is it?"

She looked at him. "I haven't the slightest idea. It's a list of names. But I've never heard of these people."

Fozzie took the list. "Do you think it's important?"

"She wrote this in the hospital. In Isla Caribe. Maybe on her deathbed. It's got to be important. But maybe only to her." She turned the paper over and over, as if willing an explanation to appear. "You think there's something written in invisible ink?"

Fozzie took the paper. "I really doubt it. If she was that sick, where would she get the wherewithal to write in invisible ink? And if she did, why not write the whole thing with it?"

"You're right. I'm just . . . confused. Maybe these people were supposed to get something from her. Like add them to her will. Or maybe I'm supposed to let them know she died." She thought about that for a moment. "That makes the most sense to me. Maybe she didn't finish the list, and she was going to add the instructions at the end."

"Well, most homemade invisible inks are activated by heat. We could try." He crossed to the kitchen. She jumped up and hurried behind him. He lit the gas burner and held the paper above it, moving it slowly back and forth.

"Careful," she said. "Don't burn the paper. Maybe I should have copied the names first."

"No worries."

She tried to peer around his shoulders to see if anything magically appeared. "Anything?"

"Nothing. Sorry." He pulled the paper away from the burner and fanned the air.

"Maybe it's some kind of code?"

"Usually the simplest explanation—"

"I know, I know. Occam's razor. So these would just be names."

"That would be my first guess. You did say she was very sick.

I don't know how much energy she would have had to create a deathbed puzzler. Or why she'd feel the need to. These are probably friends of hers. People she was thinking of."

"So, how do we find out who they are?"

He stared at the paper. "It'll be tough," he said. "These are fairly common names. But I can give it a shot."

"Maybe I should try to track down her parents first. Ask them. Unless you think it might cause them more grief?"

"Tough call without knowing who these people on the list are. But why would someone who's very sick want to list people who don't like her? Or that she doesn't like?"

The effects of the second glass of wine were slowing her thought processes. She broke down and pulled a package of assorted cheese cubes from the minibar. Trying not to think of the prices, she unwrapped it and slid a piece of cheddar into her mouth, then extended the plastic tray to Fozzie.

She thought as she chewed. "That makes sense. I'll bet Kathy's boss would have contact information. He really cared about her. He's the one who hired your company to find her. He even came all the way to Isla Caribe when he found out she'd been hurt."

"You know him well?" Fozzie stood there, working on the cheese.

"No. I met him for the first time at the hospital. Derek Wingard. He's head of a research company that's looking for cures for the diseases nobody else cares about. I had dinner with him the night Kathy died. God, she probably died while we were enjoying our meal." Another wave of regret slid over her. She took the paper and read the names again.

Sandy Johnson. Melissa Norton. Edward Singleton. Stephanie Carter. Chris Logan.

"So, what first? You look for these five people, or I ask Derek Wingard how to get in touch with Kathy's parents?"

"Wingard's probably a faster option. But do you think it'll be okay if it waits until after dinner?" Fozzie asked, setting the empty cheese container down. "I'm starved."

Torie folded the paper and put it back in the envelope. "It's waited this long. If it was urgent, it's already too late, I guess. Another day won't hurt. Besides, we've got that two-for-one deal at the restaurant." She grinned. "Tell you what. I'll try to get contact information for him while you change into your new sweater."

He looked down, obviously puzzled. "What's wrong with what I'm wearing?"

"Let's just say, I love a guy in a sweater, okay?" Something she didn't see often in Miami.

He grabbed a huge JCPenney bag from the table and hustled toward the bathroom. She smiled again and went to the computer.

She found a contact link on the company Web site and sent a quick message asking Derek Wingard to get in touch with her. "We met in Isla Caribe," she wrote. "I'd like to get in touch with Katherine Townsend's parents. If you could either supply their e-mail, or forward this to them and ask them to respond, I'd appreciate it."

She heard the bathroom door open. She clicked Send and hurried to find her shoes. Toeing them out from under the table, she caught a whiff of decidedly masculine aftershave. She raised her head.

Whoa.

Fozzie. He'd changed from his baggy cargo pants to new black denims. And underneath that scrumptious cable-knit sweater that wasn't really blue and wasn't really gray, he wore a button-down shirt. Charcoal-gray cuffs peeked out at his wrists. The collar of the shirt was open enough to tease her with the chest hair she'd enjoyed up close and personal last night. His hair seemed—tamer, somehow. Slightly damp. He stepped closer, his scent growing more delicious. Clean shaven, too, registered at the back of her mind.

He raised his arms to his sides. Gave her a nervous smile. Did a slow pivot. "Satisfactory?"

She decided that she might like a man *out* of a sweater better than in one. She tugged at her turtleneck, all too aware her headlights had popped into high-beam. "Um . . . definitely. More than satisfactory."

"You about ready?"

"Right with you." She grabbed her purse, her shoes, and bolted for the bedroom. She surveyed herself in the mirrored door of the closet. Okay, the department store makeup job was hanging in. She did a quick de-shine, dabbed a little more gloss on her lips. Fluffed her hair. Dashed into the bathroom and swished mouthwash. When had dinner turned into a *date?* And when had Fozzie gone from teddy-bear cute to hands-off-my-man handsome?

Another *whoa.* Where had that come from? *My* man? No way. But his smile hadn't been that confident, cocky grin. It had been like—like he wanted her approval.

Calm down. She looked at her reflection again. Short. Bottom heavy, even though the black narrow-wale corduroy slacks and the horizontal black and white stripes on her turtleneck followed all the rules for looking slimmer. She was still dumpy To-rie. And Fozzie was still being her self-appointed bodyguard, even though he'd repeatedly told her the odds were slim to none someone could track them down. And he was hungry, and she'd merely said to put on the sweater.

Of course he would. Because he was hungry, and putting on the sweater was the price he had to pay for dinner. Okay, he'd shaved, too. And used the aftershave from the hotel's toiletry pouch. Big deal. It was probably automatic before going out to

217

dinner somewhere other than a fast-food joint. Not meant to impress *her*. To blend in.

He could have suggested room service, she told herself. Did he actually want to go somewhere public with her? Because if he wanted sex, she was willing. As a matter of fact, she was all but ready to tell him to lose the sweater, the pants, and if he'd opted to wear them, his sensible cotton briefs.

Which, she reminded herself, they could do *after* dinner.

"Torie?" Fozzie tapped the door. "You okay?"

"Coming." She snapped her purse shut and opened the door.

He guided her to the door with his hand at the small of her back. They strolled to the elevator and she paused. "We can walk."

He shook his head. "Elevator's fine." He pressed the call button. He shifted from foot to foot. He clenched and unclenched his fists.

"I don't mind. Really." The elevator's ding announced its arrival. The doors swooshed open, revealing an empty car.

"I said it's fine," he said, his voice gruff. Pressure on her back pushed her inside.

She pressed the button for eighteen and watched Fozzie struggle for control, his eyes fixed on the floor lights as the door shut. She pushed him against the wall. Panic filled his eyes. She stood on tiptoe, pulled him against her. Pressed her lips to his. Ran her tongue along the seam of his lips, coaxing. When he opened his mouth to protest, her tongue plunged deep. She ground against his groin. His hands found her bottom. His breathing grew heavy, but she didn't think it was for the same reason it had been when they'd entered the elevator.

The chimed dinged and the door opened. She stroked his jaw and led him out of the elevator by the hand. "Was that so bad?"

Fozzie swallowed. Hard. There were words trying to get out, he was sure, but nothing got past his mouth. Which was still tasting minty-fresh Torie. And part of his brain was dealing with the too-obvious reaction to the kiss. He stopped, dropping Torie's hand. "Wait." Good. His voice was back, even if it sounded like a sick frog. He maneuvered Torie in front of the bulge in his pants and let another couple pass on their way to the restaurant.

He tugged her to a telephone alcove. "What was that all about?"

"I thought I'd try some desensitization exercises. At least I think that's what you call them. You know, when you distract your mind so it can't deal with the fear. Or maybe it's conditioning." She gave him a sweet, innocent smile. Those gold streaks in her eyes sparkled. "Did it work?"

"Sunshine, you definitely gave me something else to think about. Now we're going to stand here for a few minutes until I can walk."

Conditioning? Like Pavlov's dogs? Just what he needed. Instead of a cold sweat when he got into an elevator, he'd be stuck with a boner. And would this *conditioning* carry over into any enclosed space? On an op, surrounded by his teammates? Which was a scary enough thought to deflate him.

Then again, during the adrenaline rush of their typical hostage rescue, most of them carried lumber in their pants, so he wouldn't stand out. He winced at his bad pun. "Let's go eat," he said.

As they shared the dessert Fozzie knew Torie wanted but for some reason was ashamed to order, he contemplated the Torie sitting across the table. Yeah, she looked better—that lady at the makeup counter had brushed and dusted and patted Torie with a dozen different ingredients. But if he hadn't seen it all being applied, he might not have noticed.

Kind of the way you never really thought about all the

ingredients in a chocolate cake, like the double-death-by-chocolate cake they ate. Flour, eggs, and who knows what else. Everything did its part, and you ended up with a delicious dessert. The woman was still Torie, but she seemed more confident, not cowering. And she hadn't apologized once.

Good lord, he was starting to sound like his grandmother telling him all about beauty being on the inside, and never judging a book by its cover, and any one of a hundred other clichés she used to spout. When had he become the philosopher?

He motioned the waiter over and ordered two cognacs. Torie's eyes widened. "I shouldn't," she said. "I had those two glasses of wine before dinner—"

"And nothing but water since."

"Well . . . all right. If you want one."

Confusion filled her face. Over a cognac? Did she think he was a drunk? He'd had one glass of wine with his dinner.

Crap. Just say it. "I'm enjoying being here with you. I'd like to enjoy it a little longer."

He watched the retreat into her shell. What had he said?

"You and me. Here?" she asked.

"What's wrong with that?"

She poked at the cake with her fork. "I thought you'd be . . . you know . . . in a hurry to get to the room. The way you were in such a hurry to eat."

"Torie, that's the way I *always* eat. I can't do that little nibble thing you do. And if you think—what *did* you think? That all I wanted was to jump your bones? That I was going to pay for it with dinner?"

Crap, crap, crap. Smart move. She's having second thoughts, and you stick both feet in your mouth. Up to the knees.

He took a regrouping breath. "If that's all I wanted, we'd have ordered room service. I thought you wanted to get out."

Confusion turned to resignation. Most of the sparkle left her eyes. "I did. This is fine. The cognac will be great."

He was *not* going to let her retreat. Not after she'd made such progress. He called the waiter back. "Sorry, please cancel our drinks. I'll take the check."

When he'd signed the check, he walked around the table and offered his hand. Now she looked confused again, but she took it and walked with him toward the elevator.

She gazed at him, then the call button, her eyes speaking the question. She'd kiss him again, he knew. But why? Because she thought he needed it? Or expected it? Last night, she'd come onto him like there was no tomorrow.

Which is what she'd been afraid of, dolt. That her last tomorrow might be a lot closer than she'd ever thought.

"Can you manage the stairs?" he asked.

She nodded.

Back in their room, he poured them each a brandy and settled her next to him on the couch. He left the light on over the kitchen counter, but didn't turn on the lights in the living room. "What happened?"

"What do you mean?"

"One minute we were having fun. Then, out of the blue, you disappeared. Did something scare you?"

"Not really."

"Torie, talk to me."

She swirled her drink, staring at the amber glow. "I got— confused."

"About?"

"About what I'm feeling. Guys don't . . ." She tried to get up, but he held her.

"Stay. Please."

"Guys don't want me for *me*, if you know what I mean. Kathy always had guys at her beck and call. I was on the fringes. And sometimes, I'd get the ones who realized they weren't getting anywhere with Kathy, so why not make it with Torie?" Her forced laugh quavered. "Not only when I was with Kathy. My whole life."

He knew the sort. "And you let them?"

"Sometimes," she whispered. "If I got . . . lonely enough. Sometimes I'd try to believe them when they said they loved me. But I knew they didn't mean it. Nana taught me that much. 'Men only want one thing, and they'll say what you want to hear to get it.' " She met his gaze. "I haven't said yes in a long time."

"You assume I'm the same?" And why wouldn't she? To her, guys were nothing more than generic louts with dicks.

"That's why I'm confused," she admitted. "I'm not sure who I am anymore. I kind of like it, but I don't know if it's real."

He'd been on the receiving end of *very real* last night. "We both needed something last night. But if you're afraid it's moving too fast, I'll take the couch tonight." Damn, whose brain was sending those words out his mouth?

She shook her head so emphatically she almost spilled her drink. "No." She looked at him. "Unless you'd rather?" she added.

Crap. The puppy dog was back. "Torie, what do *you* want?"

"To feel like I did last night," she whispered.

This is where, if she'd been wearing glasses, he'd have slipped them off and placed them on the table. If she'd had long hair, all pinned up in some formal do, he'd have found the keystone hairpin that would have sent her hair cascading down her shoulders.

He forced himself to go slow. He pried the snifter from her hand and put it next to her imaginary glasses. He ran his fingers through her short hair, bringing her lips closer. And he kissed her. Slowly. Gently. A brush of soft lips. Chocolate-flavored lips. Then, a little more than a brush. A touching. But his tongue was *not* going anywhere. Not without an invitation. He threaded his fingers more deeply into her hair, the strands brushing over his hands, every strand firing a nerve ending.

Her lips parted. Her tongue peeked out, touched the tip of his, then darted back. But her lips parted. He slipped his tongue along the seam of her lips. She opened wider, met his tongue with hers.

Bells rang. She jumped away.

Crap. The room phone? Now?

CHAPTER TWENTY-TWO

Heart pounding, Torie waited while Fozzie reached for the phone. The fact that he'd gone and grabbed one of the guns first didn't do anything to calm her. She barely breathed as he answered.

"Hello?" His tone was guarded.

After a short pause, he said, "That's right." He listened some more. "Not a problem. I'd forgotten myself," he said, then flashed her a grin. "No, everything has been perfect. Tomorrow morning will be fine. Ten o'clock? Thanks for checking." He replaced the receiver and put the gun in the drawer in the end table. The other one, she knew, was in the nightstand drawer. Along with the condoms he'd bought at the drugstore when she purchased some rudimentary first-aid supplies. Talk about protection.

"What was that?" she asked.

"Aside from interrupting what was turning into a very promising kiss?"

The dim light couldn't hide her blush.

"Seems the waiter in the restaurant didn't catch the two-for-one special, and management wanted to make sure I knew they were taking care of it. They also wanted to know when we wanted the champagne that comes with the package." He grinned. "But I think it was an excuse for our motherly desk clerk to check up on us. I recognized her voice."

He held out his hand, a questioning expression on his face.

Do you want to pick up where we left off? was clear enough.

If she only knew the answer. Her body screamed yes, but the doubts spread a layer of anxiety over all the warm—ok, hot—feelings she had when she looked at Fozzie. He'd seemed confused, almost hurt, in the restaurant.

You're a chronic runaway. You've got issues with trust.

Right now, she was the one she couldn't trust. She'd known the few men she'd had sex with never saw her as anything other than a convenient body, and she'd accepted it. *Close your eyes and think of England.* But if she had sex with Fozzie again, would she be able to walk away? Or bear it when he did?

Fozzie had picked up the hotel television brochure and was browsing the contents. "At least sit and finish your drink," he said.

"Be right back," she said and took refuge in the bathroom. Was she creating something out of whole cloth? Should she listen to her body, with its aching breasts and tingling between her legs? Or her brain, which was trying to protect her from being hurt? One night, she'd said last night. And this was why.

She'd go out there, find the books she'd bought at the mall, and leave him to his television while she read. She'd even tell him he could have the second bed instead of the couch. And in the morning, she'd insist they leave and go their separate ways.

Oh, wait. There was that pesky detail of people who might still be looking for her. And Fozzie seemed to be the one who knew how to elude them. All right. She'd stick with him until Monday.

She marched out to the dining room, searching through the bags for the one with her new books. She couldn't help but glance his way. He tilted his head and patted the couch. And as if she was connected by some invisible string, she crossed the room and sat. He punched a button on the remote and she watched the opening of *Casablanca* unfold.

225

"They have movies on demand," he said with a casual shrug. "Thought you might like to watch. I'm making rooibos tea."

They'd always have the Plaza in Eugene. She curled up alongside him. He put his arm around her shoulders. She rested her head against his chest.

Later, snuggled into him in bed, she toyed with the sweat-matted hair on his chest. "Can I ask a question?"

"Sure. Can't promise I have the brain cells left to answer, though."

"Is it normal . . . to get . . . aroused . . . when I'm . . . you know, touching you, but you're not touching me anywhere?"

"You mean is turning someone else on a turn-on?"

"Yes."

"Lord, yes." He picked up her hand and kissed it. "Wake me in a tick and we can experiment, though. Just to make sure." He curled her into him.

She lay there, feeling his warmth, feeling the arm across her go dead weight and his breathing slow. Guys never spent the night with her after sex. They finished, got dressed, and went home with some lamebrain excuse about having to be at work early. Yeah, everyone worked on Saturdays and Sundays.

She wasn't ready to sleep, though. Carefully, she lifted Fozzie's arm enough to slide out of bed. She cleaned up, then put on a robe and went to find her books—the ones she'd never taken out of the bag after Fozzie had called her over, and they'd watched about twenty minutes of the movie before they started kissing. He hadn't done anything but kiss her, but she'd touched him and she'd felt him grow hard, and she couldn't wait.

She closed the bedroom door and turned on the lamp by the couch. Before she settled in with a book, the hum from her laptop reminded her she hadn't shut down before leaving for dinner. She tiptoed to the desk and checked her e-mail. Most of it was spam, which she deleted. A few routine hellos from friends, who would have received her automatic vacation response. Should she deactivate it now that she was back in civilized territory? Probably not. No telling where she'd be next. She scrolled to the newest messages. Her pulse quickened, and she opened the first.

Yes, I recall our meeting. Thank you for getting in touch. I forwarded your message to the Townsends. Also, while going through Katherine's effects, there seemed to be some research notes missing on our current project. I wondered if perhaps she'd left them behind by mistake, and you might have picked them up.

Sincerely,
Derek Wingard

Torie searched her memory of that day. It was fuzzy, what with the aftereffects of food poisoning and seeing her friend so ill. Kathy had said they were important. But she also told Torie not to let anyone know she had them. What could it matter now? Kathy was dead, and others would be handling the research. She couldn't get in trouble for letting someone else look at them. And they might be important.

She clicked Reply. How to word it so Kathy's memory wouldn't be sullied?

I'll look. If I find them, I can have the hotel business office send them to you in the morning, if you'll send a fax number.

She sent the message and turned her attention to the next, which came from a Hotmail account. Seeing "townsend" in the return address quickened her pulse. Holding her breath, she opened it.

Mr. Wingard gave us your e-mail address regarding getting in touch with us about our daughter. You can respond to this e-mail.

Quickly, Torie found the list of names and began typing.

Dear Mr. & Mrs. Townsend. We met briefly after Kathy's tragic death. I am so sorry for your loss. I found a list of names that Kathy gave me through her doctor. I hoped you might know who they are, and if you can give me any contact information.

After inserting the names, she added,

Thank you and, again, my condolences.

Torie Stoker

With a feeling that she might finally get some answers, she hit Send.

She went back to her book, but kept listening for another e-mail alert. After an hour, suitably drowsy, she closed her book and turned off the lamp. Maybe the names had upset them, or they had to look them up. She'd check again tomorrow. She shut off the laptop and crawled into bed.

Fozzie stirred. He got up and used the bathroom, then came back. "You ready to try that experiment?"

She smelled the minty mouthwash on his breath.

Fozzie lay in bed, hands folded behind his head as Torie slipped into her robe. He could lie here for weeks, watching her. Good plan. After last night, lying here was probably the limit of his abilities.

"I thought I'd run the Jacuzzi," she said. "What time are they bringing the champagne breakfast?"

He checked the clock. "You've got an hour."

Torie disappeared into the vast bathroom, and the sound of

water surging into the Jacuzzi echoed into the room. He yawned. Maybe the hotel delivered a paper. He collected the strength to throw on a robe and stumble out to the living room. A few stiff muscles. Not surprising after the workout of the last two nights. A hot Jacuzzi would feel good. So would a cup of coffee. He went into the kitchen and was pouring water into the coffee-maker when the phone rang.

"Mr. Mayhew?" He hooked the phone between his ear and shoulder and added the packets of coffee to the basket. Enough hotel stays had taught him that if he doubled the coffee, the brew was passable.

"Yes?"

"This is Edith Dennison from the front desk. I checked you and your wife in. I hope I'm not disturbing you."

"No, not at all." *American accent, idiot.* He cleared his throat. "Is there a problem?" He eyed the drawer by the couch where he'd stashed the SIG. And why was he assuming it was bad news? Hell, the mother hen probably wanted to know if he and Torie had kissed and made up. He smiled. Oh, yes they had.

"I know there's a privacy block on your room, but late last night, there was a call, and someone was looking for your wife. Is her name Torie? They were asking for a Torie Stoker, which of course wouldn't show up in our computer at all, but he did describe her quite well, and he mentioned the car you listed on your check-in form. I'm sure your privacy is intact, but I did want to let you know that it sounds like her parents are trying to reach her. I thought she might want to call and put their minds at ease."

"Thank you. I'll tell her right away." He hung up. How the fuck had they tracked them so soon? Had they called every eff-ing hotel in Oregon?

Bags still covered the table. He opened one of the new suitcases and started cramming stuff inside.

"Torie!" He dashed into the bathroom. She was submerged in froth, her head laid back, her eyes closed. He found the power switch and turned off the jets. Her eyes opened. He must have looked like he felt, because they filled with alarm.

"What?"

"Sorry, Sunshine. Bath time's over. Pack up. We're leaving. I'll explain later." He handed her a towel.

Thank goodness she didn't hesitate. She stood, dripping foam and water. Like that goddess again, rising from the sea. She held out her hand, and he helped her step out of the tub. Wrapped in the towel, she scooped everything from the bathroom counter and carried it to the bed, then went to the closet and dumped the contents into a pile.

"I'll get the suitcase," he said. When he came back, she was dressed in new jeans and a hooded sweatshirt. He hefted the smaller suitcase onto the bed. Unlike the time she'd packed at the cottage, she skipped the neat folding routine and simply threw everything inside.

"Isn't there a tote?" she asked. "It was a three-piece set, right?"

"You need it?"

"I thought we should put the important stuff in it. In case we have to go somewhere in a hurry and travel light."

"Smart. Bare necessities and one change of clothes apiece."

She opened the nightstand drawer and gingerly lifted the Smith & Wesson. "And this?"

He cupped her face and kissed her forehead. "And that."

"You can add the other one."

Minutes later, their belongings were packed and the room was as empty as when they'd arrived. He did one more check, opening all the drawers, checking the closets, and under the furniture to make sure they had everything.

"Should I call down and have them bring the car around?"

Torie asked. "Save time?"

And they mentioned the car on your check-in form.

"Your car," Fozzie said. "A rental, right?"

"Yes. I've still got a couple of weeks left."

"Does it have LoJack? OnStar?"

She shot him a withering glance. "I was avoiding my father, remember? Why would I ask for that?"

"Just covering the bases. Okay, here's what we're going to do."

She listened solemnly as he explained. No questions, no objections. As if he was team leader, giving the briefing before an op, and she was a part of his team.

Somehow, there was comfort in the thought.

Twenty minutes later, they sipped lousy vending-machine coffee at the Amtrak station near the hotel. He'd accepted Torie's hand, but nothing else as they'd ridden the service elevator to the ground floor. This was an op now, and he stepped behind the mental wall that kept most of his demons at bay.

After emerging from the elevator, laden with suitcases, and being told they were in an off-limits area, Torie had apologized and played a delightful airhead as they'd snaked their way to the rear loading dock and then walked the two blocks to the station. From there, he'd used a pay phone and called a different rental-car company. Torie would have to make arrangements for her Fusion to be picked up from the hotel.

Fozzie watched as a man in an Enterprise jacket approach the station. "I think that's our ride. You ready?"

"As I'll ever be."

Once they'd dropped the rental-car driver off at his office, Fozzie checked the GPS.

"So, we're going to Idaho?" He hadn't objected when she'd told him that's where she wanted to go, had accepted it, but he was curious. "Why?"

"Because I've never been there. It seems remote enough, but might still let me look for Kathy's lichens. Which was the whole reason I went to Aspen Corners in the first place."

He picked up his cell phone and dialed Jinx's direct line. Got the expected voice mail. "Hey, Jinx. Know you're busy. Do we know anyone in Idaho? Need a place to stay for a few days."

He ended the call and turned to Torie. "We should cross the border by nightfall. If Jinx doesn't have a place for us, we'll find a motel." He attached the suction cup and positioned the GPS on the dash of their new Nissan Rogue. Not the greatest in the mpg department, but the tank held enough to take them about four hundred miles before they needed to fill it again.

"Are you going to check us out of the hotel?" she asked.

"Our room's paid through tonight. We'll do that tomorrow. If someone does manage to get our room number from the desk, they'll show us as still there."

"You're good at this, aren't you?"

"Not as good as I should have been, or we wouldn't be driving to Idaho. I'm still trying to figure out how they found us."

"Maybe your credit-card information was compromised after all."

He shook his head. "No way. No, there's something else. I'm leaning toward your car having a locator installed by the rental agency. One they don't bother to tell drivers about. That would let them find their cars if someone tried to skip."

She seemed content to let him mull it over as they drove out of town and onto the interstate. She finished her coffee and set the empty in one of the cup holders. "We should have brought a bag for trash."

"Next time we stop."

She was quiet for a few moments, then asked, "What do you do if your job entails rides in elevators?"

"Hasn't come up yet," he said. "I'm usually in a helicopter."

"And that doesn't bother you? They seem small."

"I can see out," he said. "And most of the time I'm watching instrument panels. And the team—we cover for each other's weaknesses. We all deal with them, or we'd never be on the teams, but we try to make it easier. One guy hates heights, so we'll keep his attention focused up, not down. If we're in a closed-in space, the guys tend to gather round with me in the middle."

"Doesn't that close you in more?"

"No, because it's being alone in tiny spaces that gets to me. So if I see the guys, I'm not seeing walls closing in. But it doesn't happen often. It was only because of being locked in that truck that the memories came back. If I ever thought I was a danger to the operation, I'd quit."

His phone announced an incoming text message. He picked it up and squinted at the display. Jinx. He handed the phone to Torie. "Read it to me."

She read an address in Twin Falls. Looks like they had accommodations for the night. "Text him back 'OK', will you? And then program the address into the GPS."

The phone chirped its confirmation tone. Torie took the GPS from the cradle.

"Hit Menu," he said. "Then follow the directions to add an address."

He listened to the GPS lady confirming each of the steps as Torie programmed their destination.

"Doesn't that voice annoy you?" she asked as she put the unit back in place.

"You can turn off the speaker if you want."

"No, it's probably safer if she warns you so you don't have to keep looking at it. But if I ever got one, I'd want a man's voice." She giggled. "With an Aussie accent."

233

He shifted in his seat. Ten hours, give or take, sitting next to Torie. Who apparently had dealt with her own demons last night, enough to giggle again. And now, the new-car smell didn't mask the hotel soap and shampoo that would forever remind him of Torie.

He, on the other hand, hadn't taken the time to shower. He figured he was enjoying her scent a lot more than she was enjoying his.

If she minded, she didn't say anything. Didn't crack the window, either. She kept looking at him and smiling. It was going to be a very long ten hours.

In reality, it was more than eleven hours before the GPS lady told them they were approaching their destination. Eleven hours along a route Fozzie decided was as boring as driving from the sheep station to Port Augusta when he was twelve.

On their one real meal break, Torie, bless her heart, had actually eaten a sandwich at normal human speed. Otherwise, they'd munched on snacks in the car. As far as he could tell, they hadn't been followed, and no way anyone but Jinx and their hosts knew where they were. Not based on one text message exchange. Nobody had started archiving those yet.

Obeying the GPS voice, Fozzie turned onto a dirt road. An empty dirt road through some farmland. "You sure you programmed the address Jinx gave you?" he asked.

She gave him an emphatic yes.

He continued and as the voice announced he had arrived, a light appeared, illuminating the approach to a large farmhouse. Fozzie nosed the Rogue closer and stopped near the large wooden porch. "This must be it."

When she released the car door and the dome light came on, he saw the "And you doubted me" look.

Fozzie unfolded himself from the driver's seat, glad to stretch out tight back muscles and a numb arse. A male figure stood on the porch, an imposing bear of a man. Even more imposing was the shotgun he held at the ready.

CHAPTER TWENTY-THREE

"Hold it, Sunshine. Get down."

Fozzie's words, uttered in a low but commanding tone, sent prickles of fear across Torie's neck. Something was wrong. She froze, letting the door handle slide from her fingertips. Slid low in her seat, straining to see him until her eyeballs burned. Her mind raced. She thought of the two guns in the small case on the backseat. Could she get them out without being noticed? No way. Not with the interior lights of the car highlighting every move. And even if she could, would she be able to get one to Fozzie? She remembered the night at the cottage, where she'd held a gun for the first time in her life. She'd never wanted to before then, and she hadn't changed her mind. But could she if she had to?

Fozzie didn't speak. She held her breath, waiting for some sign, some signal.

"Where's your hat?" A deep male voice came from the direction of the house. She couldn't see him. His gruff voice demanded answers.

"Stolen," Fozzie said. "Cryin' shame, too. Loved that Akubra."

"What's your sister's name?" the man asked.

Fozzie's torso, all she could see from her scrunched down position, turned toward the house. "I have two," he said. His voice was steady, calming. Definitely *not* the cocky, teasing, cajoling man he'd been when he'd approached that rainy night when he'd appeared in her life. He wasn't in charge here, and he knew it.

"The older one," the stranger said.

"Margaret," Fozzie replied. "Meg."

Was this some sort of code? A test? Would he ask her something, too? Heart thumping, Torie waited. Fozzie would have made sure she understood something this important. Since the phone call this morning, he'd become the man calling the shots, and she'd gladly deferred to his experience.

"And what did you call her?" the man said. He seemed less gruff, but still wary.

"M and M," Fozzie replied immediately.

"Come on up, then," the man said. "Bring the woman."

Before she could move, Fozzie circled around and helped her. Not that she wasn't capable of getting out of a car on her own. But somehow, her legs weren't moving. Fozzie reached behind her and opened the back door. With their small case in one hand, and his arm around her waist—not supporting her, she told herself, because she was fully capable of walking, even if her knees were shaking just a little—they strolled toward the porch. She stumbled when she noticed the gun slung across the man's arm. A large man. A very large gun. That arm around her waist came in very handy as Fozzie steadied her. "It's okay," he said.

"*Okay?*" she whispered. "He has a gun. Bigger than yours, which are in the suitcase."

"No worries, Sunshine."

As if. She'd worry if she wanted to, thank you very much.

The man held the door open for them, and Fozzie guided her inside ahead of him. Rustic, was her first thought. Lots of wood. And homey. Comfortable blue couch, definitely well used. Likewise a blue-and-brown-plaid easy chair that straddled the line between shabby and cozy. A cat rubbed up against her ankle, and she leaned down to scratch it. "Hi, kitty."

"Dixie," the man said. "Doesn't normally take to strangers." He lowered his gun into an umbrella stand beside the door, along with several walking sticks. "Sorry about the welcome. Isolated out here. Not many visitors at this hour. Had to make sure it was you."

Fozzie had been standing in the center of the room, turning slowly, as if absorbing it. He blinked. "No worries, mate. I'd have done the same."

"Drink? Coffee?" he asked.

Not much with words, Torie thought. As if he was being charged for each one. "I'm fine," she said.

"Loo would be much appreciated," Fozzie said. "Then a beer if you've got one."

The man grunted and pointed toward a hallway. "Left."

The man wandered off toward what she assumed was the kitchen. Torie crouched and busied herself with the cat.

Calm down. Fozzie trusted someone named Jinx, and Jinx had sent them here. If Fozzie was okay imposing on this man's hospitality, it had to be all right. She assessed the room, with the lace-edged throw pillows on the couch, and what appeared to be family photographs on the mantel and bookshelves. A needlepoint canvas with a half-finished bowl of flowers worked into the design, suggested he didn't live here alone. Of course, nothing said big, gruff men couldn't like lace-trimmed pillows, or do needlepoint, but it didn't match his image.

He came back into the room carrying two beers. Craggy face, leathered by the sun. Gray-white stubble. Thinning silver-white hair. Jeans, cowboy boots, a plaid flannel shirt. A thick handlebar mustache curled up at the corners. Definitely not your stereotypical needlepointer. He set one beer on the wide wooden arm of the couch, popped the top off the second and positioned it on an end table beside the easy chair. He toed off his boots, carried them to the door, and dropped them beside the umbrella stand. He returned, running his gaze along her body. Taking her in, sizing her up, but not undressing her.

She rose and crossed the room, hand extended. After all, *she* was civilized. "Thank you so much for putting us up. I'm Torie Stoker." No sooner had she spoken than she panicked. Was she supposed to use her real name? Fozzie definitely would have told her if she wasn't.

"Figured. Brad." He eased himself into the chair, grimacing as he stretched his legs onto the ottoman. Had he been limping? She'd been so busy worrying about the gun, she hadn't noticed. Realizing her hand hung in space, she let it fall to her side.

Fozzie ambled into the room, spotted the beer and settled onto the couch. "Thanks, mate. I'm Foster Mayhew, and this is Torie Stoker. We're grateful for the shelter. Jinx didn't give us anything but your address."

"Brad Escobar," he said. "Orange County Sheriff's Office. Retired."

"California?" Fozzie asked.

"Florida. Got sick of the heat." He tapped his leg. "Bum knee. Took my retirement, bought this spread from my wife's uncle about ten years ago."

Wow. A whole bunch of words all at once. Torie joined Fozzie on the couch, but at a civilized distance. Dixie jumped onto her lap, curled up, her motor running.

"I can put her away," Brad said.

"No, she's fine. I like animals."

"You're with Blackthorne," the man said. Not a question. "Worked with them a couple of times, years back. Good outfit."

"So, what did you do with the Sheriff's Office?" Fozzie asked.

Not "what did you do with Blackthorne?" Torie had caught a brief nod, an exchange of knowing glances. A silent language the two of them understood. Some topics were not to be discussed, not while she was around.

"Detective. Homicide, mostly, until I busted up my knee."

"And now you're doing what?" Fozzie asked. "Growing potatoes?"

"Hay," Brad said. "Got my PI license. Do a little work on the side now and then."

"You have an Internet connection we can use tomorrow?" Fozzie asked.

"Satellite."

Fozzie tilted his beer to his mouth. Torie watched his Adam's apple bounce as he chugged the contents. He stood. Stretched. "Thanks for the beer. We're keeping you up. If you'll point us to where we can bunk, we'll be out of your hair."

Brad grunted. "Your colleague didn't say much, but I'm thinking you want to keep an eye on her."

Torie's face heated. Fozzie kept his gaze fixed on Brad. "Until we resolve our problem, she's not to be left alone."

"Figured." Brad grabbed both arms of the chair and hoisted himself to a standing position. "Old cook's quarters in back. Not much, but it's private," he said. They followed him through a spacious kitchen dominated by an oak table, through a doorway and down a short, narrow hall. He opened the door for them, flipped a switch. A light glowed from a hobnail milk glass lamp on the bed table. "Towels and stuff in the bathroom. Extra blankets in the chest at the foot of the bed. See you in the morning."

"Thank you," Torie said to his retreating back.

Fozzie placed their case on the chest. "This enough for tonight, or should I get the others?"

"Tomorrow's fine," she said.

Their room was small, painted white, with two framed needlepoint pictures, one a spring forest scene and a similar one in fall colors the only adornments. White curtains fluttered in front of a half-open window next to an alcove with a second door. Fozzie opened it, letting in more of the chill night air. He stepped outside, turning left, then right. When he came back in, moments later, he closed the door and threw the dead bolt.

A four-poster double bed covered much of the floor space. She pulled the white chenille spread back, revealing blue flower-sprigged sheets and a dark-blue blanket. The sheets had that freshly laundered smell. The pillowcases were ironed crisp. Done for their benefit, or was this room always at the ready for unexpected guests?

"Cook's quarters, he said. You don't think he'll expect us to cook, do you?" she said, trying to lighten the mood darkening around her.

Fozzie chuckled. "I doubt it."

"Good. Because we'd be out on our ears in a heartbeat—unless you're a gourmet cook?"

"Nope. I can grill a mean steak, though."

"I thought Aussies barbequed shrimp," she teased. Normal conversation. Keeping things light. Pretending they hadn't driven over six hundred miles to hide with a total stranger.

He laughed. "Not many shrimp where I came from."

"I'm going to use the bathroom first, if that's okay." She grabbed the toiletries from the suitcase, trying not to think about the two guns that lay beside them.

As she stood at the sink in the tiny bathroom, brushing her teeth, questions bubbled through her brain like this morning's aborted Jacuzzi soak. Brad had a room ready for fugitives? He had Blackthorne connections, but Fozzie hadn't asked about them. Brad was a licensed PI. Would he help her figure out who those names on Kathy's list belonged to? Or why she'd been captured? What was next Monday?

Too many questions. Not enough energy to worry about

answers. She rinsed her mouth, washed her face and stepped back into the room. She opened the small walk-in closet. No robes, silk, terrycloth, or otherwise. She sat on the edge of the bed, tugged off her sneakers and unzipped her jeans.

"I need a shower," Fozzie said. He ducked into the bathroom. While he was in there, she checked the suitcase. It was mostly the non-clothing stuff. Toiletries, first-aid kit. Her laptop, assorted chargers. The guns, ever-present reminders that this was anything but a vacation getaway. She hadn't been thinking when she'd thrown in some clean underwear and an extra turtleneck. Because if she had, she'd definitely have included something to sleep in.

She stripped and crawled under the covers, taking the side closer to the wall, leaving the lamp on for Fozzie. Comforted by the normal sounds of someone in the shower, of teeth being brushed, a toilet flushing, she drifted off. Footsteps padded across the room. A thunk. She opened her eyes. Fozzie had closed the window.

"All snug," he said as he slipped in behind her. He flipped off the light.

Fozzie draped his arm over her and drew her against him, sharing his warmth. The accommodations were more appealing than Al Abbott's basement. And the warden was a whole lot nicer. Somehow, though, she couldn't shake the feeling that she was as much a prisoner here as she had been there.

Fozzie snapped awake at the sound of low voices from the kitchen. Daylight registered immediately, as did Torie's absence. He leaped out of bed, grabbing his pants. How had he slept through her leaving? Not enough of his brain had made the switch to protector, and he cursed himself. Soft beds with warm women were *not* acceptable reasons for dropping his guard, awake or asleep. He zipped his pants as he checked the dead bolt. Still fastened from the inside. The window was shut.

The aroma of coffee brewing and bacon sizzling sent him toward the kitchen. He peered around the doorway. Torie sat at the large wooden table, hand wrapped around a coffee mug. Across the room, a bird of a woman stood at the stove, cracking eggs into a skillet.

Relief cascaded through him. He told himself if anyone had come into the room for Torie, he'd never have slept through it. But the seeds of doubt had been planted. He dumped mental weed killer over them. He might have been tired from the drive, but there was no way he'd lost that much of his edge.

He stood there a moment, out of sight, taking in the way the sunlight played over Torie's hair, shimmering it with gold highlights. Loud, slightly uneven footfalls approached. The woman at the stove turned. A smile lit her face even before the owner entered the room.

The way his mum had smiled at his dad. With her entire soul. His throat swelled and his eyes burned. Damn, was he coming down with a cold? And there was one other morning problem. He retreated to the bathroom and waited for his erection to fade so he could pee.

He finished dressing and strolled to the kitchen. "Mornin'."

Three pairs of eyes—make that four if you counted the cat—turned and stared at him. He gave a quick downward glance to make sure he'd zipped up.

The woman smiled at him. Friendly enough. "You must be Mr. Mayhew. I'm Caroline Escobar. Brad's wife. But, please, call me Carrie. Would you like coffee?"

"Please. And I'm Fozzie."

She pointed to the chair next to Torie. "Sit. How do you like your eggs?"

"Whatever's easiest for you." He exchanged a glance with Torie, whose expression said, "Just go with it."

"I'm sorry I couldn't greet you in person last night. I trust you slept all right?"

"No worries, ma'am," Fozzie said. "Slept like a babe."

Brad stood and went to the coffeepot and refilled his mug. Standing beside his wife emphasized the woman's tiny stature. Gray hair in a long braid hung down her back. She wore red knit pants—not quite slacks, not quite sweats—and a matching top with daisies embroidered around the neckline. Round wire-rimmed glasses enlarged her twinkling blue eyes. Her freckled complexion said that, unlike her husband's, her family tree didn't have Hispanic roots.

Brad reached for a slice of bacon from a platter beside the stove. Carrie slapped his hand away. "You sit down at the table and eat like a civilized person."

Fozzie took his time enjoying the breakfast Caroline had set in front of him. When he'd finished sopping up the last bit of egg yolk with a piece of buttered toast, he took his plate to the sink.

Brad followed, taking both plates and putting them in the dishwasher. "We should talk." He filled his mug, his eyebrows gesturing that if Fozzie wanted more coffee, he should do the same. Fozzie topped off his mug. Brad headed toward the door. As they passed the table, Torie stood.

"Fozzie, may I have the car keys? I'll get the suitcases."

"On the bed table, but I'll fetch 'em. I'll be back in a tick," he said to Brad.

Torie followed Fozzie, closing their bedroom door behind them. "What's going on?"

"I don't know." He twisted the knob on the dead bolt and went outside. Circling the house, he found their rental car. "Think I'll move it around back," he said. "Closer to our door."

"Am I allowed to wander, or are we still joined at the hip?" He heard the concern in her tone.

"If you're outside, I want to be with you. If we're inside, I guess you're all right as long as you're within hollering distance. And I don't like to holler too loud indoors."

"I get it. We're still joined, but with an elastic band."

He parked the car about ten feet from their door and laid the two suitcases on the bed.

"We're not going to have to stay here long, are we? Or should I unpack?"

"Night or two more, I hope will be enough." He locked the door again.

She gave a resigned sigh. "All right. I'll straighten out the mess in these suitcases." She unzipped the first case, scooped everything out of one and dumped it onto the bed. He grabbed her by the shoulder and kissed her. Hard. "I'll be with Brad. Come find us when you're done."

In the kitchen, Carrie directed him to the den. Definitely masculine. Probably three times bigger than Brad's office when he'd been a cop. Dark paneled walls, massive desk with a huge leather chair behind it. Brad stood, gazing out the window, sipping his coffee. An infinitesimal tilt of his head indicated he'd noticed Fozzie's arrival.

"You were more than a homicide dick," Fozzie said.

"Did some covert-ops work. Long time ago. Rangers."

"I don't think we'll need those talents. Couple of penny-ante thugs. We know who, but not why."

"Good. Don't need trouble out here."

Fozzie caught the quick glance toward a picture of Carrie on Brad's desk. "Look. We appreciate the place to stay. We've probably managed to stay under the radar, but if you're uncomfortable, we can be on our way. A few hours on the Internet would be helpful, but if you'd rather we leave now, say the word."

Brad settled himself into the leather chair, which shrank to average size under his bulk. "Names?"

Fozzie gave him Palmer and Abbott, and what little he already knew. "We think they're being controlled by a third party, but we don't know who."

Brad's sausage-sized fingers flew across the keyboard. "You want, you can take care of the lady. This'll take a while."

Fozzie swore the man heard his eyebrows lifting in surprise, because Brad immediately answered the question Fozzie had barely formulated.

"Did a lot of desk work after I blew out my knee. I still have contacts."

"Do you know Jinx? Did he tell you what we needed?" How had his colleague picked this man to shelter them?

Brad shook his head. "Nope."

"Seems we were lucky to end up here, then, considering your . . . skills."

Brad raised his eyes from the monitor, and his lip curved upward a millimeter. "Doesn't take all that much luck. You can't go five miles in Idaho without running into an ex-cop. The state's one fucking-big retirement home."

"I heard that, Brad." Carrie's voice preceded her as she walked into the room, Torie behind her.

"Sorry," he said, a chagrined expression on his face.

Fozzie stifled a laugh.

Carrie crossed to the desk and kissed Brad on the cheek. "Torie has some names she'd like me to research. We'll use my computer upstairs. There's fresh coffee in the kitchen."

They disappeared. Brad said, "Carrie worked research for the *Orlando Sentinel* nearly thirty years. If there's a fact hiding somewhere, she'll ferret it out."

Feeling about as useful as slippers on a snake, Fozzie flopped onto the recliner in the corner of the room.

Chapter Twenty-Four

Torie followed Carrie to a small bedroom on the second floor of the house. A neatly made daybed was tucked into a corner. Most of the pink coverlet was hidden beneath a mountain of stuffed animals. A bentwood rocker with a needlepoint cushion sat in the opposite corner, next to a basket filled with yarns.

"This used to be my getaway room," Carrie said. "Now I have to share it with my granddaughter when she visits."

Torie picked up a maroon plush rabbit. "How old is she?"

"Six. Going on thirty. But God forbid anyone moves one of her menagerie."

Torie dropped the rabbit, trying to put it exactly where she'd found it. Carrie walked over to a computer desk, sat down, and jiggled the mouse. A picture of a grinning child, who Torie assumed was the granddaughter, filled the screen.

"Let's see those names," Carrie said.

Torie handed over the slip of paper, saying, "I don't see how you can find them from just names. I imagine you'll get hundreds of thousands of hits."

"Search engines are powerful, but you have to ask them the right questions or you'll spend weeks going over all the matches. The names you gave me are fairly ordinary, so I expect we'll have to figure out which ones belong to the people you're looking for."

"Yeah, and it would probably help a lot if I had a clue who they were. Chris and Sandy could be either sex."

Carrie clucked. "Yes, there is that. We'll have to look at all the matches rather than eliminate obvious males or females. What's your friend's name? I'll look for connections."

"Kathy Townsend. Katherine."

Pairing each of the first three names with both Kathy and Katherine didn't find Torie's Kathy. Many of the hits, Carrie explained, were sites designed to make life difficult for spam bots.

"There are other options," Carrie went on. "Maybe she went to school with them. Do you know when she graduated from high school or college?"

Embarrassed at how little she actually knew about someone she considered a good friend, Torie explained that they'd met relatively recently. "We hit it off, but our relationship started at that point. We never talked about our pasts." Probably because Torie never shared hers with anyone. Until Fozzie.

"All right. We might try the Classmates site. And if your friend had a MySpace, Facebook, or any of the other social sites, these names might be on her friends list. Do you have a page?"

"No," Torie confessed. "I couldn't get into that scene. I've always been a loner."

"Not a problem. If it comes to that, we'll use ours."

Torie couldn't hide her surprise. "You have pages?"

"Yes, we do," Carrie said. She twisted her head around and smiled, laugh lines deepening around her eyes. "Brad takes an occasional case where it comes in handy. He's caught a number of predators that way."

Footsteps on the stairs, quicker and lighter than Brad's gait, caught Torie's attention. She felt a stupid grin spread across her face. Willing it away didn't work.

"Torie?"

She went to the door and poked her head out. "We're in

here." She searched his face for signs that new problems were about to descend, but he smiled when he saw her. He held a piece of paper.

"You found something?" she asked.

"Some connections." He nodded at Carrie. "Your husband's still got his chops."

Carrie took her eyes from the monitor. "He was a good cop. He hated being chained to a desk, although he did the job well. He was respected and keeps in touch."

"I hope he didn't waste any favors hunting this out. But"—he showed the paper to Torie—"Palmer and Abbott both did time at Tehachapi. There were two others they hung with, Stuart Freeman and Hector Garcia. Garcia's living in Ohio now, works in a garage and seems to be a decent citizen. Freeman's dead, died in a robbery three months after he got out."

Torie handed the paper back. "What does this have to do with me?"

"I wondered if either name rang a bell."

She shook her head. "Sorry. Never heard of them."

"Got something," Carrie said.

Torie hurried to the computer. "A blog?"

"It's an old entry, but the blog belongs to Stephanie Carter, and there's a comment by Kathy Townsend. I've scrolled down to the first of Stephanie's entries on the subject."

Fozzie put his hand on Torie's shoulder, positioning her in front of him so they could both see the screen. Gently, his hands massaged her neck.

Torie read Stephanie's words.

February 1: I'm stoked. I got the notice today that I'm accepted into a clinical study testing a new drug. I really hope this will be the answer. More next time.

She scrolled up the screen to follow the posts in chronological order.

February 8: Got my new meds two days ago. So far, so good.
February 21: I'm feeling great. I'm trying not to get my hopes up too high. It's still really early. But I haven't had an attack in two weeks, and that's a record. Wouldn't it be great if I could be normal. "J" sat with me at lunch. Offered me a chocolate chip cookie. I know I shouldn't have, but I ate it. And . . . drum roll . . . No ill effects.

"This is where Kathy commented," Carrie said, and she clicked the link.

Fingers crossed for you, Stephanie. I'm so glad things are working out. Keep me posted. E-mail me if you want.

"Is that your Kathy's e-mail address?" Carrie asked.

"Yes," Torie said.

"Bingo," Carrie said. She clicked to another site. "Two down, four to go."

"But I didn't read all the entries," Torie said.

"It's bookmarked. Right now, I'm trying to find as many of these people as possible."

Fozzie dropped his sheet of paper on the desk. "I hate to make more work, but can you find any connections to these names?"

"No problem. It's fun to be back in the game."

"Guess I'll go see how Brad's doing," Fozzie said. "He was tracking down the owner of the house where they took Torie." He rested his forehead on Torie's. "I think we're getting closer."

"I hope so," she said. Before leaving, he brushed her cheek with his lips. Fingers to cheek, as if holding the kiss in place, she wandered across the room to the rocking chair. If they did figure everything out, what next?

"Do you have a wireless connection?" she asked Carrie. "I'd like to check my e-mail. And maybe I can read the rest of the blog entries from Stephanie's site."

"Sure. Give me a minute to allow your computer to access our network. By the time you power up, you should be good to go."

Downstairs, she saw Fozzie leaning over Brad's computer, much the way she'd been an observer of Carrie at work. Outsiders looking in. Not that unusual for her, but she noticed an edginess to Fozzie's demeanor. Not someone used to relying on the kindness of strangers.

Leaving them to their work, she went to the bedroom she and Fozzie had shared and powered up her laptop. A quick burst of excitement surged through her when her e-mail contained a reply from the Townsends. She clicked it open.

It's so nice to hear from one of Katherine's friends. We're still adjusting to the loss. None of the names you sent are familiar. Is there any more information, something that might trigger a memory? I would love to help you. Strange as it might sound, your message brings Katherine closer.

A dead end? With Carrie working upstairs, it didn't seem to matter as much. But Torie couldn't shake the feeling of being useless. She surfed the Net for a while, trying to duplicate Carrie's expertise, but got nowhere. Too bad she didn't have Kathy's laptop. She bet Brad and Carrie could have tracked down all the answers. Wait. They weren't the only ones who could play detective. She went back to the Townsend's e-mail and hit Reply.

Thank you for your prompt answer. I know this is an imposition, and if it's too much trouble, or if you don't have the information, don't worry about it. But if you still have Kathy's laptop, could you e-mail me her list of bookmarked sites?

Why would she be asking that? She thought for a few moments.

I noticed she commented on a blog I was interested in, and thought she might have more sites. Where I could spread the word and let people know of the tragic accident. Thanks, one way or the other.

Torie

Feeling like she'd finally done something to contribute to the search, she hit Send.

Fozzie handed Brad a beer. The two men stood on the wooden deck behind the ranch house. Brad popped the top and took a healthy swig. The aroma of grilling meat filled the air. The fading light filtered through the hazy smoke of the barbeque.

"You're going to a lot of trouble for us," Fozzie said. "We've kept you from your normal routine."

Brad grabbed a pair of tongs and flipped the steaks. "Felt good to spend a day finding answers." He poked a steak. "If you like 'em on the rare side of medium, they're done."

"Sounds fine."

They gathered around the table, which Carrie and Torie had set with salad, a platter heaped with corn, a basket of hot biscuits, and a bowl of green beans. Fozzie couldn't help but notice the way Torie followed the friendly conversations, not participating, but drinking in the atmosphere. This was probably something very different from her own childhood.

Fozzie cleaned the last crumbs of apple cobbler from his plate. "You worked way too hard, both of you. First with research, now with all the cooking."

"Nonsense," Carrie replied. "Torie shucked the corn, the

beans were frozen, the cobbler's from the bakery, and the biscuits came out of a tube." She grinned. "But if you tell anyone, I'll deny it."

"Guess I should do the dishes, then," Fozzie said. "Since all I did was carry some beer."

When nobody objected, Fozzie laughed. "I can take a hint." He started collecting plates.

"I'll help," Torie said.

"Carrie and I will go over our notes while you two youngsters pay for your supper, then," Brad said.

Carrie threaded her arm around Brad's waist and they strolled out of the room.

Fozzie started rinsing and loading while Torie finished clearing. "This is the last," she said, placing the glasses on the rack. "You seem to know what you're doing."

"Mum didn't allow slackers," he said. "And she wasn't one to divvy the labor by gender. Tony and I were older, so we got put to work as soon as we were big enough. Dishes, laundry, shearing, dipping sheep—didn't matter. Jobs needed doing, we had to do them."

She leaned her elbows on the counter, a wistful expression on her face. "This is taking you back, isn't it? The way you looked at the place when we first came in. It was like you were someplace else."

She inched closer. Despite the cooking smells and the lemon-scented dish soap, Torie's aroma was the one that registered. "It did trigger some memories," he admitted.

"Good ones?"

He finished rinsing the oversized pot the corn had been cooked in and set it in the rack. By fifteen, he'd been sick of the station life. Wanted to see the world. As soon as he finished school, he applied to every college and university he thought might take him in the US. His parents hadn't stood in his way, although he knew it hurt that he wanted to go so far. But they scraped together enough money to get him started when the agricultural school at Cornell offered him a small scholarship, and sent him away with proud but teary smiles. Money and distance kept them apart. He'd walked in last night and homesickness he'd never felt while at school had surrounded him like a fleece blanket.

"Yeah," he said.

Torie picked up a towel and dried the pot. "You see yourself living the family life?"

Not until this week. "Never gave it much thought. My job has me bouncing around, sometimes with no notice. Didn't seem fair to involve anyone else."

"I never had anything like this," Torie said. "Families were in books or on television. Nothing real. Hardly anyone I knew lived that life, so I figured it was all make-believe anyway."

He closed the door to the dishwasher. "We're done. We should probably go see what they've found."

She folded the towel neatly into thirds and slipped it over the oven handle. "Guess so." But she didn't move to leave. The wistful expression hadn't left her face, but there was heat in her eyes.

He'd given up telling himself he shouldn't. He simply closed the short distance between them and cupped his hands around her wonderful round arse, pulled her tight and kissed her. She returned it with a tenderness that made his chest ache.

"They're probably wondering what's taking so long," she murmured.

He released her. "I have a feeling they're not wondering." He kissed the tip of her nose. "You go on. If I go out now, they'll definitely not be wondering. I'll just be a tick."

His gaze lingered on the sway of her hips as she left the room. Damn, was he going to be hard for the rest of his life? Thinking about her was enough to make his jeans painfully tight. He forced his thoughts elsewhere, but Torie's image appeared wherever he tried to escape. With a sigh, he yanked his shirt free from his jeans and hoped for the best.

He found everyone gathered around the dining room table, which had been covered with a huge sheet of white butcher paper. Thankfully, all eyes were on the table, not his stiff cock. Carrie's laptop was fired up. He joined the group, taking a position next to Brad and away from whatever spell Torie cast over him, and surveyed the diagrams and notes on the paper.

In the upper center was Torie's name, with Kathy's underneath. To one side, Brad had written the names from Kathy's notes. Palmer and Abbott were written on the other side, circled, with a line connecting them. Another line led to Stuart Freeman and Hector Garcia. There was a big X drawn across Stuart Freeman's circle, and a question mark under Garcia's.

"You don't figure him for the third guy, do you?" Fozzie asked.

Brad shook his head. "Model citizen according to his parole officer."

"So we're still looking for another player. Someone calling the shots," Fozzie said. He followed another line on the paper.

The address of the house where Torie had been held was written in a square, with lines pointing to both Abbott and Freeman. Fozzie tapped the line between Stuart Freeman and the house address. "You got something new?" Earlier, they'd found the property tax rolls, which indicated the house had belonged to Abbott.

"Stuart Freeman's sister was married to Abbott. They divorced about three years ago."

"He got the house?" Fozzie asked. "Isn't it usually the other way round?"

"Apparently she'd had enough and wanted out," Carrie said.

"House has been on the market, empty for six months. But Abbott still owns it, has a key. Told the realtor he was going to be doing some repair work."

"How did you find all this out?" Torie asked. "This can't all be on Google."

Carrie's laugh was like a bird chirping. "Called the realtor. If they think there's a sale in the offing, they can be very informative."

"Okay," Torie said. "We know who had me, and how they're hooked up. But why?" Her gaze moved from one person to the next around the table.

"They didn't hurt you, right?"

Torie touched her jaw. "Not really."

Fozzie clenched his fists. "Who? What?"

She ducked her head. "Abbott slapped me, that's all. I was talking, and he didn't like it. It was only once, and not all that hard. He never tried anything . . . you know."

Lucky for him, Fozzie thought. Or he'd be dingo tucker. "Palmer's firebug episode says much the same. He wasn't trying to burn the house down. Just chase us out. And my money says he's the one who came back and put it out."

"Best guess?" Brad said to Torie. "Keep you quiet."

"Quiet about what?" Torie's voice raised half an octave. "I don't know anything to keep quiet about."

"You might, and might not know it. The relevant factor here is that these guys think you know something."

"Or they were searching for something," Carrie said. "Which would explain why the guy put out his own fire. Gets you out, gives him some time to look around."

"So, do you think they found it, whatever it is? And if they did, why did they still need me?"

After a moment of thoughtful silence, Brad spoke. "If it was something you were aware of"—he nodded in Torie's direction—"then they'd still need to keep you under wraps, because you might talk even if they found what they wanted."

"I think I'll put on some coffee," Carrie said. "My brain needs a jolt." She whisked away.

"If they were looking for something in the cottage, it didn't have to be mine," Torie said. "I'd only been there two weeks."

"We already discussed the possibility they wanted Kathy, not you, but as you said, Kathy's death was no secret," Fozzie said.

"So, did anybody find anything happening on Monday that involves any of these guys?" Torie asked.

Carrie came back into the room. "No, nothing. Couldn't find anything connecting them to each other except for their time in prison."

"And you cross-referenced all the names with Epicurean, right?" Brad said.

Carrie shot him a look. He raised his hands in surrender. "Just recapping."

"What about Stephanie Carter?" Torie suggested. "Maybe we could get in touch with her, ask her how she knew Kathy."

Carrie cast another look in Brad's direction. "Good idea. I might have already done it if *someone* hadn't needed all those other searches." After scrolling and clicking, she looked up at Torie, shaking her head. "I'm sorry. She died. The last entry was in August. Her parents left the blog up as a memorial."

"How did she die?" Torie asked.

"Something called Willamette Syndrome," Carrie said.

"Never heard of it," Fozzie said. "Have anything to do with Oregon?" He looked for signs of recognition from the others, but they seemed as clueless as he was. Carrie was already tapping and clicking.

"It's a rare disease," she said. "Nothing to do with geography. Some kind of metabolic disorder, first described by a Doctor Willamette. I've found a support group site where Stephanie was a participant."

Brad said, "What about—"

"Hold on." Carrie's tongue peeked out of the corner of her mouth. Her brow furrowed in concentration as she worked her magic. Fozzie crossed the room to stand behind her. Torie sidled in beside him and dovetailed her fingers with his.

"They're all there," Fozzie said, pointing at the screen.

"So, they all had the same disease," Torie said. "That's their connection."

Pages flitted across the monitor as Carrie went back and forth to the search engine and plugged in the names along with Willamette. After the third search, Torie's hand grew cold in his.

"Those were all obituaries," she said.

CHAPTER TWENTY-FIVE

Torie stared at the screen as Carrie located all five names from Kathy's list. All dead. "That's so sad." She became aware of Fozzie's arm around her, drawing her closer.

"Can you look for the other set of names?" Fozzie asked.

"Cost you a cup of coffee," Carrie said. "Splash of milk."

"I'll get it," Torie said. "Anyone else?"

"Black," the men said in unison.

Torie assembled mugs on the counter, then poured the coffee. Why did Kathy have those names? Stephanie, at least, had died several months ago. Why had Kathy given them to her now?

She grabbed two of the mugs and brought them to Fozzie and Brad, then went back and fixed ones for Carrie and herself. Not that she needed caffeine. Her heart was pounding enough without the added stimulation.

She hurried back to the dining room. "Did all these people die at about the same time?"

"Let's slow down," Brad said. "Make a list of questions. Keep things logical. Don't waste effort." He tore a sheet of paper from a tablet.

"Wingard Research," Torie said.

"What's that?" Brad asked even as he wrote it down.

"The company Kathy worked for. They research drugs to cure orphan diseases—rare diseases that the big companies can't be bothered with."

"You think they were working on this Willamette disease?" Brad asked.

"I don't know," Torie said. "Kathy always said they kept everything hush-hush."

"Makes sense to me," Fozzie said. "Big company gets wind of a new cure and might jump in, go for the glory."

"I could call Derek Wingard," Torie said. "I met him in the hospital the night Kathy died," she added when Carrie and Brad threw questioning looks her way. "He was very nice, and very concerned about Kathy. To find her, he hired the company Fozzie works for. Even flew all the way down to Isla Caribe to check on her."

Brad's expression changed from curious to . . . *cop* was all that came to mind. Suspicious?

"What?" she asked.

"Seems a bit much for a CEO to take time to fly down. You think he and Kathy had anything else going on?"

She tried to control her indignation. "Like a sexual thing? No way. Kathy had guys swarming around her in Miami. She had an active social life, and from what I gathered, a decent sex life. I'm sure she would have mentioned it if she had anything going on with her boss."

"Work related, then?" Brad said.

"Kathy did research. Derek raised the money and ran the company. I don't think he understood how the scientific stuff actually went down, only that they were getting results."

Brad moved to his computer. "You said his name was Derek? About how old?"

"Fifties, maybe," Torie said.

"I'll look into the company," Carrie added.

Frustration at feeling useless amidst all the frenzied computer work overcame her. "I might have some new information my-self."

"What's that?" Carrie asked.

"I e-mailed Kathy's parents and asked them if they'd send me a list of the bookmarks in Kathy's laptop. I haven't heard back yet—"

"You did what?" Fozzie said. She recoiled as he spun around, his face inches from hers.

"The other night, back in Eugene, I couldn't sleep, so I found the site for Wingard Research, where Kathy worked." She looked at him, the first inklings of doubt threading through her brain. "I sent an e-mail through the contact address on their Web site and asked him to put me in touch with Kathy's parents. I figured he'd have had that information in her files."

Fozzie stepped closer. He didn't look angry, but a muscle in his jaw clenched. As if he was trying not to yell at her. "And he answered?"

"Right away," she said. "I was surprised, because it was late, but he'd said their experiments ran around the clock sometimes." Not able to meet Fozzie's gaze, she directed her remarks toward Brad and Carrie. "I asked him to either pass my message to Kathy's parents or to have them e-mail me directly. Which they did. I gave them the names and asked if they knew who they were. So, this morning, while everyone was working, I got an answer."

"Which was?" Fozzie said.

"That they didn't recognize the names. But I thought if we knew more about Kathy, we might find more connections from her end."

She looked from one face to the other. For several moments, no one spoke. Carrie broke the silence.

"You e-mailed them from here?"

Torie nodded. "That . . . Fozzie said . . . you were all on computers . . . on the Internet—" She met Fozzie's eyes. "You said regular people can't trace people through computers or cell phones or credit cards. That only the cops can do it. I thought . . . I wanted to help."

"No need to panic," Carrie said. "May I see your laptop?"

No need to panic, Torie repeated to herself as she hurried to the bedroom. Okay, not panic. But a huge boatload of dread settled over her.

She yanked the power cord from the wall and it dragged behind her as she rushed back to the dining room. She felt it wrapping around her ankles as Fozzie reached forward and rescued the laptop when she started to stumble. She managed to catch herself before she went down, and given the circumstances, she'd forgive him for saving the laptop over her.

In the endless minutes it took for her laptop to come to life, Torie imagined Palmer and Abbott bashing down Brad's door. Fozzie had their guns, but that didn't mean they couldn't have more. She paced from one end of the table to the other, hugging her arms around herself as if she could cram everything back inside.

"I'm so sorry. I didn't know," she whispered.

Fozzie grabbed her by the elbow, swinging her around. "No apologies. You *didn't* know, and it's still damn hard for anyone to find you because you sent an e-mail."

"But the possibility is there, or Carrie wouldn't be doing whatever it is she's doing." She craned her neck, trying to see past Carrie's back and onto the laptop screen. Fozzie dragged her to the living room and sat her on the couch.

"Very slim odds, Sunshine. Did you send any other e-mails?"

"Just to Derek Wingard and to Kathy's parents. Derek asked me if I had any of Kathy's research notes."

"And did you?"

"Only one set she gave me when we were at Isla Caribe. I never got around to looking at them, and then when she died, it didn't seem to matter. I almost threw them out, but they seemed a link to Kathy."

"What did you tell him?"

"I said I'd look, and if I found them, I'd fax them to him."

"Do you have them here?"

Realization clanged in her head like a Chinese gong. "You think that's what those thugs were looking for? But why? Did you find a link between them and Derek Wingard?"

"Trying to keep things simple. You have something someone might want. People are coming after you. Makes sense that they're related."

"What about my father? The Epicurean connection?"

"Still a possibility, but the Wingard connection seems stronger. And simpler."

"I think I'd like to slit Occam's throat with his razor." She put her elbows on her thighs and lowered her head to her hands. Fozzie rubbed the tight muscles in her neck. "So, all this time it's been Wingard, not my father. Did I screw up? Is everyone in danger because of me?"

He gathered her into his arms. "No, no, no. Everything we did entailed a risk. Sometimes, no matter how careful you are, things happen. Like the electric repair guy being called to the shop where we stopped for lunch. That was pure luck—bad for us, good for them."

"I can't stand this. Sitting around. Waiting."

"Why don't you try reading?" Fozzie said. "Pass the time, take your mind of things."

"I couldn't concentrate."

"TV?"

She shook her head. "Just stay with me."

He stroked her hair. "No problem. I'm feelin' a bit superfluous myself."

She didn't know how long they'd been sitting when faint footfalls approached. Carrie entered the room. Torie jumped up. "What did you find? Should we pack and leave? I don't want anything to happen to you or Brad. You've been so generous."

Carrie eased herself into a chair opposite the couch. "Do you know how e-mail headers work?"

"No," Torie said.

"Well, they're like return addresses on envelopes. You need an IP address to get onto the Internet, and those IP addresses are part of the message. Most people don't bother to look at them. Your e-mail system was set to the normal display, so you can see who sent the message, but if you expand the headers, you can follow the e-mail's path from sender to you."

"Oh, God. So they know we're here?" Torie said.

"No, not here. Your first message went to info at Wingard Research. It was sent from your hotel. If the person receiving the e-mail knew what to look for, he'd be able to know the e-mail originated from a Plaza hotel."

"Which explains how they found us there," Fozzie said.

"But beyond that," Carrie said, "all they can see is our Internet e-mail provider's headquarters, which is in Virginia, so they can't find you here. Not without demanding that our Internet provider turn over the records, and they won't do that without official cause."

Torie almost collapsed with relief.

"See," Fozzie said. "You worried yourself half sick for nothing." He patted her thigh, then addressed Carrie. "We left the hotel a day early, left her rental car there, and got a new one delivered to the train station. By the time they realize we're gone, it'll be too late for them to track us."

"Unless they were watching the back door of the hotel, or the train station," Torie said.

"In which case, they'd have been here already," Fozzie said. "But we probably should leave tomorrow anyway. All we have to do is keep moving until after Monday, and whatever this was all about should have blown over."

"But what if it's something important?" Torie said. "Don't you think we should at least figure out what it is? What if it's something bad?"

"Bad for who?" Carrie asked. "It might be something bad for Abbott and his buddies, but good on a wider scale."

"All the more reason to figure it out," Torie said.

"Then I think you should come see what we've found," Carrie said.

Fozzie tried to curb his own anticipation. Torie was freaked out enough for the two of them. He hooked an arm around her waist in a sideways hug. "Easy, Sunshine," he whispered into her ear.

She slowed her pace, avoiding a rear-end collision, but he sensed her impatience as Carrie preceded them into the dining room. Brad looked over the top of his coffee mug, a hint of pride in his eyes. And maybe something more when Carrie glanced his way. Fozzie snugged Torie a little tighter against him.

"Here's a possible connection," Carrie said. She sat in front of the laptop. "Stuart Freeman has a brother, Lonnie. Who happens to work for Wingard Research."

Fozzie peered at the screen, at Wingard Research's Web site, where Carrie had selected their About Us page.

"I found an obituary for Stuart Freeman, which, after much digging, led me to Lonnie, which led me here," Carrie said.

Brad conspicuously cleared his throat.

"With help from the neighborhood PI, of course," Carrie said, turning to Brad and winking.

On the screen, a middle-aged man, balding, wearing black-framed glasses, had smiled stiffly for the camera.

"And there's Kathy," Torie said, her voice hushed. Her cheerful blonde image was framed in black, with a brief mention of her years of service and untimely demise. And, Fozzie noted, a link to making memorial donations.

"You could get a job working for Blackthorne," Fozzie said. "Jinx couldn't have done better."

"I'll keep it in mind," Carrie said. "But this reminds me why I was glad to leave my old job." She stood, stretched, and rubbed her neck. "Eyestrain, headaches and sore back muscles."

Brad stood. "It's late. I think we're going to call it a night. I've checked on Lonnie, and his record seems clean. I can make a few follow-up calls in the morning." He rested his hand on Carrie's shoulder and kneaded the muscles. "Good work, kiddo."

"You're no slouch yourself, retired detective." Carrie tilted her head up and beamed at him.

"You two should get some sleep," Brad said. "It's been a long day."

"Good night," Torie said. She hadn't taken her eyes off the laptop monitor.

Carrie initiated the shutdown process. "Brad's right. You should get to bed." She folded the laptop screen down. Torie continued to stare at the space as if the images were still there.

Fozzie waited for the couple to leave the room. He couldn't help but notice the way Brad's hand laced with Carrie's as they walked. Images of his mum and dad twirled around his head, dissolving only to rematerialize as Torie.

Danger. Danger Will Robinson. Commitment Alert. L-word ahead.

Lust. That was the L-word. Had to be.

"You think we're safe?" Torie asked once they lay together in bed. "Really?"

He kissed the top of her head. "I trust Brad and Carrie. If they called it a night, so can we."

"You think they're . . . doing . . . you know . . . upstairs? The way they were looking at each other?"

"Oh, yeah." He gazed toward the ceiling. "I hope their room isn't right above this one."

"It's sweet, though, isn't it? That they're still obviously in love. Somehow, I can't imagine my parents *ever* being in love, much less—"

"Everyone knows parents never have sex," Fozzie said. "Although Brad and Carrie do remind me a bit of me mum and dad."

"Do you think you'll ever find someone like that?"

I might already have. "Don't know. Haven't really thought about it."

She sighed. "Guess we should try to sleep."

"Guess so." With a valiant effort, he turned his back to her. "G'night, Sunshine."

As if he could sleep. She'd opted for the cotton sleep shirt, not the satin nightie he'd added to her purchases. Taking that as a sign, he'd put on a pair of briefs. In the small bed, his bare back pressed against the warmth of hers. Sign or not, the cotton layer between them seemed very flimsy.

He forced himself into sleep mode. His training meant he could tell himself to sleep, and he would. He'd slept in the hot, sticky jungle with its raucous background noises of squawking birds and buzzing insects. In the cold, dry desert nights with the wind howling. In a makeshift shelter with rain dripping in. And countless combat naps grabbed on the helo, with the engine and rotor noise nothing more than a distant lullaby. But, now, in a warm, comfortable bed with only the soft even sounds of Torie's breathing, sleep taunted him like a lamb bolting from the flock.

When she turned over and it wasn't her back, but her breasts, pressing against him, he gritted his teeth. When her arm draped over him, he sucked in a breath and captured her hand, moving it out of range of his aching cock. When she wriggled closer until he didn't think there was a cell in his body unaware of her presence, he surrendered and placed her hand where he might find some relief. Slowly, gently, he rocked his hips against her hand. Her fingers slid inside his briefs. Her thumb swirled around his tip, spreading the slick evidence of how aroused he was.

"You can't sleep either?" she asked. "I'm still wired. Must be the coffee."

"Mmmh."

"It feels kind of weird, though. You know, with them upstairs."

It felt anything but weird. He couldn't stop his hips, and his erection slid back and forth along her fingers. "They're . . . um . . . probably . . ."

"Actually, it's kind of a turn-on. Is that crazy?"

Lord almighty, how could she *talk?* He found a couple of brain cells that weren't connected to his cock. "Then I must be ready for the funny farm."

"Touching you is a turn-on, too." She slid his briefs down. He kicked them off. She gripped him tighter. His pace increased. Her hips ground against him in a matching rhythm. Her breasts rubbed along his back. What had happened to her shirt? Her breathing grew faster, her breath fanning his skin in short, hot bursts.

One more stroke. He'd enjoy one more stroke, and then he'd find a condom, or at least do his part for Torie. One more. Okay, maybe two, but that was it. Only she did something with her thumb at the end of the stroke. Oh, that felt good. Just one more time with that extra bit. And oh, oh, Christ, he came. And came. And came.

Lord, he was a weak, self-centered, selfish sod. No self-control.

Torie nuzzled his neck. "Did you like that?"

"I think it's obvious. Altogether too obvious. But—" He flipped around and found a breast with his mouth. Sucked, licked, nipped it until she squirmed. His fingers sought the cleft between her legs, opening her to him. He found his target, hot, slick and swollen beneath his touch. Abandoning it, he explored her depth, stroking her in a slow, easy rhythm. She wiggled, silently begging him to touch her where she needed it most. "You do it," he said.

Her eyes popped open. "What?"

"You heard me."

"I . . . can't. Not with you . . . watching."

His fingers continued to tease. "You're not going to tell me you never have."

Even in the dim moonlight filtering through the curtains, he knew she blushed. "But—"

He slipped a second finger inside her. Her hand approached her goal. A tentative touch. Her eyes closed. Her finger moved in tiny, rapid circles, then back and forth, then in circles again. Her nipples stood on end. As did his cock.

He withdrew his fingers gently and reached into the drawer of the end table where he'd stashed his condoms. Sheathing himself, he slid inside her. Her eyes opened and she smiled.

"Don't stop," he said. "Double your pleasure."

And his.

Sleep was no longer a problem. By the time he registered the distant ringing as a phone, it had stopped. Not his phone, that's why it hadn't awakened him. Right. He was in Idaho. And, from the way he was hot and cold at the same time, and his stomach was doing the two-step, he was either coming down with the flu or in love with Torie. He ran the back of his hand over his forehead. No fever.

When the ringing in his ears picked up again, he realized the sound came from their overnight case.

Chapter Twenty-Six

Torie clutched the sheet to her chest. Fozzie crouched in the corner of the room, rummaging through their small suitcase. At four in the morning?

"Damn, I'm an idiot," he said. "A total, bloody idiot."

"What? What's wrong?" She dug through the covers and found her sleep shirt. Pulling it over her head and struggling to get her arms into the sleeves, she rushed to his side.

"Abbott's bloody cell phone. I chucked it in here along with Palmer's. His was dead, but I totally forgot Abbott's. Never gave it another thought."

"So, someone called him?" She sat at the foot of the bed waiting for her heart to stop pounding. "At four in the morning?"

Fozzie stared at the display and pushed some buttons. "Something to write with?"

She crawled over the bed and found her purse. Her new purse that had yet to accumulate the normal clutter. "No worries. I'll find something. Back in a tick."

He smiled. "See you're learning to speak Strine."

She padded out to the kitchen and found a notepad and pen by the phone. She hurried back and turned them over to Fozzie. He pushed some more buttons, scribbled something on the paper, then tossed the phone into the suitcase. He shoved at his hair.

"Well?" she asked. "Tell me what it means."

"It means we might have a way to figure out who Abbott was reporting to, assuming they were using this phone. And I'm sure they were. There's not much battery left, so I copied the numbers of the last few calls. No point in waking Brad and Carrie at this hour. We'll check it out in the morning."

Technically, it *was* morning. "I'm not going to be able to get back to sleep. Isn't there anything we can do on our own?"

"I don't know. Brad's got all the PI connections. But I suppose we could Google a bit."

Why did it sound so suggestive the way he said it? She watched his bare bottom as he sauntered into the bathroom. Very fine.

When he came back into the room, he said, "We should work in here. No need to disturb anyone."

"You can start the laptop." She brushed past him on her way to the bathroom. Tendrils of desire snaked through her. Again? She was tired, and sore, and sticky, and . . . and she still wanted more of him. To be with him. To feel his warmth in bed. Of course she would. It was only logical. He'd rescued her. He was protecting her.

She considered that as she cleaned herself. Protecting her? Yeah, right. As if what they'd done earlier was for her protection. She waited for the inevitable regret or embarrassment to descend. Yet he'd been kind, not demanding, and had her enjoying things in a way she'd never have thought she could. She felt . . . satisfied. Confident. And for some reason, confused.

She dried off and folded the towel. She would definitely have to do the laundry before leaving. Now, thinking about the sheets they'd messed up, the embarrassment hit. Great. Embarrassed by laundry, but not by the act that created it.

Smiling, she found Fozzie sitting cross-legged on the bed, her computer in his lap. He looked up long enough to give her one of those lazy, bone-melting grins. Well, her bones had melted enough for a while. "Find anything?"

"Just getting started. I'm checking a few reverse directories for the numbers I found on the cell phone. Only most cell phones aren't listed on the free public sites."

She crawled up beside him, watched him work. He smelled a little like soap and a lot like musky sex. He frowned, clicked, frowned, then stared at the screen. "Find something?"

"Abbott sent and received calls from a Miami cell-phone number. Trouble with cell phones is they don't stay where they're registered. We can't be sure it was actually placed from Miami. Not without some help."

"Wingard Research is in Miami."

"So is Lonnie Freeman. That goes along with what Brad found. If Abbott and Palmer and Stuart Freeman were buddies, then it's reasonable to expect Stuart's brother might have known them as well."

"Wasn't Abbott married to the sister? But what about the other guy? Garcia?"

Fozzie shook his head and scrawled something on the paper she'd brought in. "He was in Ohio according to Brad. And no calls from there that I can find."

"So we should be looking at Wingard Research," she said. "I'll go get a bigger pad of paper."

"Any coffee left?"

"I hate to go clunking around in their kitchen, but if there's any from the last pot, I can nuke it."

He didn't look up. "Thanks."

She turned the light on in the kitchen and found enough coffee in the pot for a cup. While she waited for the microwave to heat it, she tiptoed into the den and found the tablet Brad had been writing on.

She padded back into the bedroom, set the coffee on the night table, and the tablet and another pen beside Fozzie, who grunted something unintelligible.

"I'll take that as a thank-you," she said. Refusing to become nothing more than a gofer, she dug out the notes Kathy had given her. The night air chilled her and she dragged on a sweatshirt and pulled the blanket over her legs, settling in beside Fozzie. She leafed through the technical-jargon filled pages. It looked like two copies of some kind of case report but dated several months apart. She separated the pile into two stacks, then picked up the first page of each.

The words "Willamette Syndrome" leaped off the page.

"Fozzie." When he didn't reply, she nudged him.

"Huh?"

"Geez, were you asleep?"

"Taking an eyeball break is all." He reached for the coffee and took several healthy swallows.

She waved the papers in his face. "Wingard Research is connected to Willamette Syndrome. These are clinical studies. Confidential clinical studies. No wonder Derek Wingard wanted to know if I had them."

"What do they say?"

"How the heck should I know? Kathy's got some notes on the newer set. But, judging from the date, she probably didn't get these until right before we left for Isla Caribe. Her notes stop after the third page. Most likely, she planned to study them on the trip."

"Why did she give them to you if they were confidential?"

"Fresh eyes, I think. I found some typos and discrepancies in a report she was writing once—nothing confidential—and Kathy broke the rules and had me proofread for her occasionally. But this is a clinical study, and it's not her department."

"You think you can figure out why it's so important?"

"I'll try. But not here." Not with his distracting presence. "I'm going to have to spread out. I'll work in the kitchen. Why don't you see if you can find any more of those Willamette sites?"

She dug through the suitcase for her sweatpants and socks. "I might have to risk clunking around the kitchen and waking Brad and Carrie, because there's no way I'm going to get through these reports without coffee."

"I'm sure they'll understand."

"Understanding won't make them less tired." She rubbed her eyes and carried the two stacks of paper to the kitchen. As quietly as possible, she set a pot of coffee to brew, then plunged into the task. Each report was over twenty-five pages long. Picking up page one from each stack, she sighed and started reading. For now, she'd ignore Kathy's notes and form her own impressions.

She didn't know how much time had passed, only that she was on page eleven when strong, warm fingers, accompanied by Fozzie's scent, massaged her shoulders. She lowered her head. "Okay, but in twenty minutes, you're going to have to stop."

He nuzzled her neck. "You going to share the coffee?"

"Help yourself."

He filled his cup and brought it to the table. Pulling a chair out, he sat across from her. "Find anything?"

She chewed on the end of the pen. "Maybe. What about you?"

"Same."

"Good morning." Brad, a white T-shirt showing at the neck of a plaid flannel robe, crossed the kitchen and helped himself to coffee. "You're up early."

"I'm sorry. We tried to be quiet," Torie said.

"I'm up early most mornings," Brad said. "Never could see much point in wasting the day. You've been working, I take it?"

After explaining what they'd discovered, Fozzie retreated to the bedroom and returned with Abbott's cell phone. "Forgot I had the bugger. And it's been on for a few days, so there's not much battery. You think you can get his contacts and trace his recent calls? I got as far as Miami, but the rest of the information is off-limits to private-citizen blokes."

"You know," Brad said, "a lot of people think hacking into computer systems is how the bad guys get their information. In reality, social engineering is much more efficient and effective."

"Social engineering?" Torie asked.

"Fancy highfalutin word for schmoozing," Brad said. "Much easier to convince someone to *give* you information than to break into computers and find it yourself."

"So, did you do a lot of . . . social engineering . . . when you were a cop?" she asked.

Brad grinned. "My lips are sealed." He took the phone. "Miami, you said? It's past nine there. Let's see what I can find."

"So, anything popping?" Fozzie asked. Torie's eyes were rimmed in red, and her hair stuck out in unruly spikes as if she'd been yanking on it. She had four stacks of paper in front of her—two faceup and two facedown.

"I've got two clinical study reports," she said. "Three months apart. Everything is written in Science-ese. They've listed all the test results, everything that might be a side effect."

She took a sip from her mug, grimaced and carried it to the sink and dumped the contents.

"And?" he asked.

"And I see some differences in the wording here and there, but nothing remarkable. Some differences in the side-effect percentages."

"Well, if the studies are three months apart, that's not unexpected, right?"

She went back to the table and sat. "I'll have to wade through the rest before I can draw any conclusions. What about you?

Find anything useful?"

"Useful? I don't know. But interesting. I spent some time reading that support group site for Willamette Syndrome. Not everyone used their names, but I'm fairly sure all the names from Kathy's list were there. There were about ten contributors who mentioned being part of a clinical study. I wonder if it was Wingard's."

"No way to tell from this report," she said.

"So, there are no names on what you have?"

"No. Everything's encoded. All numbers. But given how little attention is paid to these orphan diseases, I can't imagine more than one company researching a treatment."

He took a breath before broaching the next topic. "And you're positive that these reports Kathy gave you originated because Wingard is doing the research into finding a treatment for Willamette Syndrome?"

"Why would I think otherwise? Kathy gave me the papers." Her eyes shot open to saucer size. "Are you insinuating that Kathy was into . . . industrial espionage, or whatever you call it? That she was trying to steal this report and—no, that's impossible. And if she were, she would *never* have let me see it. But she wouldn't do anything like that. Not Kathy. Not ever. How could you even *think* that? And besides, this is a report about results. Not a how-to manual on creating a drug."

He grabbed for her flailing hands. "Hey, take it easy. I didn't see the report, remember? It's one possibility that came to mind. One we'd have to eliminate."

She jerked her hands from his grasp. "Well, consider it eliminated. Wingard Research is trying to find a treatment for Willamette Syndrome. End of discussion. Tell Occam to put that up his razor and slice it."

His jaw hurt from trying not to laugh at the intensity of her outburst. A genuine spitfire. But cute. Too damn cute.

"I believe you," he said. "We take the simplest explanation, which is that the ten people from the Internet support group are part of a case study testing a treatment developed by Wingard Research. They were all excited about it, because the survival rate for the disease is low. Most people with it die within ten years of diagnosis. The gist was they felt that anything that extended their life expectancy was a good thing."

"So, they died, but they might have died sooner without the treatment?"

"Sounds like it. Does your paperwork give any of those details about the subjects?"

Torie worried her lower lip and flipped through the pages. "No, only that there were eighty subjects. It gives age ranges, gender breakdown and says that all have been diagnosed within the last five years."

"Which means some might have been too far gone to save."

A sadness filled Torie's eyes. "Did they talk about how they were doing? Did they compare notes?"

Fozzie shrugged. "A little. Not a lot of details. I guess they all knew the symptoms so they didn't need to rehash them in depth. They'd write things like 'took the stairs today' or 'no problems after dinner.' Like they'd all know what the typical problems after dinner might be."

"Did Kathy post anything to that site?"

"Not under her name," he said. "I checked. But if she was trying to get an inside scoop on how the treatment worked, it wouldn't be kosher for her to admit who she was."

Torie gave an acknowledging nod. "Doesn't mean she didn't hit the site. I don't suppose you checked my e-mail to see if the Townsends sent Kathy's bookmarks?"

"No. But you can if you want a break."

"Maybe when I finish going through these files." She yawned and pressed the heels of her hands against her eyes.

"You should eat something. Give yourself an energy boost."

"I feel like I've overstepped the boundaries by making coffee. I'm not going to help myself to food. I'm fine."

She picked up another page from each of the faceup stacks. He watched her intense concentration as she tracked a paragraph with her pen on one page, then repeated it on another.

"Too bad they're not computerized. You could let the computer compare them."

"Don't think I haven't thought of that." She didn't take her eyes from the page. "About a hundred times."

"What if I read it out loud? Would that save time?"

She looked at him as if he'd handed her a diamond necklace. Her smile was ten times brighter than any jewels. Without saying a word, she passed one of the stacks of paper to him.

He took the top sheet and started reading. Lord have mercy, this was dryer than the specifications for an infrared sensor. He stopped trying to comprehend and simply read the words.

"This next bit's a bunch of numbers," he said after picking up the next sheet. Almost the last sheet.

She turned the one they'd just finished into her facedown pile and picked up the next. "Got it. Just take it slow."

He read them off as Torie ticked things on the page, nodding as she went. "Wait," she said. "What was that?"

"Males, thirty-six, females, forty-four," he repeated.

"You're sure?"

He rubbed his eyes. "Yes, thirty-six and forty-four."

Her eyebrows came together and she picked up the paper. "I've got twenty-six and thirty-four." She scrabbled through the previous pages searching for something, then shoved the second facedown stack at him. "Go back. Look at page four."

He found the page. "What am I looking for?"

"Read the fourth paragraph."

"For this study, eighty subjects, all diagnosed with Willamette

279

Syndrome—"

"Stop. Read this." She handed him her page.

He shrugged. "For this study, sixty subjects—ah—the numbers are different."

"I missed it. Expected to see an eight and so I didn't notice it was a six."

"It's not a typo?"

She glared at him. "Do the math. The totals add up correctly in each report."

"So, the newer one used fewer subjects. Why is that a big deal?"

She grabbed his stack, dug out a page, then found what he assumed was the comparable one from hers. Her gaze moved back and forth between them. "Stupid, stupid."

"What's wrong?"

"I glossed over the opening bits. I assumed, like you did, that these were separate studies. But it's not a new study," she said. "Only a new *report*." She thrust the first pages at him. "See. Same dates. Same study code number."

"And what do you think it means?" he asked. "Assuming it's not a mistake."

"I don't see how. I think someone deliberately changed the data so the results would make the drug look good. Those twenty missing subjects probably didn't respond the right way."

"As in, maybe they died?"

"Died, got sicker, who knows?"

"Maybe they dropped out."

"I'm no expert, but I'm pretty sure that studies like this are supposed to keep everyone in the data. They can't pick and choose which results they want to use. You've got the newer report. Does yours say anything about dropouts, or mortality? Anything about the number of subjects?"

He scanned the rest of the pages. "Nope. No disclaimers, no

nothing. It's based on sixty subjects."

Torie pushed her chair back, got up and paced the kitchen. "I can't believe Kathy would be involved in something this . . . unethical."

He let her work off steam, then stepped into her path and put his hands on her shoulders. "Look at it from the other side. She saw the reports, something didn't ring true. But she didn't have time to check them out word for word the way you did. Or she didn't want to, not with a vacation starting. And as long as you're there with her, she asks you to do an impartial read."

Some of the tension left her face. "Right. And someone else knew about the report. And that's what they've been looking for. Lonnie Freeman." Her eyes widened. "Now I remember. When Derek Wingard was there, in Kathy's hospital room, he told her Lonnie Freeman would be taking over. But what if he was already involved? If anyone found out, Kathy would take the fall, because it was her project."

"Maybe we need to look at Lonnie Freeman a little closer," Fozzie said. He took Torie's hand and headed toward the den.

CHAPTER TWENTY-SEVEN

Brad looked up from the phone when they walked into the den. He held up a finger, motioning them to wait. Torie felt Fozzie's hand on her back and searched for patience. After drinking three cups of coffee, the caffeine coursing through her bloodstream and the acid churning in her stomach made that one a tough sell.

Finally, Brad hung up the phone. "Talked to some folks in Miami. Rumblings that Lonnie Freeman owes some bucks to the sharks. He was hospitalized for a broken leg a few months ago. Claimed he fell down a flight of stairs, but the docs didn't think the injuries were consistent with a fall."

"Kathy said he was accident prone," Torie said. "He'd smashed his fingers in a car door before she and I left on vacation."

"Maybe he had some help," Fozzie said.

"This is starting to sound like a television show," Torie said. "Big, ugly loan shark comes collecting debts with a baseball bat."

"They may get the forensics wrong on television," Brad said, "and play fast and loose with the legal system, but they usually get the human nature part right. There are lots of nasty people out there who think the rules don't apply to them."

Fozzie's hand slid down to her butt before he crossed the room and sat down. "How does this play out? Lonnie Freeman needs money, and he goes to a loan shark for it, so it must be urgent. He must also assume he's going to be able to pay it back."

"Or he thinks what will happen if he doesn't get the money he's trying to borrow is worse than what the sharks might do to him," Torie said. "But, right now, don't you think it's more important to figure out what's going on with the Willamette drug? And with Wingard Research?"

Brad nodded. "When Carrie gets up, I'll see if she can talk to some of her contacts at the *Sentinel.*"

"Thanks," Torie said.

"And the reason we came in here," Fozzie said, "was to tell you we found what looks like falsified clinical study data. Reports Lonnie Freeman undoubtedly had access to."

"You think he forged them?" Brad asked.

"We don't know," Torie said. "Maybe he . . . socially engineered . . . someone to manipulate the data. We could be wrong. For all we know, there's another report lying around somewhere that explains the discrepancies we found. Don't you think we should tell Derek Wingard?"

Brad shook his head. "Not yet. If there is something fishy going on at Wingard Research, we can't assume Derek Wingard isn't in on it as well."

"I met the man," Torie protested. "He seemed to want to find real cures, not cheat. He'd want to know if someone in his company is falsifying data."

"I have to agree with Brad," Fozzie said. "Until we know for sure, it's better not to trust anyone. He could have come to Isla Caribe to make sure Kathy didn't survive to blow the whistle on his scheme."

Torie remembered him at Kathy's bedside. Could he have done something that made her sicker? Done something to kill her? Her stomach roiled, not only from the acid. She'd had dinner with the man and hadn't suspected a thing. What if he'd wanted to get rid of her, too?

Carrie entered the room on a cloud of a fresh, fruity scent, braiding her wet hair. She strode to Brad's chair and kissed his cheek. "Sorry I slept so long. I'll fix breakfast."

Torie saw the look they exchanged. The way Carrie . . . glowed. Heat rose to her face as she thought of what probably caused that glow. Carrie turned and looked directly at her. Then at Fozzie. And back at her. And smiled.

Oh, God, was it as obvious on *her* face? Fozzie was studying his fingernails. "Please, don't go to any trouble," she said. "We've put you out so much already."

"We'll fend for ourselves. I've got a little job for you," Brad said to Carrie.

Torie couldn't wait for Brad to explain. "Rumor has it that something big's going on at Wingard, but everything is hush-hush," she blurted out. "We think it might be related to a new treatment for Willamette Syndrome."

Carrie lifted two fingers in a mock salute. "Then I'd better get to work. Help yourself to anything in the kitchen. Cereal's in the pantry. Bagels in the freezer."

"One more thing," Brad said to Torie. "Can we borrow your laptop?"

Fozzie zipped away, returning seconds later with Torie's computer. "Here you go. What are you looking for?"

"Just dotting the i's and crossing the t's. I want to check Torie's e-mail again," Brad said.

"If there's another message from Kathy's parents, let me know," Torie said, hovering over Brad's shoulder.

Fozzie took her hand and tugged her out of the room. "We'll grab some breakfast and let you work."

"Do you think it showed?" Torie asked Fozzie as they sat at the table eating cereal.

"What showed?"

"You know. On us. What we did."

He tossed her a grin. "Had some mind-blowing sex, you mean?"

She hid behind a mouthful of cereal. Brad and Carrie looked like they were in love. Like they might have shared some mind-blowing *love*making. Surely Fozzie knew there was a difference.

Of course he did. And to him, she was an outlet for mind-blowing sex. Nothing more. She chided herself for feeling more for him than he could possible feel for her. Right now, finding out what was happening with Wingard Research was more important.

"Do you think it's Wingard or Freeman?" she asked.

"Why not both?"

"I don't know. I guess I'd be embarrassed to have been taken in by Derek Wingard."

Fozzie shrugged. "People lie all the time. Especially if there's something important at stake."

Like mind-blowing sex? Forget it. He'd never offered anything other than protection, which was his job. *But he said he wasn't on the job.* No, he'd said he wasn't working on a Blackthorne assignment.

"Hey, Sunshine. Come back to earth."

She gave a brisk head-clearing shake. "Sorry. Tired and confused. My mind's all over the place."

"No wonder. It's been a hell of a few days. But it should be over soon."

"Mmph." She swallowed her last bite of cereal and scraped her chair away from the table. "I forgot to ask Carrie and Brad about mystery Monday."

She hurried to the den, halting in the doorway. Oh, Lord. Carrie sat at her laptop, and Brad stood over her, nuzzling her neck. And his hand—was it grazing her breast? Thank goodness their backs were to the open door. She backed up, cleared her throat loudly and tapped on the jamb.

Brad straightened. But slowly. Casually. Without a hint of embarrassment. Which was fine, because she was embarrassed enough for all three of them. "Yes?" he said.

"Um . . . I don't think . . . that is, we didn't mention that Abbott said he was going to keep me in his basement until Monday, and then he'd let me go. So, we thought something important was going to happen on Monday that I might know something about, but I didn't, but now—"

He laughed. "And now you think it might be related to Wingard Research and the drug study."

"Yes. Exactly."

"I might have something," Carrie said. "But it's for Friday, not Monday."

"What?" Torie's heart thumped.

"All of this is unofficial, you understand," Carrie went on. "Rumor, but I'm getting it from more than one source."

"Let's hear it." Fozzie had wandered in, leaning against the doorjamb, one foot resting on the other.

"What do you know about the process of getting a drug approved for the market?" Carrie asked.

"Virtually nothing," Torie admitted. "Except they have to be tested and approved by the FDA, right?"

"Right," Carrie said. "I don't know much myself, but it's a long process, and can be very expensive. What I'm finding is that Wingard Research developed a drug and started running the first two phases of clinical trials. If everything looked promising, they were going to turn it over to one of the big pharmaceutical houses to take it the rest of the way. For a hefty fee up front and a portion of the future revenue."

"Why not do it all themselves?" Fozzie asked.

"They're still too small," Carrie said. "With the profits from this drug, they can expand and do more in the future."

Torie mulled that over for a moment. "So, the big companies don't want to deal with the orphan diseases because there's not much profit in it—not enough people with the disease—in their bottom-line mind-set to justify the expense. But if someone's already got the foundation established, then they're willing to follow through."

"That's how I see it," Carrie said.

"Makes sense," Fozzie said.

Torie rested her hands on her hips. "Well, it would be nicer if the big companies put the bucks into curing the obscure diseases in the first place, but this sounds like a reasonable compromise. But the drug might not be effective. It's possible the report left out some of the people in order to make the data look good."

"And Wingard or Freeman thought you had the report and couldn't risk you figuring it out and blowing the whistle and killing the deal."

"Word on the street is that the deal goes down Friday."

"So, they keep me quiet until Monday, when it's too late to do anything."

"Makes sense," Fozzie said again.

"I still don't think Derek is in it," Torie said.

"It's moot," Brad said. "Lonnie Freeman had the connections to the kinds of people who wouldn't mind doing the dirty work. Whether Derek started it, or Lonnie did, that doesn't change the fact that the report is falsified." He set the mouse aside, stretched his arms skyward and rubbed his jaw. "And the e-mail from Kathy's parents had the same IP as the one from Wingard Research."

Torie's head spun. "You mean Kathy's parents are in on it?"

"No," Brad said. "What I mean is that whoever received your initial message probably set up that free Hotmail account so that you'd think it came from the Townsends."

"Can you tell who at Wingard Research sent it?" Fozzie asked.

Brad shook his head. "Not without probable cause and a warrant. We're nowhere near that yet."

"Well, we have to stop it," Torie said. "People could die if the drug goes into production."

"How?" Fozzie said. "We don't even know which pharmaceutical company it is. Or how the ten people we found on the web support site died. It could have had nothing to do with the treatment. And there are ten other missing subjects."

"Isn't that in the report?" Brad asked.

"The data are there, but we don't know who those missing subjects were. Or why they were left out of the new report." Torie looked at Carrie. "Should we leak something to the press?"

"Unsubstantiated rumors? Coming from someone who knows nothing about either the disease or the drug?" Carrie shook her head. "I don't think so. And certainly not in time. It's already Wednesday."

"But they abducted me. Us." She turned to Fozzie, imploring. "That has to prove something."

"We have no proof," he said. "Your word against a prominent businessman."

"Well, we've got to do *something*. I'm not going to sit here with my head in the sand until it's too late."

"But what if we're wrong?" Fozzie asked. "We could ruin a deal that might save lives. And if we destroy Wingard's reputation groundlessly, that might cost even more lives, considering all the future drugs he might discover."

"So, what we need is someone with clout, but not the police or the media?" she said.

"Even if you knew someone, I don't see how they could pull it off before Friday," Brad said.

Torie stormed off to the bedroom, closing the door behind

her. She sat on the edge of the bed, head in her hands, trying to think.

She couldn't sit by and do nothing. Kathy had died, believing in what Wingard Research was doing. Now Torie understood the urgency of Kathy's words to her. She'd known there was something wrong. And Torie had blown her off, thinking it was because she might get caught letting an outsider look at Wingard Research files.

She exhaled a shaky breath. She knew what she had to do. She found her cell phone. With trembling fingers, she pressed the keypad.

Fozzie found Torie in the bedroom, sorting, folding, and packing clothes. Sorting as in his and hers. "We going somewhere?" he asked. He set the laptop on a clear spot on the bed.

"I am," she said without looking up. She spent a long moment meticulously smoothing out one of her shirts. Finally, she met his gaze. Her face was three shades paler than normal.

"Are you all right?" At his approach, she ducked her head again, repositioning a pair of her jeans in the suitcase. He stepped closer. Her hands gripped the jeans until her knuckles turned white. "What happened?"

She shook her head and added a stack of neatly folded underwear to the case. "Nothing. I have to go, that's all."

"Not alone," he said.

Still making a point of deliberately arranging every item in the suitcase precisely so, she said, "If you want, you can give me a lift to the airport. The car's rented in your name. You can either keep it, or turn it in if you want to go home. And I'll need an address so I can send you the money I owe you."

"Torie. Sunshine." He reached for her, but she shrank from his touch as if he'd burned her. He retreated to the door and closed it. "What's going on?" he asked, keeping his voice low.

Fierce determination was engraved on her face. "I have to do something. I'm doing it. Period. If you want to drive me to the airport, fine. Otherwise, I'll call for a cab."

"Fine." He grabbed his own possessions and crammed them into the smaller suitcase. "We'll talk on the way."

She grabbed a handful of clothes and disappeared into the bathroom. He heard the lock snick shut, then the shower turn on.

Crap. Was she thinking of confronting Wingard? Or Freeman? Damnation, not alone she wasn't. He searched the room, making sure he'd left nothing behind. He yanked the bed table drawer open. *Fuck.* The bloody guns. Their luggage didn't come close to the TSA regulations for checking them. Would Brad have a gun case he could borrow? But then there was all the hassle of getting it back to him.

No matter. The guns weren't his to begin with. If he and Torie were going to Miami, he'd have Blackthorne resources available. He'd leave the guns with Brad. It wasn't like they'd be getting into a shootout at the airport.

He finished packing, sat on the bed and waited. When Torie emerged from the bathroom, she wore her new black slacks and a turtleneck. Carrying a bundle of towels, she scuttled to the far side of the bed giving him clear access.

"All yours," she said.

"Torie—"

"I'm going to thank Brad and Carrie for their hospitality." She waited, trapped between the bed and the wall, for him to enter the bathroom.

"Fine." He walked into the steamy bathroom and closed the door behind him. For someone who always wanted to talk, who insisted he tell her everything, she was being annoyingly closemouthed. He stood under the shower spray a good long time, letting the hot water wash off some of his irritation.

Showered and dressed, he felt only slightly better. Was he upset because Torie wouldn't speak to him? Well, yes, but even the silent shouting going on in his head wouldn't stop telling him he was upset because she was leaving and didn't want him along. He opened the bathroom door and found the smaller suitcase, the one Torie had designated as his, lying empty on the floor. Hers was zipped and standing by the outside door. The bed was stripped, all evidence of what they'd shared gone.

He collected his towels and headed in the direction of voices. Carrie smiled and took the towels from him. "This really wasn't necessary."

"Not a problem," he said. "We're most appreciative of everything you did for us."

"We enjoyed helping," she said. "Helps keep the brain from stagnating. Not that I don't enjoy retirement, but the days have a tendency to blend into one another."

"I'll take the towels to the washer," Torie said. She ignored Carrie's protests and whisked them away.

"Would you like something for the plane? Sandwich? Apple?" Carrie asked.

"No, we'll be fine," Fozzie said.

Torie returned. "The washer's not done with the sheets yet, so I couldn't start the towels. If you have another set, I'll remake the bed."

"Don't worry about it. I'll take care of it. I have your cell number, so if we find anything more, we'll be sure to let you know."

"Thanks so much." Torie flung her arms around Carrie. "I guess I'll go say good-bye to Brad." She walked past Fozzie as if he were invisible and left the kitchen.

Carrie came over, stood on tiptoe and gave him a friendly hug. "You keep an eye on her. She's in a new place and hasn't quite put everything together."

By "new place," he was darn certain Carrie hadn't meant Idaho. "You can count on it," he said. Brad came into the room, Torie almost hiding behind him.

"Guess we'll be off, then," Fozzie offered his hand. "My thanks."

"Any time," Brad said, gripping Fozzie's hands in both of his. "You're always welcome."

Moments later, they'd piled everything into the car. Torie clicked her seat belt shut and clutched her purse in her lap as if she was afraid it would jump out the window if she let go.

Brad and Carrie waved from their front porch, his arm around her waist. Jinx knew how to pick them.

Torie remained annoyingly distant. Once they hit the interstate, he'd had enough. "This silent treatment isn't like you, Torie. Will you at least tell me where we're going? You're scaring me." To lighten the mood, he shot her a quick grin. "And it scares me worse not knowing."

She wiped her hands on her slacks. "Sorry. I know. I'm scared, too."

"Of what? Tell me so I can help."

"I thought I could do it myself. I really wanted to prove that I could."

"Do what? You don't have to prove anything to me."

"I called him this morning. I have to see him. Face to face."

"You did what? I won't let you talk to Derek Wingard or Lonnie Freeman by yourself."

She looked at him for the first time since breakfast. "Why would I do that? We already decided we didn't have enough information to confront them. And they'd deny it. And maybe lock me up again."

At least she understood that much. That shaved some of the rough edges off his apprehension. "Over my dead body," he said. "But I'm sure glad to know you're not doing anything foolish."

"I wouldn't be so sure."

CHAPTER TWENTY-EIGHT

Torie pressed her fingers into her temples where a headache pounded. "I called my grandfather."

"Why would you do that after all the efforts you've made to avoid him and your father?"

"It wasn't easy. But I couldn't think of anything else to do. And I know Kathy wasn't involved in any wrongdoing. She would have tried to make things right if she was alive. I have to do this. For her."

"Do what? What can your grandfather do?"

"You know what FDA stands for, right?"

"Sure. Food and Drug Administration. They're the ones who have to approve Wingard's drug."

"That's the D part. Epicurean falls under the F. Food. Grandfather has contacts. And clout. He's the only one I know who might be able to make sure everything is on the up and up, and he can do it discreetly. But he insists on a face-to-face before he'll agree to help."

"Can I do anything?"

She wanted to say no. That she could march into her grandfather's house and ask for help as the new, confident, empowered Torie. But inside, she was jelly. She always felt twelve when she dealt with her father. But Grandfather? He didn't belittle her the way her father did. Just dismissed the fact she might possibly have a brain. Or feelings.

They swung into the airport parking lot. "Don't see an

294

Enterprise return," Fozzie said. "Hand me the rental agreement from the glove box. I'll call and tell them to come pick it up."

"That's going to cost extra. Be sure to save the receipt. I'm paying half."

"Torie—" He stopped. Ran his fingers through his hair. "Fine."

Visions of marching into her grandfather's house sent a hive of bees buzzing in her belly. Even though she was still sitting in the car, she knew her knees would shake when she tried to stand. Stern, gruff, and no-nonsense, Grandfather bent his rules for nobody, not even a four-year-old who barged into his study without knocking and waiting for permission to enter. All she'd wanted was to show him a new dress. Maybe for him to say it was pretty. Not even that *she* was pretty. Tears stung her eyes at the memory. She blinked them away.

Grandfather had no place for tears. She wasn't sure she could handle facing him without her voice catching. And if it did, it wouldn't matter what the request. His answer, as always, would be no.

Fozzie sat beside her, not making any move to leave the car. He stared into the distance.

Ask him. He's not Grandfather.

She took a breath.

"I know you're probably antsy to get home, but would you be willing to come with me?" she asked. "For moral support? I feel stronger when you're around."

His eyes blinked into focus. "Of course I will. I'm surprised you think you need to ask." He reached over and touched her waist. "We're still joined at the hip, remember?"

Right. She was the one who needed protecting. Damn it, she didn't want to need protecting. But this was too important. If Derek Wingard was innocent, then she couldn't let his company, the one Kathy believed in, be ruined. And if he was guilty, then he deserved to be punished. But innocent people shouldn't have to die while another round of clinical studies was being run.

"I don't want you to do it because you feel obligated. I mean, I'm going to do it with or without you, but—"

He cut her off with a finger to her lips. "Obligated? I stopped feeling obligated about an hour after I met you."

"But your job?"

"Was secondary. And I told you, I'm not on the job now. I'm doing this because I bloody well love you."

Her heart stopped. Her mouth was probably doing that fish thing.

"Crap," he said. "That didn't come out right."

He sat there, frozen, looking scared to death. "That's all right," she said. "You can take it back. I'll understand."

"Take it back? Bloody hell, I'm not taking it back. I kind of figured there would be flowers, candles and some mushy music playing. But . . . well, it's done. I'm not exactly a poet, but I love you."

He *loved* her? He'd said it. Out loud. "I love you, too," she whispered. Her heart started beating again, triple speed.

He unfastened his seat belt and leaned across the car, dragging her into a kiss that curled her toes. She let herself be swept away. He said he loved her. Not as a way to get her into bed. Not in the heat of mind-blowing sex. Here, in a car, in an airport parking lot. The kiss didn't end as much as it tapered off, with promises of more. "We have to go," she said, her lips still against his.

"Right. Um . . . where are we going?"

"Los Angeles. Where Grandfather lives."

"Guess we should go buy some tickets."

Who needed a plane? The way she felt, she could fly straight to Los Angeles under her own power. Luggage and all.

His arm stayed wrapped around her as they stood in line at the ticket counter. "I'm still going to pay my share," she said when he presented his credit card.

"I've finally figured that one out." He handed her the receipt. "For your collection."

"Do I have a goofy grin all over my face?" she asked once they had boarded and settled into their seats.

"No more than mine," he said, touching his brow to hers.

"Grandfather is going to have a cow when he sees you."

"Not exactly the impression I want to make. Or the image I want in my head."

"No, I mean, you're . . . together. You'll be able to look him in the eye. I've never been able to look at anything but the floor when I'm in the room with him." She squeezed his arm. "I know I'll be able to get him to check into Wingard if you're there."

He brushed his lips against hers and ran the back of his hand along her cheek. "You've got the strength to do it. You don't need me. I've seen what you can do."

She shook her head. "You didn't grow up the way I did. I wish I had your confidence."

"You know what you want. You tell him. Go in strong. Chin high. Let your grandfather meet the Torie I know."

The way he said it, she almost believed it.

When the plane landed in Salt Lake City, she still felt airborne. Only the clicking of her loafers under her feet told her she was walking on ground, not air. She felt . . . ethereal. Passing the restrooms made her aware of the not-so-ethereal pressure on her bladder. "Be right back," she said.

Why were lines in ladies' rooms so long? And three of the stalls had "Out of Order" signs on them. The people running water to wash their hands and the toilets flushing only made the time seem more endless. Finally, she was next in line. When the stall door opened, she scurried toward it, her fingers already on the button of her slacks.

Relief at last.

Washing her hands, she looked at her reflection, almost expecting to see "This Woman Is In Love" flashing in bright neon on her forehead. And, yes, she still had that goofy grin on her face. She hurried out to catch up with the man who'd put it there.

When she couldn't spot him, she waited outside the men's room for a few minutes. Checking her watch, she realized they didn't have a lot of time to make their connection. He'd probably gone to the gate. She quickened her pace, scanning the throngs of people for his familiar head of curly hair.

At the gate, they were calling boarding zones. She checked her boarding pass. Zone three. She waited, trying to quell the rising panic. Only ticketed passengers could be in this section of the airport. Abbott, Palmer or Freeman couldn't have found them and grabbed Fozzie. She approached the counter.

"Excuse me?"

The clerk looked up from her computer. "Yes."

"Can you tell me if Foster Mayhew has boarded yet?"

The woman checked and shook her head. "No, not yet. But if you're taking this flight, you need to board. We'll be departing shortly."

Where had he gone? How could he disappear? Should she wait? No, she'd already made up her mind she had to see Grandfather. She'd planned to do it without Fozzie anyway.

As she stood in line to board, constantly looking over her shoulder, the man in line behind her chatted merrily on his cell phone.

Duh. Her phone. She'd turned it off when she'd boarded the plane in Twin Falls. If something had happened, Fozzie would have called her.

She fished the phone from her purse, cursing how long it took to turn on. After seven eternities she got the welcome screen and scrolled to her messages.

"Please find your seat," a flight attendant said, and Torie realized she was standing stock-still in the aisle.

"Sorry." She checked her boarding pass and moved to her row. A mountain of a man had the window. Hers was the middle seat. She dropped into the aisle seat, which should be Fozzie's, and pressed the button to retrieve her voice messages.

"Come on, come on," she muttered as the recorded voice told her more than she ever wanted to know about how many messages she had and which one she was listening to. She crammed the phone against her ear and plugged her finger into the other one, straining to make out Fozzie's voice.

"Torie. Look, something urgent came up with work. I can't talk now, but I'll call as soon as I can. Good luck with your grandfather. Be strong."

Be strong? What happened to "I love you"?

"What bloody happened?" Fozzie shouted as he barreled full tilt across the tarmac toward the waiting Blackthorne, Inc. Premier 1 jet. The one the boss used.

While he'd waited for Torie to finish in the loo, a phone call from the boss himself had sent Fozzie racing through the airport. He grabbed a cab, pissing off the driver who kept muttering there were shuttles to the nearby private strip every thirty minutes. When the boss called, you didn't wait thirty minutes, no matter if it meant a cabbie might be stuck with a short fare. You didn't wait five minutes for someone to finish in the loo. And you didn't go rushing into the Ladies and try to explain that you really, really had to leave. Now. Because if he'd seen Torie's face, gazed into her eyes, he'd be stuck explaining things she wasn't ready to deal with. Or was it things *he* wasn't ready to deal with?

At the jet's open door, an outstretched hand, attached to a man he'd never seen before, welcomed him. The boss had said a new pilot would be meeting him, yet Fozzie hesitated, one foot on the step, before climbing aboard. The boss had given him the pilot's name, but he wasn't getting into an airplane with an unidentified stranger. Even the boss's plane.

"I'm Charles Edwards," the man said. "You must be Foster Mayhew."

The name was right. Didn't mean it belonged to the guy standing there. "No offense, but how do I know you're legit?"

The man laughed. "Hotshot said you were careful. How about my pilot's license? Or do we do the secret Blackthorne handshake?" He flashed his ID.

Dropping Hotshot's name eased Fozzie's skepticism, but he checked the name and photo against the man in front of him. "Close enough," he said. The military cut in the photo had grown out, and he had a few more years on him, but they were the same man. Fozzie ducked and stepped into the jet. A glance established the plane was otherwise empty. He headed forward. "Second seat all right, or do you want me in back?"

"Up front's fine," the pilot said. He secured the door.

Fozzie stowed his bag, then climbed into his seat and settled a pair of headphones over his ears. He noted the casual competence as the man went through takeoff procedures. Once they were airborne, he repeated his original question. "What the bloody hell happened?"

"Grinch is down. We're going to get him out."

That last part was obvious. Blackthorne, Inc. left no man behind. The pilot hadn't said dead, and Fozzie was afraid to ask. But to pull Fozzie off mandatory vacation time indicated Grinch was still breathing. Body retrieval wouldn't be so urgent. Not unless there was something sticky going on and discovery of Grinch's body would make things dicey for Uncle Sam.

"Where are we going?" Fozzie asked.

"To the compound, then to Nicaragua," the pilot said. He turned toward Fozzie and smiled. "We haven't worked together yet. I've only been with the company three months. You can call me Cheese."

The pilot must have noticed the puzzled expression on Fozzie's face. "It's Charles Edwards, but folks called me Chuck. So, Chuck Edwards became Chuck E, which turned into Cheese."

Recognition dawned. "Ah, like the pizza place."

"Fun place if you've got kids."

"Back to the subject, mate. What happened in Nicaragua?"

"Missing person. Small-time local-government official claimed no knowledge, no help, no nothing. We got the call, we went in."

"And who was this missing person?" Fozzie asked.

"Travel photographer."

"For real? Or taking pictures of things more interesting to our esteemed uncle?"

"Not our place to ask. While Uncle was trying to follow the rule book, a Blackthorne team went in and whisked the guy away," Cheese replied.

"Who was on intel?" Fozzie asked.

"It wasn't that kind of a problem. We located the target, everything ran like clockwork for extraction. But the guy had stashed his camera and—"

"Those better have been some damn fine pictures," Fozzie said.

"The guy was hurt—not bad, but bad enough he couldn't be discreet about sneaking in for his camera. We moved to Plan B."

"So much for clockwork," Fozzie finished.

"Grinch played decoy. Manny got the camera. But they got Grinch."

"And whatever was on the camera—" Fozzie didn't need to say more. He knew how the game was played. It was obviously worth more than waiting around to pick up an expendable operative.

"We lost Grinch's signal," Cheese went on.

"How long?" Fozzie asked.

"Thirty-six hours."

Even with the distortion of the radio, Fozzie heard the grimness in his voice. He kicked up the upbeat level in his tone when he answered. "Well, no worries. I'm here now, and it's in the bag."

He checked the time. Torie would be in the air for another hour, assuming she'd left on time. And he assumed she had, or she would have called. Wouldn't she?

Damn, he should have warned her about what he really did on the job.

Talk about second-guessing after the fact. He stifled a yawn. Last night hadn't been much of one for sleep, and no telling when he'd sleep again. Cheese seemed a competent pilot. "Mind if I get some shut-eye?"

"No problem. You'll probably be more comfortable in back."

Fozzie released his seat belt. "Holler if you need me."

"Shouldn't be any problems. Clear skies all the way to the compound."

Fozzie hooked his headset over the yoke. He moved back, reclined the plush leather seat, and closed his eyes. Images of an injured and helpless Grinch vied with visions of Torie, each begging for his help.

Crap. This was why he didn't do relationships. How do you tell someone you love they're not your first priority?

He struggled to let go, to find the detachment that would let him doze. He owed it to the mission to go in as rested as possible. He slowed his breathing, turned the images into fuzzy black-and-white photos and tucked them into a photo album which he closed and placed on a shelf. A very high shelf, in another room.

A thud brought him to full alert. "What's up?"

"We're on the ground," Cheese said. "Sleep well?"

"Well enough," he said, surprised that he hadn't noticed the descent. He dragged his hands through his hair and waited while Cheese taxied the jet into position. Once they'd stopped, Fozzie got up and twisted the latches to release the door.

Hotshot stood on the tarmac. "Wheels up in thirty," he said. "Surveillance gear's on board, but if you want anything other than what's on your back, go for it. Briefing once we're airborne."

Fozzie loped to the barracks-like quarters on the compound and transferred essentials from his carry-on and the contents of his locker into an available ruck. A quick run to the loo, and he was good to go. Almost.

For the next however long it took, he'd be living in close, no-privacy quarters. He found an empty briefing room and punched Torie's number into his cell. It rang straight to her voice mail.

"Crap. Wait. I didn't mean that. I meant crap about voice mail." Double crap. He hung up and tried to regroup. What could he say? *I'm going away, someplace I can't tell you about, to do something I can't tell you about, and I'll probably be fine and back in a couple of days, but I don't know that for sure, either.*

As if that would fly. He got up and paced for a minute. Hotshot poked his head in the door. "You about ready? Everyone else is on board."

"Give me a tick," he said. "I need to make a call."

Hotshot gave him an understanding glance and backed out,

closing the door behind him. Fozzie stared at the phone. He clawed through his hair, then redialed Torie's number.

CHAPTER TWENTY-NINE

Torie drifted awake at the captain's announcement that they were on final descent. She'd closed her eyes to avoid talking to the man seated in her row, and the lack of sleep caught her. She made sure her seat belt was fastened and adjusted her seat to its full upright and locked position, thank you very much. She squeezed her cell phone, waiting for the wheels to thunk onto the runway so she could check her messages.

Her finger hit the button almost simultaneously with touchdown. Nothing.

She retrieved his contact information, but couldn't bring herself to press the call button. She had no idea what she could say to him. He was the one who disappeared. Shouldn't he be calling her?

But what if something had happened? No, if he had a phone, he'd call. If he hadn't called, that meant either someone had taken his phone or . . . or he'd realized he'd acted in the heat of the moment, and had time to recognize he'd made a big mistake.

All around her, phones dinged, chimed, and sang. She shoved hers into her purse and maneuvered her carry-on from the overhead compartment. As she exited the jetway into the terminal, her phone beeped its voice mail tone. She rushed to an empty chair and went through the rituals for retrieving messages. Two of them. Heart thudding, she listed to Fozzie's voice.

"Crap?" That's the first word out of his mouth?

She heard out the brief message, which wasn't a message at

305

all, and moved to the second one. At first, she heard nothing but someone breathing. Then, Fozzie's voice came through.

"Torie. I wish I could explain. This is something that I can't say on the phone, much less on voice mail. When I get back, we'll talk." Then she heard someone telling him to get moving, and the call ended.

Anger and hurt jockeyed to dominate her emotions as she followed the signs toward baggage claim. She boarded the escalator, scanning the crowd waiting to meet arriving passengers, hoping to see him, knowing it was impossible that he'd be here. She almost missed the sign. It took a moment to register that she was Victoria Hamilton. She hurried over to the uniformed man holding it.

"Miss Hamilton?" he said.

"Yes." He wasn't much taller than she was, with a slender build that made her feel clunky. His Asian features revealed nothing.

"I am Trang, Miss Hamilton. Do you have baggage?"

She nodded, and he immediately started walking. She followed, hurrying to keep up as he strode purposefully through the crowd as if he expected people to clear a path for him. "Who sent you?" she asked while she watched the luggage drop down the chute onto the carousel revolving in front of them.

"Mr. Hamilton," he said. "He is expecting you."

Of course he'd send a driver. He wouldn't have bothered to mention it. He was probably unaware that there were other ways to get places. A possible suitcase slid onto the carousel. "I think that's mine," she said. "The red one." Checking the paper tag the airline had provided, she confirmed it.

Trang reached forward, grabbed it and set it at her feet. "Any more, Miss Hamilton?"

Fozzie had put his things in the middle-sized bag and had carried it on board. "No, just the one."

Trang whisked the small tote from her hand, piggybacked it with the larger case, and headed for the exit.

Half-surprised that he hadn't defied the rules and parked in the passenger loading zone, she followed him to the nearest structure where he popped the trunk of a gleaming black Rolls Royce Phantom. Opening the rear door for her, he waited as she slid onto the soft gray leather seat. She inhaled, triggering vague memories of riding in the back of a car like this with Nana. It smelled the same, like leather and lemon and something more masculine. A scent that heightened her anxiety. Grandfather's scent.

She remembered a tall man in a black uniform opening the doors for them. For some reason she'd felt like Cinderella then, going to the ball. Now, she felt more like the Cinderella who scrubbed the hearth.

The trunk closed with a soft click, and Trang took his seat behind the wheel. They wound their way out of the airport and to the freeway, where even Grandfather's arrogance couldn't eliminate the evening traffic.

"Have you worked for my grandfather long?" Torie asked when she couldn't stand the silence any longer.

"Five years," he said. He pressed a button and classical music filtered through the sound system.

All right, she could take a hint. She crossed her arms and stared out the window at the hills rising in the distance. They exited the freeway at Sunset Boulevard. The Rolls hugged the curves, passing the entrances to gated communities on the left, the UCLA campus on the right. Mansions lined the streets, sitting on grass-covered slopes, peeking through wrought-iron fences or hidden behind massive walls.

Trang rolled the car into an easy right turn and along a tree-lined street. An iron-barred gate swung open at his approach to a curving driveway. It closed again once they'd passed, and she couldn't shake the feeling she'd entered a very elegant prison.

Looming ahead like a stately British manor, the white stucco home with the dark wood trim sent her pulse racing. Trang eased the car to a gentle stop at the top of the drive and had her door released before she could collect her thoughts.

Strong. She'd be strong. She stepped out of the car. The massive carved wooden door threatened more than it welcomed. It opened, revealing a tall, black-suited figure standing ramrod straight. Her eyes were immediately drawn to the shock of white hair on his head, but as her gaze drifted down to his clear blue eyes, she remembered. "Hutchings?"

The faintest trace of a smile creased his face. "Miss Victoria. It is good to see you again." He stepped around her, taking her bags from Trang, who vanished like a wisp of smoke. "It was such a pleasant surprise to learn you're returning to the fold after all these years. Everyone is assembled in the study."

"May I freshen up first?" she asked. Hutchings had always been kind to her, sneaking her a cookie when she'd been sent off to think about how to behave like a proper young lady after some inevitable rule infraction.

"Most certainly."

"Down that hall on the left?" She caught herself before she pointed—young ladies *never* pointed—as she tried to remember the floor plan.

"Perhaps you would prefer the one off the kitchen." He gave an elegant wave in that direction.

She realized that she would have passed the study had she gone the other way and probably would have been required to enter, regardless of her needs.

Once she'd bolstered her courage, refreshed her makeup, and convinced herself she was twenty-nine, not five, she straightened her shoulders and strode toward the study.

The open door made her give a silent thanks to Hutchings

for sparing her a confrontation with Grandfather in a less than composed state. Not that she was actually *composed,* but at least she wasn't going to be hopping from foot to foot.

She forced a smile and entered the room. Only then did she recall Hutchings had said, "Everyone."

Thinking about Torie wasn't going to do him or the mission any good. Fozzie turned his immediate attention to Manny, team leader for this op. Manny unfurled a map onto the table in Blackthorne's custom King Air 300.

Manny tapped a point near the center of the paper. "This is where our initial target was picked up. It's an old hotel, currently being used as a brothel."

"Well, if Grinch has to be holed up somewhere, there could be worse places." Cheese's voice came from the open cockpit over the headset radios.

Several pairs of eyes glared at the pilot. Cheese shrugged and turned back to his instruments. "Just trying to keep things light," he muttered.

"On task, gentlemen," Manny said, tapping the map again. "This is the designated extraction point." Another tap. "We're going to land here, where we can refuel for the return trip. Hotshot and I will take land transport to the village, where we have reservations at a legitimate hotel. Fozzie and Cheese will take a helo, from which, we hope, Fozzie will do his voodoo and confirm Grinch's current location."

"Voodoo?" Fozzie said, feigning indignation. "You call my superior prowess with the latest technology *voodoo?*"

"Our cover?" Hotshot asked.

"Scientific researchers studying the three-toed sloth," Manny said. "*Bradypus variegatus,* if anyone asks."

"What the—" Fozzie said.

"Best we could do. Their habitat gives us credibility to move around, and since we're doing research, it's normal to be carrying all your latest *scientific technology*. And we wanted to avoid repeating our target's photographer cover, although photographs are part of the researcher's arsenal."

"What the bloody hell do we know about sloths?" Fozzie asked. "I'm not interested in being someone's lunch."

Hotshot laughed. "They hang around upside down in trees and eat leaves. And I think their top speed is clocked at a tenth of a mile an hour. Even you can outrun one, should you find yourself up a tree. They hardly ever come down to earth."

"Great," Fozzie grumbled. "Let's find Grinch and get the hell out of there before someone expects me to answer questions about these critters."

Manny twisted around and rummaged through his ruck. "Here you go." He passed around a file folder full of paper. "Sloth cheat sheets. I suggest you familiarize yourself with the basics."

"Nobody can say working for Blackthorne, Inc. doesn't expand your mind," Cheese said. "Last mission I learned more about French impressionists than I ever wanted to know."

"And," Manny continued, "here are your IDs and letters of authorization from SINAP, the organization that oversees protected areas. Cheese stays with the helo, because there's a strong possibility we'll be doing a grab-and-go once we locate Grinch."

"And I make sure everyone stays connected," Fozzie said. "In and out like the wind."

"Wham, bam, thank you, ma'am," Hotshot added.

"Questions?" Manny asked.

A collective head shake.

"Then make sure you understand your assignments, check your gear, and get some shut-eye. Cheese, Fozzie will relieve you in three hours."

"Roger."

Fozzie allowed a quick thought of Torie. Very quick, because they were already way too high for any kind of cell-phone connection, and until the job was done, Grinch was his concern. He found the lockers with his instruments and began checking them. Once he was satisfied they were in good operating condition, he stretched out in one of the seats to take advantage of what might be the only semi-comfortable sleeping accommodations until the op was over.

Fozzie took the paperwork Manny had given and scanned the first page. Two paragraphs into the dietary habits of *Bradypus variegatus,* he was out.

Just as quickly, he snapped awake when he heard a loud boom, followed by an equally loud "oh, shit" from the pilot over the PA.

He had his seat belt unfastened before he heard Hotshot call, "Fozzie, up front. Now."

"On it." Fozzie rushed forward. The right side of the sky glowed through the porthole. The plane tipped in that direction, and he grabbed the nearest seatback to keep his balance. He felt the plane losing airspeed.

"Bad thing. Number-two engine," Cheese said. "Need some help."

Fozzie slid into the second seat and slapped on a headset. The plane yawed more toward the right. The red master warning light came on. In too-rapid succession, the displays showed systems shutting down.

"We're flying heavy," Cheese said. "We need both engines or we'll have to go down."

Ditching was definitely not an option. Fozzie knew they carried extra fuel to cover the distance. Any delays might cost Grinch his life. But, now, Fozzie was more focused on his own.

"Shut off the damn buzzers," Cheese said. "Can you get a

visual on the engine? See anything?"

Fozzie glanced out of the cockpit seeing individual blades where there should have been a blur of propellers. "No obvious damage."

Cheese grabbed the lever beside the throttle. Fozzie watched the angle of the propeller blades shift as the pilot feathered them to reduce drag.

"Trying a restart," Cheese said.

"No worries," Fozzie said, sweat filming his palms.

Cheese flipped the starter switch. Nothing.

Lots of worries.

Three men rose when Torie stepped into the study. Grandfather wore a dark suit, a crisp white shirt and a perfectly knotted tie striped in two subdued shades of red. His eyes moved across her face, then took in the rest of her. Neither approval nor disapproval registered in his expression. Aside from a thinning of his perfectly combed steel-gray hair and a few more wrinkles, he looked exactly as he had every time she'd seen him.

Her father, on the other hand, looked twenty years older than the man she remembered. Strain carved furrows in his forehead and creases around his eyes. He'd developed jowls, and a paunch his suit coat didn't hide. He glanced away when she fixed her gaze on him.

The third man was a total stranger. Attractive in an almost too-meticulous way, he had dark blond hair, styled, not merely combed. Deep blue eyes and a dimpled chin. Lean, tanned, and someone who spent hours at the gym, she guessed. Much closer to her age than to either her father or grandfather. The sort of man who'd have been among the swarm Kathy attracted, the kind of man who'd never notice someone like her. But, now, he was definitely noticing. Assessing. Judging. He had her as uncomfortable as the other two men, but not for the same reason. Who was he?

Young ladies didn't speak first. Chin lifted, head high, she waited. And waited a little longer. She was strong. She was not four years old. Or twelve. She was a grown woman. At least on the outside, and she was working like crazy for her strength to burrow inside.

"Good evening, Victoria," Grandfather said. He sat behind his massive walnut desk, and the others followed his lead, taking seats in the leather chairs across the room alongside a matching sofa. Grandfather's head bobbed a fraction. "You're looking well."

"You are, too, Grandfather. Thank you for seeing me at such short notice." She turned toward her father. "Hello, Father."

"Victoria. Or is it Torie now?" His brown eyes were cold.

"Either is fine," she said. "I trust you were informed I was safe."

His eyes darted to Grandfather, to the stranger, and then to a point somewhere above her shoulder. "You're here now. That's what's important." His smile held no warmth. Only resigned satisfaction. As if he'd achieved his goal, and the method didn't matter.

And, she realized, it probably didn't. She eyed the sofa, but she hadn't been invited to sit. The stranger seemed nervous, his fingers drumming on his thighs. She watched Grandfather glare at him, and the drumming stopped. Inwardly, she smiled. Young men, apparently, didn't fidget any more than young ladies.

"Please take a seat, Victoria," Grandfather said at last. "You'll be joining us for dinner."

She sank onto the plush leather, perching on the edge so her feet reached the floor. "Thank you."

Hutchings appeared out of nowhere, as he always had. "I'll have my usual," Grandfather said. "Drinks, gentlemen?"

"Scotch, rocks," her father said.

"Gin and tonic, please," the stranger said.

Hutchings looked at her with a barely discernable smile. "Miss Hamilton?"

Not "Miss Victoria" any longer. She smiled, the first genuine one she'd felt since she'd first landed in Salt Lake. "A Sauvignon Blanc, please."

From her seat, she noticed Grandfather's neck muscles tense. She'd been tempted to order a beer, simply to get a rise out of him with such a "lower class" drink. Heck, she'd almost ordered a whiskey, neat, but she didn't think she could pull off drinking it with the necessary aplomb. She gave Grandfather a toned-down version of the smile she'd shown Hutchings.

"Thank you, Hutchings," Grandfather said. "I'm guilty of forgetting that Victoria is no longer the child she was when we last saw her."

Touché.

Hutchings returned with their drinks on a silver tray. Torie accepted her wine, tempted to gulp it to ease her dry mouth. Instead, she waited.

After he'd taken a sip of his drink, Grandfather set down his glass, folded his hands on the desk and leaned slightly forward. "I understand you have a problem, Victoria. What can I do to help?"

Help? Already? On the phone, he'd insisted she present her request in person, nothing more. Her wine glass shook, and she set it on the table. She plunged into the speech she'd run over in her head at least dozen times. "A friend and I discovered something that could be killing people."

His eyebrows lifted. "Explain."

She went through what she and Fozzie found, how she thought the drug Wingard was researching hadn't been tested properly, that people might actually have died during the testing, and that she also wanted things done discreetly, in case her

314

fears were unfounded.

"And why did you come to me?" he asked.

"Because you have contacts in the FDA. You can get people to listen. And because the rumors say that Wingard Research is going to turn over their findings to one of the big pharmaceutical houses tomorrow, and they need to know that the drug might need more work."

"Why not warn them it's a bad drug and have it dropped?"

"We have no proof that it's bad, only that the preliminary research data have been altered to make it look better. But there's a possibility someone altered the data to hide the deaths of some subjects." Her arguments seemed lame now. All *ifs* and *maybes* and *we thinks*. "But someone was willing to kidnap me to keep me from telling anyone what I knew, so it must be important."

"Kidnap you?" The stranger spoke for the first time.

She nodded, brushing her hands through the air to swat the conversation away from that topic. "Grandfather, believe me, if I knew who to talk to, or if there was more time, I would never impose on your generosity."

He tilted his head and scowled.

All right, you laid that one on a bit thick, and he knows it.

"But I can't bear the thought that even one person might die if I didn't at least make every effort to stop it."

"Commendable," he said. "Very commendable. And if I do this favor for you, are you prepared to pay the price?" He nodded to the stranger and smiled.

Nothing was ever free, nothing came without strings. She'd known that the minute she'd made the call.

She downed a large swallow of her wine in a most unladylike fashion. "What did you have in mind?"

"A yes or no, Victoria. Your own words said that you were willing to make every effort to stop it. Assuming I can do what you ask, will you do what I ask in return?" The knowing smile he sent toward the stranger sent a chill down her spine.

CHAPTER THIRTY

"Okay, let's go to plan B," Cheese said. "Restart protocol. Book's behind my seat."

Fozzie snagged the notebook. Quickly flipped to the emergency section. Read each step aloud. Focused on Cheese responding "Roger" each time.

"Need more airspeed," Cheese said. "Watch the N-one indicator and tell me as soon as it hits twelve."

Fozzie glued his gaze to the small circular gauge. Instead of a healthy ninety-five, the needle hovered at the four-percent mark.

"Hang tight," Cheese announced. "We're going to play roller coaster. The E-ticket kind."

Fozzie tightened his harness as Cheese tilted the plane's nose down. He concentrated on keeping his breathing steady as his stomach plunged. He watched the needle creep across the dial. Six. Eight. Ten. Eleven.

"Now," he said as soon as it hit twelve.

Cheese pushed up on the fuel-condition lever.

Fozzie heard the engine whine as it came back to life. Outside, the propellers shifted angle and picked up speed. He fought the increasing g-forces, and his stomach did a reverse trip as Cheese pulled out of the dive and brought the plane to altitude.

After several reverent moments contemplating the familiar sounds and vibrations of normal flight, Fozzie turned to Cheese and slipped the notebook back into its pocket. "Good onya, mate."

"Would rather not have to do it again," Cheese said, rubbing his thigh. "Man, keeping her steady is a bitch on the quads." Sweat trickled down his face. He ran his fingers over the instrument panel as if stroking a lover. "That's my girl."

"Everyone all right?" Fozzie asked, twisting in his seat. He caught a glimpse of Manny disappearing into the loo.

"What the hell happened?" Hotshot asked.

"Engine indigestion," Cheese said. "My best guess is we picked up some volcanic debris."

"Volcanoes?" Fozzie said. He hadn't been paying a lot of attention to the news over the past week, but he thought he'd have noticed any headlines about an eruption. Then again, who knew what the folks in Aspen Corners or Twin Falls considered newsworthy.

"We're flying through the Ring of Fire," Cheese said. "Ash drifts around for days, over thousands of miles. Fragments can be sharp as a knife blade. Because we restarted, I'm thinking the engine's okay. Probably a starter issue."

"Any problems continuing?" Manny asked. He lumbered up the aisle, holding onto any available handholds, and took the most forward seat. "Or should we put down for repairs?"

"I think we're fine," Cheese said. "The compressor stall probably caused enough of a jolt so the starter failed. She's flying all right now, and I'd hate to delay the mission."

He had that right. Fozzie recalled a recent mission when it had taken over a month to locate and extract an operative Fozzie would trust to cover his six any day. Not something he wanted to repeat.

"Shouldn't maintenance have caught it?" Hotshot asked.

"Hard to say. We've had a lot of back-to-back missions, and things that check out on preflight can still fail. This bird's flown her share," Cheese said.

"I'll defer to your judgment," Manny said. "But we're going to alter the plan. Cheese, you'll stay with the plane. Fozzie, can you handle the helo solo?"

"Bucket of piss," he said.

"Damn, I wish you'd find a better expression," Hotshot said. "Why can't you say piece of cake?"

Fozzie grinned. "Don't go dissing my heritage."

"We'll debrief again an hour out," Manny said. "Best safe speed, Cheese."

"Roger that," the pilot replied.

Fozzie stayed where he was. Both he and Cheese would be keeping an eye on that engine for the rest of the trip. But at least there was going to be a rest of the trip. He prayed they'd find Grinch in good shape and wouldn't have to take any risks to rush him home.

"Let's hope it's an easy fix," Fozzie said. "And that if we need parts, we can get them quick smart."

"And if not?" Hotshot asked.

"How are we set for duct tape and baling wire?"

Torie met Grandfather's gaze. She'd come too far to back down. "If you can do it, then yes."

"Very well," he said. "Perhaps you and your new fiancé would like to move to the parlor and begin getting acquainted while I make some calls."

"Fiancé?" The word barely made it past her lips.

"Allow me to introduce Rhys Ainsworth," Grandfather said, nodding to the stranger.

"Fiancé?" she repeated.

"No need to sound like a parrot. Your father is retiring, and Mr. Ainsworth will be rising to fill the vacancy. As you know, my desire is to keep the Hamilton bloodline in the company. If there are no Hamiltons, then I will simply dispose of Epicurean Unlimited in a manner I deem fit. It's done very well for me, but I'm no longer able to put the necessary energy into maintaining its high operating standards."

He shot a scathing look at her father, who turned bright red and ducked his head. Despite all her problems with her father, Torie cringed at his embarrassment.

Get with the twenty-first century. Nobody in this country arranges marriages anymore. She almost spoke the words aloud. But then she thought of Kathy in the hospital, of Stephanie Carter and all the names on Kathy's list. Their hopes for a cure, for a normal life. Their lives cut short. She looked at Rhys, who studied his fingernails. He didn't seem any more excited about the prospect than she did. This was *not* the time to raise a scene. Once she could think straight, she'd find a loophole somewhere. A way out. She had to.

Rhys stood, drink in hand, and gave her a polite smile. She rose and took her wine glass, hoping Hutchings would show up with the rest of the bottle. He stepped aside at the door, indicating she should go first. In the hall, she paused. "Do you know where we're going? I haven't been here since I was a kid, and I'm sure I was never allowed in a *parlor.*"

He nodded, giving her a brief smile. Friendly enough, but the awkwardness between them was thick as the mud she'd slogged through in Oregon.

Hutchings stood in the hallway, and as they approached, he opened a door. "I think this room is more suitable than the formal parlor. May I refresh your drinks?"

"Please," she said.

Rhys followed her into the room. She paused two steps in, and he brushed against her. "Sorry," he said.

She ignored him as memories swirled around her. This was where she and Nana sat when she visited. The same pale-blue-striped wallpaper with the floral border near the high ceiling. She inhaled deeply, trying to recapture the long-buried scent of the room. Could there be any vestiges left? Probably not, but she could swear she smelled lilacs. She scanned the room for floral arrangements, but the round table by the door held only silk plants, not the live flowers Nana always had in here. She strode right to the rocking chair where Nana had read to her. Sat in it, eyes closed, rocking gently. The smooth wood armrests were cool under her touch.

The sound of a throat being cleared brought her back. Hutchings stood before her, a fresh glass of wine in hand. He reached for her half-empty one. "No, leave it, please," she said. He nodded and left the room, but didn't close the door. No, that would have been improper.

"Are you all right?" Rhys asked.

"Fine," she said. "Just remembering."

"Good memories?"

She smiled. "About the only good ones I have of this place. This was where my grandmother sat with me. Taught me to read. Made me feel important."

"I take it you're not overly fond of your grandfather."

She laughed. "Oh, you mean it showed?"

He sat on the loveseat, his fingers drumming against his thighs again.

"Worse than a blind date," she said, trying to chip away the glacier sitting between them. "Because not only do you have to go out with the frump, you're expected to keep going out with her. Again and again."

"I'd hardly call you a frump," he said. "A little serious, perhaps, but that's understandable given the circumstances."

"Circumstances? That's what you call being told we're supposed to be engaged? Or did you know about it before I got here?"

"It's been discussed," he said. "Although I've haven't been privy to many of the discussions. My parents—"

"Your parents, my grandfather. Where do they get off planning our lives?"

"I don't think anyone ever says no to them," he said. "At least I've never been able to."

"Well, I hear you there." So much for him being the one to put his foot down and tell Grandfather where to stick his plans. "So, what do we do?"

"Is what you said in there—that you want to make sure there's nothing dangerous about that new drug—really that important?"

"Important enough to let Grandfather arrange a marriage? To be honest, I don't know why I agreed. I figured there had to be a way out. I mean, once he makes his calls and alerts the right people, then it's done, right? He can't take it back. They'll investigate the drug."

"But he can dump Epicurean. Which would leave your father almost broke."

"Is it my fault he can't manage his money?" But, as she feared, coming back made it impossible to keep him some abstract, distant figure. Seeing him, how pathetic he'd looked, and knowing she'd be responsible for sending him even lower, hurt almost as much as accepting responsibility for people— total strangers—dying. "Never mind. He's my father, and somewhere deep down, the blood ties come into play."

"I know how it goes. My parents have been counting on my promotion."

From the way he avoided her eyes, she suspected there was more. "And how do *you* feel about the promotion?"

"Frankly, I don't really want a promotion. I'm happy where I am."

"Which is?"

"I'm the advertising director. In charge of ads and catalogs for the trade. But, considering it's likely I won't have a job at all if your Grandfather ditches the company, it's not really an option."

"Good grief, I hadn't even thought of that. Hundreds of people out of work."

"Rocks and hard places," he said. "Not that you're either, of course," he added quickly. "I'm sure you're very nice, and we might even be good friends."

Friends. She thought of Fozzie. They'd kind of skipped the friendship step. Which is probably why he wasn't calling. First a job, then a lover, then some words of commitment he undoubtedly regretted by now.

"So, what are we going to do?"

Hutchings entered the room, standing at attention by the door. "Dinner is served."

"Have dinner, I guess," Rhys said, extending his arm.

Torie accepted it.

People could play football on this table, she thought when they entered the room. She looked down the expanse of white linen. Grandfather stood at one end, her father at the other, nodding stiffly as she and Rhys entered. Torie took the seat Rhys held for her. He circled the massive table and took a seat across from her. The two older men sat as well. For the first time, it occurred to her that her mother was absent. Not surprising, given Grandfather's attitude that women in business were superfluous.

Grandfather nodded to Hutchings. He poured a bit of red wine into Grandfather's glass. Torie feigned interest in the ritual as Grandfather approved the wine. As if it would dare turn to vinegar in his cellar.

"Would you prefer to continue with the white?" Hutchings asked as he came by.

Why not? Who cared if Grandfather had decided his red would go with whatever the meal was. "Yes, please." Of course, going against Grandfather wasn't effective if she didn't throw him a defiant look, but she wasn't *that* strong.

Torie thought of dinner with Brad and Carrie. Food piled on the table, people helping themselves, smiling, laughing. Here, it was a single course at a time, and one didn't converse, much less laugh. One answered Grandfather's questions as the dinner dragged on. And on.

"I trust you and Rhys had a pleasant conversation," her father said.

"Yes, we did. Although I did wonder why you would promote someone in Advertising to your position. Wouldn't your second-in-command have been the logical choice?"

"Rhys is suitably qualified," Grandfather said. "His job means he's familiar with our entire product line. And Mrs. Isaacs will remain in her position to offer assistance."

So, the second-in-command was a woman. That explained it. She wondered if this Mrs. Isaacs person would be miffed about being passed over by someone in Advertising. Assuming she didn't already know.

After Hutchings cleared the main course plates, Grandfather cleared his throat. "Victoria, I've called an acquaintance at the FDA, and explained your concerns. He assures me that he will look into the reports and assign someone to confirm the study. He will also contact the pharmaceutical firm buying the rights to the drug and suggest they delay the sale until the matter is resolved."

"So soon? Grandfather, thank you. I truly appreciate it." She exchanged an uneasy glance with Rhys. Grandfather had done his part. Could she do hers?

Hutchings reappeared with a bottle of champagne wrapped in a white cloth, and another silver tray with four crystal flutes.

Grandfather nodded, and Hutchings popped the cork. After Hutchings served everyone, Grandfather stood. "I would like to propose a toast to the new general manager of Epicurean Unlimited and his bride to be."

Did a toast count if the glasses didn't touch? Because there was no way anyone could reach anyone else at this table. Rhys gave a tiny shrug and lifted his glass.

"And," Grandfather continued, "I called the *Times* and notified them of the upcoming personnel changes at Epicurean."

"That was fast," Torie said.

"In addition," he went on, "your engagement will be announced in Sunday's paper. They'll send a photographer tomorrow morning." He gazed at Torie. "I didn't specify a wedding date, but Valentine's Day seems appropriate." He turned his focus to Rhys. "That way you won't have to remember too many dates. The commercial fuss makes it hard to miss that one." He smiled. He actually smiled. And his face didn't crack. But there was no joy in his expression. His face was merely a mask.

Torie downed her champagne as if it were soda. Her head spun. "If you'll excuse me," she said, pushing away from the table.

"We haven't had dessert," Grandfather said, shocked disapproval in his tone.

She concentrated on keeping her gait steady as she hurried to the bathroom. Inside, she splashed her face with cold water. She would *not* get sick. This was all temporary. She was strong. In control. Valentine's Day. Easy to remember, ha. Far enough away so it wouldn't look like a rush job, which would keep the gossip mongers from innuendo and speculation. And with enough lead time before her birthday in May, just in case anyone knew about Grandfather's will. She wondered if her father had anything to do with picking the date. Making sure there wouldn't be a loophole in case something delayed the wedding.

Valentine's Day. Five months to figure a way out.

Hutchings was nearby when she came out. "Are you all right?"

"Fine." She flashed a weak smile. "My purse. Do you have it?"

"One moment."

She waited, not ready to go back to the dining room and face the men who sought to control her life. When Hutchings returned with her purse, she found her phone. No messages while she'd been otherwise occupied. She set it to vibrate and slipped it into her pocket.

"Is there anything I can do, Miss Hamilton?"

"You can call me Torie," she said. "Other than that, no. I was expecting a message, but he—it hasn't come through yet." And even if it did, it would be too late. "I guess I'd better go back."

"Your grandfather is expecting you. It's not often that someone leaves the table before the meal is officially ended. And he did request a chocolate mousse for dessert."

"*He* requested it? I didn't even know what a chocolate mousse was the last time I was here. I'd have thought it would have been something akin to a chocolate Easter bunny."

"I do recall you enjoyed chocolate pudding. Perhaps I hinted that might be a wise choice for tonight."

"Why are you being so nice to me?" she asked.

His face saddened. "Your grandmother cared for you deeply. And I couldn't help but notice your reactions as a child to the gruff demeanor of your grandfather. Since your grandmother is no longer with us . . ."

"You've stepped in as my champion." She stood on tiptoe and kissed his cheek. "Thanks."

"If you can endure dessert, you should be excused immediately afterward."

"Don't tell me—the men are going to go have port and smoke cigars?"

Hutchings smiled. "I'm afraid Mr. Hamilton's physician put a stop to the cigars about five years ago."

"I'll bet that pissed him off."

His smile widened to a grin. "It did, indeed. Would you rather I make your excuses?"

"No, I'll get back and face the music."

Not only were all eyes on her when she returned, but the three men stood as she approached her chair. Rhys almost ran to get there in time to pull it out for her. He lowered his face to her ear. "Are you okay?"

Was he worried? She searched his eyes. Concern, yes, but for her? Or that if things fell apart, he'd be out of a job?

"I'm fine." She gave her grandfather the sweetest smile she could find. "I'm sorry to have held up your dessert. There was no need to wait on my account."

"Nonsense. You are the guest of honor, after all. I can understand a bit of distress after a grueling travel day, not to mention the excitement you must be feeling."

Oh, yeah, she was really excited.

Under ordinary circumstances, the mousse would have been delicious. Instead, it resembled chocolate-flavored glue. She forced it down, smiling politely between bites, keeping her left hand below the table, resting on her cell phone.

And what would she do if he called? Her bed was made, so to speak, not that she had any desire to lie in it with Rhys.

"Your father and I have agreed that it would be most sensible for you to remain living here until the wedding," Grandfather said.

"I couldn't impose," she replied.

"It's hardly an imposition. The house is certainly big enough. Hutchings has seen to it that a guest room is ready for you. Miss Neville, the housekeeper, will see to your needs."

"Yes, sir." Until she saw proof that he'd held up his end of the bargain, she'd comply.

"Shall we retire to the study?" Grandfather asked.

Rhys and her father stood. "If it's all right with you, sir, I'd like to spend a little more time with Victoria."

"Most certainly." His smile was more of a smirk.

They found their way back to Nana's sitting room. "If you wouldn't mind," Torie said, "I'd like to make a call."

"Of course. I'll . . . um . . . I'll just . . . freshen up."

She glared at the phone, giving it one more chance to ring before she pressed Fozzie's number.

CHAPTER THIRTY-ONE

Fozzie stood with Cheese and watched the cloud of dust fade in the distance as Hotshot and Manny sped to the village.

"I've confirmed your preflight twice," Cheese said. "Everything checks out. Give the word and you'll be airborne."

"I need ten minutes to check my equipment." Once he was satisfied, Fozzie slipped on his headset. "Radio check. Hotshot, Manny, do you copy?"

"Five by five," both men said.

He turned to Cheese and twirled a forefinger in the air. "I'm off. Keep us posted on the repairs."

Cheese wiped his hands on his pants. "They're rushing a replacement starter from the center in Toluca, Mexico. Once I have it, it's a"—he lifted his eyebrows at Fozzie—"a bucket of piss to install. You get our man, we'll be ready, or I'll have an alternative lined up."

"Counting on that," Fozzie said. Any doubts that Cheese didn't mesh with the team had long since dissipated. He climbed aboard and put the helo in the air.

His briefing materials indicated sloths could be active—if you could call their slow-motion existence active—both day and night, which gave the team the excuse they needed to search at any hour. He had a feeling the choice of cover wasn't a lucky coincidence. Blackthorne's research team was nothing if not thorough. He sought the spot where, according to Blackthorne policy, Grinch should be waiting. *If* he'd escaped.

Thirty minutes later, Fozzie hooked up with Manny and Hotshot in the cantina adjacent to their antiquated hotel. "I scoped out the extraction point," Fozzie said. "Nothing five clicks in any direction."

"Damn," Hotshot said.

"Nothing's ever that easy, is it? We'll find him," Fozzie said.

"That we will." Manny handed him a room key.

Fozzie slipped it in his pocket. "The helo's secured in a clearing behind the church."

"Perfect," Manny said, "because the church tower's your best vantage point. Everyone ready for phase two?"

"Where one of us lucky bastards goes into the brothel and tries to convince a lovely lady to divulge Grinch's whereabouts? Yeah, I'm ready," Fozzie said. Maybe Murphy's Law was done interfering with this op, they'd locate Grinch, get him out, and Fozzie would be free to patch things with Torie. He owed her that much.

"Too early for any action over there," Manny said. "Dinner first, if you're so inclined. Or sleep, shower. Your choice. I'll head over at twenty-hundred hours. Hotshot, unless I report otherwise, you show up at twenty-fifteen, start doing what you can to poke around. Fozzie, start setting up your gear at nineteen-thirty. Don't need to risk being discovered by being there too early. Questions?"

"No worries. Be ready for a final check at nineteen-forty-five." Fozzie tossed the key in his hand, reading the room number on the tag. "I'm going to scope out the accommodations."

The room made the one at their dump at Isla Caribe look luxurious, and he hoped they wouldn't be here long. Two narrow cots flanked a narrow window, and a slow-moving paddle fan on the ceiling shifted the musty air as effectively as waving his hand.

He sat on the bed, tossed his ruck beside him, and fished out his handheld. No updates from central ops, and no alerts on Grinch's phone. He set it down and checked his personal cell phone, which held the single voice mail from Torie.

"I'm sure your job must be very important. I'm at Grandfather's, and he's already called the FDA about Wingard. Thank you for everything you did. Maybe our paths will cross again. Bye."

It hadn't changed since the last three times he'd played it. He hit the Delete key. He had a job to do, and replaying her message wasn't going to help. The one he'd sent hadn't exactly begged her to wait for his return. *I'll explain when I get back.* Brilliant. No wonder she'd written him off.

He exhaled something precariously close to a sigh. No matter what they'd said before, bottom line was they'd just met, and they'd been under a mountain of stress. Feelings grew, but theirs really hadn't had time to take root. They'd acted on passions of the moment.

And, right now, the moment said he had a teammate to find.

After a shower. Nothing like the cold sweat of fear followed by the sweat of loading equipment onto a helo in the Central American heat to cover him with *eau de* longshoreman's jockstrap. Come to think of it, showering with his clothes *on* might be a better solution. But not a viable one. He stripped and stood under the trickle of lukewarm water, rubbing the tiny bar of soap through his hair and over his body.

Slightly cleaner and barely refreshed, he toweled off and put on the fresh clothes he'd stuck in his ruck. He'd deal with the dirty ones later. If Grinch was in the brothel, they should have him out and be on their way tonight. He checked the time. Waiting another hour would do nothing but make him feel helpless. If Manny didn't want him to set up in the church tower yet, he could still work out of the helo. He grinned. After all, there might be sloths out there, and the ever-diligent researcher should be out looking for them.

He let Manny know where he'd be, then strolled through the pothole-filled main street of the small village. The spicy aromas from the cantina mixed with the dust blowing in on the afternoon breeze. He passed a small general store, a larger hardware store and a petrol station before reaching the church in the central plaza. He turned down the dirt lane, past the churchyard, then cut around the adjacent cemetery toward the helo.

A collection of youngsters played a lively game of football on a field as much dirt as grass. A few more watched, their attention shifting from the game to the helo. Since they kept their distance, he assumed they were more curious than mischievous. "G'day, mates," he called, waving, as he drew closer. *"Buenos dias."*

As he neared the helo, the game stopped and everyone ran toward him. He grinned as he tried to decipher the myriad voices babbling in Spanish. *"No tan rápidamente.* Not so fast."

"I speak English. I am Luis." The boy holding the ball stepped forward. The leader, Fozzie surmised from the way the others immediately grew quiet.

Fozzie tried to downplay the Aussie in his speech. Doubtful these kids had heard many Strine accents, either in English *or* Spanish. "I'm Fozzie. Here to study your sloths."

The boy looked puzzled. "Sloths?"

"Momento." Fozzie unlocked the helo and fetched the information sheets. He handed an illustrated one to the boy. "Sloth. They live in trees. Very slow."

The boy's eyes lit in recognition. *"Si. El perezoso."* He turned and showed the paper to the group. "Sloth."

"Sloth," they repeated in solemn unison.

"Right," Fozzie said. "But now I have work to do. You can get back to your game." He climbed into the helo and flipped on the computer. While it booted, he watched Luis toss the ball to one of the other boys who kicked it into the field. The rest of the group raced after it, and their game resumed.

Luis held back, his eyes following Fozzie's moves. "You can fly this?"

"Yes," Fozzie said.

"I would like to be a pilot someday."

Fozzie saw the yearning in the lad's eyes. He understood what it was like, living in one world and wanting to be part of another. A world where things seemed more exciting. Memories of his parents bounced across his mind, along with images of Brad and Carrie. Sometimes more exciting wasn't really better than what you left behind.

"Maybe I can do something for you, and you can take me for a ride? I can get you a woman. A beautiful *señorita.*"

"I don't think so, Luis."

"No, it is true. Where I live, there are many such women. The men come and enjoy them at night."

Fozzie stopped dead. "Where do you live?"

He pointed in the direction of the brothel. "With the *Señora.*"

"I'm not in need of a woman, Luis."

"You prefer a man? There are some at the house who provide that as well."

"No. No man, no woman. I have work to do."

"Then something else? I helped the other *hombre norteamericano.*"

Fozzie jumped to the ground. "What *norteamericano?* What was his name?"

Luis shrugged. "It was a strange name. Like the story. Who steals Christmas."

Fozzie clutched the boy's shoulders. "Grinch? You saw Grinch?"

Luis grinned. "*Sí.* Grinch."

Before he could say anything, an alert buzzed from the computer. He rushed to open the mapping program. A light blinked. Grinch's cell phone had just been turned on.

"Stay right there," he told Luis.

Torie sat in the wing chair in her room and stared at the photo in the Westside pages of the newspaper. Somehow, the hair stylist, makeup artist, and photographer had made her look both attractive and happy about her engagement to the man she'd met the day before. She tossed that section aside and searched the rest of the paper for any news about Willamette Syndrome or Wingard Research.

Nothing. But it was only Sunday. It probably wouldn't hit the papers until tomorrow at the earliest.

She looked up at a tap on the door. "Come in."

The pucker-faced Miss Neville bustled in and opened the silk draperies. "Your grandfather suggests that you take the day to shop for some suitable attire. Your mother will be here at eleven. I believe she's already arranged some private showings on Rodeo Drive."

Shopping with her mother. On Rodeo Drive, no less. She remembered her recent trip to the mall with Fozzie. She could see her mother's face if she mimicked his shopping system and simply walked into a single store and grabbed.

No one seeing the newspaper photo would guess that below the frilly blouse materialized by Grandfather from who knows where, she wore jeans and sneakers. Rhys had arched one eyebrow but hadn't complained as they'd posed.

Grandfather suggests, my eye. Grandfather ordered. And she obeyed.

Only until she confirmed that Wingard's research was being verified and that nobody's life was in danger. Meanwhile, she had to survive a shopping trip with her mother. That basement with Mr. Abbott didn't look so bad anymore.

She sighed. "Thank you, Miss Neville. I'll be ready."

"Very well." She got as far as the door before asking, "Is there anything else?"

"No, thank you."

Precisely at eleven, Miss Neville stood, starch-stiff, in Torie's doorway and informed her that her mother was waiting in the parlor. "I'll ask her to wait while you change," she said.

"No need. I'm ready." Torie grabbed her purse and trudged downstairs.

She paused in the doorway, gazing at the woman she hadn't seen more than a handful of times in over fifteen years. Petite, blonde, and regal. And holding a cut-crystal glass half-filled with what was undoubtedly vodka. Aside from an up-to-date hairstyle, the woman standing in the parlor looked exactly the way she had when Torie had last seen her. How many nips, tucks and injections had it taken to freeze her in time?

She stepped into the room. "Hello, Mother."

"Victoria. It's so nice that you've come home at last." Her mother swept her up and down with a distasteful gaze. Torie had resisted changing into her dressier slacks and loafers. Why bother, since she knew she'd come home with an entire new wardrobe. And no shop personnel on Rodeo Drive would dare diss her mother.

Botox spared Torie the uplifted eyebrows. "I can see we have a lot of shopping to do," her mother said. "And won't it be fun, the two of us, planning your wedding. Valentine's Day. So romantic. With only five months, we'll have to hurry, and I know exactly where we should start."

Oh, yeah. Mom and me. Real fun.

She pasted a smile on her face, about as sincere as the one her mother had given her. "Then let's get started."

Chapter Thirty-Two

Fozzie hopped back into the helo. He kept one eye on the display as he contacted Manny. "Got a hit on Grinch's phone. Tracking it now. Stand by." Crap. The light blinked out. Reflexively, Fozzie tapped the screen. "Come back you little—"

"Come again?" Manny said.

"Lost the bloody signal. But there might be call to modify our original plans."

"Be there in five," Manny said.

The sun dipped below the tree line. The church bells chimed, and the rest of the kids abandoned their game, no doubt heading home for supper. Hotshot and Manny arrived a moment later.

"Anything new?" Hotshot asked. "Signal come back?"

"Not yet."

"So, what do we have?" Manny said.

"Hard to tell. All we know for sure is that we got a quick burst from Grinch's phone." He introduced Luis. "The lad says he lives at the brothel and he's seen Grinch."

Manny immediately fired off a series of questions in rapid-fire Spanish, much too fast for Fozzie to follow. Luis responded just as quickly, interjecting the conversation with nods, head shakes, and shrugs.

When they stopped, Manny tousled Luis's hair and handed him some bills. *"Gracias, amigo."*

Luis grinned and raced across the field.

Manny turned to face them. "The kid doesn't know much. Grinch was hiding in a shed behind the brothel, pretty banged up. Luis found him, brought him food and water, but Grinch was out of it most of the time. Some thugs showed up late last night. Woke Luis. He heard them threaten the women, ask about Grinch. He thinks one of the women knew. And this morning Grinch was gone."

"Does he know where they would have taken him? Who they were?" Hotshot asked.

Manny shook his head. "He didn't see. Apparently the kid's the son of one of the . . . working women. He lives there, but away from the normal night action. He says he sleeps through most of it, like it's all background noise. Last night was louder, more violent. He was afraid for his mother, snuck out of his room, but didn't get a look at the men."

"Best guess where Grinch might be?" Hotshot said.

Fozzie shrugged. "The signal came from the northwest." He pointed to a map where he'd marked the location.

"Moving toward the border?" Manny suggested.

"Until we get another signal, *if* we get another signal, there's no point in jumping to conclusions," Fozzie said.

Manny looked from one man to the other. "The helo can cover that distance quickly. Fozzie, take her up and check it out. Hotshot, go with him. I'll check the brothel. Some of the women might be willing to talk to me." He patted his pocket. "For the right price."

"On it," Fozzie said. "Hotshot, you have enough medical gear in here, or is it back at the hotel?"

"Only basic first aid at the hotel. The good stuff's in here."

"Do it," Manny said. Without looking back, he jogged across the field. "Keep me posted."

"Likewise," Fozzie said. Things might get a bit dicey. Cheese was their pilot, and while Fozzie had no problems flying the helo, he couldn't fly and watch the surveillance instruments. "You all right with covering intel?" he asked Hotshot.

"Chill, Fozzie. I might not have your degree of finesse with the search equipment, but it's not like I don't know what I'm doing," Hotshot said. "You've got to learn to trust others."

Had he been that obvious? Then again, there weren't many secrets within the team. Fozzie tilted his head. "No worries. For now, we don't have much to go on other than one spot on a map." Seconds later, they hovered above the trees, then set out toward the coordinates Hotshot read off.

"Hang on," Hotshot said. "Got another blip."

"Log it," Fozzie said. "Compare it to the first one."

"Same coordinates," Hotshot said. "So Grinch isn't moving."

"No, his *phone* isn't moving."

"Damn. It's gone again."

"Keep an eye on the monitor. And give me a terrain display of the area. See if there's anyplace to set down if we need to."

Fozzie resisted the urge to lean over and do it himself. Hotshot was right. He trusted his team, and unless a life hung in the balance, there was no point in trying to do everything himself.

"Got another signal," Hotshot said.

And, like the others, it disappeared within seconds.

"We can be at the coordinates in twenty," Fozzie said. "Maybe fifteen."

Manny's voice came over the radio. "I talked to a few of the ladies. Or I tried. They're scared about something. Only one admitted knowing Grinch was here at all. I'm going to work on her until you get back."

"And I know you mean that in the most professional manner," Fozzie said. "Your profession, not hers, of course."

"Of course," Manny said.

"We're almost at the coordinates," Fozzie said. "The signal

comes and goes, but it's not moving."

"Keep me apprised," Manny said. "Sitreps every ten."

"On it," Fozzie said. "Hang on, Hotshot. It's pedal-to-the-metal time." He pushed the yoke and pulled on the collective.

Ten minutes later, they circled the rocky shoreline where the GPS signal had originated. "Anything new?" Fozzie asked.

"Nothing," Hotshot said. "Exactly like the last ten times you asked me."

"According to the GPS, Grinch, or his phone, should be directly below us."

"I may not have your expertise," Hotshot said, "but all I see directly below us is water and rocks. I'm not getting anything noticeable on the infrared."

"Boost the gain," Fozzie said. "If Grinch is wet, his body temp is going to be lower than normal. And if he's in the rocks, it's going to be even harder to pick up a signal."

Hotshot made the adjustments. "Nope, still don't have anything. And then there's the small matter of nothing remotely resembling a landing pad down there."

"Looks like we'll be hoofin' it, then. I'll find someplace to set down." He turned inland.

After a moment, Hotshot spoke. "Fozzie, this might be crazy, but I think there's a message in these signals."

"What do you mean? Grinch hasn't made contact, has he?"

"No, I think it's the timing. We've had nine blips. The first three lasted approximately ten seconds before disappearing. The next three were about twenty. Then, the last three were ten again."

"Three short, three long, three short," Fozzie said. He coaxed a little more speed from the helo.

"Right," Hotshot replied. "SOS."

Torie tossed Thursday's paper aside. Still no mention of Wingard. Good news? If Wingard had sold the rights to the drug, wouldn't it have been mentioned somewhere? If there was a huge scandal about the clinical studies, wouldn't reporters have jumped on it? The Internet might be a better option. But the only computer in the house was in Grandfather's office, and when he wasn't in there, he kept the door locked.

Without Internet access, her laptop was useless for research. And she could *not* face another day shopping with her mother. Her closet was already packed to the rafters with more clothes than she could wear in the next five years. Of course, within six months they'd be out of style, so her mother would insist they get more. Torie used to enjoy shopping. Picking, comparing, deciding. Now, she merely accepted whatever her mother deemed appropriate for any possible occasion—"This will be perfect if Mitzi invites us to tea at her club"—and watched Trang stuff the boxes into the Phantom. Not to mention the deliveries. Hanging up new clothes seemed to be the only task that brought the semblance of a smile to Miss Neville's dour features.

As if the thought was enough to summon the old bat, the housekeeper swept in. She'd stopped knocking after the first day. Torie ignored the woman's disapproving stare. So what if it was nearly noon and she wasn't dressed yet? She pulled the belt of her robe tighter and ran her hand through her stringy hair.

"Lunch will be in thirty minutes," Miss Neville said.

"I'm not feeling well," Torie said. "Perhaps you could bring up a tray with some soup? Chicken. With rice." What the heck? If Miss Neville was a servant, let her serve.

The woman's nostrils flared. "Very well. I trust you'll be recovered by tomorrow."

"I hope so," Torie lied. Tomorrow night would be the first in what promised to be an interminable string of parties. Parties to celebrate the prodigal daughter returning home. To celebrate the engagement. To celebrate Rhys's promotion. Her stomach burned at the thought. So did her eyes. Maybe she *was* coming down with something. If only she could be so lucky.

Torie ached. Her face ached from smiling, her feet ached from hours of standing in too-high heels. And so did everything in between. Rhys took a champagne flute from a passing tray. Torie grabbed it from his hand.

"Are you sure?" he asked. "I think that makes five."

"I can still see. Hear. Feel. Must mean I'm still sober."

"You're not enjoying the evening, I take it?" He stroked a finger under her eyes. "You look tired."

She lifted her gaze to his. Saw concern. And dark circles under his eyes as well. "So do you. You think we can blow this joint without causing fireworks?"

He pushed back a sleeve and tilted his wrist, exposing his thin, gold watch. "It's well past ten. I think the guests—assuming they notice we've gone—will indulge the newly engaged couple's desire to sneak away for a few private moments."

Torie twisted the diamond ring sparkling from her left hand. Rhys had presented it in full view of all the party guests in the hotel's grand ballroom less than two hours ago. "I guess you're right. Can we go someplace quiet—your place, maybe?"

His face clouded. "Not the best idea. I've got somewhere else in mind."

She set her flute on a tray and went to find her father. He'd be the easiest target for a quick "Thanks but we're leaving" speech. Rhys could deal with Grandfather.

They drove in awkward silence until Rhys pulled off the Pacific Coast Highway and parked his Lexus. He cracked the windows. The chill night air blew in its briny smell, and the roar of the ocean calmed her like one of Nana's lullabies. Rhys slipped his jacket over her shoulders. "If you get too cold, I can run the heater."

"No. I like the atmosphere." She kicked off her shoes and stared at the moonlight illuminating the foam of the crashing breakers. "How's work? The new job and all. Keeping you busy?"

"Very," he said. He gripped the steering wheel. "I guess it's all right. Mrs. Isaacs puts up with me."

"Does she resent you? Think you took her job?"

"Actually, I didn't take her job. She's an administrative assistant, not management. She's sharp and knows everything inside and out, but she definitely prefers her role. Not a decision maker. She wants to come in at eight-thirty, have lunch from twelve to one, and leave at five-thirty on the dot. I asked her to stay a little late once, to explain a report, and she made it clear it was one time only."

"But you'd rather be in Advertising."

He shrugged. "I enjoyed it. Knew what I was doing. I'll get used to this new position. Eventually."

"I'm sure you'll do fine. But I have a favor."

"Ask."

"I need to get out of the house for a while. On my own. No mother, no driver, nobody watching over my shoulder to make sure I'm behaving like a proper young lady. Just to use the Internet." She gave a quiet laugh. "Catch up on my former life. I figured if you asked me out—you know, like for dinner or something—you could drop me at an Internet café, or the library, or anywhere I could manage some online time. If it's not too much trouble."

"How about lunch on Monday?" he asked. "Mrs. Isaacs has a dental appointment and is taking the afternoon off. I can pick you up, and you can use the computer in my office."

"Nobody will mind?"

"Sometimes it's good to be the boss."

"Thanks." The moonlight caught the flash of her ring. She

lifted her hand. "You didn't have to do this, you know. It's much too . . . much, considering."

"Considering what? You're my fiancé. That requires the proper display of our positions."

An involuntary gasp escaped her. He laughed. "Or so your grandfather and my father said when Dad gave it to me to give to you."

She relaxed. Allowed a smile. "Yes, that sounds like Grandfather all right. Your father didn't seem quite so . . . stuffy, though."

"He can play the good old boy, but the pecking order is still his number-one goal."

"I thought pecking order was for the hens and that it was alpha dogs for guys, but I get what you mean."

"Seriously, if you don't like the ring, we can pick something else out. Something you'd be more comfortable wearing."

He sounded as if she'd be wearing it forever. Had he accepted the whole package? That she was going to go through with the whole marriage thing? Did he feel so obligated to his father that he'd give up whatever he must have had planned for the rest of his life? Or maybe he meant their engagement would be long enough so it would be proper when they broke it off.

He gave her hand a quick squeeze. "It's late. I'll take you home. We could both use a decent night's sleep."

When they arrived at Grandfather's house, he left the car engine running while he walked her to the door. "I'll pick you up Monday at eleven, okay?"

"Okay." She looked at him in the yellow glow of the porch light. GQ handsome. Polite. Rich. But nothing in his brilliant blue eyes said she was more than a business deal to him. She thought about Fozzie. Unkempt hair, calloused hands. A lived-in face. With plain brown eyes that she could drown in. She fished out her key.

Rhys took it from her and slotted it into the lock. With the door ajar, he dropped the key into her palm. He kissed the top of her head. "Take care."

"You, too." She listened to him whistle as he jogged to the Lexus. When she stepped inside, Hutchings stood in the foyer. "Your grandfather would like to see you."

"Crap, Fozzie, slow down. We won't be doing Grinch any good if we break our legs. Or lose the medical gear."

Fozzie stopped. Hotshot was right, of course. Even with night vision, the rocky terrain was precarious. Fozzie checked the GPS again and adjusted their route along the bluff.

The briny ocean smell permeated the air, and the surf crashed below. "Looks like we go down from here," Fozzie said. He pointed to a narrow trail leading to the beach.

Hotshot stood beside him. "Well, that's going to be fun. And if you say 'bucket of piss,' I'm going to shove you down to blaze the trail with your *arse.*"

"No need to get your knickers in a twist. You need any help with the gear?"

"No, it's balanced the way it is." As if to verify his statement, he adjusted the straps on his ruck. "Be nice if Grinch had left the light on."

"Lots of reasons why he didn't," Fozzie said. "No light to leave on, he's not alone. He hasn't signaled again, so that's a distinct possibility." Which is why they hadn't tried to reach him via his cell. Not smart to alert anyone that help was on the way if it was the creeps you were alerting.

"Let's do it," Hotshot said.

Cautiously, they worked their way down the steep cliff to the boulder-lined beach. Fozzie checked the coordinates one more time. "That way." He pointed to the right. "I'm on point." Weapon at the ready, he moved forward, using the rocks for cover, and surveyed the terrain.

Crap. Countless outcroppings and caves. Any one of which might hide Grinch. He signaled for Hotshot to come closer. "We're going to have to split up. Cover more territory."

"Wait," Hotshot said. "Did you see that?"

Fozzie spun around. "See what?"

"Over there. Lights."

Fozzie looked in the direction Hotshot was pointing. A glimmer of light. A pause. More flashes.

"That's Grinch," Hotshot said. "Our extraction signal."

Fozzie was already running toward the source. Which, of course, was a cave. A small cave. A dark cave. Labored breathing came from inside.

Hotshot pushed past Fozzie. "I'll check it out," he said, taking off his goggles and switching on his flashlight. "Cover my six."

"I'm alone." Grinch's voice, barely audible, echoed from darkness. Then silence.

Fozzie followed behind Grinch, using his own powerful Maglite to illuminate as much of the cave as possible. Hotshot had already shrugged off his ruck and was pulling out his med kit. "Give me light, Fozz."

"Right." Fozzie directed the beam at Grinch, suppressing a gasp when he saw his teammate's battered face.

"Not as bad . . . as it looks," Grinch said. He struggled to get up, wincing in pain.

"Lie still. Since when did you become a medic?" Hotshot spoke in his best bedside-manner tone as he assessed Grinch's condition. He turned and stepped away, speaking softly. "He's dehydrated, and I'm guessing a cracked rib or two. I don't want to give him anything by mouth, and I'm not moving him outside yet. I'm going to need you to give me light while I treat him."

Inside the cave. Fozzie told himself the cave would not collapse. He swallowed. "No worries."

CHAPTER THIRTY-THREE

Torie and Rhys strolled across the plaza to the Century City high-rise. "It's like being surrounded by a park," she said. "You ever come out and enjoy the sunshine on a break?"

"As if I get breaks now," he said. "I've barely seen light of day since this stupid promotion."

They stepped through the lobby, Rhys at her side. Clusters of people waited at banks of elevators. He steered her across the glass-enclosed building, across the black granite floor, to a grouping of slender palms flanking a single elevator door. He slipped a key card into a slot below a small plaque that said, "Epicurean Unlimited."

The elevator doors slid open, and he inserted the key into another slot inside. Torie noticed the buttons went from thirty-nine to forty-four. Rhys pressed forty-four. The doors shut with a whisper, and the elevator ascended.

"Private elevator," she said. "Not bad."

"A perk for management. And, lately, it's more reliable than the public ones. Last week, some people got stuck for half an hour in one of them."

Moments later, as quietly as they'd closed, the doors opened. She followed him down a hallway with a beach of carpet so thick she wanted to take her shoes off and wiggle her toes in it. "Nice digs."

"Your father believed in keeping up appearances." He stopped at a door with a tasteful brass plate engraved with "Executive

Offices" beside it, and used his key card once more. "Here we are. Home, sweet home."

They entered an anteroom where the carpet seemed even more luxurious. Smaller than she'd expected, with only two upholstered chairs. "Where do people wait?" she asked.

He nodded to a door at the side of the room. "Oh, there are at least two rooms through there, where I can make people cool their heels if I so desire." He guided her past Mrs. Isaac's tidy desk and swiped his keychain beside a panel by the door at the rear of the office.

"Geez, nothing like keeping the riffraff out," she said.

"I only keep it locked when nobody's here. Mrs. Isaacs has a fob, so she has access to my space."

She noted a couch, a table with two upholstered chairs, a wall full of bookshelves, and gleaming wooden cabinetry. And then there was the view. She stepped to the window—more like a glass wall. "I'll bet you can see Catalina from here."

He laughed. "Maybe, on a clear day. To be honest, it seems all I ever see is the computer monitor and acres of reports." He picked up a stack of file folders and crossed to a sofa. "I'll catch up on my reading while you work."

She checked the online edition of the *Los Angeles Times* and couldn't find anything about either Wingard Research or Willamette Syndrome. She opened Google, tried a few more sites and finally found, in the *Miami Herald,* mention of a "minor setback into research for a new treatment for Willamette Syndrome."

Apparently Wingard Research and Willamette Syndrome weren't important enough to warrant much coverage, at least outside Miami. Not surprising. An orphan disease nobody cared about to begin with wasn't going to make headlines because research into treatment hit a snag. And, apparently that was what they considered it. A snag. A minor setback. But it seemed

Grandfather had done what she'd asked.

The thought brought a scramble of emotions. Pride and satisfaction that she might have made a difference. But there was also apprehension and dread that she'd paid too high a price. She glanced at Rhys, who frowned as he read. Until now, she hadn't noticed the tension he carried.

The more she thought about it, the more she wondered what was really behind Grandfather's decision to put Rhys in charge. True, the company had floundered under her father's reign, but how could putting someone like Rhys at the helm save it? Why him?

Or maybe he didn't want to save the company. Could Rhys's father and her own grandfather have something else in mind? Saturday night, when he'd summoned her to his study, he'd pontificated on the importance of her being the proper corporate wife, of doing good works and being seen in the right places by the right people. She felt like she'd come away with at least a few points. He'd been pleased when she wanted to work with Adult Literacy, and he'd even acquiesced when she'd demanded—okay, politely but *firmly* requested—she have her own car. He even approved her choice. But he hadn't said word one about Epicurean.

She got up from the desk. "What are you working on?" She had to repeat herself before Rhys looked up. Even then, it took a moment for her question to register.

"Oh, departmental reports. Profits and losses, quarterly business projections." One corner of his mouth twisted upward in a rueful smile. "I miss the pretty pictures in my old job."

"You don't really like it, do you?"

He shrugged. "It's still new. I'll learn."

"Would you mind?" she asked. She held out her hand. "I might be able to help."

★ ★ ★ ★ ★

"It's been a long ten days. I'm ready to go home," Fozzie said. He signaled to the waitress for the check and looked at the team's weary faces around the cantina table. "So, 'fess up. Which one of you invited Murphy to the op?"

"He doesn't need an invitation," Hotshot said. "I think that's why they call it Murphy's *Law*."

"Have you ever had an op without a snafu?" Cheese asked.

"This wasn't really a snafu. Grinch stumbled onto some gunrunners and plans for a coup in El Salvador."

Manny said, "The boss decided we should extend our 'research expedition' and deal with returning their cargo to its rightful owners."

"Consider it dealt with," Fozzie said. "Of course, that doesn't address the bigger failure of the mission."

Heads snapped in his direction. "What are you talking about?" Manny asked.

Fozzie grinned. "We never found a single sloth." After the groans died down, he looked at Grinch. "You all right?"

"Good as new," Grinch said.

Hardly, Fozzie thought. Underneath his tan, Grinch was pale. His face was drawn, evidence of pain he refused to acknowledge. When they'd found him in the cave his eyes had been swollen shut from beatings. Grinch had refused medical treatment beyond what Hotshot provided. "We leave here, no telling what will happen," he'd said. "And I trust Hotshot more than any local doctor."

The boss gave them new orders, and they'd continued their cover as research scientists while they awaited the return of the gunrunners. Beach-dwelling sloths were a bit of a stretch, so they took turns traipsing around the forests by day, then assembling to keep watch on the coastline by night.

The waitress dropped the check in the center of the table.

Fozzie passed it to Manny. "You're team leader, you get the honors."

Manny reached for his wallet. Fozzie stood. "I'm calling it a night. See you at oh-seven-hundred."

Grinch finished the last of his tonic water and shoved his chair back. "Sounds like a plan."

Fozzie followed Grinch out the door and across the lobby of their motel. The man walked gingerly, like someone who'd downed a few too many and didn't want to stagger. Fozzie held back as they climbed the two flights of stairs, ready to support Grinch if he stumbled. Grinch leaned on the railing, but he made it to the top without faltering. Fozzie slid the key into the lock and opened the door. "After you," he said.

Grinch crossed the room to one of the twin beds and eased himself down.

"Busted ribs are a bitch," Fozzie said.

"Cracked, not broken. I'm fine. Sore from sleeping on the ground." He didn't bother mentioning the physical side of dealing with twelve gunrunners who had other ideas about surrendering their cargo.

"Hey, tonight it's a real bed." Fozzie sat down and bounced on the mattress. "Although I'm not sure how much better it is than the beach."

"You could have slept in the cave with the rest of us," Grinch said quietly.

"I preferred the fresh air. The smell of an ocean breeze beats the aroma of a refried-beans diet from four other guys."

Grinch barked a quick laugh, then winced and sucked air through his teeth. "You might have a point."

Fozzie stomped into the bathroom and found the vial of pills in Grinch's kit. He brought one to Grinch. "Take the damn thing," he said. "I don't need you groaning in your sleep."

Grinch dry-swallowed the tablet. That he did so without comment told Fozzie more than he wanted to know about Grinch's pain level.

Fozzie stripped, then slid under the covers. Grinch simply lay back, fully clothed, on top of his bed. "Get the light?"

Fozzie reached over and clicked off the lamp.

"Good night, Fozz. And thanks for finding me."

"The SOS was a nice touch. Why the bloody hell did you wait so long to start signaling?"

"Didn't get the phone back from the dirtbags until after I convinced them to let me go."

"By letting them beat you up?"

It took a little longer for Grinch to answer. "I gave better than I got. And it took a while to find the phone. They'd dragged me into that goddamn cave. Too dark to see, not that I could see outside in broad daylight since my eyes were swollen shut." His words came out slowly, muffled. Good. The pill was kicking in.

"Maybe we should get the boss to issue us all seeing-eye dogs," Fozzie said.

"Would have been . . . nice . . . have company . . . warm."

Fozzie waited until Grinch's breathing evened out before allowing himself to drift off.

By noon the next day, they were well underway in Blackthorne's King Air 300. Manny had vetoed Grinch's insistence that he could fly copilot. Hotshot had threatened Grinch with promises he'd file a doctored medical report exaggerating Grinch's condition if he didn't shut up and take his pain pills.

"They knock me out," Grinch complained.

"Which is the whole idea," Hotshot retorted. "It's a long enough flight. This way, you arrive bright eyed and bushy tailed."

"Bleary eyed and groggy's more like it," Grinch said.

"I could always strap you to the medical gurney and put you

on IV painkillers," Hotshot said.

Grinch had swallowed the pills and was snoring peacefully at the rear of the plane. Fozzie busied himself keeping a close eye on the instrument panel with frequent glances out the window at the engine. Cheese had gone over the engine with a fine-tooth comb. Fozzie had done his own checking before they'd taken off. They'd had more than their share of Murphy's Law this trip.

He itched to call Torie, but had no clue what to say, or if she'd even talk to him. He listened to the comforting drone of the engines and the familiar chatter from air traffic control. They'd be home in a few more hours.

"Debriefing in thirty," Manny announced as they landed at the Blackthorne compound.

"I'm going to start the washer," Hotshot said. "Feel free to add any clothes you don't think need burning."

Fozzie stuffed his dirty laundry into the machine, then stowed the rest of his gear. Jinx caught up with him on the way to the debriefing room.

"Touch and go there," Jinx said.

"Been worse. Mostly it was staying out of sight while we waited for the next drop."

"Grinch okay?"

"Yeah, he's healing. The gunrunners were going to drag his arse to El Salvador, but he got away. Hid out in a damn cave by the ocean until we found him. He insisted on carrying out the mission, over Hotshot's protests."

"Sounds like Grinch all right." There was a moment of awkward silence.

"What?" Fozzie asked.

"Um, I wondered if you'd heard from the woman you'd been protecting."

If only. "No, we got busy and out of range." He waited. Jinx knew something.

"I think you should see this. Before you make any, you know, personal calls." He handed Fozzie a plain white envelope, then spun around and walked away.

Something about Jinx's halting tone and hasty departure made Fozzie stick the envelope in his pocket where it could wait until after the debriefing.

He sat at the conference table, only half hearing the discussion. Someone would deal with the disposition of the confiscated weapons. Maintenance would do a thorough inspection of the entire fleet. Any suggestions Fozzie offered for future ops revolved around better equipment, comments he'd made before. Ones that could spurt from his mouth with his brain barely engaged. The envelope burned like a hot coal in his pocket. He begged off the usual round of beers at the local pub and went into one of the small conference rooms. Kicking the door shut behind him, he snagged the envelope from his pocket and ripped it open. Inside were several sheets of paper, folded neatly into thirds.

He unfolded them and stared at a copy of a newspaper article. A picture of Torie. Smiling into the camera next to a man with perfect hair and a mouth full of shiny white teeth. The word engagement leaped off the page, searing his eyeballs. He leaned against the wall, his legs suddenly unwilling to support him. He read the caption under the photograph. Victoria Hamilton and Rhys Ainsworth. Engaged. He'd been gone ten fucking days and she was *engaged?*

What kind of a fucking name was Rhys Ainsworth? He ripped the page into tiny pieces and tossed it in the trash. He scanned the rest of the pages. Society clips and business reports about Rhys fucking Ainsworth as the new general fucking manager of fucking Epicurean Unlimited.

He made confetti with the other pages and added them to

the bin. He rubbed his chest, where it felt like someone had punched a hole in his heart.

He rushed out of the room. Found the team loitering around Hotshot's van. He ran toward them. "Hey, mates. Wait up. Changed my mind about the pub."

CHAPTER THIRTY-FOUR

Torie set the bag on Rhys's desk. "Brought you some lunch."

"Smells great." Without looking up from his computer, he tilted his head toward the table and chairs under the window.

Torie crossed the office and moved a stack of folders off the table. "Buddha's delight, hot-and-sour soup, brown rice." She set the containers on the table. "And chopsticks."

He scrubbed his hands across his eyes.

"Eat," she said. "While it's hot." He moved to the table, and she slipped into his chair. "How's the presentation going?"

"Very well, thanks to you. I don't know what I'd do without you."

She looked to where he sat, spooning mouthfuls of soup as if he hadn't eaten in days. She sighed and focused on the reports in front of her, flipping between them and the PowerPoint slides. "Looks good. Maybe add another couple of slides about the proposed new Home Cooks Division. Stress how Epicurean understands that the economy sucks right now, and people aren't going out to eat, but they still want to enjoy good meals. Ordinary people will now have access to some of the secrets of restaurant chefs, from affordable but quality cookware, to conveniently packaged meals and ingredients." She made a couple of adjustments to one of the slides, deleted two others. "In your talk, you want to stress where we're going, not where we've been. And I wouldn't mention that you're bringing in another outside auditor. Not until we confirm the discrepancies."

"I repeat. What would I do without you? My presentation is in two days, and you're making me look like I know what I'm talking about."

"Hey, I enjoy this." And she did. Who'd have thought when she'd come to Rhys's office for the first time two months ago, that she had a knack for corporate management. Rhys tried, but for him it was a struggle. And it showed. His hair needed a cut, and his tie was loosened at his neck. Bluish-purple crescents sat below his eyes.

She made some notes, saved her changes and copied everything to her flash drive. She flipped to his Internet browser. Wingard's reputation had taken a slight hit, but they'd fired Lonnie Freeman and were moving on. The pharmaceutical company had delayed signing any contracts but hadn't closed the door on the deal.

She clicked to the *Herald*'s site and searched for updates. A tiny article mentioned that Wingard Research was now collaborating with the pharmaceutical company to continue the research. They cited the previous problems as errors in statistical reporting, not problems with the treatment itself.

Well, she didn't buy that, but with the FDA breathing down Wingard's necks, and having to repeat the early trials, she felt that her debt to Kathy was paid. An article about cancer cures being found in chemicals produced by sponges caught her eye. Kathy's lichen research nagged at her. Could lichens produce other lifesaving drugs?

Should she dig out Kathy's old notes, mail them to Wingard Research? Let them take it from there? Kathy had wanted to find the lichens herself for preliminary testing. She was far more qualified than Torie would ever be. Wingard Research could do something about them.

She heard Rhys snoring softly. His head lolled against the back of the chair, and his chopsticks dangled from his fingers. She shut down the browser, stepped soundlessly across the plush carpet and eased them from his hand. She checked the clock on the bookshelf. He had another half hour before Mrs. Isaacs would be back from lunch. She'd let him sleep for another twenty minutes. After he got through his presentation, she'd insist on the heart-to-heart about the marriage thing.

In the past two months, they'd met several times a week, having dinner and often working well into the night. Several more times a week, she brought lunch in for Rhys while Mrs. Isaacs was out of the office. If his assistant thought they were up to anything, doing company work was probably the last thing on her mind. But Rhys had never shown her anything other than polite, almost brotherly affection. Everything revolved around Epicurean and his new position.

Not once had he invited her to his home, or even given her more than a perfunctory kiss on the forehead or cheek. Always had her back by midnight, like she'd turn into a pumpkin. She wondered if Grandfather had dictated ground rules of pre-wedding acceptable behavior.

Then again, she'd never tested him, never tried making the first move. Instead, she slept alone in her bed at Grandfather's house. When Fozzie didn't invade her dreams and keep her awake.

Torie nibbled at a few of the vegetables Rhys hadn't finished. He stirred.

"Mmh." He blinked. "Must have dozed. Sorry."

"No worries," she said. "I've saved everything for you, and I'll look at the files later. It's my literacy tutoring day. And then there's a final meeting for the Adult Literacy fund-raiser."

"Saturday night. I remember."

"Your mom's been great about setting things up. I think this is one party I might actually enjoy."

"She likes you," Rhys said.

Torie shook her head. "No, she likes that you're marrying me. She's made it clear how glad she is that her darling Rhys is finally letting go of bachelorhood at the ripe old age of thirty-six. I don't think it's really me she likes, per se."

"Well, she should. And my dad likes you, too."

"Same goes for him, I think." She smiled. "But it never hurts to be liked." The outer office door opened. "Sounds like Mrs. Isaacs is back. You know, from the way she looks at me when I leave, she probably thinks we're having mad, passionate sex on the desk."

Rhys flashed a quick grin, the first she'd seen in a while. "I'm sure she thinks we're respectable enough to use the couch. I'll pick you up at seven on Saturday."

On Friday, Torie spent too much of the day taking care of last-minute preparations for tomorrow night's ball. Considering the Los Angeles traffic and multitude of stops she had to make, she'd almost asked Trang to drive but relished the independence her new Prius afforded her. She left the florist after approving the centerpieces and making sure everything would be delivered and set up on schedule.

She realized she'd been so busy that she'd totally forgotten Rhys's presentation at three. She'd wanted to be there when he finished, to offer her congratulations. In truth, she'd wanted to be there for the entire thing, but he'd vetoed that, saying it would make him too nervous, and besides, it was closed to all but the department heads.

Get real. You want to know how your work was received.

Well, she wasn't far from his house. Why not surprise him? She programmed her GPS for directions and followed them as they led her from Sunset to Beverly Drive, then up into the foothills. She drove past a small orange grove, a surprising rustic touch for an area where land for new homes didn't exist.

As she drove, it was obvious that many of the homes had been remodeled and enlarged so they sat shoulder to shoulder with their neighbors. After she worked her car into a parking place a few houses down from Rhys's address, she wished she'd brought a bottle of champagne. He'd worked hard; he deserved it. The sun had gone down behind the surrounding hills. Jasmine filled the air with its sweet, almost cloying perfume. She locked the car and walked up the street—no sidewalks here. Real estate was too valuable to waste space for the occasional pedestrian. Everyone in LA lived in their cars.

Rhys's address proved to be a much smaller, older home. One of the non-enlarged ones. He'd said his parents had bought it in the late fifties and sold it to him at their cost. She realized nobody had discussed where they'd live after they got married. Assuming they were actually going to get married. She found Rhys comfortable to be around, a friend, but did she really want to live that way? Still, she evaluated the house as if it might be her home someday.

White stucco, Spanish tile roof. Red-tile walkway to the entrance lined by boxwood hedges. Carved wooden door, windows framed with wooden shutters. Cozy. She rang the bell. Soft music played inside. She rang again. Knocked. No answer. She tried the door, and it opened at her touch.

"Rhys?" she called. "It's Torie."

When there was no answer, she stepped into the red-tiled entry foyer. "Rhys?" she called again. To her right, the living room was unoccupied. To her left, half-burned candles flickered on the dining room table, which was covered with dirty dishes. A champagne bottle sat upended in a silver cooler. Service for two.

Her stomach clenched. No wonder he'd never made any

advances. She had her hand on the door to leave when Rhys rushed into the room. He was barefoot, wearing a thigh-length silk robe, with a serious case of bed head. "Torie, please. Don't go. We need to talk."

"It's pretty clear to me. I don't think I need an explanation."

"Wait." He took her arm. Gently. He led her to the couch. "Please sit."

She sat in a chair across from him, not beside him on the couch. Where she could look him in the eye, but not feel his body heat. Or smell the mixture of his aftershave and after sex. "I guess this means the wedding is off. Which is a good thing. Arranged marriages went out a hundred years ago." She was proud that her voice didn't quaver, that her eyes didn't brim with tears. After all, she'd been looking for a way to bring up the subject, and he'd done that for her.

She heard footsteps behind her. Great. He was going to parade her competition out here in front of her? She refused to turn and look.

"It's not what you think, Torie," Rhys said. "I've been trying to figure out a way to tell you. I . . . I didn't know how." He extended his arm toward the person behind them. "I want you to meet someone."

She schooled her mouth into a smile, called upon every polite gene she had, and stood, ready to greet Rhys's lover. Turning, her gaze collided with a bare chest. A hairless, but very male bare chest. She wasn't sure whether to look up or down. Up, she decided.

"I'm Phillip," he said. Tanned, dark-haired. Stubble-jawed, dimpled cheeks. Where Rhys was handsome, Phillip was pretty. She didn't know whether to laugh or cry.

"Torie." She sank onto the chair, and he crossed the room and sat next to Rhys. Rhys looked at him the way Fozzie had looked at her. Phillip crossed a jean-clad leg over his knee and waited.

"My parents don't know," Rhys said.

She swallowed the urge to say, "Duh." "So, what are we going to do now?"

Rhys lowered his head and yanked his hair with both hands. "Assuming we're not hit by an earthquake and I'm not swallowed alive?"

"Yeah, let's assume that's not going to happen," she said. "How long have you and Phillip—you know?"

"Five years," Rhys said.

"And were you planning to come out?"

The two men exchanged uneasy glances. "We'd been thinking about it. But my parents—let's just say they're not very progressive. Nor are a lot of their social circle."

She wondered what Grandfather would think. He couldn't abide the idea of a woman in an executive position; what would he say about a gay man?

"So, what did you think? That the three of us would live together?"

"I didn't think," Rhys said. "I was too busy working. Damn my father anyway, for—"

"For what? For making you feel guilty for not living your life the way you want? Was that why you didn't object to the new job at Epicurean? Do what your father wants, and maybe he'll accept the rest of you? It doesn't work. I've lived my life that way, too, remember."

"Take it easy," Phillip said. "We can't undo what's done. Let's figure out what we do next."

"Tomorrow night's the fund-raising ball," Torie said. "I'm not abandoning that." She looked at Rhys. "If you don't want to come, I'll understand, but it's important to me."

"I'll be there," he said.

"And afterward—no, on Sunday—we're going to meet with Grandfather," she said.

Rhys blanched. "And tell him what?"

"Phillip, can you make some coffee?" she asked. "Rhys and I are going to have a nice, long chat."

CHAPTER THIRTY-FIVE

Torie looked up from her desk when Mrs. Isaacs tapped on the door before walking in. "You've got lunch with Mr. Jacobson at twelve-thirty, and a meeting with Noreen Ellis from accounting at three."

"Thank you," Torie said. "And I could use the month-end reports from Advertising, New Accounts, Appliances and Cookware, please."

"Of course." From the hallway, a shrill bell chimed several times.

"Not the elevators again," Torie said. "What's that? Third time this week?"

"At least. Maintenance swears they've fixed it." She spun efficiently and strode to the door.

"And leave the door open, please." Closing it was a habit, leftover from Torie's father, she thought. Torie preferred to feel she wasn't alone.

She got herself a cup of coffee from the pot in her mini-kitchen and worked her way through her correspondence.

"Sir. Sir! You can't go in there." Mrs. Isaacs' normally unflappable tone was decidedly flapped.

"I bloody well can, and I will."

Torie jumped up, knocking what was left of her coffee onto her desk. Ignoring it, she raced to the outer office, where she almost plowed into a wide-eyed Mrs. Isaacs. "I'm sorry, Miss Stoker. He barged in. Shall I call Security? Or maybe Health

Services. He doesn't look so good."

He looked wonderful. Okay, so he was pale and sheened in sweat, and sat on one of the chairs with his head down and his shoulders heaving as he gasped for breath, but he still sent her pulse racing. "Get him some water. Quickly, please." Torie knelt next to Fozzie and put her arm across his shoulders.

"You work on the bloody forty-fourth floor?"

"You didn't walk up, did you?"

Mrs. Isaacs returned with a glass of ice water. Fozzie took it, although his hand trembled. "No, of course not."

"Mrs. Isaacs," Torie said. "This is Foster Mayhew, a friend I haven't seen in quite a while. We're going to catch up."

"How do you do," Mrs. Isaacs said, giving him a glance that was both wary and curious.

"Can you manage to walk about twelve more feet?" Torie asked. "We can go into my office."

He looked around. "This isn't it?"

She smiled. "No, I'm in there." She bobbed her head toward her doorway.

He gulped down the water and wiped his mouth. "I'm fine." He met her gaze. "Now."

"Tell me you weren't in one of the elevator cars that stuck."

"If I did, I'd be lyin'."

She led the way into her office and closed the door, afraid to speak. Afraid to ask him why he'd appeared when she hadn't heard from him in months. Why he'd simply disappeared from the airport. Afraid to admit how her heart had tumbled at the sound of his voice.

He didn't seem to find speaking any easier. So they sat on the couch and stared at each other.

Fozzie sucked in a huge breath, then blew it out. Mortification at how he'd almost passed out caught up with him. He'd gutted it out in the elevator, including all twenty-three minutes and seventeen seconds of being trapped between floors. Alone. When the doors finally opened, all he could think of was Torie. Instead of stopping by the men's room to compose himself, he'd plunged down the hall, light-headed and weak-kneed.

He'd opened the office door expecting to see Torie, and instead, there was another woman. Older, prim. The thought that he'd lost her, irrational as it might have been, was the kicker. His brain had shifted into op mode. He'd spied an open doorway at the back of the office, and staggered toward it as if he were clearing a building, making sure there was nobody left behind. Running on sheer adrenaline, which chose that moment to abandon his system.

"Crap," he said, breaking the awkward silence.

Torie's eyes widened.

He dragged his fingers through his hair. "I said it out loud, did I?"

A smile flickered about her mouth. "I'm sure Mrs. Isaacs heard it, too."

"It was about me, not you," he said. "I'm . . . out of my element here." He looked at her, at the posh surroundings. At her silky green blouse tucked into a slim gray skirt. A new hairstyle. Still brown, but with subtle streaks of gold, which were reflected in her eyes. She appeared totally in her element.

"I guess we should talk," she said.

He tried to answer. Everything he wanted to say, all the words he'd repeated in his head turned to alphabet soup, floated around like so much gibberish.

"I can make tea," she said. "I even have rooibos."

He nearly came undone. "No thanks," he croaked.

"Would you rather we go someplace more . . . informal?" she said. "If you can handle the ride down so soon."

Her expression said she remembered the last time she'd

helped him deal with his panic attack. But he couldn't read her well enough to know if she'd be willing to do it again. He had no right to expect her to pick up where they'd left off. Not after the way he'd disappeared. He wouldn't blame her if she sent him packing. Then again, she could have already sent him packing, leaving him on his own to deal with forty-four flights of stairs, because it would be a cold day in hell before he was getting on that elevator alone.

"I made it up. I'll make it down," he said.

She picked up the phone. When she did, he noticed the absence of a ring on her hand. Did that mean she was no longer engaged?

"Please reschedule my lunch," she was saying. "And have Sam Baxter take the meeting with Accounting. He should have a copy of the files. And clear my calendar for tomorrow as well."

Before his brain exploded with running all the possibilities, she hung up. "This way."

She led him into a workspace, smaller than either her office or Mrs. Isaacs'. A comfortable sofa, a round table with a leather chair. A coatrack in the corner held a jacket that matched her skirt. She slipped it off the hanger. He stepped closer, helped her work her arms into the sleeves. Her scent invaded his senses. Their hands touched briefly. A mere touch, quickly released, but it sent a jolt through him as if she'd hit him with a cattle prod. She opened a drawer in a console and extracted a small black purse and a pair of black heels. He noticed she wore flats. Despite her executive trappings, a trace of the Torie who put comfort above fashion lingered.

She opened a door and they were in a hallway. He followed her to an elevator door. "This one's more reliable," she said, pressing the button. "And more efficient. We'll be on the ground in nothing flat."

The doors slid apart. The car was maybe a quarter the size of the public ones. He swallowed.

"You all right?" she asked. "I could wait in the lobby while you take the stairs." Was she concerned or teasing?

He thought of the bare ring finger. "I'm fine."

She watched him warily when the doors slid shut. After she pressed the button for the lobby, she slipped her hand into his. As the elevator descended, he concentrated on not squeezing it. Instead, he fixed his gaze on her eyes, trying to see through them into her brain. She offered no small talk, no distractions, simply the warm hand that said she was there.

He hadn't found the right words when they exited the elevator, or walked to the parking garage. He managed the brilliant "nice car" when she unlocked her red Prius, and the equally brilliant "nice place" when she unlocked the door to an apartment somewhere near enough to the ocean that he could smell the sea air. Not much better was the "yes, please" when she repeated her offer of rooibos tea.

So, here they sat, sitting on bar stools at her kitchen counter, sipping tea and trying not to think of the elephant in the room with them. "Crap," he muttered.

"That seems to be your go-to word."

"I'm sorry," he said. "Not for my limited vocabulary. For screwing up. I'm so bloody sorry."

"I'm listening," she said.

"I don't know where to start."

Her mouth flattened. "How about the Salt Lake City airport?"

He set his mug on the counter and forced himself to look her in the eye. "I never really told you what I do. You only saw a small piece of my job. The rest . . . gets complicated."

"I'm still listening."

He explained the less public side of Blackthorne, Inc. How they never left a man, and how he and Grinch had saved each other's arses more than once. Slowly at first, but as she seemed to accept what he'd done, he continued to fill in details. At least the ones he was allowed to talk about.

"I wanted to talk to you, but I wanted to do it face to face. And then the mission dragged on, and when I finally got stateside, you were engaged."

"It was the only way I could get Grandfather to do what I asked, so I agreed to his terms. Maybe if you'd been there, you might have helped me find another option. But since you didn't seem to think I was important enough to bother with, I went along with what he demanded."

"I saw your picture in the paper. You looked happy." He forced himself to admit the truth. "And I was a bloody coward. I was afraid that if I came back and begged you to give me another chance, you'd send me packing."

"Well, we'll never know, will we?"

He held her left hand in his palm, fingering the spot where a ring would have been. "What happened, Torie?"

"I'm no longer engaged." She pulled her hand away. "And I finally managed to stand up to Grandfather. To prove that a woman can do the job of a man. And, considering the way my father handled the job, that she can do it better."

"I'm proud of you," he said.

Her face turned pink. "I remembered how you believed in me. I'd knuckled under the first time, but that was because there wasn't time to think. And there wasn't time to wait. I didn't want anyone else to die if the Wingard research was flawed. What I did made a difference. But, later, when I was helping Rhys with his new position, I saw what I was capable of. We went to Grandfather and told him that I'd been the one responsible for all of Rhys's accomplishments, and that we weren't going to get married. Rhys was more unhappy about the marriage than I was."

"He didn't want to marry you? The man's a fool."

"Well, the fact that he's gay might have played a teeny tiny part in that."

Fozzie nearly choked on his tea. "What? Your grandfather arranged a marriage between you and a gay man?"

She favored him with the first smile he'd seen. "He didn't know. And Rhys didn't tell him then. He simply said he didn't like the new position and wanted his old job back, and that I'd already shown I had the potential. We showed how there had been some shady dealings involving kickbacks from vendors. Lots of spreadsheets and graphs, and Grandfather always loved statistics. So he agreed, on a one-year trial basis. Not that he had much to lose, since he'd already planned to give up the company. But I enrolled in an MBA program, and Grandfather has been receptive to my ideas for change."

"So why did your grandfather give Rhys the top-dog job in the first place, if Rhys didn't want it and wasn't good at it?"

"Long story. My father had been benefitting from those kickbacks. He wanted a successor who wouldn't find them. Rhys's father had been hounding my father to give his son a career boost. My father thought Rhys becoming general manager was the safest course of action, and since the Ainsworths and the Hamiltons go way back, Grandfather felt it was a good opportunity to repay an old family obligation. His future is secure and doesn't depend on Epicurean. And," she added ruefully, "at first, I think he enjoyed watching me meekly do his bidding."

"I think there are more details in here."

"And I think you've done an admirable job of turning things around so I'm doing the talking. Where have you been for the past four months, and why are you back now?"

Trapped by the lightning bolts in her eyes, he gave her the short version. "For the first part, I was working. I begged for any assignment Blackthorne would give me. Anything to keep from thinking about you with another man. Then, I went home."

"Australia?"

He nodded, remembering the punch to his gut when he'd gotten his mum's call. "Tony—my brother. He'd been in an accident."

She gripped his hand in hers. Her eyes asked the question.

"He's okay now. But he'll be in a wheelchair for the rest of his life."

"Oh, Fozzie. I'm so sorry."

"He's doing fine. Nothing gets Tony down. But, early on, they needed me to be there." And, it had turned out, he'd needed them.

"Will you be going back?"

"No. My life's here. I'm not cut out to live on a sheep station, and my family knows it. They've always had plenty of help. Tony's a whiz at management, and he can do that from a chair." He shoved his hair back. "Torie, I know I have no right to ask, not after the way I let you down. My job means I'm away a lot. Sometimes I can't tell you where I'm going, or when I'll be back. But . . . do you think we could give it another go? Slow, easy, see how we fit?"

Her cheeks flushed bright red. "I don't think so."

CHAPTER THIRTY-SIX

Torie took perverse pleasure in watching the flash of hurt in Fozzie's expression. Almost. All those nights, thinking about giving him a taste of what he'd put her through. If he ever had the nerve to come back. But seeing him—just hearing his voice when he'd stormed into her office—had her responding to a far different emotion. A reaction that slammed into her like a runaway train.

"I . . . I understand," he said. "I can catch a cab. Be out of your hair." He stood. "It was good to see you again. You're lookin' fine."

The heat flooding her destroyed the need to punish him. She slid off her stool and positioned herself between his thighs. "I already know how we fit. And slow and easy isn't what I have in mind right now." She yanked his head down to meet hers, pressed her mouth against his. His opened with a gasp and she dove inside, her tongue seeking, demanding.

"I wanted to hate you," she said between frantic kisses. "I can't." She fumbled with the buttons on his shirt.

"Torie—"

"Man comes back, woman can't resist. It's so romance heroine. Damn it, I'm a cliché, okay? I need to touch you. I want you to touch me."

He framed her face with his hands, tilted it, then covered her mouth with his. His tongue met hers, probe for probe, stroke for stroke. He cupped her bottom and hoisted her onto his lap, her skirt bunching around her hips. Blood pounded in her ears. Her breasts ached. She reached for his hands, put them against her chest. Not waiting for him to caress them, she pressed her hands over his, rubbing her breasts, sending bursts of desire to her groin.

Beneath her, she felt his hardness. Her panties were wet. She parted her legs further, squirming, needing contact with that spot between her legs where her universe was centered. They fit like two pieces of a puzzle. She wriggled, squirmed, did everything she could to create the friction she desperately needed. His hand gripped her hips, pressing her against him, moving her against his length. His other hand found her nipple, fingers teased it, massaged it, pinched it, each movement sending the flames higher. He drove her up, up, up, and she surrendered to the demand for release.

Shuddering, she sank against his chest. His heart thudded beneath her ear. His hand moved gently up and down her back. "You okay?" he asked.

"God, I don't think I've ever . . . not that fast . . . not even when . . ." She pulled away, embarrassed. She'd done little more than gratify herself.

"Can we try for slow, now?" He tugged her back to him, rested his forehead against hers, while unbuttoning her blouse. He stopped after three buttons, brushed his fingertips over the top of her breasts. Thumbed her nipples through the nylon. She stilled his hand.

"Let me touch you." She slipped his shirt over his shoulders, splayed her fingers over his chest, moving them outward, finding the nubs of his nipples. She leaned forward and scraped one with her teeth. On a sigh, he leaned back, eyes closed.

"Come with me," she said. She slid off his lap and tugged on his hand.

"We're going fast again, are we?" He smiled the cocky grin

she hadn't seen in months, and she nearly dragged him onto the kitchen tiles. An iota of practicality prevailed.

"Just come on." She unfastened her skirt and let it slide to the floor. Unencumbered, she lengthened her stride and pulled a laughing Fozzie to the bedroom. She yanked the covers down, trying to get out of her clothes at the same time.

"Hey, Sunshine, take it easy. Let me help." He gripped her waist and set her on the bed. Kneeling at her feet, he unbuttoned the remaining buttons of her blouse. Agonizingly slowly. Her nipples peaked under her bra. He continued the gentle caresses he'd begun in the kitchen, grazing his fingertips across the tops of her breasts. He leaned forward, kissing where his fingers had stroked.

He ran a fingertip from her ear to her chin, then kissed that route as well. Soft lips replaced calloused fingers. She reached for him, but he shook his head. "Slow and easy. I want to enjoy this. It's been too long."

"Not my fault," she muttered. "Kiss me."

"I will." He started at her chin and worked his way south, slipping her blouse off her shoulders. She shrugged it all the way off. Lips and tongue covered her with delight. He swirled his tongue around her navel, then skipped the piece of real estate yearning for his touch and went to her bare thighs above her nylons. One at a time, he slid them down, still caressing and kissing. She shivered when he reached the back of her knees. Groaned when he massaged her arches.

He rose, scooped her up, and laid her on the bed. "I like your hair," he said, pushing it away from her face. "And your nose." He kissed its tip. "But I love your mouth." He lay beside her, cupped her head and pressed his lips to hers.

Greedily, she took him in, deepening the kiss. Hot kisses, gentle kisses, frenzied kisses. She tangled her fingers in his hair, trying to get him closer. "I want you. All of you." She fumbled with his belt. "Too many clothes."

"I'm not finished with you." He hit her with that devilish grin again. "And I only brought one condom."

She struggled to rise. "I still have the ones we bought in Oregon. Bathroom drawer." She pointed.

Fozzie rolled off the bed and found the condom box. His cock throbbed, begging for attention. He kicked off his shoes, tugged off his socks and shucked his pants. Slow and easy would have to wait.

Returning to the bedroom, he opened the box, grabbed a packet and dumped the rest on the bedside table. Torie had denied him the pleasure of removing her bra and panties. Another time. He sheathed himself, then stretched out alongside her, cupping her mound with his hand, nuzzling a firm breast with his mouth. His fingers delved into her hot, wet silkiness. She moaned and lifted her hips, already setting the rhythm.

His thumb rubbed circles over her swollen bud. She moved faster. She pressed his head tighter against her breast. He nipped, scraped, and sucked.

"Inside. Now. Now. Now!" She reached for him. The touch of her fingers on his cock, stroking. Her other hand fondled his balls.

He forced himself to enter slowly. To savor each centimeter. She was hot, wet, and tight. She tilted upward, grabbed his arse and pulled him in to the hilt. Wrapped her legs around him. Clamped him like a vise. He gasped.

She rocked, and he followed. Bit by bit, he slowed the pace, gliding in and out with long, smooth strokes. He'd survived on memories of their lovemaking, but the memories didn't begin to compare with the delight each thrust delivered.

When the inevitable threatened, he lowered himself to her breast again, fondling one, nibbling the other. Her short, shallow breaths warmed his face. She moved faster, took him higher.

Her eyes squinted shut.

"Open your eyes," he said, hanging by his toenails to his last shred of control. "Look at me. Look at me."

He watched those brown eyes, shot with lightning bolts of gold, go blank as she went over. And with one more thrust, he followed her.

He crumpled on top of her, unable to speak. Barely able to breathe. And since he was dead weight, she probably couldn't breathe at all. He rolled over, taking her with him. She snuggled against him, all warm and soft. The empty feeling, the indefinable ache he'd felt for the last four months was gone. He wrapped his arms around her and kissed the top of her head.

"I love you, Torie. I know your granny told you not to believe anything a man says in bed, but I loved you before, and I've never stopped. I've been an idiot, but an idiot who loves you."

"I know," she whispered into his chest. "You rode up forty-four floors to find me."

"Good thing your office wasn't at the top of the Sears Tower." He tousled her hair. "I'm not sure I could love *anyone* that much."

She punched his arm. "I suppose we should finish our conversation."

"Can we do it after lunch? Airlines don't feed you worth a damn."

"In or out?"

"In. Definitely in."

"I'll fix us something," she said. "After I shower."

He grinned. "Don't bother. I have a feeling you'll need another one soon enough."

CHAPTER THIRTY-SEVEN

Fozzie absorbed Torie's warmth, enjoyed her scent, before he opened his eyes. Six-fifteen. Wednesday morning. Two glorious days of Torie. He trailed the back of his hand along her cheek. "I'm so fucking in love with you," he murmured. "Mum was right."

"About what?"

"I thought you were asleep."

"Don't change the subject." She turned over and traced her fingers along his jaw.

He hugged her tight, speaking to the top of her head. "I slept last night."

"I would hope so."

"No, I didn't mean that. I've been more exhausted before, gone days with hardly any sleep. But I've never—" He searched for the words. "I've never felt like I could let go. With you, I slept . . . safe. Me mum said that's how I'd know it was real. When my mind trusted enough to shut down completely, I'd know I found the one."

Her eyes brimmed. "I feel the same way. When you touch me, everything untangles inside."

"What are we going to do about it?"

She sat up. "I don't know. I like my job, Fozzie. I really do. And I'm good at it."

"So am I."

"I know."

"I'm gone a lot."

"I work long hours, and I've got my MBA classes."

"I'm based out of San Francisco."

"Epicurean's been in LA for over thirty years."

"I don't have to be at work until Monday," he said.

"I took two days off. I have to go in today."

"Would you be willing to have a houseguest for the rest of the week? Kind of a test run?"

She flashed a mischievous smile. "I suppose. But I have work to do. You can pretend I'm off on some top-secret mission and stay out of my hair. No more joined at the hip stuff."

"Sounds fair."

"And you'll need a tux for Friday."

"Not a problem." Her look of surprise at his immediate answer sent a quick thrill through him. Didn't she know he'd do whatever she asked?

"I suppose we wouldn't be the first couple with a long-distance relationship," she said.

"Relationship." He grinned. "I like the sound of that." He ran his fingers over her breasts.

She slapped them away. "No you don't. I'm going to shower and go to work. Assuming I can walk as far as the bathroom."

"If you'll let me borrow your car, I'll drive you to work. I have a tux to rent."

Fozzie circled Torie's living room until he was afraid he'd wear a trench in the carpet. He ran his finger around the collar of his tux. He should have asked Grinch or Hotshot to go to his apartment and get his own tux, overnight it to him. If a man had to wear one of these penguin suits, at least a custom job was less uncomfortable than a last-minute rental.

He fingered the velvet box in his pocket one more time. Two days hadn't given him time to do what he wanted, but no way was he leaving town without giving Torie something that said she was his. His? Who was he kidding? He was hers. She owned his heart.

Which thudded through his chest like a red kangaroo bounder when she appeared in the doorway.

Slinky dress. Red. Hot. His mouth went dry. She stood there, not moving. Her eyes widened. "You clean up nice," she said. "Are you ready?"

Was he ever. "You're gorgeous. You sure you don't want to stay home? Or can we be late?" Very late.

She crossed the room and slipped her arm around his. "Sorry. This is business."

"For you, maybe. I'm seeing the pleasure side of things."

"A boring exclusive cocktail reception at a preview of the Restaurant Show? You think that's a pleasure?"

He kissed her throat. "No, looking at you, and thinking about after the reception. That's the pleasure. I . . . um . . . I thought we could go out afterward. Unwind. The two of us."

"I guess," she said. "We'll see how it goes. Usually, all I want is to get my shoes off and go to bed."

"Which is also an excellent idea."

She giggled. She'd been giggling a lot lately. It set that kangaroo in his chest bouncing again.

The doorbell rang. "That'll be Trang," she said.

"Trang?"

"Our driver. I borrowed him from Grandfather for the evening." She pulled some sort of loosely woven shimmery fabric off the back of the chair and wrapped it around her shoulders.

"Can we neck in the back?"

She punched his arm. "Maybe on the way home. I can't show up looking like—" She stroked his jaw. "Like we've been doing what I've thought about all day."

"Hold that thought." They walked to the door. God, she smelled good. He rested a hand at her waist, letting her walk half a pace ahead of him as he tried to get his arousal under control.

Two hours later, he was still walking around at half-mast. Torie worked the crowd like she'd been bred to it. Which, he realized, she had. She may have rejected it, but the roots were there. Every now and then, she'd smile at him, and his blood supply took a nosedive. She didn't need him to hang onto, and aside from some introductions when they'd arrived, she'd sent him on his way.

"Enjoy the food. Look at the gadgets," she'd said. "I have to schmooze for a while, and no point in both of us being bored."

As if watching her could ever be boring. He grazed his way through the food displays, observing. He'd done his share of security gigs for Blackthorne, and he occupied himself making a mental catalog of the guests, dividing them into three categories. There were the ones who were here to be seen, the ones who were here for the free eats and drinks, and the ones who were here to work, like Torie. She mingled, cleverly steering guests toward the Epicurean booths and displays.

A shapely redhead approached. Definitely in the "to be seen" category. Legs to her neck, hooters the size of melons. She smiled. He smiled back. Nothing. No spark, no electricity, no desire. After exchanging a few words of polite conversation, he excused himself and headed to the men's room.

When he returned, he had a momentary panic when he couldn't spot Torie. Her red dress had made her an easy target. When he located her talking to a group of men across the vast hall, he felt the bong in his chest he didn't think he'd ever get used to—or want to. He strolled in their direction, shaking off an offer of champagne from a passing waiter. He wanted a clear head tonight.

Torie had no sooner taken her leave from one group than another stepped in. This time, she appeared to be the goal of a solitary man Fozzie pegged as the "here for the food" type. Dark suit, slightly rumpled. Graying hair, thin, with a low part just shy of screaming comb-over. Cold, hard eyes behind black-framed glasses.

Fozzie quickened his pace across the floor of the exhibit hall. Torie could use a buffer between herself and a boor. And maybe he could convince her it was time to go. His hand went to his pocket, to the velvet box that had been his touchstone all evening. Could he make her understand? That it wasn't about sex. Since she went back to work, they'd barely seen each other and hadn't had sex. But just waking up next to her, falling asleep beside her, filled him with a contentment he'd never known before. And thinking about her had him grinning like an idiot, he realized.

From her friendly smile and outstretched arm, Fozzie could tell Torie had spotted the man approaching her. But instead of stepping forward, she stepped back, dropping her hand. He looked more closely at the man and moved more quickly through the clusters of guests. There was something vaguely familiar about him. When the man grabbed Torie's arm, Fozzie's grin fell away. He broke into a run, not caring who he jostled, or if he knocked plates of canapés out of their hands.

"Hey, watch it, buddy," a man said.

"Call security," Fozzie said, pushing past. He dodged the huge chocolate fountain in the center of the room. Torie's captor had her arm wrenched behind her back and was pushing her toward a small breakout room.

"Freeman!" Fozzie shouted. "Stop!"

The man spun at the sound. He shoved Torie into the empty room. Torie stumbled to the ground. Fozzie slid through the door before it closed. Freeman knelt at Torie's side, a knife pressed to her throat. "Get away or she dies."

Fozzie slowed. Lifted his hands. "Take it easy, mate. You don't want to go doing something stupid. This place is packed with people." He kept his gaze fixed on Freeman. "You all right, Sunshine?" he said.

Her "yes" was a faint gasp.

"What does it matter?" Freeman said. "My life is ruined, and it's her fault. All I needed was a little more time. I owed people money. Too much money. The drug needed a few tweaks, that's all. We'd have worked it out, but she had to blow the whistle, get me fired. Lost my wife, my house, and I'm a dead man anyway when the sharks catch me. I'm not going alone."

"Let's talk about it," Fozzie said. "We can work something out. I know people who might be able to help."

"Yeah, like I'm supposed to believe that. And even if I was stupid enough to believe you, the bitch needs to be punished for what she did to me. I've watched her, with her fancy job and all that money. She has to pay."

Torie gasped. Freeman kicked her aside and stood, facing Fozzie, a large chef's knife in his hand. Blood stained the tip.

Fozzie's own blood approached the boiling point. He moved forward slowly, urging Freeman to attack, to move away from Torie. He didn't dare look at her, didn't dare think about what Freeman had done.

Freeman's eyes were wild, glassy, rimmed in white. He lunged forward, slashing the knife at Fozzie, then again, this time with a backhand strike. Fozzie used his forearms to block the blow, to control Freeman's arm. Only then did he feel the burning in his upper arm. Crap.

"That was *not* a nice thing," Fozzie said. He touched his arm. His fingers came up sticky with blood. "Definitely *not* a nice thing. This is a rental."

Half-blind with fury, Fozzie recaptured Freeman's knife arm, twisting it so the blade pressed against the man's neck.

"Go ahead," Freeman said, breathing heavily. "But make it quick. Not like what the sharks will do."

Fozzie lessened the pressure. He didn't kill pathetic jerks like this. "Let go of the knife," he said. "Now."

Freeman brought his other hand atop Fozzie's and pressed. "It's better this way," he said.

Fozzie eased back the knife, still twisting Freeman's wrist. He moved his right leg against Freeman's, sweeping it out and bringing the man to the ground. Freeman's grip on the knife relaxed. Fozzie hurled it away. The door opened.

"What's going on?" a deep male voice asked. "Event Security."

"Restrain this man," Fozzie said. "And call the cops." He left Freeman slumped in a heap and rushed to Torie's side.

"Sunshine, are you all right?"

"Cold," she said.

He looked at her. Pale, her lips almost blue. Sweat beaded her face. Her hands were folded across her midsection. He rested his over hers, only then seeing the dark stain spreading across her red dress.

"Call an ambulance," he shouted, one hand pressed against her wound. "Now!" Not trusting a rent-a-cop, he used his other hand to fish for his cell phone, and found the velvet box in his pocket instead. He reached across his body for his other pocket, grabbed the phone and dialed 9-1-1.

"Hang on, Torie."

She smiled weakly. "We have to . . . stop . . ."

Torie snuggled against Fozzie in the back of the Rolls, resting her head on his chest. His heartbeat, strong and steady, was more effective than the painkillers the doctors had given her. The sky began to pink with the rising sun.

"Long night," she said. "Not what we'd planned."

Using his good arm, Fozzie tucked her closer. "Not even close. But you should have spent the night in the hospital."

"It's morning. We did."

Freeman had been taken into custody. She and Fozzie had spent hours talking to the cops and getting treated in the ER.

"You do stuff like this a lot, don't you?" she asked. "Disarm men with knives, come to the rescue of damsels in distress."

He rested his forehead on hers. "Torie, I've never been so scared in my life. All I could think of was losing you, when I'd just found you." The corners of his mouth twitched upward. "Although I wish it hadn't been on the forty-fourth floor."

Tonight, she'd seen the alarm in his eyes when he'd come to her aide. And the love. Heard the panic in his voice when he'd called 9-1-1. She'd never tell him she hadn't been worried about her injury until she saw his fear. But in that moment, absorbing his terror, she knew he'd become a part of her, too.

Even when her wound was officially proclaimed non-life-threatening, he'd refused his own treatment until the doctors patched her up.

"It wasn't supposed to be like this," he said. "But I screwed up the first time I told you I love you, so maybe it's going to be our tradition. To do things unconventionally."

"What do you mean?"

He cleared his throat. "I had reservations at Cicada. Someone said it was the most elegant joint downtown. We were going to have champagne and caviar, and I was going to give you this." He handed her a small velvet box. "I know it's been fast. And we're still in the trial phases. But . . . crap . . . I can't say this right."

She laughed. "Shall I open it?"

"Please. It's not real . . . I mean, it's real, but it's not *the* real. It's a promise ring. Because I promise to be there for you until you're ready. And then you can pick out any ring you want."

She flipped open the lid and saw the loops of gold forming a six-petal flower, with a diamond in each loop and another in the center. "It's beautiful." She took the ring from the box and held out her finger. "You put it on."

When he took her hand and slipped the ring over her finger, she felt an almost electric connection. As if the ring was setting roots in her soul.

"I thought it might remind you of the way we met—flowers and plants and all—"

"Fozzie." She clapped her hand over his mouth. "Shut up and kiss me."

ABOUT THE AUTHOR

Terry Odell lives in the mountains of Colorado, where she enjoys watching the wildlife from her window as she plots her next book. Visit her at http://www.terryodell.com.